Vendetta's Rise

The dragon realms saga book I

PART ONE

VENDETTA'S PATH

1

Elucard hopped off of the rickety old boat with the day's catch slung over his shoulder. The seaworn planks of the dock creaked as he bent down to tie up his father's boat.

"Tie the knot tight, Elucard. Last thing we need is to have the boat drifting away. Storms haven't been too kind to Ravenshore as of late," the boy's Father said sternly.

Elucard peered out towards the horizon. Winds blew through his dirty blonde hair. Dark heavy clouds were rolling in from the Eastern Sea and the air was laden with moisture. A cool salty film lined Elucard's fair skin. His elven ears perked up as he heard his father call over to him.

"Get those fish to your mother before you scamper off and be home before dark."

"Aw, Pa, but me and Jetta were going to catch fireflies to sell for ca–" Elucard caught himself. Candy wasn't the ideal way to spend his hard earned coin in his father's eyes. Angus' general store had a selection of the stickiest and most dazzling candy in all of Ravenshore; not only this but he also moonlighted as the local ale master. He traded bubble brew and the best mouth watering butterscotch for a jar of fireflies. Angus let them go when the children left, but Elucard didn't know that. Elucard usually spent the allowance he earned from fishing with his father on peppermint sticks. Not a wise investment, but that was the way of the youth of the old fishing village. And just another reason to keep his trap shut.

"For new trousers? A good idea, since you've run those worn." His father hid a smile as he gave his son a roguish wink, while stroking his bushy dark red beard, "Hurry up now, I'll convince your mother about extending your curfew since you're planning a business venture with Jetta."

"Thanks, Pa!"

***

"Salene, I'm home, what's for dinner?" River called out as he entered the small cottage.

"River, don't you dare enter this house without taking off those boots, you know they make this home stink of fish, and I won't have it anymore!"

River smirked, setting his rubber boots outside the door, before hanging his long coat on a hook. They'd been married for twenty-four years, and every day she scolded him for not taking off his boots. That's why he never did it; he liked consistency in his life. The cottage was small but cozy. Shafts of light illuminated the old shelves that held wooden figurines. River carved them himself for his wife when they were just children themselves. A carving of a stag or mermaid was a sure fire way to swoon Salene in their youth. These days they collected dust on the shelves, but they also had quite a collection of memories within them as well.

"Elucard went off in a hurry. Gave me a line of fish, pecked my cheek with a kiss, and was gone," Salene said with a slight quiver in her voice.

"They won't pick him this year, they didn't last time. He's small and skinny. They'll pick the blacksmith's apprentice, but not Elucard." River walked over to comfort his wife.

She embraced him and began to sob. Another visit by the Black Rabbits fast approached and each time she struggled more and more to keep herself from falling apart.

"Why do they have to come here? Why do they have to take our children? We should fight back!" she said almost weeping.

River rubbed her back gently, attempting to calm her down.

"They protect our town and many others. Our country doesn't have an army. We're all unfit to fight. We are tradesman, not warriors. Leave the fighting to them. They take our kids and turn them into–"

"Criminals!" Salene interrupted, "They take our children and they turn them into criminals!" She still remembered the day that her brother and cousin were taken by the assassin clan. They were forced to walk the dark path of the Black Rabbits and were never heard from again.

"This is the price we must pay for safety, Salene," River said stoically. He may not have agreed with their methods, but he couldn't argue with results. Bandits and raiders hadn't dared to strike their town since the Black Rabbit clan started providing Ravenshore with protection.

"I know, River. It's just that…It's not Elucard's price to pay," Salene whispered in a slight daze as she thought about her only child being stolen away.

River cupped her hands as she stared hopefully into his magenta eyes. It was the only feature that Elucard had inherited from his father.

2

Although River's eyes were steely and had seen a lifetime of work, Elucard's eyes were as soft as his nature. Elucard's heart desired no violence or toil, but wonder. He was a child, not a soldier.

"Salene, He won't be picked," River reassured her, "They'll see he is no killer, no assassin, and he'll be passed by."

Salene was quiet. She believed him. Not because she knew he was right, but that she needed the hope he was giving her. The same hope that had sustained her for the last four years.

"River, I just can't do this much longer," Salene sobbed.

"Come now. We have to be strong for him…for Elucard," River said softly. Yet he didn't know if he believed the words himself.

***

Elucard dashed down the gravel roads of Ravenshore. The small fishing village had been the only home he'd ever known. He passed by the old tavern that was down the alley from his house. It reeked of ale and the salty sweat of the sailors that occupied its stools. Elucard wrinkled his nose as he hurried past it and whipped around the corner. He heard the clanking of the blacksmith's hammer as he and his apprentice worked on various iron wares. The town was especially bustling recently, from the good catches over the past few weeks. New travelers stabled their horses by the Calming Tide Inn and Elucard watched them get settled. Many had traveled a fair distance to taste the only sprite moss chowder on the azure coast of the Eastern Sea.

Elucard ran past the old schoolhouse before finally getting to the outskirts of Ravenshore. He slowed to a walk as he reached the old willow tree with its long drooping branches that hung over a tiny pond that had formed from an inlet. This was where he and Jetta spent the majority of their time together.

"You're late." A small girl said doing her best to look angry with her skinny arms folded across her chest and her face squished up in a pout. She was about two years younger than him. Her auburn hair was wild and messy, a stark contrast to when Elucard first met her. When they were toddlers, Jetta was a squeaky clean girl with her hair always tied in a yellow ribbon. She would never dare get her favorite dresses dirty – or any dress for that matter. They were all her favorite. However, over time her exposure to the rambunctious Elucard caused Jetta to come out of her shell. From then on it would be Elucard who needed to keep up with her.

3

"Sun's still out! I say I'm on time." Elucard plopped down by the roots near the pond's bank. He inspected two makeshift fishing poles perched in the grass, "You remember to use bait this time?"

Jetta thrust her hands to her hips, "Yes! You take me for an idiot?"

Elucard cracked a smile as he playfully leered at his friend.

"Well, I couldn't find any worms…" Jetta mumbled.

"Jetta…."

Jetta raised a fishing wire out of the water; a round chocolate ball had a hook poking through it, "Malt ball. Fish gotta like chocolate!"

Both kids burst out laughing.

***

The sun dipped beyond the farthest reaches of the horizon as it made way for the night. Fireflies flickered over and around the pond. A few bobbed inside a jar that rested in the grass while crickets chirped in the reeds and Elucard lay lazily on a bough.

"Elucard, my grandma says the Black Rabbits will be here in the morning," Jetta said softly.

Elucard nodded, his parents had told him the same thing the other day. They attempted to reassure him by saying that he was too scrawny for the Black Rabbits. However, he wasn't. He was twelve, and he was growing stronger every day. His back might have been weak compared to Myler, the stable boy, but it was stronger than Jetta's. His parents thought he'd stay in Ravenshore forever, but he wasn't so sure.

"Elucard, are you scared?" Jetta voice was tiny now. The older they got, the more likely they were to end up with the Black Rabbits.

Elucard feigned a smile, "Scared? Me? I'm not a fraidy cat, like you!"

"I'm not scared!" Jetta protested.

"Ya, I bet you still sleep with your stuffed bear!" Elucard teased poking Jetta in the side.

Jetta paused shyly.

"You do, don't you?" Elucard laughed.

Jetta's voice cracked as she shivered, "Elucard, I don't want to leave home."

Elucard slid over to wrap an arm around his little friend, "Remember what I promised you?"

Jetta harkened back to the day her father was being buried. It was only three years ago, but she was still old enough to experience the pain of losing a parent. She remembered how her mother couldn't handle the sudden loss of her husband, and how she failed to take care of Jetta.

4

And even though her grandmother took her in, it was Elucard that made Jetta feel safe. It was he who made her feel like everything would be alright.

"You said you'd always be there for me," she said in a still small voice.

Elucard nodded, hugging her tighter, "I meant that promise. No matter what happens tomorrow, we'll still be together and I'll always be there for you."

Jetta smiled brightly, once again comforted by her best friend, "Thank you, Elucard."

***

"Come again?" Dest stared blankly at the trio of bandits. Her comrades scanned the scene as they sized up their situation. The bandits were clad in green leather tunics with iron rivets studded along the seams. Two of them stood by their horses, blocking the wagon's path. The third pointed his dagger at Dest's face.

"This here is our road that you be usin.' Gotta pay a toll if'n you want to pass," the bandit spat.

Dest looked back at the two men in her wagon. Vemrick smiled thinly, the other did not look amused. Dest looked back at the highwayman, "We have to make Ravenshore by morning. It would benefit us all if we were on time. Please remove yourself."

The three green-clad men burst into a loud belly laugh. The bandit grinned, showing off his yellow teeth. His breath stunk of wine and rot, "You talk slick. Pay up. You don't want to mess with the Black Rabbits, do you? We be the most feared men in these lands. Cross our path, we make widows of yer wives and orphans of yer children!"

Dest raised an eyebrow, "Oh, you be the Black Rabbits? I've heard of your exploits. You are certainly not to be trifled with."

Vemrick was a bit younger than Dest. He slicked back his red hair and twitched his elven ears. He nudged his companion before poking his head out next to Dest, "Ya know, Dest. We should just pay these fine men. The last thing we want to do is evoke the wrath of the spooky Black Rabbit clan."

The bandit's grin grew wider, "Aye, pay us and ye can live."

Dest fidgeted with her haversack taking out a few gold coins from a small pouch within it, "We never wanted any trouble…" she said coyly.

The bandit scrunched his face in confusion, "Weren't there three of you?" he said pointing at a missing body in the wagon.

5

Vemrick mockingly raised his brow, "Weren't there three of *you*?"

The bandit whipped his head around and gasped in horror. His two compatriots were sprawled out on the ground. Their necks were slashed and their thick red blood soaked into the earth. A single shadowy figure slowly moved himself closer to the remaining thug. In his hand he had a long two handed sword dragging in the dirt.

Dest spoke calmly as the mysterious individual raised his weapon, "We would have paid your silly tax. We would have left you alone. We would have gone about our business, but then you had to claim to be Black Rabbits."

The sword drove through the cowering man in a wild blur. Blood spewed from his mouth as he crumpled onto his back.

Dest continued as the victim slowly died, "Legion doesn't appreciate our name being dragged through the mud. None of us do. We earned the right to be called Rabbits. You did not."

The bandit gurgled as blood sputtered and dripped from his mouth.

"We've wasted enough time. Ravenshore awaits our arrival," Legion said flatly with little emotion in his voice.

"No rest for the weary, eh, Legion?" Vemrick asked.

"None."

2

Wiccer gripped the wooden sword tightly as he lifted it to parry an overhead attack. His dark skin glistened from the sweat that covered his face. His older brother constantly taunted him, "You'll have to be quicker than that if you want to survive going toe to toe with a Rabbit, little brother."

Avren swung his training sword deftly, striking Wiccer on the side of his arm, "Still too slow, brother!" Avren shouted.

Wiccer rubbed his arm as pain pulsed beneath his flesh. He brushed back his tightly curled hair and wiped away a layer of sweat. He may have only been thirteen but his brother was treating him as if he were a fully grown man.

"Hey, Avren, you're going too hard," Wiccer said exhausted.

"Too hard?" Avren scoffed, "We Newsun are trained at a higher standard. You think our mother would have settled with our father if–" Avren caught himself. He knew the subject of their mother was sensitive around Wiccer. He hadn't known her as long as Avren had. After all, Wiccer was merely a toddler when she died, but still they were close.

Wiccer spoke up, "You don't have to pretend that she didn't exist." Her memories weren't fresh, nor were they faded.

Avren grinned awkwardly, "You think I'm going hard on you? Mother's training was so hard on me that my hands were bloodied and blistered from holding onto that training sword." He laughed, "I wasn't allowed to call her 'Mother' either. It was Lieutenant Cutter…" He was quieter now as he recalled his Mother's face, "Lieutenant Vivian Cutter…"

"Avren?" Wiccer prodded his brother who was clearly lost in thought.

"Right, back to training, little brother."

Avren's white cloak danced in the breeze of his flowing movements, in sync with his long, dreaded hair. He spun on his heel, whipping the practice sword around, glancing across the back of his younger brother's tunic, "You're still not getting it. Stop trying to over-analyze my steps and pay attention to the blade in my hand, Wiccer. The White Cloaks will never accept such sloppy swordsmanship. Just because our father is Captain Marcus Newsun doesn't mean we get special treatment!"

Wiccer took a step forward. This was his daily routine for the last two years. After breakfast he would practice swordsmanship and footwork. He would endure the bombardment of lectures and insults from Avren and later he would receive lessons on politics and history from his father. All this was so that he could earn a white cloak of his very own. It was a family tradition. The only family tradition he'd ever known.

A sharp rap to the side of Wiccer's head snapped him out of his thoughts, "Dead again, Wiccer. Are you even trying?"

Wiccer rubbed the side of his head, "Let's go again, I think I'm getting the hang of this!"

Avren barreled towards him whipping the training sword over his brother's head. Wiccer barely managed to block it in time. Avren pressed his weight down on until Wiccer's legs buckled down into a kneeling position. Avren knocked his younger brother onto his back before pressing his foot down on his chest.

"You were saying?" he said jokingly.

"Why do the Elves even need us? Why can't they just defend themselves and go through all this training instead of me?" Wiccer roared in frustration.

Avren tossed his brother a waterskin, before taking a seat on a nearby stump, "Father hasn't covered Long Whisper politics yet?"

Wiccer shook his head after inhaling a mouthful of fresh stream water, "History of the human nations; not much on the elves."

"He talk about his time in Alva?" Avren said, cracking a wide smile.

"Nothing specific. Just about the history of the war between the Queen of Chains and the Gladiator King. Why, is that important to Long Whisper? Isn't Alva in the desert realm of Scorch?"

"No, they aren't related. I was just curious how much Father told you about our roots."

Wiccer edged closer to his older brother, "I know Mother and Father are from the desert lands of Scorch, but did Father fight in Alva? Did Mother? Why did they leave for Varis? It's such a long trek to the realm of Cypress."

Avren shook his head, "Forget that I brought it up, it's a long tale and we don't have that kind of time. Let me answer your original question and you can have Father tell you everything else." Avren took out a small leather pouch of deer jerky before giving Wiccer a quick lesson, "About thirty or forty years ago, Long Whisper was a land that was occupied by various tribes of elves. They had no central leadership of any sort; not even a council. At some point, an elf by the name of

Jaelyn Dawnedge united the tribes under one banner and was crowned king of Long Whisper. Not everyone agreed with such a change, particularly the warrior tribes who left for lands elsewhere." Avren paused, "Do you see where we come in?"

Wiccer examined Avren's cloak – an alabaster color with a silver trim, "The White Cloaks are their warrior tribe now?" he asked, "Why don't we at least train a militia or a body of law enforcement? Surely they could at least solve their own minor problems."

"Minor problems are indeed solved. Thievery and other small squabbles are dealt with leaders who are elected by the people of Long Whisper. Think of them like the mayors of Varis. The White Cloaks are used for much larger problems such as protecting villages from bandits and rendering justice to murderers. We also protect the crown from all threats – foreign and domestic. Do you now see why we must train so hard?"

Wiccer nodded intensely.

"Good, now pick up your sword. Back to training." Avren said, tying his jerky pouch tightly.

"Come on, Avren, five more minutes! I want you to tell me about Alva and our parents' role in it," Wiccer pleaded.

"Dammit, Wiccer. Don't give me that look," Avren sighed.

Wiccer raised his brow and puffed his lower lip like a sad puppy.

Avren laughed, "Alright, let's make this quick. I'll be the one getting a beating if Father finds out I've been slacking on your training!"

Wiccer cheered before getting comfortable.

"Father was a sergeant who was assign–" Avren began before getting interrupted.

"Sergeant? Father wasn't a Captain?" Wiccer said wide eyed. He had only ever known his father as a Captain.

"Back before I was born, our father was only Sergeant Newsun and he was assigned to the desert country of Alva across the Serpent Sea. Alva was at odds with the Queen of Chains, herself, Isana. Alva's leader was Traven, who was the–"

"The Gladiator King!" Wiccer interrupted, happy to show he learned something from his lessons on political history.

"That's right, little brother. Now quit interrupting, or else this story will take until sundown to tell." Avren waited to see if Wiccer was going to sit quietly before continuing, "Isana was declaring war on Alva and our guild was chosen to assist King Traven. At the time, Father was to serve under Lieutenant Vivian Cutter."

"Mother..." Wiccer whispered in awe of the story.

Annoyed, Avren briefly glared at Wiccer, "They fought countless battles together until one day Marcus was grievously injured in an ambush during a routine patrol. Vivian was the only other one left alive. She fought tooth and nail and dragged him into a nearby nomad camp. There they stayed, for months, until Marcus was ready enough to walk back to base."

Wiccer's face was plastered with wonder. His Father never told him war stories, "Is that where Mother and Father fell in love?"

Avren chuckled, "Not at first. She saw him as nuisance for being so easily injured, but over time, the Newsun charm worked its magic."

"But they didn't stay in Alva; you and I were born in Varis…"

Avren took a deep breath. Wiccer was starting to tread on 'that' story. A story that he wasn't ready to tell, "It's true, our mother and father were married and set to be stationed at the guild headquarters in Varis. They had me and then later they had you."

"And the rest is history." A new, deeper, sterner voice chimed in, ending the tale before it could continue.

A muscular man with a finely trimmed black beard stood behind the two boys. His white cloak draped over his shoulders, his black leather boots were polished to a shine, and his blue dyed leather armor had a silver trim that went well with his pearl colored cloak. Their father, Marcus, was the leader of the Guard of the White Cloaks for the Long Whisper division. He was a legend within the guild for his countless missions and unrivaled swordsmanship.

"Wiccer, show me what you've learned." Marcus said, folding his arms over his broad chest.

He watched as his two sons sparred in the cool autumn morning. It was an idyllic setting. He nodded his head as Wiccer made a thrust at Avren's chest, but the blow was met with the clunking sound of oak slapping oak. Marcus again nodded at both of them before he put up a hand, halting the lesson.

"Avren, a word."

Avren tossed his practice sword to Wiccer, who made a clumsy catch. Wiccer eyed his father and brother as they walked into their cabin. The stone house smelled of moss and rain from the past couple of days. Smoke billowed from its chimney as sounds of a lightly flowing river crossed by their small patch of land. Wiccer headed inside to hear what his father had to say.

Marcus sat down in a chair by the wooden table where they ate their meals while Avren sat parallel from his father. Avren put his hands on the table, "Well?

Marcus stole a glance at Wiccer, who was still holding the practice swords. Eagerness to hear the news was plastered on his face. Marcus made a shooing motion to his youngest child, "Wiccer, this is Guild business."

Wiccer's face drooped, "Aw, but Father, I've been training real hard. The White Cloak is in my blood. I'm practically a member!"

"Quit your whining, boy, before I tan your hide! Now be gone with you. Your brother and I have much to discuss," Marcus said sternly.

Wiccer lowered his head and sulked away into another room. Once out of sight, he crept to the edge of the wall and held his breath to strain his hearing, hoping to eavesdrop on any bit of information he could gobble up.

Avren smiled and whispered, "You know he's still listening?"

Marcus shook his head chuckling, "If he wasn't born to be a Cloak, He'd probably be a Rabbit." Raising his voice, he continued, "Now listen up son, I bring news from the Guild. King Jaelyn requests more Cloaks. The city he's building around the elven home tree needs more security. I want you to take over leadership there, while I stay here to finish Wiccer's training."

Avren grinned widely. He always wanted a chance to prove his leadership skills. Although he wasn't taking over the Guild, this was a step in that direction, "You want me to take over duties in Lost Dawns? Father, I'm honored. I won't let you down."

"See that you don't. Also, more importantly, be careful. You shouldn't trust half of those Elven Lords. Not all of them wanted to unite the tribes, let alone build a city around that tree of theirs."

"You suspect that they've been hiring Rabbits?" Avren asked.

Marcus crossed his arms and nodded, "Aye. Though, of the eight tribes, I know not which one. So, suspect all of them until you can manage any proof."

"When do I leave?"

"Tomorrow at sunrise, so get some good sleep. I've arranged a squad of Cloaks to go with you. Roads are dangerous these days." Marcus turned his head to the doorway of the kitchen and the living room, "Wiccer, come in here."

Wiccer jumped a bit, not knowing how his father knew he was there. He poked his head around the wall and shuffled in, hoping he wasn't in trouble, "Yes, Father?"

"I'll be taking over all your training. Your brother is leaving on a mission to Lost Dawns. Go prepare dinner. This will be the last meal we'll have as a family for long time."

3

"Do you feel it, Grandchild? It flows through the earth as it would flow through your soul. It is the essence of life, it is the Magi. Do you feel it?"

Koda strained his hands as he spread his fingers, reaching for any synapse of Magi that might exist in the ground. Sweat beaded down the side of his face as he struggled, "Grandfather, I don't... I don't feel it."

The ancient elf threw back his massive deep blue cape to reach for his grandson's hand, "Let me help you. Together we are bound by blood. Feel what I feel, see what I see."

A jolt of energy spasmed up the young elf's arm as a flash of vivid lights blinded him turning his vibrant blue eyes to a pale white. A sound hummed as it bounced through his long ears, then it all went quiet. The lights faded until he could only see the old twisting forest. His hand felt as if he were in a warm bath: relaxing, calm, tranquil.

"Do you feel it?" His mentor asked again.

"I do! I feel it!"

His grandfather released Koda's hand, "Concentrate. Do as I say. Concentrate, young one. Do you still feel it?"

Koda melded his mind with the aether's steady flow, "Yes, I still feel it."

His grandfather nodded, "Hold onto it. Envelope it into your hand and embrace it."

A fluxing shape of light transversed through Koda's body. His eyes gaped open with awe, "Grandfather Xile, what do I do with it?" Koda asked, somewhat frightened.

"Wield it carefully, Grandchild. It is volatile in this form, for it is pure and raw. Quickly, pass it to me!"

Koda, gingerly locked fingers with Xile and the magic rapidly passed over to the more experienced elf.

"Raw magic is found only in the rarest of mana streams within our world. Only a true master can tame it. Magic that a mage uses is not in its raw form, but bred over countless generations. It is weaker in nature, but much more malleable than its raw brethren." Xile shot his hand out towards the sky. The magic sparked in a brilliant shower of lights before firing into the air and exploding in a crack of energy.

Koda gasped at the display, "Amazing!"

The old elf hid a smile within his cowl, "You were not the first to be amazed by such power."

Koda turned away from the remnants of the spectacle, "My Father and Uncle Tull?"

Xile waved a hand in dismissal, "If only my sons had half the interest in the Magi as you do. No, I speak of my first two students. Boys no younger than fourteen, about your age, Koda."

Koda looked up inquisitively, "Were they Dawnedge elves?"

"They weren't elves at all. That was my first mistake, but not my biggest... teaching them anything was my greatest failure!" Xile spat in disgust before regaining his composure, "We must keep our secrets within the family. Remember this and never make the same mistakes that I've made, my grandchild."

Koda had never heard of such students and prodded his elder further, "What did they do? Why haven't I heard of them before? What ever happened to them?"

Xile rubbed his brow, "I think it's time for bed, Koda. We have much to do in the morning."

Koda persisted, "Please? History is as important as anything else you are teaching me!"

"It isn't important what became of them as long as you know whom you are to become and what you are meant to do. Koda, you must always respect the Magi; not merely as a weapon, but as something to revere, to respect, and to uphold above all else." Xile kneeled down to Koda's level, "Can you do this?"

Koda nodded.

"Good. Now, off to bed with you. At first light, I will have a gift for you."

Koda began to walk away, but his curiosity got the best of him as he turned to ask a question, "Will you ever reveal all of this island's secrets?"

Xile did not answer.

"Grandfath–"

"To bed. Now."

Xile walked into the shadows of the forest, leaving Koda without an answer.

***

The sun rose as the young elf boy was shaken awake. His grandfather's silver and white braided beard tickled Koda's nose as he shifted from a sleepy daze.

"Rise, grandchild. They will not wait any longer for you to make a choice," Xile said excitedly.

Koda groggily rubbed his eyes as he sat up in his moss pile bedding. He tied his long golden hair in a braid, keeping his bangs in strands behind his ears. The cave was still dark, but a dim fire glinted off the many crystal shards that jutted from the stone walls.

"Who?"

Xile smirked, "Follow and see."

***

The forest of the isle of Nashoon was the lushest forest in all of Long Whisper. Its ancient trees twisted and wove its roots among themselves forming intricate paths. Moss dangled from the boughs as will o' wisps floated within the cool mists. Streams that trickled into tiny ponds carved through the grass creating several banks. Each bank was blanketed in wild flowers and clovers. In the distance, the cracking sound of wood twisting and turning could be heard echoing through the deeper parts of the forest, for deep in the belly of the forest lay mystical beasts never seen by the elven eye. According to many tall tales, unicorns, drakes, and hippogriffs were said to take up shelter in the depths of Nashoon.

The Wolves of the Eclipse were a special breed of wolf that were infused with Magi. Their fur coats came in all sorts of exotic colors and patterns. Their blood was so potent with magic that it flared from their eyes.

"A litter of cubs were born a few moons ago. They await for you to choose a familiar." Xile picked up a green and red colored pup. The newborn licked his face, excitedly, "This one would make a fine companion, but you must make that choice yourself."

Koda knelt down to play with several pups. A pack of large wolves watched patiently off to the side, eyes glowing in the shadow of the trees.

"Grandfather, what is a familiar? What does that mean to me? Is it like a pet?"

Xile let the wolf pup loose to romp with his siblings, "Koda, you are training to be an Arcane Guardian. Charged to protect this island and forest from anyone that would do harm to its inhabitants and the

14

powerful forces that lie within this land. A Wolf of the Eclipse is a partner, meant to protect and share your burden. They are not pets. You will have a lifelong bond, and from that an alliance will be born. You feel its pain, as it does for you. So, Koda, look into the eyes and hearts of each wolf. The choice will be clear once you lock onto your soul mate."

Koda stared intently at each rascally pup, but no such connection was made. He was too distracted by the pack of larger wolves that stood by. He walked slowly to them. They sat frozen, with their eyes following Koda as he walked. Each one seemed to fade away in Koda's mind, until a lone female was his focus. She had a deep midnight blue coat. A single eye sparked with Magi, while the other eye was fully black with a sliver of a silver iris.

"Wildeye." Koda whispered, as he slowly reached to touch the wolf. His hands carefully caressed the wolf's head and chest. She made a long howl in the morning air.

"You have chosen. She is a loyal one. She is well trusted by my familiar, Moon Treader."

An old, scarred, red and gray furred wolf made an appearance from a nearby cave that served as the wolf den as he heard his name mentioned.

"He is the pack leader. And he approves of your choice." Xile said, a wide smile across his face.

***

Dusk approached the island of Nashoon. Along the beaches of its shores Koda sat, his bare feet sunk into the cool sands. His new found familiar lay across his lap. A fire blazed as embers crackled from the ashy wood. Xile stood over the fire enchanting his grandchild with a wild tale.

"Long ago, before the gods were born, dragons bigger than mountains roamed a world. Each fed on the stars themselves. Each more powerful than any deity that would live. Each a lone wolf not trusting any of the others. They endlessly roamed the aether searching for power to feed on until a dragon was born, so immense, so powerful, that it let loose a torrent of destruction onto their world.

Countless dragons would be vanquished by the cataclysm and all but seven perished. Five lay in the oceans so badly injured they were near death. The others used their powers to to heal their fallen kin. They grew forests and mountains on the backs of these dragons to cover and mend their heavy wounds, but the dragons were too far gone to awaken.

More and more lands bloomed across the dragons: deserts, swamps, rivers, and lakes. But to no avail. All seemed hopeless. Despite their best efforts, the five dragons were still dying until a being from across the skies came upon them.

He was a curious deity of great knowledge and power. He imbued the comatose dragons with the Magi, keeping the dragons alive, but putting them in an eternal slumber. He then gave the dragons purpose by forging life on them. Finally he bestowed names upon these new dragon realms: Cypress, Stratus, Blight, Abyss, and Scorch."

Koda's eyes widened in delight from the story, "The realms we live on are actually dragons?" he asked amazed.

"A story, but it may yield truth." Xile harkened back to the elder Dragon Walkers that told him the same story eons ago before pulling out a small scroll from his belt, "Koda, a carrier hawk bearing the crest of a sword and sun came this morning." He passed the scroll to the young elf.

Koda read the message carefully, "A message from my father!"

Xile nodded sternly. "Your father wishes you to come to back to Lost Dawns. He wishes you to begin to learn your position as Prince of the new nation."

Koda was silent.

"You don't have to go, Grandchild. You have much to learn before you take over my role as Arcane Guardian. Being prince can wait."

Koda wrapped his arm around Wildeye, "I have not been home in nearly five years. I have not seen nor talked to him during that time. I miss him, but–"

"He does not understand the importance of your training. He never did, nor did his brother. I urge you to stay."

Koda hung his head, "I know you do, but becoming an Arcane Guardian is a lifelong commitment. I need to see him, it will only be for a couple of years. Then I'll be back! I promise!"

Xile lifted his chin. Both his sons left the island and the path of becoming Arcane Guardians. Neither had interest in the forest's history or its many secrets, but Koda was different. He relished in magic and the lore behind it. He would be back, Xile knew this, "Go, grandchild. Be with your father. Learn about your people. Then return to me and continue the path to your destiny."

Koda hugged Wildeye in a fit of excitement, but then gasped, "What of Wildeye?"

"The bond has been made; she is affixed to you now as a nail to a cedar block. Try not to keep her in your chamber all day. She is a friend, not a pet, always remember this." chuckled Xile.

Koda smiled, hugging his wolf, tightly, "Ready for a trip, girl?"

Wildeye let a long howl of excitement.

4

It was a sunrise that most Ravenshore villagers would see as just another day, but for a select few, it would be the beginning of a long and terrible nightmare. Clouds rolled in from the Eastern Sea, heavy and black. The cool air was thick with the smell of rain; perhaps an omen of things to come.

Dest steered the horse drawn wagon into the town center of Ravenshore. There the people of the small fishing town were already crowding around the traveling Black Rabbits. Some of their faces were worn with the experience. Others wore a scowl of distaste. Mothers hugged their children tightly as if this was the last time they'd see their offspring.

"Denizens of Ravenshore, we are representatives of the Black Rabbit clan. The time has come to call upon your town to help serve our deity Alanna and our clan. But it is also your chance to help serve your town, your family, and yourselves," Dest said.

No one dared to speak out. In the beginning there were hints of protest, but the clan truly did keep the bandits at bay.

Dest, Vemrick, and Legion hopped down and started to grab the young children and line them up. Dest continued to address the people as she worked, "Your cooperation is greatly appreciated, and this won't take long. Have your children line up quickly and quietly so that we can begin the inspection."

Standing up straight in a single file line, the children of Ravenshore stood side by side with anxious faces, waiting for the Black Rabbit clan to take their pick of new recruits. Their mothers sobbed, watching as their fearful children flinched while being prodded and inspected for any flaws that would hinder their training.

The recruiters moved down the line, either denying a potential recruit or taking them out of the line and ushering them into their horse drawn cart.

Elucard held Jetta's hand tightly. He looked into her face and whispered assurances that they wouldn't be picked, not this year. Jetta nodded, too stricken with fear to say anything. Despite his own promises, he still had a nagging doubt in the back of his mind that pestered him like a mosquito. He couldn't doubt that this could be the year he was picked. He shook away these negative thoughts. He needed courage now.

Courage – that's what Elucard had to show Jetta. Courage that they would get through this; and that for another year, they would be free to fish, chase ladybugs, and sleep under the shade. Elucard squeezed her hand tighter as the recruiter stepped closer. Eventually he stepped in front of Jetta. The small girl squeaked as his face loomed closely in front of hers. He pawed her tiny shoulders and picked up her arms and hands. He looked into her wide, innocent eyes and shook his head, "No good, not yet."

Elucard sighed in relief. Jetta let out a weak smile, still not fully grasping that she was to stay in the village for at least another year. Elucard nodded, smiling back. He turned to look at the gruff recruiter. He was an elf, like him. Stern with weary eyes, the recruiter's short silver hair waved in the stormy air. He was strong with a cold demeanor and an eerie presence. Several scars crisscrossed over his face and his eyes were a deep hue of red. His sword rested, sheathed, strapped to his back. It was a long, heavy two handed blade that looked sharp enough to chop Elucard in two. The man performed the same inspections that he did with the other children. Finally, he looked into Elucard's worried eyes, but Elucard did not flinch or blink. The man smirked, "You're a bit tame now, but I see potential in you."

The boy's jaw slouched open, gasping. The man pointed, making a motion for his companions.

"This one!"

Elucard gazed in silence, his short life was moving in slow motion as his mother screamed, clawing for her son. River grunted as he held back his hysterical wife.

"Be strong, son! Don't let them get the best of you! You're a Freewind! Never forget where you came from!" River shouted over the cries of Salene.

"You can't have him! You hear me? He's mine! He's not like you! He's not a Rabbit! He'll never be one!" Salene shrieked at Legion

"He will, or he'll die." Legion sharply replied.

Jetta embraced Elucard tightly, tears streaming down her cheeks.

"Elucard, you can't leave, you promised you'd always be there for me!"

The men wrestled the kids away from each other. Elucard was still stunned in disbelief that he was chosen. He was herded to the cart where three other boys sat silently. He recognized them as his schoolmates. The butcher's son, Geven; Izian, the blacksmith's apprentice; and Myler, who worked at the stable.

"You were chosen too, Elucard?" said Myler, who shivered with uncontrollable fear, "We're never going to see Ravenshore again!"

Izian, a very strong kid from working with iron and hammers all his life, placed a worker's hand on Myler, "We need to stick together, don't let the Black Rabbits see our sadness. They feed on that. We got to be strong for our families, they can't watch over us anymore."

The three other boys nodded.

Vemrick and Dest hopped on the front of the cart, snapping the reins of the horse to move out. The man with the large sword jumped on the back of the cart with the boys. He smirked at the sorrow-filled kids, pointing at their soon to be former home.

"Say your goodbyes now, this is the last you'll see of your village."

Izian hid away a scowl at the statement.

Elucard moved to the edge of the cart and saw his best friend running beside it. Her eyes were swimming in the tears that rolled down her cheeks. Her voice became hoarse from shouting.

"Elucard, don't go! Please!"

Elucard's emotions flooded through him as he called back, "Jetta, I'm sorry! I won't forget you! Please wait for me!" he turned back around, trying hard to fight the knot in his throat as tears quivered in his eyes. Ravenshore was his entire life. Everything he knew was being stripped away from him in a single moment. There had been countless children who were taken by the Black Rabbit clan, and none ever were heard from again. Black Rabbits turned them into thieves and murders. This would be his fate too.

He wouldn't ever forget about Jetta, but maybe it would be for the best for Jetta to forget about him. Elucard sat down hard and hugged his knees.

Legion watched the boys saying their farewells. He knelt down to Elucard's eye level. Putting a heavy hand on Elucard's head, he spoke in a reassuring tone, as if he had been through something like this before, as if, he too, had once experienced this day.

"If you are to forget everything about your life here, don't forget about her. A shred of humanity could give you an edge against your enemies."

Elucard eyed the man's grizzly features fiercely.

"And you… Did you hold onto any humanity?"

Elucard searched his eyes; the man was silent briefly before speaking. "No."

Camping for the night under an outcropping of granite, the four boys sat on the ground, their ankles cuffed and chained together. Dest, who was assigned to watch the boys, stared sleepily at them, while the other two were out hunting for food. Her head bobbed as she tried to keep from dozing off. However, to no avail. The hypnotic drizzling of the raindrops outside the rock was soothing to someone without much sleep.

The boys looked at each other. Careful not wake their captor, they slowly got up and tiptoed out of the camp. With Geven taking the lead, they awkwardly dashed through the forest. The boys rushed under fallen trees and past boulders. The faint moonlight seemed faded from the heavy clouds. Thoroughly soaked, the tired boys collapsed on the muddy ground. They were out of breath from trying to gain as much distance from the Black Rabbits as possible in a dead sprint. Myler struggled on the chain.

"It's no use, we should have grabbed the key!"

"We couldn't risk the chance of getting caught. No doubt they will cut off our hands for making a break for it." Izian said, trying to catch his breath.

Geven glared at the ever calm Izian.

"Cut off our hands? Are you thick? They need us for recruits."

Izian grabbed the collar of Geven's tunic, bringing their faces close to each other. Izian's hands were thick and callused from working with a forge hammer. His grip was strong – too strong for the squirming Geven to break free.

"Call me thick again, I dare you."

"Thick." Geven spat, testing Izian's threats.

Myler shoved himself between the two boys, "Guys, this is what they want! They want us fighting against each other!"

Elucard ignored the bickering of his companions. He was more fixated on a warm glow coming from further up ahead. Glancing back towards the camp, he couldn't tell if they were being chased, but now wasn't the time to risk taking a break. They needed to find safety and shelter.

"Hey, you guys need to listen, Myler is right. Fighting won't solve anything and we need to get moving. I think there's a camp up ahead.

Maybe there will be some people who can help us out and even give us a ride back to our village."

Izian and Geven glared at each other, but both nodded in agreement. A truce between the two seemed best. They picked up the pace and headed for the light in the forest. Their legs were sore from the weight of their wet trousers and the iron chain shackled to their ankles, but they trudged on.

***

Dest sat up from pretending to be asleep. Her performance was flawless as he scanned the camp for the four elven recruits. The slight jingling sound of chains echoed in the distance, nearly drowned out by the rain. Two figures appeared by her side. She looked over her shoulder before speaking to them, "Vemrick, Legion; It's good to see you again. The recruits have taken the bait. How long do we give them before we go after them?"

Vemrick, a handsome, olive skinned elf, rubbed his hands by the fire, "I scouted the woods surrounding our position, there's a camp of some thieves nearby, no doubt they'll head that way."

Legion, who recruited the Ravenshore boys, tightened his sword strap. The sound of leather cracked lightly, "Did they bother to take the key?"

Dest swung the iron key from her thin neck, "Funny. Most do, but not this batch."

Legion moved closer to the edge of the forest and Vemrick called out to him, "Remember, we're to break their spirits, not their bodies."

Legion nodded, without turning to look.

***

Nero gripped his stomach as it grumbled in pain. He took stock of the two dead squirrels tied on the stripped branch that his companion was carrying, "Brim won't be satisfied with dese two rodents. Can't ye find bigger game, Lorken?"

Lorken, a scraggly man, stirred the small campfire with his sword in frustration, "Oi told yer, ain't no critters in dese woods. Dem haunted. No animal gonna go anywhere near dese woods. We be wastin' our time!"

22

"Brim is gonna be losin' his patience with us. Yer don' wanna see 'em when he's lost his top. He'll skin us and feed us to the gang 'imself." Nero whined with wide, fearful, eyes.

"Ya tink I don' know dat, Nero." He stood up and paced back and forth in an abysmal mood. Flustered and down to his last nerve, his own hunger and the stress of finding little food was driving him over the edge, "Jus' need to find some fat…" He began to stare at the husky bearded Nero, "Plump…game. Somethin' dat will feed all of us…dat won' put up much of a fight…"

Nero began to grow nervous as Lorken stared at him with his beady eyes, "Lork, buddy, ya lookin' a bit stir crazy. Mayhaps we search the woods a bit more. Maybe a boar or deer will wander our way."

A shaking in the bush snapped Lorken back to reality. He drew his sword and dagger and turned towards the noise. To his surprise four elven boys stumbled into their encampment, their faces covered in scratches from passing through the brush and thicket. Their clothes were ragged and covered in muck, and a long chain interconnected shackles around their ankles.

Nero grinned at Lorken. A gift from the gods had landed in their laps. The boys fell to their knees, breathing heavily.

One of them looked up with pleading eyes, "Please, Sirs, we need help."

Lorken swayed to the escapees, twirling his dagger, "Luck be fallen ya dis day, young'un. Oi be Lorken, dis here be my associate, Nero. We'd be 'appy to help your predicament."

Myler gleefully smiled, "Oh thank the All-Father! You hear that, guys? We're saved."

"Can you help get this chain off us?" Geven asked, tugging at the bond.

"Aye, we can. Oh, but our tools be with our compatriots back at our main camp." Lorken said, stifling a wicked grin.

The four boys looked at each other and hesitantly agreed.

Elucard spoke up, "Can you lead us there? We would greatly appreciate any help you can give us."

Nero and Lorken smiled and bowed.

***

The rain had simmered down by the time the group reached the thieves' encampment. A large bonfire illuminated the area where three more men sat around on logs. They stared at the boys with deep hunger in their eyes. A short, stout man with a great, wide-brimmed buckled hat welcomed the Ravenshore boys' guides. Lorken whispered in the man's ear. Elucard was able to make out the man's name as "Brim."

Brim nodded keenly at the four boys, "Lorken tells me you need our assistance." Immediately after speaking, he beckoned the other thieves to join him as they surrounded the boys.

Brim spoke much more eloquently than Lorken and Nero, an aspect that comforted Elucard and his companions.

"Can you lead us back to Ravenshore?" asked Elucard. Hopefulness heightened in his voice. Things seemed to be going his way.

Brim flashed a toothy smile. His teeth were well taken care of and were an ivory white, "Aye, something can be arranged, provided we eat first."

"Oh, boy! I'm starving!" Myler said as he leaped with joy.

"What's on the menu?" Geven asked, looking around for any sort of kettle or pans.

Lorken brought his dagger under Geven's chin, "Actually, you are!"

The elves scrambled in shock as they tripped over themselves, getting their legs tangled in the long chain. The men grabbed the children, who struggled helplessly in their grips as Brim moved closer, baring his sword.

"Hold them still, I'll begin the carving."

Elucard gritted his teeth in fear, now fully realizing the dire straights he and the others were in, as he tried in vain to tear himself away from Nero's grip on the collar of his tunic.

"That's it boy, make this easy for – Arrrgh!" Nero threw Elucard away as he trembled, holding his hand in the moonlight. Light glinted off a small dagger driven deep in his hand.

A calm voice echoed around the camp, "Leave the boys, it is not their time to leave the threshold of this world."

Lorken unsheathed his cutlass and quickly swiveled his head, searching for the source of the voice. The rest of the men drew their knives and hatchets.

Brim sneered, spinning around and calling out, "Who are you? Show yourself!"

The voice continued, ignoring the question, "You have acted against my clan. The only outcome for you all is death."

Brim shot an enraged glance at Lorken, "Clan? What clan?"

Lorken trembled, stuttering, "I-I don' know, boss."

Brim swerved his head back to the blackness of the shadowy woods, "These boys belong to us, who else claims them?"

Nero, shivering in his boots, shouted at his partner, "Lork, we've upset the spirits!" Nero fell to his knees, dropping his sword. Sobbing, he pleaded with the mysterious voice, "Please Master Spirit, we ain't meant no harm! We weren't gonna eat dem elf boys!"

Brim snatched Nero by the ear as he yanked him back up to his feet, "Get a grip of yourself, this isn't some specter!"

Elucard's eyes were elven, much more adaptable to the night then the human bandits. His mouth slowly opened in awe as he saw a shadowy figure drop silently between two of the thieves. Pulling out a large sword from its back, a flash of steel cleaved through the misty air as it lopped the head off of one of the men. Blood sprayed from the severed neck of the now headless bandit as he tipped over and slammed on the forest floor.

Brim furiously shouted for his men to pay attention to the assailant in the center of their view. The figure wasted no time dispatching another thief as he thrust his blade within his gut.

A hatchet swung in the night, as the ghostly figure sidestepped and connected with a fierce back kick to a bandit's jaw, hurling him into another as they both crashed into the camp fire. A blood curdling scream erupted from the tragic victims.

Lorken cried out, his face a sickening white with fear, "What are you?!"

The threatening individual slashed expertly across Lorken's throat. As he fell to his knees, choking on oozing blood, the attacker answered his question, "A Black Rabbit."

Brim pushed Nero in front of himself, "Nero, my friend, do me a favor and slay him and you'll forever be my right hand man!"

Nero, blubbering in tears and snot, slid to grovel at the assassin's feet, "I beg ye, Master Rabbit. Spare me, I ain't know dem boys were yer kin. I'm innocc–" His pleas were cut short as the Rabbit snapped his neck.

The assassin approached Brim, staring him down with an emotionless face, "These woods belong to us. These boys belong to us. You..."

Brim dropped his rapier and took out a coin purse. He tossed it to the Black Rabbit's feet and groveled, "You can have my weapon and my money, leave me be. Let's just forget this night ever happened."

Elucard watched as his savior dashed in a shadowed blur and cut down Brim in a single, bloody, motion.

"You belong to Alanna." the assassin finished.

Geven, Izian, and Myler hugged each other, frozen in fear as their mysterious elven rescuer stepped forward to them. He sunk his long sword into the ground, and went to one knee, rummaging for a cloth from Nero's bag. Without taking notice of the shivering boys, he wiped the blood off his sword.

Elucard shook his head in astonishment, "You took on six men at once! What are you?"

Legion discarded the rag, "I am that which can not be seen. You must tell stories of my acts to truly believe I exist."

"A ghost?" Elucard asked, taken aback by the riddle.

"An ideal."

Elucard looked up at the older elf. He was dressed in black with a deep purple cloak draped over his broad shoulders and a mask that covered everything below his eyes. Staring in wonderment at his rescuer as he sheathed his weapon, he looked away only when the elf noticed him gawking.

The man smirked, "Legion."

Elucard looked back at him with puzzlement, "Huh?"

"My name is Legion."

***

The tree line on the outskirts of Lost Dawns was still. The only movement came from the slowly ebbing shadows of the branches caused by the shifting clouds that passed through the white moonlight. There, the two assassins held themselves just within reach of that glow.

Vada was First Blade, a position that was the right hand of High Blade Avalon, third in line to commanding the clan. A heavy mask hid her scarred but beautiful features. She was human, but her training allowed her senses to be sharp enough to be comfortable with the night. She did not command the same presence as her High Blade did. Although equal in skill, Vada prefered to stand in the wake of Avalon to lend her support and skill from behind the shadows.

Elisa appeared Vada's side. Unlike her First Blade or other Black Rabbit peers, Elisa Moonshard was a Shadow Elf. A rare breed of elf that bore gray skin and deep purple hair, Shadow Elves hailed from a distant land. While most Black Rabbits were drafted from villages as children, Elisa came to the clan of her own volition to seek the skill to one day bring the clan's services to the kingdom she left. With exotic beauty and the cunning to match, she was slowly making a name for herself within the Rabbits. If she were to succeed in her mission, her dreams would become a reality.

"Elisa, what have you found out?" Vada spoke in a low, emotionless voice.

"My First Blade, a roaming patrol heads to the north, they won't trouble us."

Vada nodded as she spotted a faint glow of a lantern bobbing towards the north.

"A traveler approaches us. He wears rags and a long cloak. Despite his clothing, he wears a nobleman's signet on his finger. No doubt he is whom we are waiting to speak to." Elisa continued.

"Well done, Elisa. Is he armed?"

"A dagger hangs from a belt behind his waist."

The traveler came into sight as he drew closer to the assassins. His clothes were indeed, shoddy, but a gold ring glinted in the moonlight. Vada beckoned him to follow her deeper into the forest until they could be no longer seen from the road.

Vada made a subtle gesture, signaling Elisa to unleash a blade's edge at the traveler's neck.

"You dare draw a blade on me? Is this how the Black Rabbits do business?" The traveler's shrill voice cracked, flabbergasted with his situation.

Vada reached for his dagger and tossed it aside, "You were requested to bring no weapons. The last thing we need is to be double crossed before business begins."

The man chuckled nervously before the sword's edge dug deeper into his chin, "What I'm about to pay you for is treason against my king. The least I should be allowed to do is arm myself."

"Elisa, let him go." Vada waited for her companion to sheath her blade, and return to her side, "Your signet – It's not of the eight. We were under the impression that one of the eight tribes would be hiring us."

The traveler fidgeted with his ring, "I am of a lesser house, but a nobleman all the same. However, you are correct. One of the eight does wish of your services."

"Which." Vada had a hint of annoyance in her voice.

"I can not say–"

Elisa began to draw her blade again.

"But, know that I represent that tribe in this transaction. Despite all the secrecy, you shall be greatly compensated." The nobleman sped up his words before Elisa could act.

"You have our payment ready at the disclosed location?"

"For a payment that size, my employer expects results." the man said folding his arms.

Vada turned to Elisa, "Are you sure that you want to do this mission alone? The city is large. There is no shame in asking for help."

"First Blade, I work best alone. No chance for someone to get captured and spill my secrets. A bigger city just means more places to hide and strike. To rely on just myself, I can do; relying on others will be a hindrance," Elisa said, bowing to Vada.

"Construction of the city must not be completed. King Jaelyn must suffer for his arrogance!" The nobleman spat

Vada turned and bowed to her customer, "He will."

5

The Black Rabbit compound was a retreat deep in the forests of Long Whisper. It was a broad, square structure with sparring grounds spanning across its center. It housed recruits and veterans, as well as officers. The camp was built out of a clearing in the woods. It was laid out like a temple compound, with several barracks buildings surrounding a main structure. Two small lodges off to the sides served as an infirmary and an armory. Within the compound were various training grounds and set down a secluded path was a small shrine dedicated to the clan's patron deity, Alanna.

Past that, a waterfall poured into a river that fed into the city of Lost Dawns. However, the compound served as more than just a training camp. The stalwart fortress of the Black Rabbits also contained a school where the younger recruits were educated in the complex politics and history of the realms. The clan itself was headed by three figures: the Silent Master, High Blade and First Blade. The Silent Master was rarely seen. He ruled the clan from the shadows and did not make an appearance unless it was truly needed. Most commands came from the High Blade or the First Blade, who served as their lieutenant.

The Ravenshore recruits joined a set of recruits from other villages as they lined up in front of a small cadre of senior Black Rabbits. The other boys and girls were just as terrified as Elucard and his fellow villagers. The children cowered and sniveled as the Black Rabbit veterans snickered and smiled at them. A loud aggressive command broke through their minds.

"Shut up and listen!" a man said, pacing by the recruits. His loud voice and angry demeanor made it clear that he was some sort of drill instructor. He wore a tight black vest with silver buckles. His arms were muscular and bare except for the swirling pattern of intricate tattoos that wrapped around his bicep, "Welcome to your new home, kiddies. Your old home is just a fragment of glass that, in time, will be crushed into a fine powder to be blown away by the wind."

"Says you!" cried a rebellious recruit. No sooner had the words escaped his mouth than he was left sprawled out on the ground by a swift, heavy fist.

The drill instructor continued, "Your families want you here. They want you to become more than just farmers and tradesmen. They want you to become Black Rabbits so that you can serve this world on a larger scale than just milking a cow for some nameless village. If this weren't true, they wouldn't have given you up."

Several younger recruits broke out into sobs.

"Your family doesn't want you, but we do. We want you to be ambitious and strong. We want you to survive, to serve. Rebel, and you'll slow your training. A poorly trained Rabbit is a dead Rabbit. When a Rabbit fails, it fails everyone, not just itself. We don't tolerate failure. Failure means death to a Rabbit."

Elucard gritted his teeth, hanging on to each word. He needed to survive for himself, but more importantly he needed to survive for Jetta. She was waiting for him, counting on him.

The instructor pointed his finger at Elucard's chest, "You, where is home for you?"

"Ravensh–" Elucard started but was violently interrupted by a fast punch to his gut. He agonized in pain as he coughed and sucked in air.

"Do you not listen, boy? This is your home!" The instructor loomed over the crippled Elucard, "Help him up," He commanded, pointing at Myler and Geven, "You'll be divided into classes and given instructors. They'll teach you how to both handle weapons and use your body as a weapon. You'll learn to harness silence and shadows. We'll educate you on politics and how to manipulate the weak minded. By the time we're done with you, you'll be why children are afraid of the dark."

***

"You better not be taking a nap, Myler! Get off your stomach and finish that push-up!" Baines shouted. Elucard and the Ravenshore boys were under the watchful eyes of the Blade Brothers: Ridge and Baines. The two human instructors were well built and wore black leather armor with gray masks that covered up the lower parts of their face. Baines had black hair that he had styled in a spiky mohawk, while Ridge had blonde hair that he tied in a long braid that fell down his back. They were Blade Brothers, bound by the sword instead of blood. Partners that knew each other well.

They promised brutal training conditions, and Elucard's first week in the compound proved to be relentlessly agonizing.

His first week was stamina training; building up strength and speed so that he could take more and more physical punishment each day.

"I-I can't lift my body, Drill Instructor Baines" Myler spat a mixture of words, sweat, and saliva as he collapsed from sheer exhaustion.

Baines grabbed a tuft of the boy's chestnut hair and forced him to pull his body upwards, "Get to your feet, recruit. You disgust me!"

Izian had been holding back his spite and frustration for the Black Rabbits all week long. He saw himself as the leader of their small crew, and he considered each of the three to be his brothers. Each day his nerves were pushed a bit further and each day he swallowed the humiliation cast by the two instructors. However, now the ward was cracking, and he couldn't take it anymore.

"I'm going to stand up to them," he whispered to Geven, who was standing to his side in the formation.

"Izian, don't even think about it!" hissed back Geven.

Izian stepped forward from the line of recruits. His actions were immediately spotted by Ridge, who asked, "You have something to say, Recruit Izian?"

"I've had enough of your bullying and this life. I'm going home and my friends are coming with me!"

Ridge nodded as if he was in understanding with his words. He walked up to Izian and looked down into the boy's eyes, "You've got guts, kid, but you won't leave. You know why?"

Izian didn't flinch, "Why's that?"

Ridge placed a firm hand on his shoulder and gently spoke in his ear, "Your friends won't follow you."

Baines called for Geven, Myler and Elucard to come front and center. All three stared blankly at Izian, "Well, Ravenshore Recruits, will you be leaving us to join your leader?" asked Baines with a thick helping of mockery hanging in his voice.

All three bowed their heads to look away from their friend. Izian was crushed, "Guys, come on, we have to leave. Our families are waiting for us!" Izian pleaded.

"They fear us more than they respect you, recruit," Ridge said while chuckling.

"Myler, you don't want to be here. Come on now, I can protect you! Let's go home," Izian said trying to reach Myler's thoughts.

"You can't protect us, Izian. We tried to escape, and if it weren't for Legion, we'd have been dead! There's no leaving the Rabbits, No one has, no one will!" Geven asserted.

Izian ran to Elucard, "Elucard, think of Jetta."

Elucard looked at to Izian with sorrow in his eyes. Izian's words stung him. Of course he thought of Jetta, that's all he had ever thought about since he was brought to this dark place. But it was the reality of the situation that nailed him down. The Black Rabbits were a strong gale that could not be broken through. If he was going to see Jetta or his home ever again, he needed to survive the storm that was set before him.

"Elucard, let's get out of here." Izian tried again.

"Izian, stop. It's over. They're right." Elucard said in a low, broken tone.

Ridge walked over to Izian, "Will you be leaving then?"

Izian balled his fists and fought back tears. The weight of his situation came crashing down on him, but he tried to stay strong for the other recruits, "I won't leave my friends behind," he said as he fell back in line.

"A wise choice, Izian," Ridge said, "Now, let's continue. One hundred crunches, then fifty laps around the compound... Go!"

***

Three weeks had passed. Elucard kept himself occupied by trying to stay awake during history and politics lectures. He had little free time with physical and agility training squished in between his schooling and chores. Over time, his scrawny body was turning toned and strong. When he first arrived, he struggled to manage even five push-ups, but now he could do ninety without breaking a sweat. Mentally, he was getting to be as sharp as the blades he trained with. He found it hard to believe that there was a time that he couldn't name a single elf of nobility, but now he was well versed in the entire political history of the eight noble tribes. He gobbled up every lesson that the Black Rabbits fed him. The life that he saw as an enemy was turning into a valued ally.

"A Black Rabbit kills without thought or remorse and fears no man," said Ridge as he paced around his class, "The moment in which a Black Rabbit chooses to fight decides the success of the mission. You must choose the proper time to strike, and when it is wiser not to fight, you must rely on stealth."

Ridge stood with his class looking down at a path of twigs and dead leaves. The forest towered around them and rays of light stretched their long, shimmering fingers through the woods. Shadows, still fearful of the light that reached through the canopy, hid among the debris on the forest floor.

Baines stood at the other end of the path and called back to the class, "Navigate the path slowly and silently. Move with lightness in your step. Breathe steadily and avoid what light you can. Embrace silence and shadows and you will learn to master stealth."

Ridge shoved a recruit forward, "Recruit Crev, you first."

Crev took a single step on a twig and it broke under his weight. A resounding 'snap' echoed in the woods. Crev instantly fell to a knee as a leather strap whipped across his back.

"An incentive not to fail," Ridge said as he recoiled the leather whip. He turned to the rest of the students, "Begin."

Night turned to morning as the recruits gingerly moved through the path. Elucard winced, his back raw from his share of failures, but took note of all that went wrong and practiced to overcome each flaw found in his technique. After a couple of days, the recruits were able to pass through the trial with little sound – albeit very slowly – and please their proctors.

"You've done well, recruits. It would behoove you to practice this course in your free time. The more effort you put into each aspect of your training, the better an assassin you'll become as a whole."

***

A raw knuckled fist bludgeoned Elucard in the side of his face. He spun around helplessly as part of his vision faded to black. The elven boy collided into the stoney ground as his blood splattered across the rocks.

"Recruit Elucard, what did you do wrong?"

It had been two months since he was taken from Ravenshore and inducted into the Black Rabbit lifestyle. This was the first week of hand to hand combat training, "Learn to fight with your hands before you can learn to fight with a blade," That's what his instructors told them.

Elucard's hands were tied tightly behind his back and thirty pound weights were attached to each of his legs. Moving was awkward, but that was all part of the training. He had to learn to avoid getting hit, but not because he feared the hit. His opponent did not bear the same handicap.

Elucard had been hit. A lot. His nose was broken, his left eye was swollen shut, and thick strands of blood stretched down from his chin and clung to the ground.

"I let him hit me, Drill Instructor Baines." Elucard said spitting out a mouthful of dark blood.

"Why aren't unconscious yet then? This is the seventeenth hit you've taken to the face!"

Elucard was faint from the beating, but he didn't want to give in. Rabbits frowned on weak recruits, and he didn't want to be frowned upon, "When his punches hit less like a gentle breeze, maybe then he'll be able to knock me out!"

The recruits burst with the sound of laughter. Baines shook his head and smiled, "Recruit Fallon, are you going to take that from him?"

Fallon's ears were red to the tip with embarrassment. He watched as the half aware Elucard lifted his chin and made kissing sounds that only frustrated him further.

"No sir!" he cried as he threw a flurry of punches.

Elucard anticipated the barrage of fists. He wasn't just taking hits because he was too weighed down to dodge, he was studying the sloppy attacks of his opponent. Mustering the rest of his energy, Elucard ducked beneath Fallon's attacks, and rushed a knee into his groin.

Being as big as Fallon was for a boy, he went down hard from such a severe strike.

Ridge untied Elucard before calling over the medic to look at the boy's mangled face.

"Tired of being the punching bag, Recruit?" he chuckled.

"I was done having him make me look like a failure," answered Elucard.

"Well said, Recruit."

***

"Congratulations recruits, you've learned the basics of swordsmanship. Some of you have picked it up better than others, so we'll be pairing you off based on your potential skills," Baines said.

"Hold on, Baines. I say these recruits have earned a bit of fun. Let's see what they really learned. Let's have the two most promising blade wielders among them spar." Ridge looked the batch of anxious recruits over before pointing at Elucard and Crev, "You two. Show us what you've got."

Ridge tossed the two nervous boys practice blades. Their single-edged steel blades were left unsharpened to avoid unnecessary bloodshed, but their weight was identical to the real thing. It would be very difficult to slice off a limb with blades as dull as these, but the boys could still leave a painful welt if they tried. He walked between the two boys and looked each up and down.

"Give us a show." Ridge held his arm between them and then raised it quickly into the air, marking the start of the sparring.

Elucard held his blade in an inverted position and took a shy, defensive stance. Crev rushed forward and slashed rapidly at the elf. Elucard took a quick breath and dodged backwards. Juking to the side, he slid around his opponent and hefted a heavy side kick to Crev's ribs. The boy went crashing into a tree, rubbing his side. Baines leaned over to Crev's side, inspecting the bruise. He nodded his head, "A clean kick, but it won't kill your enemy. Elucard, show us a killing blow!"

Elucard nodded slowly, breathing hard. In the village of Ravenshore, he was the son of a fisherman. He was expected to be meek and quiet, never to take up arms and kill someone. He was Elucard Freewind, a good kid with no bright future, but a rather dull, peaceful one. Dull like the blade he held in his hand. However, here his future was one of a killer; being taught to hone a non-existent blood thirst; being taught to have a keen eye for weaknesses to exploit. Now his future had a real purpose and people would depend on him to shape the future of the world. For once in his life he was important, or at least his actions would be. But first, he needed to get through this sparring match.

Elucard rushed in and delivered a blow of dull steel to Crev's already bruised side. Crev dropped his blade and held his ribs, taking a knee. Elucard smiled and bowed to him. Baines patted Elucard's shoulder, "Very good. That strike would have cut through his stomach, spilling his guts. Only divine intervention could have saved him then."

"And the gods know not to interfere with Black Rabbit's marks." A figure dropped from the branches above and landed by the side of Baines and Ridge. Elucard immediately recognized him as Legion. He scanned the dirty and beaten faces of the new recruits until landing on a still smiling Elucard, "I've been watching you, boy. You pick things up well. I'd like to spar with you." Legion turned to the instructors, "Baines, give Elucard your blade."

Elucard's smile vanished as he took the sword from Baines, but he held the blade firmly in his hand. Legion unsheathed his large sword and hoisted it on top of his shoulder. With his free hand he beckoned Elucard to attack him.

The crowd of recruits began whispering amongst themselves as Elucard stood frozen in fear. Legion's ears drooped in disappointment, "Fine, I guess I'll just snap you out of your daze." Quick as a cat, Legion swung his blade in a horizontal arc. The blade was not long enough to reach Elucard, but the wind still cut into the boy's gut. The impact threw Elucard backwards into a tree, knocking the sword from his grip.

35

Legion frowned, shaking his head, "You had so much promise."

Elucard, shook off the momentary dizziness from the blow. Looking down, he pawed the wound across his stomach. An overwhelming feeling of pain set into Elucard's wound. He doubled over and dread set in: dread that there was still much more pain to come. Maybe his life back home was boring and simple, but it didn't involve this level of pain or fear. Tears began to blur his vision. In a flash Legion closed the distance and lifted Elucard's frail body higher against the tree. His grip clenched around Elucard's young elven throat. Elucard had no choice but to look into Legion's cold eyes, "To whom do you pray, Elucard? Father, god of creation? Jedeo, goddess of righteousness? Maybe you hate me right now and want to pray to the god of hate and evil, Dhalamar. That's it, isn't it? You want the dread lord himself to strike me down with a bolt of dark magic?"

Elucard could barely breathe, but he managed to gargle a weak response, "Father!"

Father or the All-Father, was who he was raised to pray to. He created the fish that his Pa's net dragged from the shore. He was a kind deity and never used his powers to smite those that didn't follow him. The other gods that shared in his covenant believed in defending peace and prosperity.

Legion tightened his grip and threw Elucard to the ground, "Father has abandoned you. None of the gods have love for you now that you're becoming a Rabbit… except one."

Elucard wanted to play possum and wish all the pain away. Legion's words were like a stake through his heart. The despair of knowing that everything that he knew and loved wasn't here to protect him any longer tore through him. Elucard shut his eyes tight while Legion's words echoed in his mind.

None of the gods have love for you now that you're becoming a Rabbit… except one.

Legion loomed above Elucard's broken body and eased in to whisper into the elf's long ears, "Only Alanna will embrace you in her wings. She is the goddess of death, and a Black Rabbit's only salvation. As a Rabbit, you will be given a spot in her army in the next life, and with our training, you will live to avoid the Roaming Plane and will be Alanna's messenger of death. However, if you wish to die now, you will die a coward and a disgrace."

Elucard's eyes snapped open, now carefully listening to Legion as he continued.

"You don't want that, do you? I saw a sense of wonderment in your eyes that night when I rescued you. You want the life of a Rabbit. You want to command respect, you want the discipline, you want your life to mean something. Elucard, it's within your grasp, all of it. But, you have to get through this first. You have to prove to us all that you deserve it. Now, get up."

Legion's words hit home. Everything he wanted from the Black Rabbit lifestyle was in those choice words. He rose to his feet, ignoring the pain pulsing from the gash on his stomach. He wanted – no, had – to prove that he wasn't a child anymore, that he was someone that could protect Jetta, that he was a Rabbit. Gritting his teeth, Elucard planned his next move.

Legion smirked as he narrowed his eyes. He was given that speech when he was Elucard's age and, like Elucard, it inspired him to take the path that led to a life immersed in the art of Alanna – the art of death. Legion positioned himself into an aggressive stance with his sword raised over his head pointing at his target. He wanted to see if Elucard was serious now. A deep cut down the shoulder would make or break the young elf.

"Elucard, you asked what I was, once. Do you remember what I said?"

Elucard shuffled his feet sideways, circling his opponent. He remembered that night very clearly. It was a keystone in his new life. Legion's words were as clear as the sky on a summer's day.

"You are an ideal."

Legion nodded, "All Black Rabbits are 'eidolons.' Anyone can be a killer or an assassin. A Black Rabbit must become more than just a shadow. We must live in one's mind and dreams. We must be the whisper in the ear; the shadow that follows the sun. We are not the reason, but the drive. Are you prepared to become an ideal, Elucard?"

"I am!" Elucard shouted.

"Then show me!"

Legion leaped forward, slashing down with a wind-sundering cut, but Elucard was anticipating the attack and dove sideways rolling towards his blade. Elucard grabbed it and charged headlong, brandishing the weapon. Legion, though taken pleasantly by surprise, didn't allow Elucard's advance and whipped Elucard in the face with a hefty roundhouse kick. The boy went down hard. Elucard growled through his teeth, sucking in the pain. He rolled to the side, and narrowly avoided a driving blade through his shoulder. Elucard jumped up and slashed low at Legion's left leg. Legion dodged nimbly, jumping backward and performed a crisscross of wind slashes that exploded into Elucard. Blood erupted from the "X" like mark on Elucard's chest.

Sliding back, Elucard fell to a knee, exhausted from the match. Salty sweat dripped from his forehead. Legion walked forward, stopping shy of Elucard, "Do you give in? You were never meant to win this fight."

Elucard tightened his grip on the blade's handle. He took a wild leap, exerting the last of his strength in a final attack, "I haven't proven myself yet!"

Legion was caught off guard from the outburst. His eyes slid to Elucard's slicing blade and caught it with his hand in mid swing, as it just grazed his cheek. Had the boy been stronger, the sword would have cut through Legion's hand and slain him where he stood.

Elucard dropped down and collapsed. Legion tossed Elucard's blade to the ground. As he turned to walk away, he coolly spoke to Ridge, "See that the boy receives medical attention." Legion took a glance at Elucard who was being helped up by several of his peers. He shook his head with an admiring smile.

***

Legion bowed his head and knelt in the presence of the High Blade, Avalon. She was pacing around him, attempting to read why he had requested to see her. Also within the quarters was Vada, Avalon's First Blade and Blade Sister. She leaned against the wall, wondering the same thing.

Avalon finally stopped in front of Legion, "Word on the wind says that you made a cameo at Baines' and Ridge's training session today. Is that what this is about?"

Legion looked up. It was only an hour ago that he was sparring with Elucard. Within that hour he thought ceaselessly about the boy's guts and aptitude. With proper molding he could get to be as proficient as Legion himself was. The clan could harness those skills. However, Legion also knew that the boy would waste away under the tutelage of a poor teacher. He didn't doubt Baines' and Ridges' skills, but they had less prowess than he. No, Elucard needed a great teacher. Someone that he trusted, but the only one he could rely on for this task was himself.

Legion collected himself before speaking, "High Blade, I–" He hesitated slightly, "I wish to take a recruit under my wing."

"So this was more than just an appearance? You took a shining to one of those kids?" Avalon grinned. In the years she had known Legion, she

38

had never known him to be a teacher. He was a good team member and a solid ally, but not a teacher.

"I see much in one named Elucard. I don't want to see his potential go to waste."

Avalon looked to her First Blade, who nodded in agreement, "Very well, Legion" she said eyeing the fresh cut on his cheek, "Consider Elucard your apprentice. If he fails, you fail. When he succeeds, you succeed. Like a Blade Brother, he is now bound to you."

Legion nodded and bowed. There was much work to be done.

6

"Dawnedge, Leafsong, Dreamstar, Baneberry, Redroot, Raindancer, Breezerunner, and…" Young Koda furrowed his brow trying to remember the eighth noble elf tribe. His teacher whacked a ruler down upon his old wooden desk. The desk rattled with the sharp noise as wood met wood. Koda snapped out of a shallow trance and rapped out the final tribe, "Moonfall!"

His teacher smiled, clearly pleased with her young student. She strolled casually to the blackboard and chalked out the eight tribes. She turned her head, glancing keenly at Koda. Tipping her spectacles down, she asked her next question.

"Young Prince, of all elven tribes found in Long Whisper, why are these eight particular tribes considered to be noble?"

Koda pondered this question, but only momentarily.

"These were the tribes that joined together to form an alliance to create Long Whisper. They elected my trib-, I mean, the Dawnedge tribe to lead the alliance. All other tribes wanted no part in the creation of a nation."

"Excellent! Now, for a harder query: Which tribe betrayed King Jaelyn?"

Looking at the blackboard, Koda carefully read each name written there. He carefully considered his choices. He knew the answer, but it was asked confusingly.

"Ms. Tabitha, you asked a trick question."

Tabitha smirked; the prince was keen.

"Did I, young Prince?"

"Yes, ma'am. There were no tribes that betrayed my father, just a single elf. He attempted to poison my father while at a dinner party. However, my father's would be assassin was betrayed by his own tribe."

"Very good, what was his name? What became of him?"

"His name was Ryjin. Ryjin Leafsong. His own tribe shunned him, stripping him of his nobility. Father exiled him from Long Whisper. What happened to him from there, I wouldn't know. I know the Leafsongs were forgiven for Ryjin's deeds. Though I hear there is still mistrust among the other tribes." Koda gave a quick glance at the clock that quietly ticked above the doorway.

Tabitha began to erase the board, chuckling, "You're right, my prince, time is up. Go meet up with that wolf of yours. She must be dying to see you again."

***

King Jaelyn strolled the bustling streets of the new city still undergoing construction. Everyday the city's economy grew and a new shop sprouted up. The gigantic tree at the heart of the city was once the elder tree of all the elven tribes. However, once the eight noble tribes crowned Jaelyn as their leader and king of their alliance, he made the unpopular decision of constructing a city around it.

Lost Dawns, you will be my shining legacy.

"My King!"

Jaelyn turned to find his brother and adviser briskly jogging to catch up to him.

"Tull, Brother! A fine day in Lost Dawns, eh?"

Tull, waved a hand, and bent over to catch his breath, "A fine day indeed, I have your report, it's not good news."

Jaelyn waved his hand ignoring the last part of Tull's response, "How goes my son's teaching? I feared Koda wouldn't pay attention to Tabitha Breezerunner unless she floated the chalk with the Magi. That boy's head is stuffed with all those magic lessons from our father."

Tull frowned at the subject being changed. He answered quickly, hoping to catch Jaelyn's attention with content of the report, "Koda's teaching goes well. He's picked up on history and politics quickly. Now for the report, my King–"

"Where is my son? No doubt his class is over by now. I want to show him the new book shop that opened today."

Interrupted again. It was as if Tull's brother was doing this on purpose, "I saw Koda walking around with his familiar. Now, about this report, it's very important–"

"Ah, yes, a familiar. I'm not sure I like him being raised to take on our old man's role as Arcane Guardian. It may have been a dream we once had, but we grew to realize it was nonsense. Remember, Tull?"

"Indeed, life changed fast when the tribes chose the Dawnedge to lead. Fiona would be proud that her son is spending time with you...take advantage of that and remember he is not some heir to be groomed."

41

Jaelyn raised an eyebrow from the remark, "My son will choose the proper path; he doesn't need to be led." Finally, Jaelyn eyed the parchment with a worried look. Since the beginning of Lost Dawns' construction, workers and townsfolk had been dying in mysterious accidents or falling ill. What kind of horrible news would befall his city today?

Tull took the silence as a cue to read, "My King, as of last night, three construction workers have fallen ill after a night of eating out. They did not survive the sunrise."

"Enough! Enough of all of this. They did not fall ill, they were poisoned! They did not die in some mysterious accident, they were sabotaged! They did not go missing, they were murdered! I am no fool, so do not treat me as such!"

Tull rolled the parchment back up. He attempted to avoid his older brother's gaze, but to no avail. Tull spoke quietly, "Brother, the White Cloak that you sent for has arrived."

Jaelyn clapped his hands to together, "I've heard much of this Marcus Newsun. His exploits are what legends are made of, let's go meet him. Where has he set up?"

"The old Ruens' temple, my King," Tull said, hiding a stressful look.

***

Ruens was the patron god of magic and insight, a favored deity of worship for most elves. The temple was a small, run down abbey that had been long abandoned after the Arcana War. It now served as a base of operations for the White Cloaks in Lost Dawns, as a proper barracks was yet to be built.

The rickety floorboards creaked as rats scurried away from the opening oak doors. Jaeyln strode in, his face plastered with excitement. Tull hung his ears low, avoiding any eye contact from his brother.

Jaeyln bellowed out a long call, which bounced and echoed amongst the large interior, "Hello, Captain Newsun? It is I, the King! I've come to welcome you to our great city!"

Avren popped his head around the corner, dressed in simple civilian attire, a pencil in the fold of his ear and a look of exhaustion strewn across his face. In his hands were several scrolls. Upon seeing the king and his adviser, he immediately dropped his papers and ran to the presence of the elven king, bowing graciously.

"My King, forgive me, I've been hard at work since I arrived yesterday morning. I inherited this mess from whoever handled the scrolls, blueprints, and documents of the city's construction."

Jaeyln looked Avren up and down. A look of confusion replaced his excitement, "You are younger than I imagined you, Captain Newsun."

"Sergeant, my king; I am not an officer just yet." Avren corrected.

"You're only a Sergeant? You were hailed as a hero during the war against the Queen of Chains. You lead Varis through the Baneblood plague. You battled the pirates on the Serpent Sea. They've written plays about your exploits and you are still just a Sergeant?"

Avren raised an eyebrow.

"My King, this is not Marcus Newsun, this is his son, Avren Newsun." explained Tull.

Jaelyn clicked his tongue in mixture of disappointment and annoyance.

"His son?"

"My king, he came highly recommended, from Captain Marcus himself." Tull said.

"My King, I've successfully lead patrols all across Varis. I know I'm up to the task of dealing with Black Rabbits!" said Avren zestfully.

Jaelyn cocked his head. He knew of the incidents happening in his city were the work of ill intent, but he never could place a face or name for that which ran rampant in his city, "Black Rabbits? What are they?"

Avren grew serious, "Not a 'what', but a 'who.' They are clan of assassins who operate exclusively in Long Whisper. We have been doing our best to look into their activities, but they have proved to be an extremely elusive foe. They are deadly and not to be taken lightly. I know, without a doubt, at least one is in Lost Dawns."

Jaelyn furrowed his brow as his temper rose, "Who leads them?"

"We don't know who leads them, but we are aware of how their infrastructure works." Avren paused before answering the leading question, "They have two high ranking officers: a High Blade and a First Blade. The High Blade works as a captain, giving out orders with the First Blade serving as a lieutenant."

"If the High Blade is the just the captain, then who is the general?" Jaelyn asked, very interested in the information.

"Someone called 'The Silent Master' whose identity is still a mystery."

"These Black Rabbits, how long have they been operating in our country?" it was Tull's turn to ask a question.

"We don't know exactly. We are under the impression that it has been as long as the Dawnedges have been in power, but this is just hearsay. Since they operate only in Long Whisper, we wouldn't know for sure since we haven't been assigned to this country for very long," Avren responded, slightly wincing at the king's agitation with the lack of knowledge Avren had of this enemy.

"Well what do you know? Do you have any idea where they might be operating from?" the king's frustration was clearer than clean water.

"My King, we still know so little of them. We have only what we've heard from word of mouth to go by."

"Well, who hired them to sabotage my city?" the king roared back in frustration.

"We don't know that either. I suspect one of your lords." Avren said, quickly regretting his most recent response.

"How dare you accuse my nobles of such treachery!" Jaelyn hissed.

Tull was quick to step in, "Brother, it is not far fetched that one of your noblemen could be behind this; do not forget Ryjin. He was a Leafsong. It was an unpopular decision to unite the tribes. It was an equally unpopular decision to build a city with our Elder Tree as the centerpiece."

Jaelyn rubbed his chin in thought.

"If I may, my King," said Avren, "You have many enemies; The Guard knew that coming here. We must suspect everyone, but I will not take any action until I have proof. Until then my number one concern is the safety of the people of this city. Trust me when I say that these Rabbits will be caught, and hanged," the young White Cloak had determination overflowing in his voice, "As we speak I have my men scouring the city for any information on these vermin."

Jaelyn spat on the ground, "Good. Rabbits make for a fine stew."

***

The crashing sound of leather boots and heavy armor bounded through the small abbey. Shouting echoed around the foyer as the cries of agonizing pain spilled through the halls.

Avren raced to meet his squad of White Cloaks, and his eyes widened when he saw the scene that was before him. Two Cloaks braced a third man who was bleeding heavily from his neck and left side. Blood soaked through his tunic and trousers, dripping into a puddle forming on the ground.

Behind them was a Cloak holding a chain that bound a shifty looking elf. He had clearly been beaten up a bit, judging by the welt under his eye and the lower fat lip that matched the shiner.

Avren assessed the chaos of the situation and first barked commands before asking much needed questions, "Clear that table, put Jefferson on it! There are towels and bandages in the storage! Grab them and get him patched up!"

"What of the prisoner, sergeant?" asked one of the men.

"Tie him to a chair. Once Jefferson is patched up, I want a full report of what happened!" Avren said.

An hour went by before the injured Jefferson's cries were just groans and he slowly passed out. Avren dried his bloodied hands and changed his shirt to a fresher one before addressing his corporal.

"Higgins, what in the name of the All-Father happened out there?"

Higgins' weary face was pale and tired from the events that befell him and his men, but he swallowed his exhaustion to unwind the disastrous tale, "Sergeant, we were following a tip that this elf: Remmin Fairfollow, was at several places before they were hit by recent tragedy."

"The Mystic Fang, the clock tower site, and Madam Sasha's Bordello?" Avren asked, listing the three most recent places a worker's murder had occurred.

"Yes, though he was spotted at the bordello thrice." Higgins said, glancing back at the bound prisoner.

"Hey, an elf has needs!" Remmin called out. An armored fist rocked his jaw, shutting him up.

"Continue, Higgins," said Avren nodding at the Cloak that socked the prisoner.

"We did some quick investigating and found Remmin's apartment in the Roots. We broke down the door and barged in and found him speaking to – and possibly doing business with – a hooded figure. Female..."

"You Cloaks are in a heap of trouble. The people I work for–" A swift backhand kept Remmin from interrupting again.

"We rushed to arrest Remmin and apprehend the hooded figure. We were four and highly trained. They were two, we didn't think..." Higgins lost his train of thought as he looked at the mangled Jefferson."

"She did that number on Jefferson, but you took care of her?" Avren filled in the blanks the best he could.

Higgins was silent.

"Corporal Higgins, is the hood figure dead?" Avren asked again, his voice raised this time.

"She escaped, sergeant…" another man piped up.

Avren looked at Higgins frantically, "Higgins, were you followed?"

Remmin started to laugh. Some of his teeth were missing, blood bubbled through the gaps. It was unnerving for Avren, who realized the full gravity of his situation.

"Shut him up!" Avren commanded. He looked back at Higgins, but gasped as the soldier collapsed in his arms. A dagger was stuck in the back of the Higgins' neck. From the rafters, a shadow moved quickly from one wooden cross beam to another.

Remmin continued to laugh as Avren scrambled to shout commands at his men.

"Draw your blades! Circle around the prisoner, we need to keep him safe! Banner, fire your bow and take her down!"

Banner was a crack shot sharpshooter with any type of projectile. Within a minute he had fired off an impressive volley of arrows that darted into the rafters.

The assailant somersaulted off of a beam, narrowly missing the attacks, and landed mere inches away from Avren. She removed her hood revealing her stunningly beautiful shadow elf features. Her deep violet eyes locked with Avren's dark brown ones. There was a moment of infatuation between the two before the assassin spoke.

"Well, aren't you a handsome soldier."

Avren shook off the charm, "Arrest her, I want her in shackles, now!"

The assassin laughed as she skillfully danced around the men, stabbing them in the thighs and backs.

"Shackles? My, you like it rough. You're a keeper, darling!" she laughed as she cartwheeled right up to Avren, pushing her breasts into Avren's chest.

Avren gawked at the gorgeous woman, stumbling over his own words, "W-who are you?"

The shadow elf gently brushed her fingers up his chest and nipped at his ear, whispering her name, "Elisa."

Avren swallowed hard before tripping backwards. Elisa back flipped away from Avren blowing him a kiss, "Until next time, lover!" she said in a sultry tone before vanishing into the city.

Avren shook his head, sweating from the encounter. He rushed to check on his fallen men, inspecting them for injuries before walking over to a surprisingly silent Remmin.

"Damn it," Avren sighed as he pulled a dagger from the throat of the now dead elf.

7

"Look around you, Elucard," whispered Legion, "The forest seems quiet, doesn't it? But listen closer. Shadows creep along the grass like cracks on an old stone wall. Roots break through the soil with their thick, armored tendrils. However, the roots are not without vulnerability. Termites and other small creatures chew into this tough hide to build their homes. All is intertwined. Nature rests on the delicate balance between life and death. It is a volatile scale, prone to wild and unpredictable swings. When the scale tips in the favor of life, death must relieve it of this excess weight. This is our role, Elucard. We are the hand of death." Legion sat on a thick branch, cutting into his apple with a small throwing knife. The nectar of the fruit dribbled down the bright red flesh and down to the forest floor. The mentor tossed a slice to his pupil, "Do you understand the importance of the task at hand? We are not simple thugs and killers. We are keepers of that balance; a necessity."

Elucard examined the apple slice. The edge was clean, thus he knew the blade Legion used to cut it was sharp. He popped it into his mouth and savored the fresh taste. It had been six months since he was taken under Legion's wing. His master made it a point to further his training on the basics, but he made sure to also educate him in academics and philosophy.

A blade is only as sharp as the Rabbit wielding it.

Elucard nodded, "A flower in a bed of weeds does not grow."

Legion tossed Elucard another slice, "You understand what that means for you, right?"

Elucard shrugged, casually, "Got to pull some weeds."

Legion grinned, but slid his face into a stern look, "Are you prepared for that task?"

Elucard plucked a leaf from the branch over his head.

"I'll do what it takes."

His master looked at him coolly, tossing him another slice of the apple.

"What if I asked you to kill one of your peers? Would you hesitate or would you give them the chance to run?"

Elucard raised an eyebrow at the question. This didn't seem to be a philosophy discussion anymore, what was his master trying to get at?

"Another Rabbit, Master?"

"No, not quite; another recruit."

Another recruit was still a Rabbit to Elucard. Although it had been nearly half a year since he'd seen any of the other recruits, he still felt like he was a part of that group. However, what if this was a test? What if not all marks were so simply laid out? What if the circumstances were more than black and white? Elucard pondered more. Legion interjected, as he watched his pupil think.

"My student, the Blood Forest fast approaches. You will be pitted against your fellow recruits and in a sanctioned trial such as this. You may have to take the life of a peer. You will be judged on your cunning, prowess, stealth, and most of all, your ability to take a life."

Elucard looked up, trying to imagine such a test, "The Blood Forest?" he asked.

Legion continued, "An eight mile stretch of twisted, gnarled woods with a canopy so dense that it is unfathomably dark. It is the perfect battlefield for a young recruit to prove they are ready to truly become a Rabbit. All recruits will be released within the Blood Forest and will be encouraged to kill or be killed. It will take all that you've learned to survive. So, my student, are you prepared to take a life?"

"If they are prepared to die, I will grant them a death."

"I assure you, they will not be prepared to die."

Elucard paused, "I shall grant them a death all the same."

Legion smiled, "Very well, young student. Now, what of the weeds?"

"What of them? I'll do what it takes."

Legion gestured to a plume of smoke through a line of trees. Elucard focused his elven eyes. His eyes were more perceptive now than when he was living in Ravenshore. Legion had trained them. Now all of his senses had been heightened.

A blade is only as sharp as the Rabbit wielding it.

The crisp dusk air nipped at his ears. Elucard looked at Legion as he pulled up his hood, "A camp?"

"A weed."

Legion beckoned Elucard to follow as he jumped to the neighboring branches leading to the camp.

A fire blazed under skewers poking into a few skinned squirrels. A ragged man with a filthy black and gray beard crawled from his makeshift tent. The shelter was as tattered as his clothes and both reeked of a foul odor. It stunk of a life full of failures.

The two assassins perched in an overhanging tree whispering to each other. Their voices were low; too low for a normal man to hear, but high enough for a trained ear to hear. A tongue the Black Rabbits had perfected.

Legion lightly touched Elucard's shoulder, "You are to kill this man. You are to make it quick, silent, and clean. This man has suffered a lifetime of anguish. His death does not need to be cruel."

Elucard gripped the leather bound handle of his sword. He gritted his teeth as he pulled up his mask to the bridge of his nose.

"May Alanna grant you grace," Legion's voice wove into Elucard's mind – a mind now heavy with a sense of duty, and a sense of fear.

Not a fear of whether he would be caught or punished for failure, a fear that this would change him forever. Was he ready to go the distance? was he ready to spill blood? Legion had him practice killing deer, but deer were different from people.

Elucard dropped down silently into the camp ground. The long shadow of the tree hid his presence. Staying light and using the front padding of his feet to cautiously feel out for twigs that could give away his presence, Elucard stalked behind the vagabond. The rookie assassin's blade quivered as it crept along the back of the homeless man's neck. The cold steel rested coolly sending a tingling shiver down the victim's spine.

"Please," a voice squeaked, "I've got nothing worth stealing. I don't want to die," the man wept.

Elucard froze. Deer never begged for their life. This man wanted to live. Elucard's hands now held more than a sword. They held this man's life.

The man slowly turned, his eyes red with tears, snot ran from his nose, the man blubbered as he formed his words, "I ain't never hurt no one. Please…"

Elucard withdrew his sword, his head lowered as his heart sank. He called to Legion, "Master, I can't kill an innocent life, this man is no weed."

Legion dropped by the side of his student, making no sound, "My student, not every innocent life has a purpose in this world. He serves no one but himself. He has no attachments. He loves no one and no one loves him. Give his life meaning, Elucard. Allow the starving wolves to feed on his carcass. Let the grubs devour his flesh. Let the soil take his bones. Let Alanna take his soul. Restore balance. Answer the call, my student!"

Elucard's grip on his blade strengthened. His eyes shut tightly. He hefted his blade into the air, but Legion halted his motion.

"No, open your eyes. You must bear witness to your deeds."

Elucard snapped open his eyes, sweat beads dripped off his soaked mask. This was the moment that would forever change his life. The fear of what he would become would now be a reality. Legion's teachings cycled through his head.

A flower in a bed of weeds does not grow.

However, in this case, he was the flower. His fear was the weeds. His blade was was the gardener. Killing this man would free him. Free him from fear, free him to flourish. The man's cries broke his thoughts.

"Why are you doing this?"

Flashes of Ravenshore gushed through his mind like the white rapids of a river that flowed into the ocean on which Ravenshore sat. Images of his parents seemed to be within reach, but as he went to approach them, they began to walk away. The faster Elucard ran, he still could not catch up to them.

'Wait, please, Ma, Pa, stay with me!'

No matter how hard he tried to get to them, his touch was just shy of his parents. Elucard stopped, alone in the void of his mind. Memories swirled around him like a drifting mist. Pictures of his childhood, his love for his friends and family, his friendship with Jetta ebbed about him.

Jetta.

The memories blew away and disintegrated like dead leaves in a harsh wind. All that was left was the tiny girl he once promised to always be there for.

Jetta, please, I'm sorry.

The girl's head was lowered, her gaze did not meet the yearning of his own. She was silent, but in that silence Elucard struggled with himself, his promise, and his new path.

Beside him, a new figure appeared. Legion. The assassin did not look at him, but simply put his hand on Elucard's shoulder.

Elucard, this life is no more, it stagnates your mind. It is a waste of thought. Memories like this will only stall your progression.

I can't forget Jetta. Elucard's mind echoed.

Then use her memory, let it push you, let it be a reminder of when you were innocent and weak. Use her as a milestone in your past to show yourself how far you've gone. Your memories have held you back. Instead, let them give you a boost up to the mountain that you're trying to climb.

Elucard looked up to where Legion stood, but found he was now alone. No memories, no Jetta, no Legion...nothing. Yet, he didn't feel alone. Was this how he was supposed to feel? Was this what he needed to to fuel his drive? The drive to kill?

Once more, the voice of the vagabond cried out to Elucard, snapping him back to reality.

Elucard's voice was a whisper. As if he still was trying to convince himself more than the man, he said, "You have tipped the scales and I must restore the balance."

A whipping sound sliced through the air as the man's head rolled onto the ground. The headless body dropped hard. Elucard let go of the sword. It seemed to weigh a hundred tons. His throat became thick and heavy, choking him as he held back the need to cry.

Legion put out the campfire, turning to smile at Elucard, "You did well. It seems you have what it takes to walk this path."

Elucard was silent.

8

"Incorruptible. That is what you must become," the voice of the commander of the Long Whisper Division rang loud and true, "When we don our cloaks, we not only represent ourselves, but our order as well. We must remain steadfast in protecting those that have placed their trust in us – undaunting in our duties, undaunting in living our code."

A line of graduating White Cloak recruits stood before Marcus Newsun. He was dressed in cream-colored finery; a saber with a gold and silver guard hung by his side, sheathed in an ebonwood case. Behind him towered the Long Whisper headquarters, a guild hall constructed by the White Cloaks merely a decade prior – a testament to the youth of Long Whisper's government and the recency of the Cloaks as a peacekeeping force in the region. Banners embroidered with the triple crossed swords were draped over the gray stone walls – one sword representing each of the three founders. Brothers bound by blood, bound by duty – a duty that was passed down to the new recruits who were here today.

Wiccer stepped forth, older and wiser than the boy that he once was. His silver tunic with its white trim looked almost regal on him. Slowly, he bent to one knee and bowed his head to his superior. The man standing before him was not only his lifelong instructor and Guild Master, but his father as well. Beneath his white dress gloves, Wiccer's hands were still bruised and blistered from constant punishment. Even the smallest mistakes in his training and lessons had earned him a swift strike on the knuckles with a wooden measuring stick or a whipping rod – whichever his father had handy. He had no chance to play with children his age, or even the opportunity to enjoy an autumn's day. Honestly the thought had never really crossed his mind until now.

For a fleeting moment, he caught himself wishing for a normal life, though he did not fully understand what that might entail. He wondered what would have become of him had he been born a farmer's son of more meager means. The idea of such a life seemed so foreign to him. Where was the glory or valor to be found in toiling in the hot sun to feed your family when a fat lordling would take a vast share of it for himself? No, this was not the life for him. Wearing the white cloak was a privilege that civilians could never understand. He banished such foolish longings from his mind. The only life worth living was one that strove for honor, duty, and the right to bear 'The Cloak of the Incorruptible'.

"Arise, Wiccer," Marcus continued. He held out a white cloak with a silver trim. The golden trim on his own cloak, a mark of leadership, glinted in the sunlight.

Wiccer's eyes were focused on the ivory cloak before him. He had desired nothing more in all of his life. He lived vicariously through the tales of his parents. He bled for the chance to earn a cloak of his very own. His very being desperately longed for this cloak, and now here it was in his father's outstretched hands. Marcus floated it around his son's shoulders.

"The boy is now a man," Marcus nodded as Wiccer raised his hand over his right eyebrow in a strong, but emotional salute.

"Thank you, Father," whispered Wiccer.

A formal dinner was being held for the new guild members at the guild hall. Although this particular hall was not nearly as massive as the one in Varis, it was still nothing to frown at. Pipers and lute strummers played a slow tune as the guests danced a traditional Varisian dance. They raised their hands together as they moved in a large circle and their bodies swayed back and forth to the melody that filled the air. On the banquet table, a feast of roasted vegetables, pheasant, and large goblets of fine ale were placed before each of the new members.

Wiccer walked in wearing a pressed white dress tunic with matching polished golden buttons that adorned him. His new pearl-white cloak was draped over his right shoulder, its silver trim glistening in the candlelight. The palm of his hand rested on the ceremonial saber that he had received along with his cloak and his boots were glossed to a shine. Many young women smiled and giggled as he made his way through the ball.

Marcus spotted him, calling him away from a night of pleasure and to a night of business. In his hand he had a long object wrapped in wolf hide.

"My son, I'm so proud of you. You've come along way and I'm overjoyed that you can now serve by my side," Marcus said as he greeted his son. He wrapped a hand around the back of Wiccer's head, pulling it to meet with his own.

"Thank you, Father."

Handing Wiccer the gift, he patiently waited for his son to unwrap it, revealing a fine arming sword enclosed in a white leather scabbard, "It was your brother's first sword, lightweight, faster than most blades. Avren wanted to give it to you himself when you earned your cloak."

Wiccer took hold of the blade and carefully pulled it from its scabbard. He inspected its edge and weighed its balance. He could tell that it was a finely crafted blade. Satisfied, he smiled, "When you write to Avren, tell him that I'll use it well."

Marcus sipped from his chalice, "Tell him yourself."

Marcus pulled a writ from a leather-bound pouch on his belt. He tossed it to his confused son,

"Read it."

With a confused look on his face, Wiccer hurriedly unravelled the scroll and scanned the finely written words it held. The words on the small scroll seemed to be too good to be true. In disbelief, he quickly looked it over a second time before looking up into his father's eyes.

"Father, Avren has sent for me!" He shook his head in shock. His brother had requested aid of him in the newly established Lost Dawns. Not only was he already receiving his first assignment, but it was with his brother in the the capital city of Long Whisper!

"You leave in the morning…Try not to celebrate too hard," Marcus replied, grinning.

***

Wiccer sat in a carriage looking out the window watching the many trees flash by. Flanking from either side of the carriage was a White Cloak on horseback. Marcus had taken every precaution to get his son to Lost Dawns safely. Reports from pathfinder patrols had told of ambushes from both bandits and Black Rabbits alike. No chances could be taken.

The carriage inched to a stop at a roadside village. Wiccer's escort had been traveling all morning and all afternoon without a break and now seemed to be as safe a time as any for the horses to rest.

The carriage door opened, "Wiccer, come out and find some lunch. We'll be resting for an hour or so." Elleneis was a tall, stern woman whose words were often as hardened as she was. Wiccer fostered a healthy mixture of fear and respect for his new superior and saluted her as she spoke.

"Keep your hand down, Private," she scolded, "Last thing I need is some greenhorn letting any lurking Rabbits know that I'm in command."

Wiccer's hand quickly fell to his side in embarrassment. Elleneis murmured curses and insults as she walked away.

Looking about the village, Wiccer scanned the various shops that dotted the sparse town: a blacksmith, a trading post, a tannery, and a tailor. Wiccer spotted a small butcher shop where several of his fellow White Cloaks had congregated. He took a moment to take in the aroma of the different meats that were cooking over several small fires behind the butcher. Mutton, steak, chicken, and even some other unidentifiable meats sizzled just feet away, and Wiccer felt his stomach rumble beneath his skin.

"What can I get you, sir?" the butcher's wife asked. Her face was worn and leathery, hinting that she had seen the many seasons at least fifty times over.

"A woman of your age and beauty shouldn't have to work," Wiccer said, smiling politely, "Surely you have a son running about?" Wiccer looked around and began to notice that the village was surprisingly quiet. Aside from the occasional hammering of hot iron by the blacksmith, there was something truly missing.

"Our son and his wife left our village when their second child was recruited." The elderly woman grimaced as she spoke and Wiccer's smile dropped. He could sense that she had never recovered from the absence they left behind.

"Recruited?" Wiccer scanned the village again, "Second child? Both were recruited? For what?"

The other White Cloaks were silent, but gave solemn looks to the young rookie.

"To become Black Rabbits. Both of them were recruited within three years of each other." She looked truly and deeply sad, "But at least they'll be together. My son and his wife just couldn't suffer the losses though." She began to trail off as Wiccer looked at the village around him with fresh eyes. He knew what caused the silence now. There were no children in this village. No children playing in the fields, no children chasing the ducks, and no children getting candy at the general store. Just none.

"The Black Rabbits take your children and you all just let this happen!?" Wiccer shouted, slamming his fist on the counter.

"And what do you propose we do, young sir? Fight them? Ha! We barely have enough strength to run this shop, much less fight off an entire clan of assassins, thieves, and murderers." The truth in her words was hard for Wiccer to accept.

Wiccer stood up, knocking his seat backwards, "We should!" He snapped his head at his strangely quiet peers, "Why aren't the Cloaks doing something about this?"

"Wiccer, you're causing a scene, take a seat and be quiet," said an elven corporal named Rahje.

Wiccer was flabbergasted by Rahje's response, "How can you be so calm when such an injustice lays right before you?"

Rahje rolled his eyes, "Wiccer, we do what we can. We protect the larger cities, but we are too small of a unit to protect every town and village. What you ask is impossible."

"We are called 'incorruptible', but we sit idly by when people need us the most?"

"The wolf does not try to eat every animal he sees. He leaves the squirrel alone to chase after the deer," Rahje said.

"The wolf makes sure to get the Rabbit, though," sneered Wiccer

"And the wolf would get exhausted chasing a rabbit instead of going for the bigger game. Wiccer, we've known for some time that we can't protect everyone. It stinks, but it's the way the world works. You can't save everyone. Concentrate on what matters. Do what you are told and hope you can make it through another day. Now sit down and just eat your food."

"I'm no longer hungry," Wiccer said as he stormed away.

***

The ancient Elder Tree that pierced the sky above Lost Dawns towered in the distance as Wiccer's carriage passed through the city gates. Though still under a great deal of construction, the cobblestone streets were heavily crowded with elves, humans, kanis, and other races Wiccer couldn't readily recognize. The crowd parted as the carriage passed. Plenty of faces attempted to peer through the carriage's windows. Wiccer kept his composure, despite his urge to gawk at the splendor of the city. Although he had been raised in Varis and had seen many wondrous places, Lost Dawns was still a sight to behold.

Buildings and small tenements dotted the sides of the roads creating a labyrinth of back alleys and side streets. Massive roots twisted over and around them. From the more low hanging branches spanned great bridges that connected the higher part of the city. The nobility of Lost Dawns resided here in their vast, extravagant homes while those of lesser stations found what meager shelter they could in 'The Roots.'

The carriage stopped in front of a decrepit abbey. Though it was clear that it had seen better days, its beauty still shined from its elegant stained glass windows and through the large moss covered carving of the angel god, Ruens. Wiccer's deity was the goddess of justice, Jedeo. He bowed and made a silent prayer before pulling his duffel bag off the roof of the carriage, not forgetting to tip the driver a silver piece. He inhaled a deep breath to calm his nerves. This was his first assignment and his first true day as an official White Cloak. More importantly though, he'd not seen his brother in nearly a year.

Before he could enter the church, the doors flung open and Avren ran to Wiccer and embraced him in a bear hug. Avren chuckled, welcoming his brother, "Wiccer, it's been seasons since I've seen my baby brother! How have you been?"

Wiccer gasped for air, trapped in Avren's well meaning clutches, "I'd be better able to breathe if I wasn't being smothered to death by you!"

Avren blinked and released Wiccer, dropping him to a clutter on the ground.

"Sorry, little brother. Life is rough in this city. It's good to see a piece of home." Avren took Wiccer's duffle bag and motioned his brother to follow him inside, "We are most likely being watched by Rabbits. I didn't send for you because you needed a vacation."

Still sitting on the ground, Wiccer looked around bewildered by the thought of Black Rabbits being in blade's reach.

With a more serious tone, Avren lowered his voice, "You're right to have that look on your face. The Rabbits have been sabotaging the construction of this city. Workers have been falling ill or going missing. Either way, they are usually found dead soonafter. I've even seen one myself, she was–" Avren stopped to think about his close encounter. His last encounter with a Rabbit left him with conflicting dreams and desires with Elisa. She haunted his thoughts with her seductive body, "She was deadly."

"It can't be as obvious as their disapproval of the leadership. Assassins don't involve themselves in politics that way," Wiccer blurted out.

"Right you are, little brother. No, the Rabbits have been hired by someone that doesn't want the city built."

Now standing, Wiccer rubbed his chin, pondering the history of the eight elven noble tribes, "Leafsong?" he asked inquisitively.

"Leafsong would be the most obvious choice, which is precisely why the Leafsong are the least likely to be behind it."

Wiccer raised an eyebrow.

Avren chuckled, "I've had a year to deal with this. The Leafsong were the tribe that betrayed their king, but they were absolved of when they banished Ryjin. You remember that from your lessons, don't you?"

Wiccer rubbed his knuckles, "Father wouldn't let me forget."

Avren clenched and released his own fists, "Aye, little brother."

"So, if the Leafsong want to keep the hides on their backs, they need to stay deep in the good graces of the king. So who's pulling the strings then?"

"Before sending for you, I sent for a platoon of cloaks. We've been able to keep incidents to a minimum, but I want to capture a Rabbit and make it talk."

9

Elucard raced his way through the twisted woods. Screams echoed all around him. Some were cut short, while others slowly withered into the clutches of the Blood Forest.

You have the skills I taught you over this last year. Stealth and combat you may think are key, but do not forget your most valuable asset: How to think.

Legion's final words were still fresh in his head.

The sun's descent was swiftly approaching and Elucard knew that soon what little light left would fall on the moon's soft glow. An elf had better night vision than a human, but even they couldn't see in absolute darkness. They still needed at least a sliver of light to see.

Elucard stopped for a moment and got to one knee, feeling the vibrations in the ground and listening for any foreign noise. Someone had been following him for the last twenty minutes or so. Now that the screams were dying down, he could make a move to dispatch his shadow.

Catching a quick glance over his shoulder, Elucard ducked behind the nearest tree and vanished into the darkness. Immediately after falling out of sight, the stranger made an appearance. Garbed in traditional black training armor, the elf had a twin scar on his left cheek, a crooked nose, and dirty chestnut hair. Elucard recognized him from when he was still training under his first teachers. This elf was named Leos.

Leos cursed as he scanned trying to find him, but Elucard continued to observe from a safe distance. Leos palmed a dirk from a sheath attached it to his thigh, still cursing under his breath.

"Master, will I be able to make it through the forest without taking a life?" Elucard asked, accepting a cup of black tea. He quickly blew to cool the liquid before drinking it, anxiously awaiting an answer. An answer he already knew the question to. Months had passed since he killed the man in the woods and yet the nightmare he was roused from felt like it had happened only the day before.

"Elucard are you afraid to take a life?" Legion answered with another question. As if this question was to open up to the truth behind Elucard's hesitance.

Elucard silently crept his way behind him and freed his sword, careful to avoid the blade gleaming in the light. With a swift action, he dashed in and sliced cleanly at his target's leg. His opponent collapsed to one knee, but before he could let out a whimper or roar, Elucard quickly covered this mouth with his hand, "Hush now, I'm not going to kill you, but I can't have you getting me killed with your yelping."

More gagged noises vibrated into Elucard's glove.

"My master would have me kill you. Would you prefer to have it his way?" Elucard asked snidely. Leos bit his lip beneath Elucard's gloved hand. He knew better than to bother with a response, "There, now hold still, I'm going to knock you out."

A quick bunt to the head with his sword's pommel left Leos out cold. Elucard made sure to search his body, but found only a few shuriken and the dirk he was wielding. He quickly stuffed the shuriken into a pouch on his belt. However, he paused as he went to pick up the dirk. A small cloud of leaves came drifting down into his sight.

"I'm not afraid to take a life, it's just that..." Elucard struggled with the question as if he were fighting Legion in a duel.

"It's just that you still question if taking someone's life is the right thing to do?" Legion finished for his student.

"Is it really our task to judge whose life gets taken? I never asked for such a responsibility!" Elucard shouted in an outburst deeply rooted in his conflicted emotions.

A blurred image fell from the canopy and a swift drop kick sent Elucard flying forward onto the rough bark of the branch he'd been standing on. Flipping through the air, Elucard attempted to stabilize himself as he thudded into a neighboring tree. The figure, already dashing after him, drew out his sword to strike, but Elucard deflected the blade into the wood next to him. Bark sprayed as the metal blade dug into the soft sapwood beneath it. Elucard answered back with a heavy fist to the stranger's face. The blow jogged loose a silver fox mask, revealing the face of young teen of Elucard's age.

His opponent jumped back, lifting several throwing stars from his back pouch, and tossing them at deadly speeds. They sunk deep, splintering the tree's bark, as Elucard nimbly ducked. Taking his own blade, Elucard stepped forth and slashed in an arcing motion, but barely caught his target's stomach, releasing a drizzle of blood in the air.

Elucard's foe slid backward along the thick, giant branch. He caught his breath, briefly checking on the close call of a wound. Elucard, peered through the darkness, taking advantage of shafts of moonlight. He gasped when he recognized the face he had been fighting.

"Izian? Izian of Ravenshore, is that you?" Elucard called out.

The boy in question looked up, and matched Elucard's gaze. Slowly it dawned on him that he had been fighting an old friend.

"Elucard? Where have you been? We all haven't seen you in forever! We didn't know if you were killed or what!" Izian exclaimed with a hint of relief in his voice.

"We?"

"Geven and Myler! They're both with me. We're teaming up to get out of this Gods forsaken forest! You should come with us. You fight pretty good."

Elucard sheathed his blade, finally happy to see a friendly face. He stepped over Leos' limp body and sprung off into the forest with his old friend.

***

Myler and Geven waited, alert and afraid, within a hollowed out tree. Izian told them to wait there while he scouted ahead. That was thirty minutes ago.

"He's dead… We should get moving" Geven said, breaking the long silence between the two. He combed his thick black hair with his fingers. He was nervous. Izian had always been the strongest of the three boys and had acted as their stalwart leader.

"Let's wait a bit longer, maybe he ran into some trouble?" Myler was antsy as well. He had not been taking his training too well, showing defiance whenever he could. However, he stuck with it for the sake of surviving with his childhood companions.

"If that's the case, we should go after h–" movement through the trees in front of them cut his words short. Geven slid out a dagger and crept forward, crouching to keep his figure harder to decipher in the cool, dark woods.

Dropping silently to the ground like an owl snatching up its prey, were two figures. Myler immediately recognized one of them as Izian.

Myler and Geven kept their distance before breaking out into a shaky laughter that resounded with relief. Izian stepped forward, waving them to come meet his guest, "Guys, guess who I found!"

Elucard lowered his mask around his collar and lifted off his hood, revealing his dirty blond hair. He gave a weak smile, unsure whether his old friends would remember him after so much time apart. His question was answered when Myler let out a big smile and slapped his arm around Elucard's neck and shoulders.

"Elucard Freewind, where have you been? It's so great to see you… alive for that matter!"

Geven shook his long lost friend's hand vigorously, "You're a sight for sore eyes. With us four watching each others backs, we'll be out of here in no time!"

Elucard nodded, "I'm game. The more people I don't have to fight, the better. No skin off my hide. Let's quit standing around with targets on our backs and move out."

The three other elves gave a short fist pump in excitement and followed Elucard further into the forest.

***

"It's true, you may have never asked for it…but the responsibility chose you Elucard," Legion said softly.

"I don't want it, Master. I don't want to take a life!"

"A true Rabbit does not want to take a life…but will," Legion said, pouring himself and Elucard another cup of tea.

Elucard knocked away the cup, "Then I am no true Rabbit!"

"That remains to be seen."

Elucard and his three companions felt as though they'd been sprinting through the forest canopy for an eternity. It was as if the woods were endless in their span and ruthless by their very nature. Massive branches covered in rough, splintery bark surrounded the boys and weaved through the forest much like giant threads of a rough, itchy cloth. The three boys had encountered no one and had heard nothing in the dense forest. The only sounds that they heard were the sounds of their heaving breaths that were muffled by their masks and the grinding thud their feet made as they dashed along the enormous branches.

Elucard grew increasingly suspicious of the quiet. He raised his hand to signal those behind him to halt. He slowly lowered his hand and motioned them to crouch and stealth. Pointing quickly to several seemingly random directions, he himself jumped a short distance to a nearby branch.

With Myler, Geven, and Izian keeping watch over several of Elucard's blind spots, he narrowed and focused his senses to better observe the area. He held his breath and calmed his heart beat to sharpen his hearing… nothing. He made use of what little moonlight glittered through the canopy to better see his surroundings… nothing. But wait, he did see something. Something faint, that glinted softly in the distance – a sliver of a silver metal line. Elucard noted that it cut across the gap of trees up ahead. Even if his group members had been paying close attention while hopping from branch to branch, they would have still been clotheslined by the thin wire.

Elucard leaped to where one end of the line was tied to tree. Undoing the knot, he inspected the wire more closely, identifying it as a garrote or choking wire. This was a trap, but where was the trapper and who was he hoping to catch? A stifled gag from behind him answered his question.

Elucard quickly jumped back to where he had left his friends, his blade drawn. Searching frantically, he found no signs of the trio, but from the shadows stepped three new faces.They wore dark blue garbs with black trims. Muffled laughter erupted from all of them as they drew a variety of weapons.

"Keth says we can't kill you just yet, but that don't mean we can't have a bit of fun," said one of them. He was a bit more husky than the other two.

Izian, Geven and Myler were the last remnants of his past. Even if the Black Rabbits attempted to beat the last inch of Ravenshore out of him, he wanted his friends to still be by his side. Rabbit or not, he needed them. Now the Blood Forest was planning to take them away. He couldn't let this happen. He wouldn't let this happen.

Elucard clenched his teeth under his mask. The obvious move would be to question these strangers. They clearly set the trap. 'Who was Keth? Where were Geven, Myler, and Izian?' That would be the obvious course of action, but not the logical one. No, he needed to dispatch them quickly and efficiently and leave only one conscious for questioning. Clearly he would need to save his energy for this "Keth."

"Ain't you going to ask, where you're friends are at?" The husky one said snarkily.

Elucard mapped out the fight in his head. His eyes were closed as his eyeballs flinched left and right, projecting imaginary images. He would move to the middle one first, running low and hacking off a leg with a clean slice; a round house kick to the now one-legged minion's chest would knock him off of the tree.

Next He would side step a vertical slash from his left and retaliate with a thrust to the kid's left shoulder. A twist of the sword's grip would ensure that his foe would be crippled in pain.

He would finally turn his attention on the one he wanted to question. He didn't know the goon's loyalty level to Keth, so he couldn't be sure that he wouldn't run. A flying jump kick to the face or the back of the head would bring him down to an appropriate position for questioning.

Elucard was silent for only a moment. Keth's allies cocked their heads waiting for an answer. The husky one took a step forward and spoke an annoyed, "Well?"

Elucard snapped open his eyes and in a matter of a few short moments, Elucard's enemies were incapacitated, save for a sniveling husky goon with a quickly forming black eye from a well placed flying kick.

Elucard pressed his sword under the boy's plump, thick neck and spat, "No, I'm not going to ask where they are, because you're going to tell me."

The blade pressed further into the neck fat, and Elucard's answer was squealed out.

"Down by the tree shaped like a spider. Keth is there too!"

Elucard threw a fierce jab to the boy's face, "How many more are with Keth?"

"Four more, I swear! Please don't kill me!"

Elucard shook his blade in anger. Who was Keth? Why did he specifically want him dead? These were questions for Keth, clearly. He needed to rid his mind of the questions and distractions that plagued him. He needed to rescue his friends, if they were even still alive.

"Please! Let me live! I told you everything!" the fat boy squealed again.

Elucard turned his attention back on his captive. Should he kill him? No, he needed to get through this forest without killing, he needed to keep a small piece of past self alive before the Black Rabbits killed what remained of his old life, "Tell me your name, if you want to live!"

"Eris!"

"You're lucky, Eris, You'll live another night in this forest. I need you to bring me to this 'Spider Tree'."

10

"The aqueducts." Avren said as he threw a dagger at a detailed map of Lost Dawns. The dagger stuck in the wooden table with a loud 'thunk.' The blade's tip landed on an empty space on the city's map. Pencil scribblings around the word 'aqueduct' with arrows signified where the structure's various segments were to be built and when. Currently, they were still under construction.

Avren grabbed the dagger's handle and ripped it from the wedged resting spot. He took a large swig of a stein full of ale as he gestured thoughtfully at his brother with the weapon, "It hasn't been struck with any misfortune yet and will be finished within a day. If the Rabbits are going to strike, it would be there."

"Elisa what are you thinking?" Avren had been in the city for almost a year now, and since their last encounter had not seen the elusive assassin. He had, however, heard accounts of an exotic elf in a purple cape moving about in the Roots. Avren knew it was her and he wanted to meet her once more, even if it were to kill her.

Wiccer rubbed his chin as he looked over the slit left in the map by the blade. They spent the entire day and most of the night going over all the places and people who were struck by the Rabbits. The city was nearly complete despite the many delays, thanks in part to Avren's best efforts. If something were to happen to the aqueducts it would push back the city's progression by at least another month. Clearly someone didn't want the city to flourish and clearly they wanted the king to suffer the fall of his beloved city – his legacy.

Wiccer nodded slowly, still locked in thought, "I think they were being smothered by our presence. It's as if they can't make their message clear. They are being choked. Soon they'll need to commit a desperate act to keep their employer happy…"

Avren's eyes widened once he got a glimpse of Wiccer's train of thought, "They are not going to poison some worker. They are not going to stop the construction of the 'ducts. They want them finished… on purpose?"

"The Rabbits want to poison the water supply!" Wiccer slammed his fist on the table, finishing the thought.

Avren slumped in his chair and tipped over his stein in shock, which sloshed his drink on the floor. A dumbfounded look scribbled over his face and his eyes fixated on the ceiling. If the Black Rabbits did plan on poisoning the city, then a security assignment just evolved into a mission to save the Lost Dawns.

"Avren, we don't have much time! The aqueducts will be finished within the next three days! We need to find their operatives now."

Avren called for the White Cloaks guarding the door, "Gather the men, we have a new mission. I'll brief you in ten."

Once they were alone, Avren turned to his brother with fear in his eyes that Wiccer had never seen before, "Wiccer, I need you to find out what these assassins are going to use to poison the water supply. That way we can make an antidote for it if we fail."

"Where do I start? Father never trained me in poisons" sputtered Wiccer.

Avren placed a reassuring hand on his little brother's shoulder, "Check the apothecary in the Roots. They wouldn't go to an alchemist or herbalist in just any part of the city to acquire this kind of poison."

Avren grabbed the back of Wiccer's neck and pulled him in for a headlock, "I love you, little brother, and I sent for you for a reason. I trust and believe in you more than any Cloak here. I know you can do this!"

Wiccer grinned, his confidence resonated back in his voice, "I won't let you down, Avren!"

"One last thing... don't bring your cloak."

***

Slowly over the course of Lost Dawns' construction, the Roots became the epicenter for crime and poverty. Avoided by the authorities and the high class, only the desperate and the lowly stepped foot onto these streets.

Not bringing his cloak was a careful warning more than a suggestion. Wiccer pulled up the hood of a ratty traveler's cloak that hid his fine pressed uniform. His eyes darted from side to side, eying the vagabonds that dotted the alleyways and stoops. There were fewer lamp posts here than in other parts of the city. Thus, the clouded night made for a more precarious scene.

Wiccer stopped in front of a shady storefront. Long curtains prevented curious eyes from peering into a slightly cracked window pane that was covered in grime and dust. The door hung slightly off its hinges and a bum lie drunk on the steps. The sign read: 'Angelo's Her-'

A wide crack splintered the sign, making the final wording unreadable. Wiccer stepped over the bum, careful not to disturb his stupor as he entered the shop.

Inside, a dim lantern emitted a glow tinted by a soft green flame. Shelves covered the walls with jars of various spices and herbs. By the counter an elderly kanis watched with one good eye, as the other was a faded white, scarred and crusty. Clearly half blind. The wolflike beastman had his long silver fur tied in tight braids, decorated with small bones and teeth, possibly his own.

"Are you Angelo?" Wiccer asked casually, making sure his cloak covered his regal tunic. His hand rested on his sword's pommel.

"Who's Angelo? There is only Loomis here." spoke the wolf, growling with a hacking cough.

"Never mind," Wiccer sneered, a poor attempt at hiding the annoyed tinge in his voice. He walked to the counter, sliding a silver trit into the shopkeeper's claws, "I seek knowledge on a vermin problem in the city."

The wolf let loose a sparse but toothy grin, "The city is full of rats, but perhaps that's not the type of vermin you speak of…"

"Lost Dawns is overrun with rabbits."

The shopkeeper cackled, "Just one, friend, just one."

Wiccer's face turned inquisitive, "What do you know, old one?"

"I know a single silver piece isn't enough for the information you seek." His claw was palm up, motioning for more money.

Wiccer jingled a pouch in front of the wolf's muzzle, "Tell me what you know, and then you will be paid."

The wolf licked his chops before indulging the information, "She comes in alone, always to purchase Wickedleaf. She pays well to make sure I ask her no questions. However, Loomis is never in the dark. She is alone in this city, and when she purchases her Wickedleaf, trouble always falls over the city within the next day."

Wiccer tossed the pouch onto the counter, "Where can I find her?"

"You seek Patches the Slim. He acts as the eyes and ears of the Roots."

***

The Roots only grew more dangerous as time passed. Soon even the drunks and homeless didn't call the corners and stoops home. Wiccer needed to find this contact, and fast. The time he spent with Loomis yielded excellent results, but he was sure that the Rabbit would learn of his prying. Perhaps she already knew.

As Wiccer passed by another alley, he glimpsed a figure enter into his blind spot. Swiftly grabbing for his sword, but not drawing it, he spun around and reached into the shadows bringing a shady man into his vision.

The man wore a tattered fedora on his head. Several scars and a stubble graced his jaw line. A long brown buttoned coat draped his body. He smirked holding up his hands innocently, "Relax, Patches the Slim is a friend to all. I can see you're looking for something. What's your poison?"

Wiccer furrowed his brow and half drew his sword that was concealed by the cape of his brown cloak, "Poison?"

The man chuckled, "Listen, I can tell by your grip you're a construction worker. And since I've never seen you in the Roots before, you've probably been brought in from Varis. You're looking for something that the rest of the city can't supply you with. You looking for some dream weed or black sap? You looking to forget your worries? Relax for a bit? The Roots can be a place of pleasure. We even have the finest women. They're experienced and know how to keep secrets."

Wiccer loosened his grip on the sword, lowered his voice to a whisper, and settled into the role of a disgruntled construction worker from Varis, "Listen mate, my boss is driving me up the wall. I want to discreetly send him a message. You get my drift?"

The merchant flashed a grin, "Aye, I get your drift. Follow 'ole Patches."

***

Wiccer kept his hand close to the sword hanging from his belt. His eyesight strained in the dark, filthy tunnels within the sewers below the Roots. The stench of waste was like a lingering fog. Rats scurried past their feet as the untrustworthy man kept up cheerful idle chat. Wiccer played along but kept up his vigilance.

"How much further Mr. Slim?"

The merchant looked back, keeping his dimly lit oil lamp at the forefront, "Mr. Slim was my father's name. Call me Patches the Slim."

Wiccer slid a weird grin, "How much further…Patches the Slim?"

"Just around this bend. When we get to her, allow me to do the talkin.' She's not too keen on the customer talking directly to her, but you insisted on doing business face to face. I don't blame ya. The business she deals in is nasty work, work that would make even Dhalamar blush."

Patches stopped around the corner and walked across a canal that divided the sewer. He rapped his knuckles on a shoddy wooden door. He did it gently for the door seemed to be suffering from cracks, mildew, and rot.

Wiccer waited carefully while wishful thinking flooded his mind. But the nagging feeling that he might be in over his head began to creep in as well. Was this the lair of the Black Rabbit? How long could he keep up this ruse?

The merchant knocked lightly again.

An annoyed voice came from the other side of the door. A woman's voice, "Patches, is that you? You just gave me your report an hour ago."

"Well–"

"Do you plan on talking through a door, come in already!"

Patches took off his ragged fedora and ushered Wiccer inside. Wiccer followed, his hand clung even more tightly on his sheathed sword.

The room was small and lit by many candles. Old, poorly made furniture decorated the area while scrolls and maps of the city were scattered about. Behind a desk sat an exotic looking elf with dark purple hair. Her skin was a light gray and her eyes were a hypnotic deep violet. Wiccer recognized her as a Shadow Elf, but he had never seen one in person. She was dressed in the traditional black and purple garb of the Black Rabbits. Surely, she was who he was searching for.

The Rabbit sneered at the sight of Wiccer, "Slim, who is this child?"

Scoffing, Wiccer was taken aback by the 'child' comment, "I'm fifteen, hardly a child!"

The woman chuckled and bowed sarcastically, "Forgive me, sir, what can I do for you?"

Patches stepped forward to explain, "He's a construction worker fed up with his boss. He wants to teach him a lesson, if you get my drift, Elisa."

Elisa slowly walked forward. A slender finger brushed under Wiccer's chin seductively. She lightly grazed over his chest with her other hand as she moved lightly around him, "Such dark features for a Long Whisper human. You aren't from here, I would gather somewhere in Alva."

Wiccer blushed from the attraction he had to such a beautiful woman, but attempted to keep his mind focused, "My parents are from Alva. I was born in Varis."

Elisa continued to slowly inspect Wiccer, lifting up his traveler's cloak, and sliding her fingers up his arms, "You have the build of a construction worker. You've seen much hard work for a human so young...but..." She stopped with her intense eyes of the night staring at Wiccer's, "You dress and are armed like a White Cloak. True, you might have left your cloak in Varis, but your tunic and sword shine with arrogant authority. Too bad, you could have grown into a very handsome man."

Drawing with life or death reflexes, Wiccer pulled his blade under Elisa's neck, "You're under arrest by the authority of King Jaelyn! Surrender, Rabbit!"

Elisa gracefully jumped backwards pulling several shurikens from her belt and whipping them through the air. Wiccer deflected several, while the rest sparked off the wall behind him. Patches gasped and crashed through the old door, making a sloppy escape.

Wiccer shuffled, keeping one hand to steady his blade, the other to reach into his pouch for a pair of small shackles. Elisa slid a pair of sais down her sleeves and into her hands, "You look familiar, Cloak. Do you have a brother?"

Wiccer blinked at the question, "You know Avren?"

Elisa circled around the young soldier, her thoughts heavy with images of Avren's muscles glistening in oils, laying in a silk covered bed: "Avren." Ever since her encounter with Wiccer's brother, he had been a guilty pleasure in her mind; a constant image that gave her company at night.

"Just curious," Elisa's mouth made a thin smile. Spinning her sais skillfully with several flicks of her wrist, she thrusted in a succession of attacks. Wiccer struggled to parry the swift attacks, still holding the shackles in his left hand. With a side swiping technique, Elisa locked her sai's guard with Wiccer's blade, pinning them both into a neighboring table. With a savage backhand, the other sai collided across Wiccer's jaw.

Wiccer released his sword and fell back against a wall. Rubbing a bruised cheek, he was caught off guard by a heavy kick to his ribs that crashed him further into the wall. Wiccer crumpled to the ground. To his dismay, his own sword's tip pressed against his neck.

Elisa grinned wickedly, "A fair attempt."

Wiccer sneered, grimacing from a cracked rib. He let loose a strong low kick, attempting to sweep her off of her feet, "I'm not done yet, Rabbit!"

Elisa somersaulted backwards, avoiding falling to the ground. However, she was caught off guard when Wiccer came barreling at her wielding a chair. Wiccer crashed the wooden chair over her head, splintering it into pieces. Blood squirted from Elisa's mouth as she hit the floor hard.

Dazed, she struggled to move, but a sharp kick to her head ended any chance for her to continue the fight. Wiccer winced as he bent over to pick up and sheath his sword. Gingerly, he examined a large purple and blue welt growing on his side.

"A fair attempt, Rabbit."

***

"Are you insane, Wiccer?" Avren was furious as he met his brother outside the cell of the unconscious Elisa, "I gave you the mission to investigate the poison!"

Wiccer raised his head and pointed his hand at his captor, "I did one better! I captured the Black Rabbit terrorizing the city. You should be hailing me a hero, yet here you are scolding me!"

"Hailing you as a hero? You could have gotten yourself killed!"

"But I didn't!" Wiccer argued.

Avren huffed a chest full of angry breath. He hung his head in a frustrated gesture, holding his hips, "Wiccer. What you did was foolhardy, and although it paid off this time, you can't always act alone. You need use your head. You were very lucky this time, but there may very well be a next time that doesn't end as well for you. I wasn't there to watch your back. No one was there to watch your back. Do you understand what I'm trying to tell you?"

Wiccer gently rubbed his now taped up ribs, "I'm sorry Avren. I'll think before I act next time."

Avren put his heavy hand on his little brother's head, "It will save your life." Avren looked towards his prisoner as she slowly began to wake up, "Wiccer, go back to the infirmary and rest up. I'll brief you on what I've learned from her later."

Wiccer nodded, wincing from his still aching ribs.

Elisa murmured as she woke to a splitting headache. She opened her eyes and found herself behind bars. She scowled, "Well, Avren, is it? Are you here to give me breakfast in bed?"

Avren hid a smile, "Breakfast? You have killed several of my men and injured even more."

Elisa moved slowly to the bars, flipping her hair away from an eye, gleaming dreamily into Avren's, "Only business, Avren. You should know that."

Avren could not help but move his eyes up and down Elisa's perfect body. She was the most ravishingly beautiful woman he had ever laid his eyes on, and her flirting with him wasn't helping him keep his concentration, "Elisa, your crimes in this city have rung high. You will hang from the gallows for what you've done... unless of course, you have some redeeming qualities about you."

The shadow elf reached to brush Avren's cheek gently, and then ran her finger down to his lips, "I have many 'redeeming' qualities about me. Why don't you come into this cell, so I can show you?"

Avren, snatched her wrist and pulled her up to the bars with a rough 'clang.'

What was he doing? No one had ever toyed with his emotions like this. He wanted her, but the militaristic discipline in him kept him from taking her on her back and thrusting himself deep within her. This was her game, she played him like a puppet, but he wanted to play this game.

Avren, swallowed hard and came in close to her luscious lips, "I'm serious, Elisa. King Jaelyn wants you dead."

Elisa, began to unbutton his tunic to reveal his bare muscled chest, "What do you want, Avren?"

Avren grabbed her by the shirt and dragged down her collar, kissing her neck. Elisa moaned in pleasure. Avren stopped, "I can't do this."

Elisa pouted her face, "You Cloaks are such sticks in the mud."

"Talk, and I may be able to save your life."

Elisa grinned devilishly, "You expect me to betray my clan for sex?"

Avren released her, "Your clan would let you swing by your neck. I can give you safety, a place to stay other than this prison or deep in the mire of the sewers. Provide us with information and work with us. You can have a better life."

"What of the sex?" Elisa said coyly rubbing the spot on her neck that Avren kissed.

Avren, still sweating, adjusted his trousers, "We can arrange something. What do you say? Work with me?"

Elisa's mind was fluttering with the thought of taking the deal. However, she would be breaking the highest law of the Black Rabbits: "Stay loyal to the clan." But Elisa's loyalty was to her Shadow Elf queen, not to the clan. The Black Rabbits were merely a means to an end. The skills she gained were to better serve Queen Ravengale. She wouldn't be able to serve her if she was sentenced to death. The Rabbits would have her marked for death for such brazen treason, but the secrets she'd learned could be such an asset to her queen and she'd never get to reveal them if the Cloaks hung her first. She needed to take the deal. It was her best option; her only option.

"I'll take your deal, Avren."

Avren opened her cell, "Excellent. Come, we have some work to do and people to see."

Elisa yanked his cloak, tugging him inside the prison room, "That can wait. We have some unfinished work of our own to attend to."

11

"His name is Elucard – a lowly brat from some shoddy no-name fishing town. He is the first student that my fool of a blade kin, Legion, has taken under his wing. I've been eying them closely. You are stronger, Keth. Know this and wield it well. Elucard doesn't have the stomach to be a Rabbit. I want him to suffer."

Malady spoke to a young elf of about fourteen years old. He had fair skin, short brown hair, and a strong back that years working as a farm boy had shaped far before his grueling Black Rabbit training. He was hand-picked by Malady along with several other lads, but it was Keth that rose to be Malady's favorite pupil.

Keth raised an eyebrow to his master. He'd been kneeling and intensely listening. He enjoyed the power that his blade had given him over others, another attribute that his master favored.

"Elucard, master?" Keth asked, eager to enter the Blood Forest and make his master proud.

"Both, dear Keth."

"But Master Malady, Legion won't be in the Blood Forest!"

Malady narrowed his one good eye. He had lost the other to Legion when they were younger. He sneered at his student's vain attempt to grasp his plan, "Fool, Legion will suffer when he finds his student's mutilated body has been swallowed by the forest. He may never take another student again." Malady smirked imagining the pain on his rival's face, "His legacy will die with Elucard."

Keth nodded, his eyes lit up with the knowledge of his actions bringing such pleasure to Malady.

"Take those that you would call 'friends' with you. Share the burden with those idiots, and do not get yourself killed. Remember, allies are like mules. They only live to serve you."

"Yes, Master."

***

The spider-shaped tree was large and had countless contorted branches that wildly sprawled in several directions. Protruding from the bark were spiky thorns. Rippled leaves carved out the tree's features like serrated razors.

Kneeling in the heavy shadows of the tree were the three elves: Izian, Geven and Myler. Their wrists were tightly bound behind their backs. Welts and bruises marred their faces and bodies. A thick mixture of spit and blood dribbled down their mouths. Only Izian's eyes were fixated on Keth. Spitting out broken pieces of teeth, he chuckled, "If I was free, I'd teach you some manners."

Keth was growing irritated as he waited for the main event. He slowly knelt down to Izian's level. Drawing a dagger from his belt, he slapped the flat of it on the Izian's face, "You were trained by Baines and Ridge?"

Izian nodded.

"Very well, it seems Elucard doesn't care for his friends, perhaps you will save them instead." Keth stood calling for his grunts to untie Izian, "Toss him a blade."

Izian checked the sword's balance and crouched down in an aggressive stance. He wondered if Elucard really abandoned them again... abandoned *him* again – but he quickly shook away his doubts to concentrate on the task at hand. He was the most skilled of the trio and a rising student as well. Without him, Myler and Geven were lost.

Keth cast a glimmering smile, "Say when."

Izian clenched his teeth with rage and let out a furious growl. He rushed at Keth, plunging his sword in the air, but Keth leaped to the side, retaliating with a smart diagonal slice up and across Izian's side. With a graceful jump, Keth spun around with a butterfly kick that crushed into Izian's jaw.

Izian was flung backwards flipping to the ground. Grasping in pain at the soil, he recovered quickly, and responded with a flurry of spin kicks of his own, each one nimbly dodged. Izian attacked again more aggressively. He saw an opening in Keth's defensive dance and swept at his feet. Keth effortlessly dodged the attack but was met with a surprise flash kick that sent his head reeling backwards.

Keth sailed into the air and crashed hard onto the ground. Stunned, Keth's minions ran to his aid, but the dazed elf violently shook them away, "Enough, you idiots!" he roared as he adjusted his jaw. He turned his attention to Izian, "Okay, enough sparring. You die first."

Taking his sword, Izian pointed it at Keth. He let out a weak grin. His body was still shaky from the excess adrenaline coursing through his body.

"Say when," he chided.

Keth, no longer in good humor, dived at Izian as he made a series of slashes, some of which clashed with Izian's blade, but some of which hit their mark. Blood sprayed from the several gaping wounds made by Keth's blade. Izian stumbled backwards from the onslaught and fell on his back from a heavy kick to his chest.

Keth stomped a solid heel onto Izian's chest and leaned in with all of his weight,"Landing one lucky kick, does not make you a victor."

Izian squirmed under the hold, "Better to die with a blade in my hands, than on my knees with one against my neck!"

"For you, you'll have neither. You'll just die!" Keth raised the blade, its tip facing Izian's chest. Izian braced himself for the sting of death. At least he had fought and not died like a rabid dog. No, he would die like a true rabbit. Keth moved to thrust his blade down but withdrew his hand in agony as he found himself disarmed by a throwing dagger that struck his blade at the hilt.

A command struck through the darkness, "Enough!"

Both Izian and Keth watched from the shadows of the trees as Elucard emerged from the darkness, a blade drawn in each hand.

Lifting Izian up, Keth tossed him into the nervous hands of his minions, "Be ready to slay them all on my command."

Keth turned to Elucard and retrieved his blade from the ground, "You killed my allies?"

"None will be killed by my hands," he shouted over Keth, to his friends' captors, "None of you need to die here. Let my friends go."

Keth snickered, "They know you are no threat."

Elucard and Keth began to circle, their eyes locked on one another. Elucard shook his head as he tried to figure out why Keth had it in for him, but no answers came to mind, "So you must be Keth. I don't even know you, why this grudge?"

"This bad blood is beyond you and me, there's a larger plan at work. However, everything hinges on your death. I'd say this wasn't personal, but really, it is."

Elucard gestured his head toward his three friends, "Let them go, they aren't part of this."

"Sorry, Elucard, every war has its collateral damage," Keth said while shrugging mockingly.

Elucard gripped the handles of his swords. The idea of escaping the forest without killing seemed more and more like a daydream. The reality was that Keth needed to be dealt with. This reality needed him to evolve or he would be left behind and so would the people he cared for.

"Very well, master, I won't hold back any longer..." murmured Elucard. His eyes were now cold, his breathing was calm. He seemed to be in a new found moment of peace.

Keth's face twisted in confusion, "What did you say, rat?"

Elucard dashed forward, folding his blades in a cross and unleashing them in a wave of wind that crashed towards his opponent. Keth's eyes widened in fear. Flipping backwards, he narrowly dodged the attack, but found himself fighting off a barrage of strikes from Elucard's twin blades. Sparks showered the air as Keth worked overtime to block each swift attack.

In the midst of his own attacks, Elucard lunged forward landing a vicious kick to Keth's chest. Keth slid backwards and barely had a moment's respite before Elucard danced amidst a storm of whirling blades, kicking up a cloud of thick dust.

Keth vaulted over Elucard's advance, but a sharp pain let him know he hadn't made it away unscathed. He tumbled onto the ground, seeking even a moment to recover. He gingerly hobbled on his injured leg, careful not to put too much weight on the weakened limb. Keth seethed with rage, "So, you do possess some skill, but not enough to keep you and your friends alive."

Elucard's mind was clear and his resolution unmoving. He took a deep breath before running forward for another set of attacks.

Using a sly reverse sidestep, Keth twisted around to be behind Elucard, and shanked him with with a surprise dagger attack. He nimbly sprung backwards and a smile began to stretch across his face.

Elucard fell to a knee. He exhaled, grimacing in pain.

"I won't hold back... I won't hold back any longer."

Elucard sought solace in his mind once more and pushed the pain to the back of his thoughts. He buried it deep in the darkness within him and gripped his swords tighter.

Keth stabbed his sword into the ground and reached for a second dagger, "My Master wishes you to die slowly. I think I'll punch you full of holes until your body runs dry."

"I won't hold back...I won't hold back any longer." Elucard's mantra continued as he stood once more and rushed for a breakneck attack, but Keth was like a mongoose, juking to the right and following suit with several more stabs to Elucard's legs, arms, and shoulders. The final attack disarmed Elucard.

He fell to his knees. How had Keth managed to bear weight on that leg? He was so sure that he'd disabled him. It would seem that Keth had a mantra of his own. Keth pulled Elucard's head back with a fiery grip and slipped his dagger under his neck. Keth called out to his allies, "Kill them. Start with the one who attacked me first." Keth leaned in to whisper into Elucard's ear, "You see, you're a gangrenous wound on an otherwise healthy body. The body can't survive with such a festering wound, now can it? No, of course not; for the body to survive, the limb must be sacrificed. I intend to be the blade that frees the body from the clutches of disease. Treasure these final moments and know that you died so that the Rabbits could thrive."

Elucard's body throbbed with pain from his many gushing wounds. His fingers were numb, and his vision began to fog over. Perhaps it was a gift that Keth's taunting words began to fade. His friends' cries bobbed above his clouded mind. His mantra seemed to fade into the same darkness he'd buried his pain. However a familiar voice cut through everything that cluttered his head.

No pain, no numbness, no distraction, just the voice. The voice of his master, Legion.

"This is you not holding back?"

Elucard was silent with shame.

"Answer me, Rabbit! This is your all?"

Through the calamity of the events outside, Elucard gave a low, raspy answer, as if he was answering the voice in his mind, "Yes, master. I have failed you."

Legion's voice became stern, *"I don't think it is. I think you're still holding back. I think you're afraid to raise yourself to a higher standard."*

"I'm afraid of what I will become," he faintly replied.

Keth grew silent. He called out for his allies to withdraw their blades. He looked down at Elucard who seemed to be mumbling to himself, "Speak up, Elucard! We're all waiting for your final words."

Legion's voice grew calmer, *"You don't have to be afraid. You were chosen by Alanna to serve on the Mortal Plane. Embrace your duty to her, Embrace your duty to yourself. Fight. Kill. Live."*

All was silent.

Legion continued, *"Are you still going to hold back, Elucard?"*

Keth asked again, "Well, what have you got to say in your final moments?"

New-found energy coursed through Elucard's body as he once buried the throbbing pain in his arms deep in the dark soil of his mind. He grabbed a large stone that lay nearby and thwacked at Keth's skull, making blood gush from the side of his head. Elucard wasted no time. He swiped the two daggers from Keth's flailing hands, flinging them at two of Keth's four goons.

The daggers violently pierced through their necks and crimson ribbons of blood gushed from the wounds they inflicted. Their lifeless bodies fell twitching on the ground as their allies rushed toward Elucard. He swiftly reached for his twin blades and made a quick set of well-aimed slices that slashed clean through their throats. They fell to their knees drowning and gurgling on their own blood.

***

Izian untied his two friends before limping over to Elucard who was standing over Keth.

"You offered me my last words. I shall do the same." Elucard tapped his blade on the back of Keth's neck.

Keth glanced over his shoulder and sneered at Elucard, "There will be others."

Elucard didn't bat an eye at the idea of this ordeal not being over, "So be it." Moments later, Keth's head rolled on the cold, blood-drenched ground.

With Izian supported by Myler and Geven supporting Elucard, the four moved to the light that flooded into the forest from the clearing ahead. They had made it out together. They had made it out alive. They had survived the Blood Forest, but they were all forever changed. There was no going back to their old lives now.

12

Koda sat at the foot of his bed staring at a letter that rested in his hand. It was from his grandfather, Xile. A little over a year had passed since he left the isle of Nashoon to visit his father. Time in Lost Dawns seemed to blur past him. It felt as though only a moment had passed since he was standing among the thick, verdant forest of the beautiful island staring up at the thousands of giant evergreen fingers that stretched toward the sky. But that was a year ago. The city was blossoming into something grand, and the fact that it was all forged by his father was something special. He was proud of him. Although their relationship had been strained in the past, he was learning to appreciate the work of a king, of his king, of his father.

The letter was written in the dead language of Ancient Fey, but Koda knew the language well. It read:

Grandchild, a full year has passed since you left Nashoon. I hope your time spent with Jaelyn goes well. The winter still does not touch our undying forest, but only because an Arcane Guardian wards the woods. You know this, Grandchild. You also know my time draws near. There was once a time when our kind would live for an eternity, untainted by age. Time, however, does not see us as equals any longer. I write to remind you that an Arcane Guardian must be trained to take on my duties – to protect the forest, its runes, and its secrets. Grandchild, I will not force you, as I did not force my own children, but I can not wait much longer. An Arcane Guardian must be chosen.

Koda lay back comfortably against Wildeye's soft fur as if she were a warm pillow. He pressed the paper against his face and sighed heavily, "Wildeye, I don't know what to do. I mean, I know what to do, but at the same time..."

He rolled onto his side to look into his familiar's flaring magical eye, "Becoming the Arcane Guardian has always been the path set before me. I was practically raised on that island. My first memories were of the runes." He outstretched his hand as if remembering the touch of coarse stone, "Why does father hate it all? Uncle Tull, too. They both abandoned their duties, for... for mother."

Koda's eyes widened as he saw a glimpse of a blurred figure. Crimson red hair is all he could remember of her. Wildeye cocked her head slanted, "I don't know her. I only know of her. She died having me..." Koda grew hoarse trying to explain things to his wolf, "She was the one that convinced Father to unite the tribes. It was her dream before his. He fell in love, leaving Nashoon for her. Uncle Tull left too, all three of them were close."

Wildeye licked off the small tears streaked down Koda's cheeks, "Father wants me close because he sees her in me. I can't blame him, but I can't ignore my destiny." Koda wrapped his arms around Wildeye, "You understand, right? This is the right decision. It has to be. But then, why is it such a hard decision to make?" Wildeye rubbed her nose on the elf's chest in response, "What's in my heart? Being an Arcane Guardian is greater than myself or even my family. That's what they never understood. It may seem cold, but it's rational. Wildeye, we have to go back. Grandfather needs me more than Father does. Greater still, Nashoon needs me more than either of them." Koda pushed his forehead into the wolf's cobalt fur, "I'll miss them, I really will, and Lost Dawns. The city has grown on me. We'll leave in the morning."

The sudden sound of of knocking surprised the two of them and Wildeye nudged for Koda to get up, "Enter, please." Koda said, pushing himself upright.

A servant walked in, dressed in a fine red tunic. He bowed before speaking, "Prince Koda, the king summons you."

***

Koda and Wildeye walked the long marble halls of the castle. A mural of the Elder Tree wrapped both walls. Images of flowers, ancient elves, and wisps were painted in brilliant hues around the center piece. Coming up to a cherry wooden door, Koda rapped quickly on it and waited for his father's response before entering.

"You summoned me, Father?" Koda looked up at his father, wondering what he could have needed from him at such a late hour.

King Jaelyn poked his head above a large stack of paperwork. A weird look hung off his face, "Summoned?" he asked, confused.

Koda chuckled at his choice of words, "You called for me?"

Jaelyn slid his chair back away from his writing desk before crossing his legs, "Your tutor tells me you've finished your studies. All high marks. Any particular areas where you might consider further studying? Perhaps politics?"

Koda's eye flinched with a sting of annoyance, "Father, I know where you are going with this, but we've discussed this. In fact, a letter from

Nashoon arrived this afternoon. My time here is at its end, I must go back."

"You are next in line to become King. You know as well as I that I won't live forever. With the amount of enemies I have, it is all too likely that it won't be age alone that kills me," Jaelyn said.

"Father, don't say that!" Koda protested. His face flushed with anger at the thought of his father meeting a clandestine end.

Jaelyn stood, gesturing with his hands, "Lost Dawns needs an heir. I need an heir, and that is what you are and that is who you are. Stay in Lost Dawns. Be by my side and prepare for your future."

"What about Uncle Tull?" Koda asked sincerely, "He'd make a much better king than I would."

Jaelyn frowned slightly at his son's words, "Tull is my brother and you are my son. As long as I have a Dawnedge child in line for the crown, Tull's rightful place is at our side, not on the throne. You know this."

"What of the Elven Lords?" Koda asked with a tinge of desperation in his voice. This wasn't his destiny. It couldn't be his destiny. Jaelyn leaned forward in a manner that did not send a welcoming message to his son. He seethed beneath the surface and Koda knew that his suggestion infuriated his father.

Before Jaelyn could respond, Koda spoke up once more, "Father, you see me as the next king, but Grandfather sees me as the next Arcane Guardian. What am I to do? I stand at a crossroads where the future of the realm hinges on my decision."

"Xile, that old fool. My son, 'Arcane Guardian' is a dead title," the king spat.

"Father! How could you say that! Guarding Nashoon and its secrets is a prestigious honor!" Koda lashed back in protest.

"Nashoon, like your grandfather, is a relic of the past! Its secrets were already exploited and plundered during the Arcana War," Jaeylen said, attempting to use the same reasoning that was used on him.

"So because you and Tull have turned your backs on your sacred duties, I must do the same?" growled Koda, angrily.

Jaelyn thrust a finger at his son, "Hold your tongue! Don't you forget who I am!"

Koda was silent, clenching his teeth and scowling. Hot tears formed in his eyes. Jaelyn leaned on his desk and and rubbed his forehead frustration, "Koda, I don't think you realize what we've created here; what your mother has created. We aren't some simple town. We are a nation and I lead our people. We aren't alone in this world either. There are many, many others – other rulers, other nations. They will be looking to us to contribute to this world. You wish to protect Nashoon? Nashoon is now part of Long Whisper, and everyone here looks toward us for protection. The time of the Arcane Guardian has passed."

"It has not passed!" Koda stomped his foot in aggravation.

Jaelyn took a long breath, "You wish to continue your studies? I will build a mage school at the center of Lost Dawns. You can study new advancements of magic as well as the further history of the Mage Council that you wouldn't be taught in Nashoon."

Koda raised an eyebrow, "A mage school?" The thought danced in his mind. He thought of robed scholars who were taught and trained to shape Magi in order to tame the elements. Fire, earth, water, air, vernal, light, and even the shadows themselves. Koda dreamt of himself draped in elegant robes, a large tome in his hand, commanding the seven elements.

"Lost Dawns is a city of both progression and tradition. We can also be a beacon of academia and magic. You say you stand at a crossroads. You say that the future of the realm hinges upon your decision. That sounds like a king's quandary to me."

A smile grew across the young elf's face, "I admit, my interest has piqued. I would be much better equipped to help grandfather if I stayed and trained as a mage first. Perhaps this could do Nashoon some good!" Koda dropped to a knee and held his familiar's paw. Wildeye whined with distress, "I'm sorry girl, but this needs to be done. Nashoon will have to wait a little while longer. I would be a much stronger Guardian if I knew about the side of Magi Grandfather refused to teach me. You understand, right?" Wildeye nudged Koda's face, a bit worrisome of being away from the isle, but nodded with the approval that Koda sought.

"Well, what did she say?" asked Jaelyn. He never had a familiar, so he was slightly curious of his son and wolf's relationship.

"She says we're staying." Koda said gleaming widely.

13

Seventeen of the thirty elves that were recruited last year stood in a long line. They wore faces that showed both exhaustion and experience. Hands once only used to play with toys or help till a field were now used only to take lives and spill blood. Their eyes no longer widened with fear and dread at the thought of killing, but instead sought after the honor it brought upon them. These were no longer children, they were Black Rabbits.

Elucard stood among them. Like his peers, the remaining scraps of his innocence had been stomped out like an unwanted flame. A week had passed since the trauma of the Blood Forest. His eyes were still weary. It was as if he had been forced to stare at the sun for an hour. Blinded by his experience, born again, and now as a killer. A year ago was now an eternity away and so were thoughts of his family, village, and of Jetta. His reward for crossing the threshold was now before him.

"Palms up!" A command echoed across the compound. Vada paced slowly in front of the remaining recruits. Avalon stood watching all of them as her blade sister went on with the ceremony. The instructors stood off to the side, kneeling and hiding the pride that they had for their students, "Draw daggers!" she roared. The recruits unsheathed their daggers, their hands outstretched with their palms facing up, "Prepare to draw blood!" Vada drew out a beautifully forged sword. It shimmered in the red light from the passing sunset. Although it was clearly as sharp as any other sword, it showed no chipping, for it was never used in combat.

She held the sword flat with with both hands and walked up to each recruit, "Shed your blood upon this blade. For it is all that you now hold dear. It is Alanna. It is your Silent Master. It is your High Blade. It is your First Blade. It is your clan. It is yourself."

Elucard trickled his blood drops onto the blade. Each command shouted at him he followed without a second thought. He was like them now, his new heroes, his new comrades, his new family. He would kill for them and he would die for them. All for Alanna, all for the clan. Never before had he felt such loyalty for a cause.

Vada passed the blade by each Black Rabbit who watched from the sidelines. Each bowed to the sword in silent reverence. Vada continued, "You are now bound to each of us, as we are now bound to you. Your hand will heal, but this binding will never be severed."

Finally, she handed the sword to Avalon, who bowed to it and sheathed it back into its scabbard. Vada nodded to her blade sister, signaling for her to finish the speech, "Even in death, you will have that bond. Congratulations, you are now Black Rabbits!"

14

"Another Autumn's moon, Elucard," said Legion, "You've been with us two years and you've been a Rabbit for one. Do you still think about that vagabond?"

"Everyday, Master," Elucard answered honestly.

Legion tossed another log into the fire. They were on the shore, miles away from any soul that could disturb them. Elucard always looked forward to these nights. Legion only brought him here when there was something to celebrate. A birthday, a solstice, an anniversary of an important mission... But there were none of these to celebrate tonight.

"Master, why did we come here tonight?" Elucard shifted a little closer to the warmth of the fire and waited for Legion to answer.

"It is important for you to remember your first kill. Never forget the pain it caused you. It keeps you mortal. It makes you cherish your own life."

Elucard leaned back and gazed up at the endless blanket of stars that wrapped the night sky, "It still haunts me. Do you remember your first kill?"

Legion looked uncomfortable for a moment before replying, "Avalon requested that I bring you on a mission. She wishes to inspect my ability to teach first hand." Legion had hastily deflected his young student's question and it seemed to have paid off. Elucard quickly sat up with a glowing smile.

"The High Blade wants me to go on a mission with her?" Elucard didn't bother trying to hide his excitement. This was an honor he never dreamed he would have.

"We are to assassinate a nobleman. Duke Cray Redroot. Apparently, his son is impatient and wants the estate now rather than later. We will strike a carriage that will be escorted by the White Cloaks."

"White Cloaks?" Elucard asked. He had heard of several other small forces that served as a paid militia, but this one he was not familiar with.

Legion stirred the fire, "It's hardly surprising that you've never heard of them. Their reach doesn't usually extend as far as Ravenshore.

The Guard of the White Cloaks is a guild of mercenaries that pass themselves as the law men in our country."

"How do mercenaries get to be the law?" Elucard asked. The people of Ravenshore more or less governed themselves as best they could. Such a small town had no need of lawmen.

"When our country was established, of the eight noble tribes who joined together in the great alliance, none were of the warrior tribes, for the warriors refused to be ruled. Once the assassination attempt on King Jaelyn failed, the White Cloaks were hired to keep the peace in Long Whisper. They act as an army and as civil servants."

Elucard took a long pause before asking his next question, "If the White Cloaks are the law, are we the criminals?"

Legion smiled, "It is true that we act outside the law, but that is because we must. We are not good, nor are we bad. We are a neutral party. We are merely a tool for those who use us. If they use us as a weapon to do evil, then they are the criminals." Elucard lay back down, satisfied with his Master's answer, "Rest up, my student. We meet with Avalon at dawn's first light."

15

Avren came into the chamber that he and Wiccer shared. He found his brother drying his hair wearing nothing but a towel around his waist. Wiccer stared at him, shaking his head, but quickly went back to his book once Avren caught a glimpse of his disapproving gaze.

"Another night with that Rabbit? The men are starting to question your judgment," he said without looking up from his book.

Avren threw the wet towel he was drying his hair with at Wiccer, "She's got a lot of useful information for us. We're learning far more about the infrastructure of that clan than we ever could have hoped to before."

Wiccer ducked the towel, "Has she disclosed the location of the Rabbit hideout yet?"

"Well, no," he admitted, "I'm still working on that…"

Wiccer balled up the towel to throw it back, "And no doubt your girlfriend told you who the Silent Master was?"

"She doesn't know their identity and she's not my girlfriend. We just have an intimate…" Avren paused while thinking of the right word, "…business relationship. Right now I'm still trying to convince her that the White Cloaks aren't mercenaries."

Wiccer gawked at the thought, "Mercenaries? Far from it! We are paid for our protection, not for our ability to put others to the sword. These filthy rabbits on the other hand…" Wiccer spat in disgust, "They are the mercenaries! Not us!"

Avren pulled up a pair of trousers, nodding to everything his brother shouted, "I agree little brother. Elisa has just been indoctrinated by this bunny cult. Give her time and she'll come around to our way of thinking." Picking up a letter from the neighboring dresser, Avren spun the envelope to his brother, "A letter from Pops arrived."

It had been a year since the White Cloaks put a stop to the Black Rabbits' attempts at sabotaging the city. King Jaelyn ordered that a guild hall be established within Lost Dawns walls and Avren had been selected to lead the newly established division.

Wiccer jumped from his bunk tossing his book onto a nearby desk. He snatched the letter in mid flight with curiosity and quickly tore it open to read the parchment inside.

"Congratulations little brother," Avren smiled.

Wiccer hooted with excitement, "I've been promoted to Sergeant! How long have you known about this?"

"Pops wrote to me a week ago asking if you were ready for the responsibility." Avren had been promoted to Captain himself after successfully protecting Lost Dawns and establishing a base in the city.

"And you kept this a secret from me?" Wiccer said, crossing his arms and arching an eyebrow.

Avren laughed a bit, "I have a mission for you, Sergeant."

Wiccer's chest rose with pride, "What do you have for me, Captain?"

You'll be taking a squad of Cloaks to escort Duke Cray's carriage back to his manor. He was here for an opera last night. Although we haven't heard a peep of Rabbit activity in Lost Dawns in a while, Elisa assures me it's only because they have been preoccupied training their new recruits. This mission should be safe enough, but be prepared to run into them. The carriage leaves in the morning. Be safe, little brother."

16

Avalon was a young human in her mid twenties which made her only slightly younger than Legion. A black mask veiled her upper features save for her cool green eyes, and a silver hood and cloak accented the mask. A crude scar ran diagonally below her left ear reaching to the edge of her mouth – a loving gift from her Blade Sister, Vada. She gripped her lightly crafted sword that was sheathed behind her waist, "Be on your guard, our target approaches."

The three Rabbits: Avalon, Legion, and Elucard were concealed within the branches of a tree that still had much foliage left to shed. The autumn leaves were turning a vivid red, bright as the sunset that broke through the dusk. The road snaked along a rocky ravine where a small stream flowed.

Avalon placed her hand on Elucard's shoulder, "Calm your nerves. You have been on missions before, and this will be no different." It was true, Elucard had completed several missions. All successful. He had been sent on them alone, with a team, and by Legion's side; however none had been done alongside the High Blade. Elucard took a deep breath, trying to rest the thoughts that plagued his mind.

Will I impress Avalon? What if I fail? I can't screw this up!

The clopping of hoofsteps making their way down the road cut through the silent morning air.

Avalon whispered so low only trained ears could pick up the wispy sounds, "I see three Cloaks on horseback leading the carriage, and two in the rear with their commanding officer; just a Sergeant by the looks of him. Elucard, he looks about your age."

"Elucard, you can handle the rear. I'll take the vanguard," Legion said, pointing at the three White Cloaks in front of the carriage.

"That leaves me with the mark," Avalon drew her blade waiting for the carriage to go under the large branch where the three were perched, "May Alanna grant us grace."

Elucard watched as his Master and High Blade dropped effortlessly from their hiding spot. Legion landed without a sound on top of the middle guard, driving his long sword in between the shoulder blades of his victim. Before the adjacent guards could cry for help, Legion launched twin daggers from either side of him into their throats.

Elucard watched in complete awe at his master, but shook his head to concentrate on the task at hand. Somersaulting and twisting into a flying drop kick, Elucard connected with a rear guard's jaw. The loud crack rocked him off his horse and onto the dirt path. He gracefully sent several daggers soaring into the neck and face of the second guard, who screamed in pain.

Wiccer's eyes widened in horror and panic. His mission was going to hell right before his eyes. He drew his blade and called for the carriage driver to make a break for it. With the snap of a whip, the carriage took off in a mad dash with Avalon clinging tightly to its roof.

Wiccer turned his attention toward the young Elucard. Storming forward with his horse, he attempted to make a sweeping slash at him, but the assassin was too agile. Elucard sidestepped the attack, grabbed Wiccer's outstretched sword arm, and yanked him off his horse. The Cloak fell to the ground with a loud thud.

Slightly dazed, Wiccer scrambled to get to his feet and raised his sword in a defensive stance. Elucard slowly began to circle him. Wiccer stood firm, watching Elucard's steps, waiting for the assassin to make his move, "Draw your blade Rabbit," he growled.

Elucard scanned his surroundings, seeing Legion chasing after the carriage, "I fear I must make this quick. Forgive me, kid." Elucard slid his blade out, flipping its grip as he rushed headlong toward Wiccer, slicing through the air. He expected to feel his blade tear through flesh as he brought it down on Wiccer, but was instead met with the hard clanking of steel meeting steel. Sparks flew each time the warriors exchanged glancing strikes.

Elucard flipped over Wiccer, switching up tactics and connecting with a roundhouse kick to his foe's head. Wiccer stumbled, his vision momentarily blurred as he dug his sword into the dirt to stabilize himself. Elucard followed through with a flourish of kicks, backing Wiccer further to the edge of the deep ravine.

Elucard smirked as he let loose a savage straight kick at Wiccer's chest. Replying with a smirk of his own, Wiccer dodged with a sidestep and made for a slashing attack. Elucard was quick to avoid the strike, but lost footing and tumbled down the jagged hillside. Elucard heard a brutish 'crack' of a bone in his arm as he landed on the hard stones. Skidding to a stop and into the shallow waters of the river, Elucard laid unmoving from intense pain. His hand shook as it strained to reach for his sword that was resting on a nearby rock.

Still inching with his good arm, the blade was suddenly kicked away as a different sword slapped the side of his face, "What is your name, Rabbit?"

Elucard grimaced from the sharp pain jolting down his fractured arm, "I did – I didn't think White Cloaks would come so young."

"Nor did I know murderers would come so young," spat Wiccer.

"I'm not a murderer. I'm a tool. We work outside the law to bring balance to the world." Elucard took pride in his words, but he struggled to get them out.

Wiccer lifted Elucard upright, by his collar, "You would have the world burn!"

"If the world were to become overgrown, it would smother itself until its own destruction. So yes, to save the world, I would burn it!" Elucard sweat as he managed to smile despite the overwhelming discomfort.

Wiccer shook his head in disbelief. He raised his sword preparing to thrust into the would-be assassin. Elucard's face turned serious as he looked with pity at Wiccer, "You'll always remember your first kill."

Wiccer clenched his teeth and tightened his now sweaty grip on his sword, "I've killed plenty!" he lied.

Elucard eased his voice, "No, I don't think you have."

Wiccer thrust the blade forward, but stopped just short of Elucard's stomach. Frustrated, he threw Elucard to the ground. Elucard grunted, gingerly rolling to avoid further injuring his arm. Wiccer stepped away from him, "Do not think me sparing your life is a sign of weakness. What is your name, Rabbit? Give it to me, I deserve to know."

"Aye, you've beat me. My name is Elucard Freewind of the Black Rabbit Clan. Allow me yours, so that I know who bested me."

Wiccer sheathed his blade and grinned from the compliment, "Sergeant Wiccer Newsun, Son of Marcus Newsun of the Guard of the White Cloaks. Know this Elucard, the next we meet, you will not be spared."

Elucard nodded before passing out.

***

The carriage careened down the path as Avalon held on for dear life. Struggling from the wind, she made a daring play and swung herself through the door of the carriage, landing inside. A startled elf with red rusted hair and a goatee to match gasped, startled from Avalon's appearance. In his lap was a small elven girl, no older than a toddler.

Avalon brought her blade's tip to the neck of the duke. Cray Redroot sobbed at the sight of the sword, "Please madame, if you must kill me, spare my daughter. Her mother would be devastated if she were to lose me and our little Bess on the same morning."

"Call for your man to stop the carriage," commanded Avalon.

With the carriage stopped, Avalon took a hard look at the saddened little girl and clenched her teeth. In the past she had killed many men, many women, and even needed to kill a child or two, but each death chipped away at her weary soul. She was tired of this lifestyle, tired of the needless bloodshed. Her soul longed for redemption, but as High Blade of the Black Rabbit clan, such a wish would never be granted.

"Please, spare my child," the pleas echoed over and over again in Avalon's head. It was as though she was caught in a shallow trance, half listening to the duke and half listening to her own thoughts. Avalon's blade fell to her side as Legion entered the carriage.

"What are you doing?" Legion's voice pierced through Avalon's heavy-hearted mindset. She sheathed her blade and stepped out of the carriage. Passing Legion she spoke softly, "Kill the mark, spare the child."

Legion coldly answered back, hiding his suspicions, "Yes, my High Blade."

A child's cry cut through the autumn's morning: a cry that would haunt Avalon for eternity.

17

Within a small room flickered the many candles of Alanna's shrine. Each half melted candle sent warm wax dripping down into tiny puddles on the floor. Dusty and broken stained glass windows depicted the Death Goddess drawing her bow before reaping the souls of those who were to pass on to the Roaming Plane.

Beneath the shadows of an altar, Avalon prayed. Five days ago her cowardice had crippled her so far that Legion was required to kill in her stead. Not only that, but now a fear festered deep in her heart that she could never kill again. While it was true that she possessed the skill and ability to kill, the *desire* was what she found herself lacking. She thought of the little girl's eyes as they peered back at her in despair. Guilt pierced through her soul and the weight of all she had done settled on her shoulders with the heaviness of an anchor.

"Alanna, I need your guidance. I fear I can not carry the burden of your task any longer," Avalon prayed, desperately seeking a sign – any sign – from the deity that she served and worshiped all of her life.

"Sister, what burden do you speak of?" Avalon snapped open her eyes and spun her head, her hand half-rested on the blade next to her. Although it was only Vada, she still felt tense by her presence. Vada stepped out of the shadows of the temple and into the dim, flickering light of the candles. She knelt down beside her blade sister and lit a new candle. She chanted a small prayer, hoping to ease her friend's troubled mind.

Alanna, please come hither,
And string your bow with lace,
Draw an arrow from your quiver,
And lay her fears to waste,
Without you she will wither,
So, Goddess please make haste,
Alanna please forgive her,
And forever grant her grace,

Vada finished before turning to her lifelong friend, "Avalon, what troubles you? You've been aloof in training and distant ever since your last mission."

Avalon tightened her eyes and went back to praying, ignoring the questions. Vada prodded further, "Avalon, we've know each other since we came here as recruits. We might not be from the same village or related by blood, but we're best friends. You know me better than I know myself. We have a connection that is as true as the bond that real sisters share." Vada took hold of Avalon's hands. They were shivering as Avalon began to cry, "Don't let this eat you up from the inside. Please Avalon, tell me what weighs upon you. I want to help."

Avalon's tears rolled down her cheeks as Vada wiped them away with her sleeve. The High Blade whispered her response at first, barely able to croak out her words. She was ashamed of the feelings she had in her heart. She felt that they betrayed everything she was taught, "I – I don't want to kill any longer. It breaks my heart each time I take a life. It's all wrong! What we do is wrong. I want this pain to end."

Vada's nurturing face turned grim, "Avalon, what you speak of is treason to this clan. You are High Blade, you can't mean these words."

"But I do mean them!" Avalon's voice was quivering. She had served the Black Rabbits since she was ten. In those years she had committed unspeakable acts, but now more than ever, she was confused as to why she had done them.

Vada put her hands on her blade sister's shoulders, "It's alright to feel lost. Sometimes we need to step back to see the bigger picture. What Alanna asks of us is–"

"Bullshit! It's bullshit, Vada! I'm done with it all. I want out! I regret everything I've done and will no longer take part in it."

Vada slowly shook her head in disbelief, "Where will you go, what will you do? You know they'll send someone after you."

Avalon stood and began to pace the temple. For years everything was within her control, but now she was disheveled. She was a mess, "There's a guild of warriors that serve Jedeo. I could join their ranks, redeem myself..." Her eyes widened, "Come with me, Vada!"

Vada looked at her blade sister with utter contempt, "Never. The Silent Master will hear of this. If you have resigned yourself to treason and cowardice, then you are no sister of mine."

Avalon picked up her blade and moved towards the archway, "Please, come with me." She spun around beckoning her blade sister to follow, "You and I, together... We don't have to repeat the mistakes of those that came before us! We can break this chain. Please, come with me, Vada. I don't want to do this on my own."

Vada turned to face away from her, disgusted by the very sight of her, "I'll give you until nightfall to leave."

"Sister, please.."

Vada mustered all her power to fight back her tears, "Go... just go."

18

Elucard woke in the infirmary with a dull pain in his arm. It had been bandaged and was finally free from the tyranny of what he considered to be the itchiest sling ever made. The sages had done a phenomenal job at repairing his arm. He had always wondered how the Black Rabbits recovered from severe injuries so quickly, and now he knew first-hand. Alanna had once walked among the sages and showed them how to stave off death, or so the story goes.

Legion sat at Elucard's bedside, lost in a complete daze. News of Avalon's defection had traveled quickly. An elite troupe of Rabbits had been tasked with putting down the former High Blade and Vada had been charged with leading them. With the seat of the High Blade vacant due to treason, the First Blade was stripped of her rank. Vada would have to return with proof of Avalon's demise in order to regain her standing and ascend to the position of High Blade. In the meantime, Legion had been personally asked by the Silent Master to serve as High Blade.

"Master, are you ok?"

Legion snapped out of his trance to a worried Elucard. Rumors filled the air like a thick smoke. Some said that Avalon abandoned the clan to form her own. Others said that she fled due to her own deep-seeded cowardice and spat on the ground. But rumors are just rumors. They may as well be tales of Alanna walking among the sages. Nevertheless, the leadership feared that dissension was sure to follow within the lower ranks in the absence of a strong High Blade.

"Elucard, how's your arm?"

"It's stiff." Elucard carefully measured his mentor's face before asking the question that had plagued his mind since news of Avalon's treason had reached him. A long silence hung in the air for what felt like several moments before he decided to proceed with great caution, "Master, why did Avalon leave?"

Legion sighed greatly. He was present when Vada informed the Silent Master of Avalon's betrayal. He learned of Avalon's doubts and how she had openly blasphemed Alanna to her blade sister, "Elucard, do you believe we are a family?"

Elucard nodded. In his early days of becoming a Rabbit, he didn't quite know what he wanted from the clan. He just knew he wanted something. Soon, he felt camaraderie with the other clan members and had a father figure in Legion; a father that had grown to replace even the memories of his own real father.

He hadn't really thought about family since he was taken from Ravenshore. His mother's face was a faded blur, his father was now just an idea, and Jetta…

The Black Rabbits were all he had now. It was clear to him as he sat and stared back at his mentor, "I suppose the clan is my family. It's more of family than I can even remember having before."

"Elucard, Avalon no longer believed that the clan was her family, and her betrayal has grievously wounded us all. If a Rabbit leaves the clan, they must be dealt with. When you take up a blade for the clan, you do it for life. Do you understand that, my student?"

"Master, I would never betray my family!"

Legion nodded, pleased with Elucard's response, "Very good. Now, let's see to you getting out of this bed and back to training."

***

"Silent Master, the morale of the clan is low. The loss of Avalon dealt a tremendous blow to our leadership. There are reports of a small group of deserters who fled under cover of the night." Legion knelt in a small, shadowy room hidden deep within the main compound of the Black Rabbit retreat. It was the meditation quarters of the Silent Master. Only those closest to him were allowed entry.

"They must be dealt with. Made an example of…" The Silent Master spoke in his low, gravelly voice.

"I'll send Baines and Ridge to track them down," Legion said, quickly.

"No, that will not do."

"Master, Ridge is our best tracker, and Baines will make quick work of the defectors. With the oncoming weather, these deserters will be tough to catch," Legion said, confused with the Silent Master's refusal.

"Send your whelp."

Legion raised his head in shock, "Elucard? Master, wouldn't it be far more efficient to send Baines and Ridge? This task needs to be carried out with the utmost precision."

"Why do you hide his talents from me?"

Legion paused, Elucard was growing into a fine assassin, and his peers could see this. Although this task would be an excellent mission for Elucard to undertake, there was still more to the situation than Legion was letting on, "Master, I fear Elucard..."

"The ones who ran, they were the boy's friends?"

Legion left a long pause hanging delicately in the air between them.

The Silent Master continued, "This will be Elucard's final test. He may be a Rabbit in name, but he is not yet a Rabbit in his heart. It is true that he learned much from the Blood Forest, but his greatest trial has yet to come. This task must be his and his alone."

"As you say, Master," Legion said, the words nearly getting tangled in his throat. The Silent Master grinned beneath a sea of shadows.

19

Elucard admired the fine craftsmanship of his new blade as he carefully inspected it and weighed its balance. The sword glinted in the dim candlelight of his master's quarters. Elucard grinned excitedly, "Master, I'm honored by this gift, but why?"

Legion lowered his eyes, unsure how to give Elucard this task, "I give you this sword with the hope that you will swiftly and fully devote yourself to Alanna. The blood you will soon spill will be heavy and the blade you formerly carried was brittle and chipped." Legion put one hand on the new blade and another on his pupil's shoulder, "Elucard, I have one last task for you. A set of marks is all that stand between you remaining my underling or becoming my equal."

Elucard looked back at his mentor with a puzzled look, "Your equal?" How could he ever be equal to the man he had looked up to and revered for so long? His expression straightened as he contemplated the prospect before him, "I won't let you down, master."

Legion's mouth formed a tight line, "I pray to Alanna that you won't."

***

Cold rain besieged the muddy earth, filling the air with the harsh sound of pattering in an otherwise ominously silent night. Nestled within a cave a day's journey from the Black Rabbit compound shone the soft glow of a campfire. Myler, Geven, and Izian huddled around its warmth. Bound by their mutual need for protection, along with a healthy helping of foolhardiness, the three fled the Black Rabbit compound soon after the defection of the High Blade.

Myler let out a sneeze, "Aaa-choo! Figures that the second time we'd run away from the Rabbits, it would rain again!"

Geven stirred the embers with a stick, "On the bright side, it's much harder for them to track us in the rain. Haven't you picked up anything from your training?"

"I learned... stuff..." Myler trailed off, trying—and failing—to think of some witty retort as he wiped the mucus from his face with the back of his sleeve.

"Enough, you two! We need to move out if we're going to reach Lost Dawns in the next couple days," Izian wrapped up his rations and went to smother the fire with his cloak.

Myler dazedly looked at the long travel ahead of him. Muddy, rainy, cold, "Aw, Izian, can't we leave at sunrise? At least wait 'til this rain has passed. Alanna's angels will reap us in an hour if we take off in this weather."

Izian pursed his lips to snap back, but a new voice broke through the cave.

"Sooner."

The shadowy figure of Elucard stood at the mouth of the cave, his blade gleamed in the moonlight. The three companions jumped and shuffled back, completely taken off-guard. Elucard stepped closer, entering the cave.

Myler cautiously inspected the stranger, "E-Elucard, is that you?"

Geven sighed, "It is Elucard! Relax guys. He's come to join us." Geven walked over to extend his hand, "Sheath the weapon, Elucard, you're among friends."

Elucard glared at the outstretched hand. A look of anger and disgust scried across his face, "You think we are still friends?"

Izian slowly reached for his blade. A sheen of metal flashed from Elucard's hand as a dagger struck Izian. Izian grimaced in pain as he grasped his wounded hand. He grunted through clenched teeth, "Elucard, the clan has been brainwashing us! Snap out of it! We *are* your friends! We're from the same village! Who are you going to trust? Us, or a group of assassins that have been teaching you to murder?"

Elucard sneered and lowered his head, examining the blade his master had given to him. Raising the sword, he pointed it at the three frightened boys, "You never understood the work we did – the divine privilege that we undertook. You are all weeds in this world, choking the life out of those who strive." Elucard walked forward, not batting an eye, and with no tears to be shed, "Those who are striving to make this world a better place. There are those who build, there are those who burn..."

Myler's eyes widened with fear, "Elucard, please..."

"Finally, there are those who do nothing. They are a waste. They sow nothing and they reap nothing. They only feed and grow fat from all the work that everyone else does. You three have grown fat!"

"The Black Rabbits have poisoned your mind, Elucard!" Myler pleaded for Elucard to see reason. He was terrified, as were the rest of them.

"No, they have enlightened me," said Elucard.

Geven took out his blade, "You can't fight all three of us."

Elucard shook his head and stared at them coldly and without emotion, "I can, and I will."

***

The rain was a soft drizzle the next morning. Elucard walked slowly back to the compound in a shallow trance. His eyes were fixated on the sky, but his mind lingered on the past night. Violent, fractured images collided with his thoughts. All were of the massacre that he brought down upon his friends.

His friends. He couldn't say that anymore. They ceased to be his friends when they abandoned his family. They needed to be dealt with. He was the only one that could deliver the proper punishment. Only he could set things on the correct path once more; to bring justice to the crime of betraying the clan.

The cries of Myler were like a loud howl in his mind. His clothes were wet and sticky with blood and the taste of iron filled his mouth. He couldn't escape the images of milky-eyed stares coming from the lifeless bodies of his... enemies. This was the true foray into a new chapter of his life. He was no longer "Elucard, the boy who wanted to be a Black Rabbit," no, now he was "Elucard, the man that became a Black Rabbit."

There was no turning back now.

***

Elucard kneeled before his master and High Blade. Ridge and his blade brother, Baines, stood on either side of Legion, "It is done." Elucard hefted a large duffle bag from his back that Geven had been carrying supplies in.

Baines crossed his arms, "They were your closest friends. It will take more than a supply bag to prove that you have completed your task."

Elucard shot a glance at Baines' unconvinced eyes and moved to open the bag. He placed three swords on the grass. His hands had shaken since the night before. Not from chill or trauma, but from adrenaline.

102

"I am still not convinced," Baines said with more than a hint of disappointment and annoyance in his voice.

Elucard rummaged further into the bag and began to pull out the severed heads of his former companions one by one. Ridge grabbed the tuft of Izian's black hair, looking at the pallid, grim face of the dead boy.

"What did you feel, Elucard?" Legion asked in a very solemn tone.

"Satisfaction," Elucard whispered without a hint of emotion.

Ridge grinned wickedly, patting Legion on the shoulder, "You made a cold hearted bastard, Legion."

Legion shook his head, "No, I made a Rabbit."

20

The Verdant Academy of Lost Dawns was the newly established school for green mages within the kingdom of Long Whisper. Koda had spent the last six months within its high walls and winding hallways, studying the ways of malleable magic. Long ago, the Council of Mages learned to tame the chaotic energy of raw Magi and shape it into each of the seven elements or spheres. Mage schools could be found all over the five realms and each one was dedicated to a single sphere. Once a student mastered their school's sphere, they were given a colored sash that represented it. Purple for light, black for shadow, red for fire, blue for water, brown for earth, white for wind, and green for vernal. Only upon earning their sash were students given the title of Mage. If they wished to further their knowledge and gain the other six sashes, they had to travel to the schools of other spheres. There, they had to earn the right to enroll by defeating a mage of that sphere in single combat. If a student mastered all seven spheres, they were given the prestigious title of Archmage. To Koda's knowledge, only two mages had ever achieved such a feat.

Koda stood in front of a small council of his teachers within a large lecture hall. He fidgeted with the stuffy green scholar robes and nervously gripped the silver sash that was wrapped tightly around his waist.

"Disciple Koda, you have shown the aptitude of one who has been around magic all his life. We are not surprised by the way you grip the concept of vernal magic. You tame like a true master. However, we are unsure if we are ready to consider you a Green Mage."

The teachers before him were human, and all of them had traveled from across the globe to teach at this new school. Despite their time studying vernal magic in vast forests, none had seen an elder tree, and never would have imagined that a city would be erected around one. These four teachers were unaware of Koda's history with with far more volatile magic. Learning vernal magic came easily to him.

"I do not understand. I'm the top of my class and have learned all there is that you could possibly teach me. I can restore the autumn leaf to its summer state. I can cause a forest to blossom in the driest desert. Why am I still not ready to be a Green Mage?"

"You are untested in applying your skills," declared a new voice coming from the entrance behind the young elf.

Koda spun around to find himself face to face with a tall human woman with broad shoulders. Her face was aged, but toned. Her hair was red with twin streaks of gray on either side of her head. She bore the robes of a Green Mage, but her sash was gold with a blue strand. She was Megan Silverson, headmaster of the Verdant Academy.

"All I have been learning is how to apply my skills," Koda said, still a little taken aback by the headmaster's appearance.

"And yet you have no combat training," she replied, sternly.

"Combat? Why do I need combat training?"

Megan's eyes narrowed as she crossed her arms, "You are young and naive. You have not seen war, but you may in the future. Magic is not a piece of art to be admired in a gallery. It is a weapon meant to be harnessed."

"Then I question your ability to teach! Magic is meant to be respected! 'A weapon, meant to be harnessed', you know nothing!" Koda shouted, thrusting his finger at Megan.

Megan paced around the student, brushing off his words, "It is true that magic is to be respected. It is a powerful energy, still not completely understood by even the Mage Council. It is a tool that can benefit this world, but if it were to fall into the wrong hands — which it will one day — what then, Disciple Koda? Do we let our enemies trample us, enslave us, and bring those too weak to fight to the brink of extinction?"

Koda was silent. Everything Xile had taught him was diametrically opposed to the ideas before him. He had always been told to treat the Magi as a force to be revered and respected, not to be harnessed for power and personal gain.

"We must arm those who are willing and able to fight with the ability to defend themselves using magic. We must also be the defenders of those who can not defend themselves. Magic is only what people use it as — a weapon..." Megan said, interrupting his thoughts.

Koda went to speak up again, but shut his mouth quickly.

"...But, it is up to us to make sure it is only used for good. What say you, Disciple Koda?"

"My grandfather warned me of mages. He told me that they were the cause of the Arcana War; that they forced their ways upon everyone else. I thought the mages had learned their lesson and had been humbled. It seems I was mistaken," Koda said, an air of disapproval in his words.

"I was a young mage in the Arcana War. I've seen what misery my people wrought on the world. The first mages were foolish to think they could control both magic and those who used it. But that was a long time ago. The council was formed to ensure that another Arcana War would not rise..."

"Who's to say it won't?" Koda interrupted.

"It might. There are those that will never see eye to eye with the rest of the world. When that day comes, will you defend the masses with your knowledge and prowess or will you cower on your island like the Arcane Guardian? People who watch the wildfire and do nothing are as much to blame as those that started it."

"The Arcane Guardian does not cower on Nashoon! He defends and protects the Magi—"

"From what? From evil?" Megan interrupted, "A mage can do that! But a mage must also share their knowledge with those who can learn from it so that we might all be better equipped to protect the Magi. No one person can be entrusted with such a monumental task. Sooner or later, when the darkness comes, it will take more than an Arcane Guardian to defend the realm." Megan ended the debate with a small grin. She knew that she had broken through to Koda and that it was just a matter of him admitting it.

Koda lowered his head. He thought about all of the lessons his grandfather had taught him. Then he reflected on Megan's words. Arcane Guardians and Mages seemed to be no different anymore. Both were using magic to keep it from falling into nefarious hands, "You are right."

"Very well then, follow me."

Koda looked up in confusion, "Where are we going?"

"Somewhere for you to apply your skills."

***

Koda never knew there was a room under the school, but there it was. The Battlefield was an impressive arena that spanned underneath the base of the large academy. Opposite sides were marked with a large circle where either mage would stand—a challenger and a defender. Under normal circumstances, the defending mage would be a top rated student tasked with testing the mettle of those who dared to challenge their sphere. These, however, were no normal circumstances, and so Megan stood before him.

The battlefield was surrounded by lush green trees entangled in twisting, flowered vines. No doubt they were all grown by magic – no need for water, no need for sunlight.

"Are you ready, Disciple Koda?" Megan called from the other side of the arena.

"I'm to fight you? Shouldn't I be tested against one of my peers?" He looked at Megan, somewhat puzzled.

Megan shrugged his questions off and widened her stance, "Hit me once and you shall have your title," she said, rolling up her sleeves.

"Excuse me?" Koda did not bother to hide his disbelief.

"Enough banter!" Megan jumped forward, rapidly thrusting her arms into the air. As if in unison, massive roots erupted from the ground around Koda and began to close in on him, attempting to encase him in a wooden coffin.

Koda was startled as he tumbled to the side before the roots could trap him. Hesitating, he stood frozen in fear. Megan did not waste time by coddling her student with encouragement; instead she magically commanded the trees behind her to fire a rushing flow of leaves at Koda.

The relentless barrage of leaves slammed into Koda's lower back and lifted him high into the air before dispersing and dropping him onto the ground with a shuddering slam.

Koda grimaced in pain, arching his back.

"You surrender already, Disciple Koda? Are you ready to go home to your large castle and hide behind your books and your father?" Megan taunted.

Tears swelled in Koda's eyes. He didn't want to give in, but he was well and truly afraid. Clenching his teeth, he gripped the earth beneath him tightly. Pain began to surge through his right arm as he began to sign an incantation. Soon his arm began to harden as bark began to cover it. He roared and shot his hand out at Megan – a giant oaken arm the size of a large tree was now gripping Megan's hands tightly, preventing her from signing any spells.

Megan was caught off-guard as the branches wrapped around her wrists. Suddenly, a line of thorns began to erupt through the bark and tiny wooden daggers rushed toward Megan's bound wrists. Thinking fast, she pressed her fingers along the branches that bound her and nimbly managed to sign a spell that withered them. She broke free just as the thorns were about to reach her.

Jolting to the side, Koda took his giant arm and tried to smash Megan with a mighty swing.

Megan transformed into a figure of leaves as the attack passed through her body. Reforming to the opposite side of Koda, she could already taste the sweetness of victory as his arm quickly began to return to its normal state. It was clear that he could no longer maintain such an exhausting form. Her hand came in contact with his chest and implanted a seed that sprouted into a myriad of vines that wrapped tightly around him, constricting them to his sides. She quickly commanded the vines from the trees behind him and they rapidly thrust forward, coiling tightly around his neck and pulling him taut against a tree.

Koda gasped for air, but managed to find little respite.

Megan shook her head, "What was that Koda?" she said as she clenched her fist to tighten the vines.

Koda squirmed, "I don't give up! I want to be a mage!"

Megan walked up to the tree where Koda was bound. She squeezed her fist once more and the vines began to force the very breath from his lungs, "No. I don't think you have what it takes. You learn from books fast, but you have no real skill in magic."

Koda struggled to breathe as the vines began to crush his ribs. Closing his eyes tightly, he began to scream in agony.

"Give in and go home, Koda!" Megan shouted fiercely.

"G-Give me..." Koda gasped as he gulped for breath.

"What?" Megan said raising an eyebrow.

"Give me your strength!" Koda roared as the trees behind him exploded into splinters and the vines that bound him disintegrated. A shockwave of raw Magi sent Megan soaring backwards, crashing into the ground splayed on her back.

Koda fell, panting for air. He writhed in pain from his broken ribs. Excess magic rushed through his body in blue flames before vanishing as quickly as they had arrived.

Megan sat up, stunned, "I've never seen such a use of magic. What was that?"

Koda struggled to rise to his feet, "I-I don't know. I-I just wanted to be free, so I tried to tap into any Magi that I could. I-I didn't know what would happen." His grandfather had warned him of the dangers of raw Magi, but he had never had cause to use it before. It was thrilling and it was a craving he never knew he had. He was afraid of it, and yet entranced by it. If this was raw Magi, he wanted more of it.

Megan gingerly touched a fresh gash on her cheek, "Fascinating. We will have to learn how to tap into this newfound power. There is much we—you can learn from it."

Koda managed a weak smile, "Am I a mage now?"

Megan helped Koda up, "Not yet, but I will make a fine mage of you yet. None of the other teachers can give you the attention that I can. I'd like to personally take you under my tutelage."

Koda nodded, still in agony, "I'd like that."

21

Seasons had passed since Avalon defected from the Black Rabbits and Vada had not been heard from in just as long. In those months Elucard had grown into a formidable assassin and the grizzly memories of slaying his friends slowly faded from his mind. No one realized this transformation more than Legion.

Elucard entered the High Blade's quarters and kneeled before his master, "You wished to see me?"

Legion sipped tea from a clay cup. He smiled fondly as the warm cup rested in his hands. Winter had been unreasonably harsh that year. Winds howled outside as a light layer of snow packed onto the the the dirt pathways.

Legion watched as Elucard brushed off drifts of snow from his shoulders and mask. He nodded and gestured for Elucard to fill a cup for himself when he caught his student eying the kettle with yearning eyes.

"Elucard, winter will pass next month. By then we expect to have a new batch of recruits. This will also mark the beginning of a new division."

Elucard hastily poured himself a cup of tea, shivering and wet from the snow. He took a long sip before finally responding, "I've heard rumors that we'll be pairing medics with our assassins on missions. I doubt they will be of any use when they are neck deep in danger."

Legion nodded, "This is true, which is why this division will be a new breed of Rabbit – Veiled Menders. We will be training them in stealth as well as a bit of combat. In the future, assassins will work in alongside Veiled Menders." Legion gestured to Elucard's right arm, "Too many missions would have gone a lot smoother had a medic been present."

Elucard looked pained, remembering the battle he lost against the White Cloak. He quickly redirected the conversation, "Master, why did you really call me? I don't believe you called me here because you dearly missed my company."

Legion smiled. He found it endearing that Elucard still referred to him as "Master." These days he had seen less and less of his former student. His role as High Blade had kept him busy and prevented him from doing many missions. So his time with Elucard was usually brief, but always time he considered well spent.

"I wish for you to be by my side when the new recruits come in. I was wondering if you had given any thought to becoming a teacher."

Elucard looked up from his drink, "Master, I don't think I'm prepared to teach. I still consider myself a student."

Legion shook his head, "You underestimate yourself, my student. You have gained much cunning and prowess over these last few seasons. Despite your lack of experience, you are able to stand toe to toe with many of the veterans here. I would urge you to think about taking at least one student under your wing. You still have much to give to this clan."

Elucard listened to each word and imagined himself as a Ridge, Baines, or even Legion. A student of his own, it might be a good move for him, "I'll think about it."

"That's all I ask," said Legion.

***

An old wagon that had seen its fair share of use pulled into the Black Rabbit retreat. In it sat children of varied ages and genders. The Rabbits driving it ushered them all out the cart and the filed into a single line.

Elucard and Legion stood off to the side, watching as several men gave the recruits the same frightening speech and directions that Elucard had heard when he first arrived. That his old life was over, a new one was to begin. Quitting meant death. Escaping meant death. Failure meant death. He smirked in amusement.

One newcomer in particular seemed to have already caused the instructors much grief. He was a teenager, Elucard's age. He had gray skin and long, deep purple hair. He wore a porcelain clown mask that hid his silver eyes.

"Remove your mask, Elf!" an instructor demanded.

"It is a memento of my true home," the teenager said, speaking in a quiet voice.

The instructor sneered and went to snatch the mask, however the disobedient elf slammed his head into the instructor's face. The thrust crushed the instructor's nose and impaled his cheeks and eyes with shards of porcelain.

He cried in agony as he fell to his knees. Immediately several other instructors brought their blades to the boy's throat.

"Enough!" A command pierced through the commotion. It came from the High Blade. Legion turned to Elucard, "This one could use guidance, Elucard. He has the spirit of a wild horse."

Elucard stared intensely at the elf, but shook his head, "I'm not the one that will break that horse."

Legion put a hand on Elucard's shoulder, "My student, you don't break wild horses. You forge a connection with them. A horse that *chooses* to bear your weight is a far greater ally than one that is *forced* to."

Elucard raised his head and looked into Legion's eyes with a satisfied grin, "I suppose so."

Legion turned back to all the Rabbits, still poised to strike down the elf, "Let him be. He will be instructed by Elucard! Medics, take your recruits to the new Veiled Mender division grounds!"

Several teenage elves were ushered by Elucard and Legion, but one confused elven maiden caught Elucard's eye. Her eyes widened with surprise when Elucard met her gaze.

"Jetta?" Elucard said, utterly perplexed. Before she could respond she was rushed away by a medic. Elucard quickly turned back to Legion and asked, "Master, was that Jetta?"

Legion raised an eyebrow, "Who?"

"Jetta Breezelark! My old childhood friend from Ravenshore!"

"Calm down Elucard. We use your old village as a recruitment point every now and then. This time we recruited potential menders for the new combat medic division. Does she have any medicinal experience?"

"Her grandmother owned an apothecary."

"So she would have been taught the basics of medicine. That knowledge will be very valuable for her," Legion said, trying to walk away.

Elucard shook his head in disbelief.

Legion pointed at the gray skinned elf, "Concentrate, young Master. Your student is him, not Jetta. Jetta will be a Veiled Mender. She'll learn quickly and serve you well."

"Or she'll fail and die…"

Legion put his hands heavily on Elucard's shoulders, "That too could be the case, but you need to trust that Jetta will do her job so that you can do yours." Legion waited for his former student to nod, "Now get to work."

Elucard nodded as Legion disappeared into his quarters. Taking a deep breath, Elucard walked over to his new student, "Elves don't usually come in gray around here. Where do you hail from?

The elf was silent, curiously peering into Elucard's magenta eyes.

"I saved you from a slit throat. I'm not your enemy. My name is Elucard. I'm originally from a fishing village a few days north of Lost Dawns called Ravenshore."

"Lost Dawns… my troupe performed there for the winter Moon Festival!" said the elf, pleased to make some friendly conversation.

Elucard smiled, "You're from a circus?"

The elf smirked, "Assassin Elucard, I was once masked, but no longer am. I think it would be fair if we stood on equal footing before I divulge any further information about myself."

Elucard smiled underneath his own mask, "That's not how this works. I am the master, you are the student. We are not equals."

The gray elf bowed down in an exaggerated motion, "Ah, but of course, Master. After all, I am merely a wild horse. You are not to break me, but make me your ally. Feed me a carrot, and I will allow you to saddle me."

Elucard smiled and decided to play along. He lowered the mask that covered his mouth and nose and then lowered his hood. The student smiled thinly at the sight of such a handsome young face.

"A handsome face such as yours should not be hidden from the world. Now that neither of us are hiding anything, I can trust you. I was born and raised in my family's troupe, 'The Ebonpath Traveling Circus.' My family couldn't afford the protection that the Black Rabbits offered while we traveled across Long Whisper. So, to avoid…repercussions, I was offered in return."

"Ravenshore, as well as other villages, offers recruits in exchange for protection. What is your name?" Elucard asked, knowing the story all too well.

"Inle Ebonpath" the elf said, still staring dreamily into Elucard's eyes.

"Well Inle, I know nothing about the life of a circus performer, but I can tell you that the new life before you is fulfilling. It will be hard at times, but if you persevere, you will find the servitude to Alanna rewarding. I will teach you skills of stealth and combat, politics and philosophy. You'll see the world through a new lens – one of shadow and truth. Are you prepared to undertake the challenge?"

Inle thinly smiled, "What choice do I have?"

Elucard paused, "I will give you a choice never offered to me or any of the other Rabbits. If you do not wish to serve as a Rabbit, you may go back to your life as a clown. But know this: There is no feeling in any realm, mortal or roaming, quite like the feeling of committing to something greater than yourself. You will become more than an assassin or a servant of Alanna."

Inle looked at the woods behind him. He didn't know his way back to his troupe, but that really didn't concern him. At the moment, Elucard's words intrigued him. He never thought a life outside of his troupe was possible, and though he had traveled the world, he felt that there was always something missing in his life. Perhaps Elucard's life offered him that missing piece.

Inle looked back to Elucard, interested in hearing the rest of Elucard's thought, "What will I become?"

"A Black Rabbit."

Inle chuckled, "Another troupe, another performance. This time as a rogue instead of a clown."

"Yes, but this time you'll juggle with life and death instead of balls and pins."

Inle's eyes lit up, "Well then, Master Elucard, show me the world of the Black Rabbits."

22

Alue, please whisper in my ear,
Guard me from the wicked in this world,
In your grace I shall find no fear,
Your mercy is my shield, your love is my sword,

"Don't let him die, Mender!" A voice broke out as Jetta tried desperately to triage the wounds of the dying man before her. Her hands were a clumsy, shaky mess. She prayed again, harder.

Alue, please whisper in my ear,
Guard me from the wicked in this world!
In your grace I shall find no fear!
Your mercy is my shield, your love is my sword!

"His life is in your hands, and your incompetence is killing him!" The voice lashed out again. The dying man did not flinch or cry out in agony as she weaved the needle in and out of his raw flesh. He just lay there – a bloody, motionless heap. A deeper, more severe panic began to set in on Jetta and she desperately tried to mend the broken body before her.

Alue, please whisper in my ear...

"He's dead," Tyric stood across from Jetta with his arms folded and a disgusted look scrawled across his face.

Jetta folded forward in agony and wept, her eyes hot with tears. Her hands were drenched in blood. She slowly lifted a blood soaked gauze from a gaping puncture wound under the ribs of the corpse in front of her.

"Not everyone can be saved. You must come to terms with this," The medic's voice was emotionless as he spoke. He gestured for the other medics to come and carry the corpse away. They swiftly moved forward and lifted the body.

Jetta was mortified at her abject failure. Her mind raced. *What could I have done differently?* A million different scenarios played out in her head at once and she found respite in none of them. Then a dark anger rose up inside of her, "There was nothing I could do, was there?" Her voice did not even thinly veil her fury and disgust. She looked up from her bloody, quivering hands, "Why would you purposefully kill this man? To teach me some petty lesson?!"

The instructor shrugged off her reproach and placed a hand on Jetta's shoulder, "He was a criminal, a no name vagabond. His life did not matter until he was used for this lesson. We gave him a purpose to fulfill. Do you weep when you tug a weed from a flower bed?"

"No," Jetta hotly replied and wiped the warm tears from her face.

"Then you do not have to weep now." Tyric passed a warm wash cloth to the student, "Clean yourself up. In the future you'll see weeds be pulled and their death will allow flowers blossom. Weep when you must, otherwise make sure that above all else, you did your job."

Jetta took the towel and walked away, shaken and angry from the ordeal. *Alue, where are you?*

***

Jetta rested under a large gnarled tree. Its branches were dotted with tiny flower buds and a crisp early spring breeze waved the leaves in a slight rocking motion. She held a medallion in her hands. Its silver linked chain was wrapped around her wrists and locked her hands together. Her eyes were shut in concentration as she whispered a set of prayers in a now forgotten tongue.

Speak to me o angel of mine,
And let the sun upon me shine,
Take me to your world above,
Fill my heart with mercy, grace, and love,
Chase away the wings like shadow,
And calm me in your gentle meadow,

The shadow of a figure broke her focus, "The angelic tongue. Your dialect is a bit off, but I can tell you were educated. You are no normal fishing village girl."

"Master Jesevik, I...I thought I was alone," Jetta said, slightly taken aback by her medical instructor's presence.

Jesevik was an elf like she was. His hair was silver and tied in a long braid that fell down his back. He wore the traditional gray and deep purple robes of a Black Rabbit medic, and was revered as such, but was classically trained. New medics, or menders, were now expected to also be present on combat missions.

"Jetta, you and your peers were given this time off to hone your skills. Yet, I find you here praying instead."

Jetta draped her necklace hastily around her neck and tucked the medallion into her tunic. Jesevik took notice of the symbol, "That is not the emblem of Alanna," he said, with an air of suspicion and disappointment.

Jetta attempted to stand and walk away before the conversation turned troublesome, "You are right, Master. I should go practice my craft."

He grabbed her by the arm, "You'd be wise to aim your prayers toward Alanna. The goddess of mercy can not help you here."

Jetta eyed the darkness in her master's eyes, "Alue protects me. I shall not fail her."

"Your prayers fall on deaf ears, child. Only Alanna listens to a Rabbit." Jesevik whispered harshly.

"I tend to Rabbits, but I am not one of them," Jetta spat, now seething with anger. She could not hide her frustration with her situation. Her master's words hung heavy on her heart. The last few weeks had been an era of darkness in her otherwise enlightened life. A year prior she had been given the opportunity to travel the world with a priest of Alue, but chose to stay with what was left of her family. Now she did not even have that. She had nothing anymore but her faith.

"Don't say such ridiculous things, Jetta. We are not your enemies. Your enemy is your own doubt. Doubt in yourself and your future. This is your new life. We are your new family and Alanna is your new god."

New life, new family, new god. The impact of this reality hit her like a heavy oak club to the gut. She stumbled back against the rowan tree, her face scrunched up in anguish. She stammered as she attempted to collect the revelation, "I ca-can't go home. I-I'm stuck here, fo-forever. My family, friends, village… Alue, why have you forsaken me?"

Jesevik lifted her chin to expose her teary eyes, "Jetta, the quicker you leave your past behind, the faster you can go on living your new one. Alue may have abandoned you, but Alanna will always embrace you in her wings."

"I want to speak to Elucard. Where can I find him?"

"An old friend from your village? And here we all thought he severed the ribbon of his past," Jesevik smiled, "It will do you some good to speak to a friend that has been where you stand. I will arrange some time for you to spend with him."

"Thank you, Master," she said calmly.

117

***

Elucard found Jetta waiting on a small wooden bridge that spanned across a brook. Jetta smiled as her old childhood friend approached her, "Elucard, it's been so long. I've nearly forgotten what you looked like. This bridge isn't exactly the old willow tree, but it'll have to do."

Elucard did not break a grin, his eyes were vacant compared to Jetta's, which were still full of life. Jetta's smile vanished in his cold presence, "Elucard, what's wrong? You and I are reunited. Friends forever, just like it's suppose to be."

Elucard cupped her hands and gave her a faint, hollow smile, "Jetta, things are never going to be like they used to be. The life we had as children is frozen in time, far in the past."

Jetta's eyes swelled up, "Elucard, not you too..."

"Jetta time stands still when you're a kid. You hold onto meaningless things, but when you grow up... when you mature, you have to let go and learn what is truly important."

"Meaningless things? Like our friendship? Like the promise you made me?" she shouted, flustered by the fact that everything she held close was now escaping her like a withered leaf breaking apart in the wind.

"Jetta, Jesevik tells me you are having trouble adjusting to your new home," Elucard said, ignoring Jetta's questions.

"Elucard, you are all that's left of... of..." Jetta stuttered, trying to keep her composure.

"I'm here Jetta, but I'm different now. I had to let go of the weak-willed child that I was. I had to let go of silly dreams. I had to let it all go in order to survive."

Jetta collapsed into his arms and sobbed. She did not want it to change, but she knew her old life would soon be just as dead as the man she could not save. The Rabbits had cut and stabbed it and left it for her to mend, and she knew already that doing so was an impossible task. No one was better at killing than the Rabbits.

"Jetta, you need to embrace your new lifestyle. This new world wants to chew you up and spit you out. It's a harsh, bleak world. It will shove you and kick you when you're down. You need to take in what the clan teaches you. The Rabbits don't want you to fail, but will discard you if you do. Please listen to me. I've seen what happens when you don't adapt... first hand." Elucard hung on those last words reflecting on that night in the cave.

118

They both fell to their knees, Jetta's crying slowly stopped, "Elucard, will you be there for me if I fall, or will you be the one kicking me down?"

"Jetta, I serve the Rabbits now. If you become a Rabbit, I'll protect you, but I can't stand by you if you defy us. Forgive me Jetta, this is my life now."

Elucard brushed her aside as she still shivered. He walked away, hoping he got through to her. She sat alone on the bridge until the sun went down, and contemplated the choice before her. Fight or submit.

23

Inle's strained to move his arm to block the incoming attack. The weights on his wrists slowed him down considerably and his body could no longer exert the energy to keep up with Elucard's quick and graceful movements. A spinning butterfly kick connected with Inle's jaw and he twirled chaotically to the ground. Inle lay motionless, struggling to find the will to stand again.

The two Rabbits had been sparring for at least three hours. Inle's wrists, shoulders, and ankles bore heavy weights that hindered his otherwise naturally agile movements. Elucard, however, was free of such a handicap.

Inle slowly rose to a knee and then managed to stand. Exhausted, battered, and bruised from the bout, he did not know how much longer he could press on. His vision was blurred from a swollen eye and his eyes stung from the sweat that dripped into them. Every inch of his body ached. Even all his years as an acrobat in the circus had not prepared him for such excruciating work, but he loved every second of it.

Elucard floated from toe to toe. He danced around Inle's worn and pathetic defenses before landing a series of jabs to Inle's kidneys and a devastating hay-maker to the side of Inle's face. The blow sent a mixture of saliva and blood whipping from the shadow elf's mouth. Inle's entire world crashed sideways as he slammed into the hard frozen ground.

"Enough. Rest," Elucard said before removing his tunic. His toned muscles glistened from the sweat that beaded down his body.

Inle watched entranced. Elucard was a young attractive elf. Even with the scars that crossed over his back and chest, it made Inle's heart skip a beat as he watched in infatuation. Since the moment Elucard stepped in front of Inle and removed his mask, every movement, every exchange, every moment, Elucard was locked in Inle's heart.

Elucard tossed a water skin to his student, "Hot day today. You're starting to give me a work out."

Inle smiled, struggling to grab the water skin that fell just shy of his reach. Even stretching his arm was a feat for Inle. He rolled to his back as he poured the reward down his throat.

"Easy Inle, don't hurt yourself."

Inle nearly passed out from the pain as he burst out laughing, "Master, you'd make a good clown. You have a knack for comedic timing."

Elucard sat down next to his apprentice, cracking a smile when he realized where the joke came from, "What was it like entertaining a crowd in Lost Dawns?"

Inle sat up, reminiscing about the life of an entertainer. The Ebonpath Traveling Circus. It consisted of his parents, three uncles, and seven sisters. He was the youngest of them all. They were a close family, which made it harder when the Black Rabbits took him. However, life in the circus, as adventurous as it seemed, slowly became monotonous. The same routines, the same laughs, the same gasps. The only thing that changed from performance to performance was the city they were in.

"Inle?" Elucard poked, seeing his student lost in thought.

"Lost Dawns is a grand city. I've never seen a tree so big. The people are a traditional crowd. They laugh and cheer when queued like marionettes. If you know which string to pull, they'll do whatever you want."

"You didn't like being a clown?" Elucard asked curiously.

"I grew bored of it. It's nothing like being an assassin. I can feel my body tightening, growing stronger. I'm reaching a new level. What's more, I'm making more of a difference now than I was delivering trite punchlines."

Elucard took back the water skin and took a sip. He fell silent for a moment or two before speaking quietly, half mumbling to himself, "I wish Jetta had your fortitude."

"Jetta?"

"An old friend from my village; my only real friend. She counted on me for everything… but then… I became a Rabbit." Elucard drifted for a moment, remembering the promise he had made to her. How he said he would always be there for her, that he would be the brother she did not have.

"She was recruited wasn't she? She must be somewhere around here training then." Inle pressed his hand to his brow and imitated the gesture of a scout searching high and low for her.

Elucard laughed and released a distant sigh, "She doesn't really understand the good we do here. She's fighting every step of the way and she's going to suffer because of it."

"Have you seen her yet, since she's arrived?"

"Yesterday."

Inle nodded, slowly seeing the picture that Elucard was painting of Jetta, "It comes down to you not giving up on her. Now more than ever, she needs you. The Black Rabbits aren't going to salvage her. You need to. You want her to survive? Well, then you have to be there with her. You must think of her as your Blade Sister."

"I see that now. You're wise beyond your years, Inle."

Inle winced as he let out a meek, bloody smile.

"Inle, the Blood Forest comes in less than two months. Veiled Menders will be assigned to each group. I'm going to arrange that you be paired up with Jetta."

Inle nodded quickly, "Say no more, Master. If she can keep me alive, I'll be sure she makes it out of that forest."

Elucard jumped up and grabbed Inle's hand, lifting him to his feet, "Well then, we'd better make sure you're ready. How about another round?"

24

Inle's polished blade moved silently and smoothly through the pale moonlight beneath the canopy. The would-be assassin choked as he retched a stream of blood onto the cool, dark forest floor. Inle's new steel mask gleamed under a ray of moonlight, spotted with streaks of blood. He thought back to the day that Elucard had given him his new mask as he slowly dragged two fingers through the warm, sticky blood that had spattered on it.

'Inle, your old mask represented the family and life that you once had. It is for the best that it was broken. However, I give to you a new symbol of the life you have now; of the family that surrounds you. Together, we will make you a stronger person.'

Inle stood motionless with eyes closed and breathed softly. His jet black leather armor would have been spotless were it not for several small, wide arcs of blood that had sprayed across his torso. He breathed a quick sigh, shaking away the memories and faces of his recent victims, then cleaned the blood from his blade. He needed to be precise. The Blood Forest was not his only test. He was tasked, like many others in the forest, to protect a Veiled Mender. He, however, had the added weight of having to protect the childhood friend of his mentor, and Jetta was making this no easy task.

"Jetta, we must move quicker. I hear another pair not far from the east." Inle wanted to keep Jetta safe, but also reveled in the idea of spilling more blood beneath the dark, dimly lit canopy. Jetta knew this but took no comfort in it.

"We could make our way quicker if you would quit killing everyone who had the misfortune of crossing our paths," Jetta said with slightly more reproach in her voice than she had intended, "This is supposed to mirror a real world escort mission, not a siege," her voice carried less edge this time. It was almost soft.

Inle grinned wickedly beneath his mask. She made a fair point. He had been going *slightly*, out of his way to kill off the competition. Elucard had regaled him with stories of the Blood Forest for past couple of months. His mentor had told him how he was originally sickened by the thought of taking a life, but Inle felt nothing inside when his blade sunk through cloth and skin. In fact, apart from his strong feelings for Elucard, he was almost completely empty inside. He did, however, revel in his role as one of Alanna's harbingers of death. The power that came with ending a life and the notion each death could tip the scales of balance in the world thrilled him.

Although Jetta's new life had left her numb and unfazed at the sight of death, she would have preferred to be fighting to preserve life. In her eyes, even the death of a Rabbit seemed a great waste. She had trained countless long hours to keep death at bay, and yet here she was, surrounded by it. Even so, she seemed to slip into the role of a Veiled Mender naturally. Her hands were steady and quick with stitching and bandaging. She also worked exceedingly well under pressure. Yet, deep inside she knew she was saving those who would go on to kill for a cause she did not believe in.

Over time, Jetta struggled less with her skills as a mender and more with identifying as a Black Rabbit. She had to pray to her goddess, Alue, in secret because praying to any god besides Alanna was treasonous. To make matters worse, 'mercy' was not an attribute praised by the Rabbits. She remembered a common prayer that she was taught:

Born of shadows, the light I'll face,
My blade is silent, swift, and sleek,
My dear Alanna, grant me grace,
And I shall slay those I seek,

A prayer that she noted even Elucard would whisper before going out on a mission. She, however, could not stomach such a vile hymn. A deity should not give their blessing for anyone to kill, especially for such nebulous reasons as the Rabbits apparently had. She simply could not fathom such a god.

Jetta whispered a prayer to clear her mind:

Fill the wicked with purity,
Find those who wander in the darkness,
Alue will give the weak security,
And breathe life into the heartless,

"What was that, Jetta?" Inle called to her as he finished scouting up ahead.

"Come on, Inle. Can we avoid any further bloodshed and just get out of here? This place gives me the creeps. I can't help but feel like we're always being watched." Jetta looked around nervously as the pushed ahead, but could see nothing behind the infinite black lurking beyond the trees.

Inle had to admit that the Blood Forest was the most unnatural forest he had ever stepped foot in. The soil was as bathed in blood as the trees were in shadow. He appeared to be comfortable deep within the wretched forest, but in truth, he wanted nothing more than to put the forest's eeriness behind him, "Fine, let's go."

***

Elucard stood high in the branches of the Blood Forest, keeping a watchful eye on a lone assassin stalking Jetta and Inle. With each step that he made, Elucard gripped the handle of his blade even tighter.

"Do not interfere with their test," he murmured to himself. He could sense the tension building within himself and was worried that he would act rashly.

Elucard's eyes darted over his shoulder. A figure emerged from the thick shadows behind him. Elucard loosened his grip, "Master, I was only–"

Legion took Elucard's hand and slowly peeled the blade away, "You were only keeping an eye on your student and your friend. You do not have to explain your actions to me." Legion watched the skulking assassin below and saw that he was quickly drawing closer to the two recruits, "Nevertheless, we shouldn't be here. You know the rules as well as I."

"His name is Keir," Elucard said, brushing off Legion's words, "He's a student of Dest. As you can see he excels in stealth and tracking. He chose not be paired with a veiled mender, and now I see why. It's much easier to stalk alone. He's been following Inle's trail of blood all night." Elucard's eyes dashed wildly through the trees as he tried to keep Jetta and Inle in his line of sight.

Legion frowned slightly as his gaze followed the two students below, "With each kill Inle has exerted more and more energy, and Jetta has apparently opted out of learning basic self defense. Instead she has honed her ability to mend her allies. But if Inle keeps going at this pace…" Legion looked up at Elucard and saw a face that was tight with tension. Elucard's face was hard as stone and a fierce protective anger seethed behind his eyes.

The trio below dashed out of Elucard's line of sight, so he jumped from tree to tree until he was looking down upon them once more. Keir was just upon Inle and Jetta now. Legion landed beside a crouching Elucard. He knew Elucard's thoughts and motives well and he knew that Elucard was fighting a deep, fiery urge to interfere.

"Elucard, you've done all you can for Inle. You've taught him our philosophies and sharpened his skills. Like yourself, Inle must walk the Blood Forest and discover his own way out; and he must do it alone." Legion placed a firm hand on Elucard's shoulder and turned to pull him away, but Elucard did not move.

"Jetta did not have the luxury of our teachings. She's a lone sapling in the storm."

Elucard's words brought about a sudden flood of realization. He was not fighting to suppress his anger. He was fighting to suppress his fear. Fear that Jetta and Inle would not have what it takes to survive the Blood Forest. No – fear that Jetta would not survive.

Legion spoke softly, "If she survives the storm, she'll grow into a tree that can survive any storm afterward. You must trust them, Elucard."

***

"You look tired. Maybe we should rest."

Jetta knew Inle could probably keep this pace going for quite some time, but she was well and truly exhausted, "The forest is silent. I think we're alone," Jetta said, kneeling down to take a swig from her water skin.

Inle crouched beside her, lifting his mask up from his mouth and panting heavily, "Thanks, I could use a few minutes," he lied. He knew she needed a break and that leaving her behind was not an option. Elucard was fond of her and so she was important to him.

Jetta tossed him her water skin, "Keep hydrated. The last thing we need is for you to pass out at the exit."

Inle caught the canteen, but seemed to stare intensely at Jetta. It was unsettling to her.

"Copper for your thoughts?" Jetta asked timidly.

"I heard your prayer a little while ago. It was not a prayer of Alanna. Why do you pray to her? Alue? You alienate yourself from your clan by worshiping a false goddess." Inle pointed at his ear to show that her whispering had failed.

Jetta was silent at first. She did not know what to say. Inle was right. Right that she continued to alienate her peers and 'allies.' They were villainous souls, but wayward nonetheless. They had good intentions, but were steered in the incorrect direction. If they focused their efforts

126

for good, then she could only dream of what they were capable of, "Alue isn't false. She's very real, and if you opened yourself to her, you'd see she has sent me to help you."

Inle smirked, "Well, you can help me by passing me a ration," he said as he lifted the canteen's mouth to his. However, only a droplet fell in. Inle's eyes grew wide when he saw that a shuriken was lodged in its side and that water was pouring from the massive gash it left.

"Get down!" he yelled as a volley of glinting iron shuriken flew in the night and sank deep into his arm.

Jetta dropped to the leafy ground, her hands rising swiftly to protect her head. As more shuriken sliced wildly through the air, Inle flipped backwards, attempting to dodge the flurry of iron. However, his exhausted body moved sluggishly. Several shuriken found their marks in the elf's thigh. Inle crashed and skidded across the moss and fern.

"Inle!" Jetta cried, as she slid to her partner's side. With a volley of shuriken flying by them, her hands dove into her haversack of medical supplies. Grabbing ointments and bandages, she examined the wounds that were in Inle's arm and leg, "Hold still, I'll get you patched up."

"Make it fast. I'll try to deflect any shuriken that I can." Inle raised his blade and prepared to block any incoming attacks.

"I'll try. Keep that left arm and that leg still!"

Inle grimaced as Jetta worked fast dislodging the star shaped metal shards. She slapped a concoction of disinfectant and medicine into the wounds, and wrapped them tightly with linen bandages, "That'll have to do for now. Go, quickly!"

"It'll do fine! Stand back!" Inle winced in pain as he began to gather himself for an attack. He drew his blade and peered into the darkness. If there was ever a time for him to be proud that he was a shadow elf, this was it. Accustomed to dark caves and tunnels, his eyes were likely more suited for low light combat than his opponent. His attacker would not be safe in the shadows for long. Inle scanned the mist of shadows that surrounded them but saw nothing. The assailant was most likely hidden in the tall ferns that overran the forest.

"Come out, I wish to dance with you!"

A long moment passed and nothing happened until the sound of movement stirred in the brush behind Inle.

Keir slowly stepped into the moonlight. His traditional black garbs had tight belts and sashes all around his waist, chest, arms and legs that were packed with foliage, giving him a makeshift camouflage. He looked past Inle and let out a toothy white grin at Jetta.

Inle slowly shook his head, "Pay no mind to the girl. I, Inle Ebonpath, shall be entertaining you tonight." Inle made a gracious bow as if he were back in the circus once more, entertaining a crowded audience.

Keir winked at Jetta and spat, "Let me deal with this clown. Don't go anywhere."

Inle smirked, "Heh, 'clown'." Inle dashed headlong, pulling out a dagger, sending it soaring in front of him whilst wielding his sword in his other hand. Keir quickly equipped a cat claw, deflecting the thrown dagger before clashing with the blade.

Inle parried a slash, spinning around with a slick roundhouse kick that slammed into Keir's jaw. Keir twisted in the air before smashing to the ground. Rolling to his side, Keir nearly missed a driving impalement that instead struck the firm ground.

Keir leaped backwards, landing in a standing position, "You move fast, clown, but I see the night has slowed you down."

Inle was breathing heavily. He did not recover during the little rest he had. He needed to finish this fast. Keir had a point. If they continued this battle much longer, it would not be on equal footing.

Keir unleashed a flurry of shuriken as Inle ran toward him. The elf made his best to avoid the attack with a skillful attempt at deflecting them, but to no avail. Stumbling, he crashed to the ground as a series of shuriken lodged in a tall arc across his chest. He struggled to raise a knee, breathing heavily as the iron stars sent furious tremors of pain scrambling through his body with each breath.

Keir laughed, "Not everyone is cut out for this life, clown."

Inle made an effort to stand, wobbling under the pain, exhaustion, and labored breathing.

Keir took out another shuriken, "You want another go? Fine with me!"

Inle mustered the last of his energy and once again sprinted sword first at Keir. Concentrating on the shuriken's path, Inle lowered his back and neck, deflecting the stars with his armored mask.

Keir gasped at the surprise deflection, as Inle drove his blade deep through his stomach, driving him backwards and pinning him to a tree.

"I guess you weren't cut out for this life," Inle said faintly as he collapsed against the tree just beneath the impaled body, chuckling to himself.

"Inle!" Jetta screamed as she scrambled to his side, "Alanna was with you tonight," she said, attempting to keep Inle in good spirits as she worked to remove the countless shuriken buried deep in his chest as painlessly as possible.

"Lucky me," Inle said, taking off his mask and giving a wry smile.

They smiled at one another and rested beneath Keir's corpse until they were ready to exit the Blood Forest through the clearing ahead.

25

"Quickly, Inle, don't lose him!" Elucard dashed past a series of thugs, his blade slicing through the legs of the men that stood between him and his mark.

"Easier said than done, master! These men are as big as bears!" Inle leap-frogged over the goon in front of him and released several daggers that sank deep into the back and shoulders of the next man blocking his path. In the distance, Inle could see the weaselly man that was their mark run down the corridor of a dimly lit safe house.

"Bears; heh, I bet they are just as hairy too!" Chided Jetta as she kept pace with Elucard, nimbly flipping over and sidestepping countless guards. It had been a year or so since the Blood Forest and Jetta had made large strides in her role as a veiled mender. She kept up with Inle and Elucard. The three had excellent chemistry as a team.

A heavy wooden chamber door crashed open as Elucard ran in, sword at the ready. Jetta followed with Inle tagging just behind. A small, thin man huddled in the far corner, breathing heavily and sweating profusely. He shivered as he sputtered, "L-Listen, I can get the money, I just need a bit m-more time. I swear; it's all tied up in my various shops. I swear to Father that I'm good for it."

Inle balanced a dagger on the tip of his finger before tossing it and snatching it in mid air, "You pray to the wrong god, my friend."

Elucard slipped his sword's edge under the frightened man's chin, "You failed to pay for our clan's protection. We are tired of your excuses. Now it's time you pay with your life."

The man dropped to his knees, "Please, I–"

His pleas were cut short by a quick swipe across his neck with Elucard's blade. Inle drooped his ears in dismay, "Master, you killed the last one. This was my turn."

"No doubt you had your share from all those hired muscles I skipped."

Jetta scowled, folding her arms, "We shouldn't revel in taking lives even though we must. This isn't a game. We don't kill for sport."

"You're right, Jetta," Nodded Elucard, "Let's head out."

Inle rolled his eyes beneath his mask, clearly annoyed, "You're just the medic. You don't even carry a weapon. Who are you to talk down to me about taking lives?"

Jetta snapped her head back to Inle, "Excuse me?" Jetta walked up to Inle and thrusted an index finger into Inle's chest, "I may just be the medic, but I am just as much an accomplice in these murders as the both of you."

"Murders? That implies we've committed a crime. Jetta, you still don't understand the work we do, even a year after you've become a Rabbit?" snarled Inle. He moved dangerously close to Jetta, lowering his masked face to meet hers.

Jetta shoved him back, "I do what's asked of me. I keep you alive! Nothing more than that."

Inle took out a dagger and thinly grazed the side of her face with its point, "Dear Jetta, perhaps Alue fogs your mind. Distance yourself from our family, and you also become lost in that fog."

"A'lunis sik mere'th J'Deio shi sahde Alann'Na!" Jetta spat.

"What was that?" Inle said, his voice now raised.

"Hope is my beacon in Death's shadow," Elucard said with disappointment in is voice. He stepped between Inle and Jetta and raised a hand to mediate between the two, "Inle, that's enough." Elucard turned to Jetta, "Relax, Jetta. Every now and again it's good to let out a bit of steam. Our work no doubt hangs heavy in our souls."

Jetta nodded and bowed to her friend, "Elucard, you are right, I didn't mean to—"

"It's alright Jetta, no harm done," Elucard shot a glance at Inle, "Inle?"

Inle bowed his head, "Forgive me, master, I was out of line. I ask forgives from you as well, Jetta." Inle's voiced seemed a bit sharper as he spoke Jetta's name.

Elucard returned the bow in respect to his student, "It's fine. Our team functions best when we are all in accordance with one another. We're going to have our differences, but we need to leave that aside when it is time to get a task done. Master Legion speaks highly of our teamwork. Let's continue to earn that praise."

***

The Black Rabbit compound was widespread with commotion as both recruits and assassins gathered in front of High Blade Legion. He raised his hands to simmer down the whispers, "The rumors are true.

We have been given a task larger and more important than any mission this clan has ever been given before."

Immediately the whispers started back up. Theories of what the mission could be spread like wildfire. Voices began to call out to Legion to lay the clan's curiosity to rest.

"We've been given the task to assassinate King Jaelyn during the Lost Dawn Completion Ball!" A sweep of silence fell over the crowd as Legion gave the announcement.

Malady stood in the back leaning against a pillar. He found this announcement more interesting than most. To him, it was a clear chance to finally prove that his students were the most finely skilled assassins in the clan. However, the past failures of his pupils to defeat Legion's students left a foul taste that lingered in his mouth. Nevertheless, this was his chance to gain the Silent Master's favor. Perhaps he could even aspire to become First Blade; a position that was still vacant with Vada's absence — and most importantly—leave him in a strategic spot to someday become High Blade.

Malady's voice broke through the utterly flabbergasted crowd, "And who, dear Blade Brother, shall be the lucky Rabbit to fell a king?" He continued before Legion could answer back, "May I suggest my apprentice, Tesha? She is a cut above the rest and has proved to be both equally precise as she is lethal."

Before Legion could consider the suggestion, the rice paper door slid open behind him. A collective gasp resonated amongst everyone in the retreat. The Silent Master had made a rare appearance.

Legion immediately collapsed to his knees, bewildered by the clan master's presence. The Silent Master gazed at his subjects as they all quickly fell prostrate before him. Most had never seen the man who commanded the High Blade.

He was an elf like the most of his Rabbits. Unlike most elves he had large imposing muscles that rippled through his body. He had a shaved head that was nearly bald, although short silver hair could still be seen. His eyes were black with a slight edge of near-white irises hugging his pupils. Decorative tattoos covered his arms and half of his face which was accented with a thin scar crossed diagonally over his lips. He was robed in black and violet silks. A pair of short swords were sheathed on either side of a red sash around his waste.

The Silent Master held quiet briefly before speaking, "The first attempt on Jaelyn's life was a failure. I was betrayed by my own tribe. However, I have since forsaken those traitorous fools. This clan is my tribe now. You are all my family." He paused for a moment and gazed out at the crowd, "I have taken some time to deliberate who should carry the weight of this mission on their shoulders. One who has shown promise over these years, one who was trained by our most skilled fighter, most of all, one whom I can trust." The Silent Master motioned his finger, "Elucard, come forth."

Elucard's eyes widened with disbelief. Inle patted him on the back and whispered for him to hurry.

The Silent Master continued as the young elf hustled forward, "Elucard, each test we've given you was performed with prowess and finesse. You've proven to be a student of our ways and philosophies. You've grown from the whelp you once were to the assassin you are today. You and your team of two others shall travel swiftly and silently to the gods-forsaken city of Lost dawns. You shall carry out your duty to slay Jaelyn and thereby cement your own legacy. When you return victorious, you will take your place alongside your former teacher, Legion, as my First Blade."

Elucard was stunned.

"What say you?"

Elucard looked back to Inle and Jetta and then smiled as he bowed before the Silent Master, "May Alanna coat my blade with the same honor you bestow upon me. Like a shadow, my team will descend upon our enemies and drown them in their own blood."

The Silent Master smiled thinly, "Very well Elucard, reap the night."

26

A dull blade smashed against a heavy iron buckler. Wiccer danced backwards as Avren recoiled from the block and struck out with an attack of his own. The training sword deftly sliced through the air, but missed its mark. No longer forced to reside within walls of the run-down temple, the Long Whisper Division of White Cloaks now had a barracks and headquarters built within the newly formed military district of Lost Dawns. There, a training ground was built in a lot outside the barracks, which was a common place to find Wiccer and Avren in the early hours of the rising sun.

"You're getting better each day, little brother."

Wiccer smiled, "Better than you," he said as he spun around, slashing at Avren.

Avren caught the blade with his own sword, and with the twist of his wrist, sent Wiccer's sword flying out of his hand.

"Not quite," he laughed.

Wiccer walked over to his sword sulking before getting back into a defensive stance in preparation for another round, "How's your girlfriend doing? No doubt she's been bored held up in the city. I'd imagine she wants to get back to her clan so she can stab us in the back."

Avren smirked thinking about Elisa's new hobby of trying on pretty dresses to impress him. Afterward she would steal the ones she liked. It was true that Elisa was not meant to be a caged bird, but the opportunity to use her in the field had not quite presented itself. Avren suggested that she become part of the Guard, and each time he brought it up she would laugh in his face.

"White doesn't suit me," she would say. Avren did his best to convince her otherwise. The White Cloaks had learned just about all they could from Elisa, and he knew that she needed to continue to prove herself useful or she would quickly find herself back in a cell.

"Although, she might prove of some use if she were to go back to her clan," Wiccer said as he ducked under a quick attack.

"How so?" Avren deflected a brutal slash with his shield.

"What we need are a well trained set of eyes and ears on the Rabbits. If Elisa is too afraid to tell us where their compound is, the next best thing is for her to be a spy in their little rabbit hole."

Avren nodded before crashing his shield into Wiccer's chest, bowling him over, "I'll run it by her. Could be more danger than she's up for."

"You're really starting to care for her!" Wiccer laughed, mimicking a hugging motion with his hands and puckering his face.

"Hey, we're just mutual partners. It's purely business."

"Business and sex," Wiccer snickered, picking himself up off the ground.

Avren smacked him on the back of his head, "Enough out of you. Hand me that water skin." Avren took a long drink and wiped the water from his mouth with the back of his sleeve, "Speaking of business, we have an order from the king."

Wiccer sat and rubbed the back of his head, "The city is buzzing about the ball that is coming up. Is that what the order is about?"

Avren nodded, passing him a scroll, "According to Elisa, the Roots are buzzing too. No doubt word will get out to the Rabbits. The king is throwing a ball to celebrate the city's completion. Jaelyn wants us to provide security and he wants us personally to be at his side."

"That's a big honor. The Rabbits wouldn't risk such an appearance with that much security. It would be foolish."

"A chance we can't take. Best to be prepared all the same. The ball is three days from now. So get your finest tunic pressed and use your ceremonial saber. This could be a night to remember."

27

"Elucard, I urge you to reconsider your team," said Malady, "Allow my apprentice Tesha and I to accompany you instead. We have more skill and experience between the two of us than your whole team. You will regret not taking us."

The one-eyed elf repeated this over and over to Elucard in an effort to snake his way into the mission of a lifetime.

"Sorry, my mind is made up. The Silent Master must see great potential in me and I must trust my own judgment. I'd be daft not to." Elucard turned to leave and signaled Jetta and Inle to follow him.

At the last second Malady pulled Inle to the side, "You and I both know you should be First Blade. Elucard has skill, yes, but I've watched you, Inle. No one has the drive quite like you. Even my apprentice admits you belonged under my tutelage. Now, I can't take you under my wing for training, but I can take you under my wing to make sure you truly grow. Elucard is going to take all the glory away from those that truly shined."

Inle smiled wickedly, "You flatter me, sir. You wish to see me grow, but to what end? Where do you benefit?"

"I do not need to directly benefit. You becoming the rightful First Blade is benefit enough. I can make this happen. Are you interested?"

Inle looked back to Elucard before giving his answer, "I have to admit, I am a bit interested."

"Just make sure Elucard does not return alive. That is it. Things can happen in the heat of battle. Accidents happen all the time. Enemies can get the upper hand…understand?"

Inle stared fiercely at Malady, "Afraid I don't. In fact, I think it would be best if you just walked away, or else I'll make sure an accident happens to you. Do we understand one another?"

"Perfectly," Malady smiled and chuckled through his teeth, before he walked away.

***

Kneeling in the shade of the Blood Forest, the silence enveloped Malady like a pair of shadowy wings. He locked himself within the depths of thought. Memories of his youth crashed through his mind like the rapids of a river.

He slowly stood, reaching for two of his five swords fanned across his back. Unsheathing them, he coolly went through the motions of a meditative kata. Flowing through different combative stances he imagined his enemies were in front of him. The image of Legion; the image of Elucard; finally, the image of Leandra. In slick fluid motions he swiped at the illusions skillfully killing his targets one by one, until they were gone.

"You held me back!" He shouted, calling out to no one but himself, "You were only ever in my way!"

"Master, who are you talking to?" Tesha asked as she slid from the shadows behind Malady. She was an elf from a similar fishing village to Ravenshore. She was dressed in the traditional black and purple clothing of the Black Rabbits. Her long red hair matched the scarf that coiled around her neck and made her stand out among the rest of the clan, as did the small butterfly tattoo on her wrist.

Malady sheathed his blades, still furious from his own thoughts. His face was covered in pure anguish, but he slid it back to his normal, more calculated demeanor. Taking a deep breath, he turned on his heel to approach his apprentice, "Were you followed?"

"Of course not, you take me for an amateur?" Tesha seethed a smile, "So what is your plan? Are we going to steal the kill from Elucard, his apprentice, and that mender bitch?"

Malady steepled his fingers as he brought them to his lips. His plan was the very definition of 'insane'.

Tesha tapped her foot impatiently, "Well, spit it out already!"

"You are to go to the king, but instead of killing him, you will warn him of the coming attack and will help him kill Elucard and his comrades." Malady shined a toothy smile.

"But Master, that's treason!" Tesha could not even begin to fathom what must have driven her master to such madness.

"It is justified treason!" roared Malady. His smile vanished in a flash, "*I* should be High Blade! *You* should have been given the opportunity to become First Blade! All this clan has ever done is humiliate me!" Malady panted in frustration before continuing, "You are still young, Tesha. Have I ever told you about my last high apprentice? A young boy about your age named Keth? Deep within the very forest where we stand, Elucard relieved my dear Keth of his head. Keth was much

137

stronger than you are, but you show boundless cunning. You have what it takes to succeed where Keth failed, I know it. The clan does not want me to thrive, it never did, and now it will not let you flourish. You have seen how everyone brushes you off. You have seen how the clan praises Elucard and Legion for even the most minuscule of victories."

Tesha was silent.

"She always praised him; I worked harder than him; Than all of them!" Malady paced back in forth, his hand waving in the air.

"Master?" Tesha was lost in Malady's ramblings.

Malady gritted his teeth, collecting himself, "My dear Tesha, you and I will no doubt become High Blade and First Blade if Legion and Elucard are taken out of the picture. However, first you need to leave at sun break for Lost Dawns. Reach the king and tell him the danger he is in. Then help him fend off and kill Elucard, Inle, and Jetta. The city will raise you up as a hero. We will no doubt earn an alliance with the King to do tasks the Rabbits had no access to before. Legion will be crushed that his beloved prodigy has fallen in the line of duty. He will step down to wallow in his misery. Good fortune will finally shine down on us. Life will be grand!"

Tesha grinned, imagining herself as the hero of Lost Dawns and First Blade of the Black Rabbits, but quickly questioned Malady's plan, "But master, if I betray the Silent Master, why would he make me First Blade?"

"The Clan will be aligned with Lost Dawns. If that old fool of a Silent Master can not see the rewards in that, I will see to it that he steps down. We must think outside of the box. They have pushed us to this road. Now child, leave at once!"

She bowed before him, "I shall do this for you."

Malady bowed back, "For us."

***

Lost Dawns was a sight to see from where the three stood atop the clock tower. The elder tree stood a force of pure beauty in the center of the city. Buildings dotted the landscape all around its mighty trunk. Elucard and Jetta were stunned by the sheer size of it all. In the distance, the Dawnedge castle watched over the slumbering city. The moonlight cascaded over the three Rabbits as they sat on the ledge of a looming tower.

"We move in three hours. Inle, scout the castle perimeter and get us a count of White Cloaks," said Elucard.

Inle bowed before dropping into the night.

Jetta folded her legs, adjusting her position on the ledge. Long ago she was afraid of climbing too high on the old willow tree back in Ravenshore. Now she was sitting on the edge of an enormous clock tower. She looked over at Elucard. He had changed as well. No longer was he the peaceful young elf boy. He was once curious and kind, but now he was a ruthless killer. Perhaps that boy was still in him, trapped as a prisoner of his new Rabbit soul. Maybe it wasn't too late for him to rejoin the living, instead of being a slave to the damned.

"Elucard," she whispered, "Do you ever think of what could have become of us if you weren't taken by the Black Rabbits?"

"Jetta, you must stay focused. This isn't some slumlord or lesser baron we are going to kill. It's the king of all of Long Whisper."

She went silent. Did he not grasp what he just said?

"Elucard," her voice was higher now, "We don't have to do this. This is terrorism. Please tell me that somewhere inside of you a shred of humanity still exists. That you haven't let the little boy you once were succumb to the killer you are now."

"I–" Elucard stopped himself short; "Humanity." Legion once told him to save the humanity in him. That it would be an edge against his enemies. He had forgotten that. He had lost all humanity until only a husk of himself existed. He needed to sever that tie to survive. But did he survive? He was alive, but he felt nothing now. Emotionless, cold, empty.

"Jetta, now isn't the time for this. I need you to focus and act like the Rabbit we've trained you to be. The moment we stumble is the moment we will fall."

"Elucard, I know the good in you is still there. I know the Rabbits haven't turned your into soul into complete darkness. The moment we assassinate Jaelyn… Well, that's something we can never turn back from. Do you understand that we'll have to live with such a deed over our heads for the rest of our lives?"

"Such a deed? Jetta, listen to yourself. Have you learned nothing? What we do must be done. It is a divine duty to kill for Alanna! I can't believe I have to debate this with you!"

Jetta reached out for Elucard, "Alanna is a neutral goddess. She doesn't wish for us to go around killing people! She is a goddess of nature. The Rabbits have twisted everything, including the will of the fates. Even I can see that, Elucard. Why can't you?"

Elucard jerked backwards in complete disbelief of Jetta.

"Elucard please. Please see reason. You can't possibly believe that what we are about to do is justified. We kill the innocent, we make widows and we make orphans. Look into your heart and see what you've become."

Elucard's eyes were blanketed with anger and confusion. How could Jetta be saying this, especially now? He thought she understood the cause. That she believed in it...

"Jetta... I thought you were with me. We are a team, you, Inle, and I... a team."

"Elucard, I'll always be by your side, but I just wish you would understand that the Rabbits are poisoning you," Jetta said tenderly. She now saw a lost little boy looking back at her on the ledge of that clock tower.

The Black Rabbits have poisoned you! Myler's words echoed in his head. Flashes of him slaughtering his friends scattered across his mind.

"Jetta, you don't know what I'm capable of. What the Rabbits are capable of. The things I've done could never be forgiven. What we are about to do... I can't protect you from the path we're about to embark on. You need to go... now! Run far away from me, the Rabbits, all of it, until you are safe."

Jetta shook her head, furrowing her brow in sadness, "Elucard, I see that you want to protect me from the life we lead, but when we separated for that first time it cracked us in two. Together we are strong. I want you to be strong Elucard... I want to be strong with you."

Elucard embraced his friend, a tear rolling down his eye, "Jetta I promised to keep you safe, but I don't know how long I can do that."

"Elucard, I've grown up. I want to be the one to keep you safe."

Elucard smiled meekly, breaking from the hug. Still keeping a hand on hers he whispered, "We'll protect each other, then."

"Elucard," Inle broke the moment like lightning through the sky.

Elucard stood and bowed to his student, the side of his eyes wet from the tears. Inle took notice, darting his attention to Jetta and scowling under his mask.

"Elucard, there were nine guards covering the wall, only four around the castle roof. I found a balcony that is unguarded. An excellent place to slip in." Inle said, hoping to have Elucard snap back to attentive state.

Elucard nodded, "We'll lea–"

"We should leave now," Inle said cutting off his master. He spoke again, still eyeing Jetta, "Before more guards accumulate."

Elucard patted his student on the shoulder, "Good job, Inle."

He stole a glance at Jetta. A new feeling was emerging from him that laid dormant in his mind for so long… joy. Not the joy from a kill or the joy from satisfying his peers and master. This was a different type of joy. A hopeful one. He could not pinpoint it, but it felt like his childhood.

Inle watched as his master's eyes seemed to wander off into his thoughts. Inle needed to take control of the situation, whatever Jetta had said needed to be undone. He needed his master's head to be in the game.

"A blade is only as sharp as the Rabbit wielding it," he said to his master, "You need to clear your head. There is a lot of madness in this mission. We are here to do what no one could do before. Kill the king. You're not doing this alone though. You have me. You have Jetta. We are the team that the Silent Master hand picked. Master, we are *it*. The true elite. We have your back. The clan has your back. It is time that we Rabbits do what we were trained to do. Purge a life and rebalance the scales."

Elucard looked through the thin eye slits of Inle's mask.

"Yes, Inle. You speak the truth."

He turned to Jetta putting a hand on both her and Inle's shoulder, "We are the true elite. We need to prove to not only our clan, but ourselves, that we can perform the most daunting task of our life. Whether we succeed or fail, this will be a trial that all will speak of for the rest of history." Elucard took out his blade and nodded to the two teammates.

Inle smiled, taking out his blade, "We are with you, Master."

Jetta lowered her head, still in doubt of the cause, but complied all the same, "Until the end, Elucard."

Elucard pointed his blade at the castle.

"May Alanna guide our blades!" Elucard roared as he dropped down.

Once Elucard was out of sight, Inle grabbed Jetta's arm, "I do not know what you said that shook him up like that, but you need to stop playing your little game with Elucard's head. He needs to be at one hundred percent to complete this mission, and if he is second guessing himself…"

"Relax Inle. Let me go. We have work to do," Jetta said, yanking her arm away, "Don't be distracted by me. Elucard isn't the only one of us that needs to be at one hundred percent to walk out of this alive. Have you forgotten? We're about to kill a king," Jetta sneered, disgusted by her own words.

Fury washed over Inle's face beneath his mask, "I'm watching you, Jetta."

28

Wiccer leaned against the marble railing of the small balcony that overlooked the blooming city below. His pearl-white cloak swam in the cool evening air and his thoughts scattered like the infinite sands of Scorch: unsteadily, listlessly, and utterly directionless. Then at once, his thoughts violently washed over him and there was nowhere he could run or hide to escape the coarse avalanche. His mind raced back hours ago, to the castle keep where he and his brother kept watch...

"Wiccer, get the king out of here!" Avren roared. His sword shimmered in the glaze of the daylight that seeped from the open window where Tesha had entered. She stood on the war table, unfazed by Avren's blade. A series of daggers whizzed into the floorboards, stopping Jaelyn and Wiccer in their tracks.

"I think it would be best that the king hears what I have to say," she said. She gave Wiccer a thin smile as he moved himself in front of the elven king, "If I wanted the king dead, I would have killed him when you two noble idiots weren't here."

"What did you call—" started Avren.

"We are losing valuable time here," Tesha interrupted, "Jaelyn, I'm here on a mission to protect you from my clan. As we speak, my clan has sent a squad of assassins to deal with you. As much as I hate to admit it, they are very skilled. Without my help, you may perish this night."

Wiccer cautiously moved his hand away from his blade's handle, "Why should we trust a Rabbit? Especially one working against its own clan?"

Tesha flipped her hand through her wavy, vibrant red hair. Her amber elven eyes gazed into Wiccer's, "An excellent question, my handsome White Cloak. My clan is much like the sun. It nourishes one flower, while the rest wither in the shade."

"What do you gain from your clan's failure?" Wiccer asked, still unconvinced.

"I would have saved the king's life. No doubt I would have gained enough trust to build the foundation of a relationship between our people; exclusive contracts, perhaps. After all, don't we all wish to be praised as heroes?"

"I would indeed hail you a hero for turning against your clan to protect me," said Jaelyn, "We shall set a trap for these villains. With my White Cloaks aligned with a Black Rabbit, they will stand no chance." The king brandished a wide smile and clapped his hands, "I want to be present for this."

"Absolutely not!" Avren gestured his hands in a motion to display that he completely disagreed with the entire situation.

"It's not your call. You may lead your Cloaks, but I hired them. You take commands from me. This isn't the first time someone has tried to kill me, and I'm sure that this will not be the last," The king turned to Tesha, "You, Rabbit, who is coming to assassinate me?"

"Elucard leads two. Inle, his student, and a medic known as Jetta."

Jaelyn scrunched his face in disgust, "This Elucard and his team will hang from broken necks in the town square tomorrow. I will personally see to it."

"Your Grace, I highly advise against this plan. If this Elucard intends to kill you, why should we give him such an opportunity?" Avren said, this time remembering his courtesies.

"Captain, I do not fear what goes 'bump' in the night. For when it does, I 'bump' back."

Wiccer anxiously thumbed the edge of his blade. *So, Elucard. My honorable deed will haunt me*. He resolved then and there that he would not spare him a second time.

"What troubles you, sergeant?" The quiet but kind voice broke up his thoughts. Wiccer turned and found himself looking at an elf, roughly his age. He was clothed in fine nobleman threads. The circlet around his forehead and a Dawnedge signet ring marked him as royalty. By his side stood a large wolf that had brilliant cobalt fur eye an eye that sparked wild with magic. It nudged at the elf's hand.

Wiccer knelt in the presence of the Prince of Long Whisper, "Prince Koda. I-I was only thinking…"

Koda chuckled, "Yes, I can see that. What about?"

"Yes, a dumb response. I was thinking about tonight, and my responsibilities, my future, everything, I suppose."

"Ah, I see. Everything often gets cluttered in one's mind,"Koda knelt down to playfully run his hands through the thick fur of his familiar. Wildeye hefted her giant paws onto Koda's shoulders and licked him mercilessly, "It helps to have a friend that can clear out that mess in your head!"

Wiccer leaned on the railing and looked towards the horizon. The sun was setting and crimson and purple clouds covered its retreat, "I have the stress of protecting an entire city, commanding men, battling for my life. You have it easy. You share little responsibilities with your father. I can't just have a dog lick me and have it all just be better."

Koda's face went stiff.

"Forgive me my Prince, I–" Wiccer bowed baffled by his poor choice of words.

Koda waved him off, putting a light grip on Wiccer's broad shoulder, "My friend, it is true that we have different worries and duties. But no matter which boots we walk in and which roads we are led down, we must always keep an open mind. An open mind is a clear mind. A clear mind is a sharp mind. A sharp mind… that is a weapon you must favor. Nevertheless, have a good night, my friend. Think well on what I have said here tonight."

Koda walked away with Wildeye softly panting at his side as Avren and Elisa stepped out onto the balcony.

"Avren, we'll have to be getting ready soon. Has she decided to help us spy on her clan?"

"As of now things are too heated. I can't risk going back to the compound. I learned from my contacts that both the High Blade and the First Blade are missing," Elisa said, slightly anxious with the mood of the night.

"High Blade and First Blade; so, Avalon and Vada, as you called them. How are they missing?" Wiccer asked, a bit annoyed by Elisa's lack of cooperation.

"Avalon left the clan and Vada was tasked with hunting her down. Desertion from the clan is punishable by death. You see why I can't go back," Elisa continued.

"All I see is a Rabbit losing its usefulness," Wiccer sneered.

Elisa looked earnestly towards Avren, who scowled at his brother, "Wiccer, enough. Elisa brings news of who this Tesha might be and whether she can be trusted."

"Well?" Wiccer said, tapping a nervous foot.

"According to my contacts, Tesha is the new apprentice of Malady. His previous apprentice was killed by Elucard. Overall I know very little of this Tesha. Malady, however, I know. He's a cunning man – a snake in the grass. He can not be trusted, but in this case he works for your advantage. But do not forget, he works only toward his own ends."

"So this isn't a trap?" Avren asked.

"No, I don't believe so. This is some sort of revenge against Elucard at the very least. At the very most it is a power play against his own clan," Elisa finished.

"Nice work, Elisa. Wiccer, let's head out and get ready for our guests," Avren said, nodding approvingly at Elisa.

***

The moon was a sliver in the night, partially shrouded by navy blue clouds. The air was laden with the thick scent of rain. Inle led Jetta and Elucard passed the guards and to a small marble balcony. The trio slipped in smoothly.

"It's all so quiet," Jetta whispered, "There should be guests arriving and music playing. The ball is tonight, isn't it?"

Inle checked a pair of double doors before scanning the stairs leading downwards, "No servants either."

"Let's check the throne room. Perhaps the king is awaiting guests there," Elucard said, beckoning his team to follow.

Elucard deftly navigated through the rafters. Slipping between the large wooden doors, Inle and Jetta followed suit. The team dropped down into the shadows of two large adjacent pillars.

King Jaelyn sat patiently on his throne. Elucard slowly retrieved a small throwing knife from his belt, taking aim at the king's throat; he let it loose.

To the shock of the three, Tesha dropped from the shadows of the rafters, deflecting the steel dagger with a throwing knife of her own. Elucard's projectile ricocheted and lodged into the pillar inches from his head. Immediately the thundering sound of marching boots flooded into the throne room and an army of White Cloaks surrounded the Rabbits. Wiccer and Avren entered from parallel doors and walked to either side of the king.

Tesha waltzed, shrugging towards the stunned Elucard, "A pity it turned out this way, Elucard. I admit, you are kind of cute." She gently brushed a finger down his black leather armor.

"Tesha, you traitorous bitch!" he furiously whispered.

"Now, now, Elucard, doesn't it feel awful to have everything you worked for just stripped away from you?"

Elucard seethed with anger as he clenched his teeth and balled his fists.

"You now know how my master, Malady, has felt for years. But don't worry, Elucard, you won't feel this way for nearly as long," Tesha continued as she walked back to the throne, taking a seat on one of its arms and crossing her legs.

"Master, what are your orders?" Inle whispered. His hands shook nervously.

"Elucard, we have to get out of here! Abandon this mission and get going while we're still able to," Jetta pleaded.

"No, we have a mission and we're getting it done. Inle, you and I will deal with these lesser Cloaks. I have a feeling the real challenge will be with those officers next to Jaelyn. Jetta, stay back, join the fray only if you have no other choice."

Inle grinned wickedly under his mask. Jetta nodded and backed into a corner, her hand hovered slightly over her haversack.

Jaelyn, silent until now, lifted a single hand, "Arrest them."

Several White Cloaks rushed headlong toward Elucard and Inle, whose hands sprung backwards before leaping forwards in perfect unison, as only a teacher and student would. They made quick work of their opponents, exerting as little effort as possible by targeting vital spots with lethal precision.

In mere minutes, the last White Cloak fell slain at the feet of the two assassins. Elucard's brow still furrowed from the betrayal.

"Inle, the king is the primary target, but do not let your guard down. I recognize one of these men. He is strong. No doubt his captain will be stronger."

Wiccer approached, sword in hand, "Ah, so you remember me, Elucard. Have you mentioned to your friend here how I left you for dead in a ravine?"

Elucard moved to meet Wiccer, "That was some time ago," Elucard swung his blade, clashing against the steel of Wiccer's steel, "You'll find it much more difficult to best me a second time!"

Inle smirked and dashed for Avren. However, his opponent was ready and rammed his shoulder into Inle's chest. Inle skidded and tumbled backwards. Jetta ran to Inle's side but he pushed her away, "I'm fine! Get back to cover!" Jetta quickly retreated back into the shadows, furious.

Avren lunged into the air, bringing down his sword with a heavy swing. Inle sprung up and quickly parried, swinging back around and viciously slashing at Avren's side. Grunting, Avren kicked Inle into a neighboring pillar, dazing him. Avren followed through, thrusting his blade into Inle's shoulder. Inle roared in pain, "Jetta!"

Inle kicked Avren backwards, tearing the blade out of his body. He collapsed into Jetta's arms, "You're going to have to make this quick, Jetta!" Avren began to gather himself for another attack.

Jetta quickly examined the deep wound. She took out a patch of cloth that glowed bright red and placed it on top of the wound. She pressed down hard as the cloth made a sizzling sound, cauterizing the injury. Inle groaned in complete pain when she removed the cloth.

"Sorry, Inle. I know blister cloth hurts like hell." Blister cloth was aptly named. Inle's wound had blistered and scarred, but he was able to tenderly rotate his shoulder again. Nodding to the medic, Inle leaped at Avren and landed a swift kick to his chest.

Avren slid back and followed through with a hefty swing, but was met with a clash of steel. Both men matched attacks with skillful parries.

Inle sent a stream of twirling daggers at Avren, some of which lodged into his arm and shoulder. Avren charged, grabbing Inle's collar and bashed him repeatedly in the face with the guard of his sword. Luckily for Inle, his mask took the brunt of the strikes, but he felt the concussive blows all the same. Inle dropped to the floor, completely dazed.

Meanwhile, Wiccer led with a flurry of swings, leaving Elucard to duck, tumble, and dodge the relentless attacks. Circling around, Elucard jumped for an abrasive counter of his own, sneaking a slash into Wiccer's torso.

Inspecting the wound, Wiccer found it was non fatal, and he rushed in close, elbowing the assassin under the jaw. Elucard grimaced and Wiccer grabbed the elf's arm and ruthlessly kicked at his chest. There was a gruesome popping sound as Elucard's right arm went limp. Elucard swiftly switched his sword into his left hand, just barely making an awkward parry from a deadly thrust. Elucard's face twisted as Wiccer backhanded him with an armored fist. Blood spewed from his mouth as he collided with the ground.

Elucard clenched his teeth in pain as he struggled to stand. Stealing a glance at Wiccer's attempt at a savage kick to the ribs, Elucard held his breath as Jetta leaped over him to land a drop kick, blowing back Wiccer. Jetta turned, "Keep still!" she commanded.

Elucard did as he was told, but arched his back in agony as Jetta pushed his dislodged shoulder back into place, "Ahh! Jetta! Are you sure you aren't doing more harm than good?!" Elucard teased, still wincing as he stretched his arm, gingerly testing his shoulder.

"I have no clue how you're supposed to be the new First Blade," she joked.

Wiccer held his broken nose from the surprise kick, as he recovered his blade, "You still lack the necessary skills to beat me."

"Then perhaps I'll quit holding back," said Elucard as he juked and slid behind Wiccer. Seizing his opportunity, Elucard drove his blade into the back of Wiccer's thigh, dropping him to the ground. While Wiccer was screaming in agony, Elucard grabbed the tuft of his hair and whispered into his ear, "You spared me. I suppose it is only right that I return the favor." Elucard slammed the Cloak's head into the ground, knocking him out cold.

Inle was now fairing better as well. Spinning to avoid another thrust to his injured shoulder, Inle backed into Avren, following up with a hand chop to Avren's throat. Avren went down hard, choking and gasping for air. Inle took the moment to run Avren through with his sword, before kicking him onto his side. Turning his head, Inle caught Jaelyn and Tesha escaping towards a side door, "Elucard, the king!"

Elucard reached into his side pouch, grabbing a smoke pellet and breaking it between Tesha and Jaelyn. Tesha shoved Jaelyn to the side, sending him crashing through a nearby door, "Make haste, I'll deal with Elucard."

Tesha could barely see through the densely clouded room. She lifted her magenta scarf over her nose and mouth, trying desperately to hold in her coughs. Several shurikens darted through the smoke. Tesha managed to deflect two of them, but a third grazed her cheek. She launched an attack of her own, sending a fan of daggers flying through the smoke. She listened carefully and heard a grunt. She smirked and careened a kick in that direction.

Elucard allowed the strike to catch him in his chest, pushing him back as he grabbed Tesha by the ankle, swinging her into a wall. Taking advantage of a stunned Tesha, Elucard thrusted his sword into the traitor's gut. Tesha smiled as blood bubbled out of the corners of her mouth. With the last ounce of her strength, she palmed two daggers and drove them under Elucard's ribs, "A parting gift from Malady."

Elucard screamed, filled with rage and twisted the handle of his blade savagely before tearing it out of her flesh. A gruesome flood of blood spilled onto the white floor.

Jaelyn scrambled down the hall calling for any help that he could find. Several shuriken found their mark in his back and he fell into a messy heap on the marble floor. He sloppily moved to get back up. Running from the end of the hall, Koda and Tull rushed to Jaelyn's aid.

"It's too late, Jaelyn," Elucard said in a low, tired voice. He limped, holding his pain-stricken side with one hand. A freshly blood soaked magenta scarf wrapped around his sword handle. The assassin mustered the last of his strength as he dashed, slicing the back of the elf king's legs. Jaelyn fell to his knees. Elucard's sword rested on Jaelyn's shoulder, tapping his neck gently.

"Spare my son," Jaelyn said in a soft voice.

Elucard locked eyes with the fallen King, nodded, and swung his blade. The loud clanging of a crown hitting the ground filled the air. Elucard lifted his eyes to find Koda standing only an arm's length away. Unfathomable sadness and fury filled the prince's face all at once. Elucard lifted his blade at the prince, warning him to stay back.

"Elucard, we need to leave now!" Jetta shouted firmly. She grabbed his arm, tugging him away from Koda, who was utterly frozen in place, "Come on!"

Elucard turned to look at Jetta, her eyes begged him to feel something, anything.

"Come on, you bastard! We have to go!"

She continued to pull on him to no avail, and silence floated between the two for a moment that felt like an eternity. Elucard's aching arm was still raised with his blade pointing at the grief-stricken Koda. Tull stood still, unable to make a move while his nephew was so close to danger. A minute, maybe more, passed. The ambiance of the rain outside was the only sound that sunk through the moment.

Elucard, exhausted both physically and mentally from the turbulent night managed a single soft word, "Sorry."

150

29

Beads of radiant energy ascended from the ground and absorbed into the thick aura surrounding Koda. He grunted as the task strained him greatly.

"Good work, Koda, now concentrate the Magi into your hands. Let your fingers be a foci," Megan encouraged from his side.

Sweat ran down his forehead and dripped off of his chin. His eyes became bloodshot as he quaked with stress. The Verdant Academy shook from the immense power being drawn. Dust and stone rumbled and swirled around the two spell casters.

"You almost have it, a little more…" she said, coaching her student. The Magi ebbed in a globular form within Koda's hands. Its form convulsed as the strain became greater than Koda could handle, "No, Koda, don't let go! Focus! Focus!"

"I-I c-can't! I-t's it's too much power!" Koda screamed as the Magi exploded in his hands triggering a surge of light to blow across the underground battlefield. Both Megan and Koda were flung backwards in its mighty wake.

Recovering slowly, Koda sat up and punched the stone floor. He mashed at the ground screaming until his hands were bruised and bleeding.

"Koda, we'll get there, we'll get there," Megan reassured him.

"What use is all this power if I can't control it?! What use is any of this if I can't use it to save the people I love?!" Koda heard a bone crack in his hand, but continued to beat the ground until his hand was a blood-smeared mess."

"Koda, stop it!" Megan grabbed his hand to restrain him, "It's broken. Come we'll get it taken care of."

"It doesn't matter. Nothing matters anymore," Koda whispered, defeated.

"Listen to yourself. Really listen. Do you hear yourself?" Koda was silent. His hand and heart throbbed in agony, "You want to know what I hear?"

Koda frowned, "I'm not in the mood for your lectures."

"Too bad," she said firmly, "I hear a boy who wants to give up because for the first time in his precious, sheltered life things have taken a dark and terrible turn." Megan manifested a thick stick and took her gold sash, wrapping her students hand tightly with the splint. Koda winced, either at the pain or the sharp reproach.

"My father was killed in front of me!" Koda protested.

"Yes, Koda, he was. Now what? Where do you go from here? Do you pick up the mantle of king and try to salvage the great kingdom that your father fought so hard to forge? Will you scurry off to Nashoon to become the so-called 'Arcane Guardian' while the other tribes fight to take the reigns of power from you? Or will you cower even lower and vanish into absolute obscurity and leave your life behind? What you do now, Koda, is all that matters."

Koda inspected the dressed hand gingerly, taking in what she had said.

"I don't know," Koda said flatly, "What would you do?"

Megan spoke without even the slightest trace of hesitation, "If it were my decision, I would have already had myself crowned."

"Will you be there with me when I address the nobles?" Koda asked.

"It's not my place to be in that room."

"It's your place if I want you there," Koda stood up, favoring his broken hand, "and I want you there."

"Well, then, I suppose I'll be there, *your grace.*"

***

"The king is dead," a cold, stern voice called out.

Koda sat in the dimly lit war room. Around him were the seven lords of the united tribes. Tull, Megan, and Marcus stood by his side. His father's blood-stained crown rested on the heavy oak table. Carved in the center of the table was an exquisitely detailed image of the elder tree. The leaves were painted meticulously with a vivid emerald green. Arching above the tree were the sigils of the seven noble tribes. In the center of the trunk was the sigil of the Dawnedge tribe.

Koda stared wordlessly at the crown, still in a daze. It taunted him. He wished that the night before had never happened. He wished he was alone in his room with Wildeye, the only one that he cared to be with at this particular moment. Most of all, he wished he was not Koda Dawnedge. He had always looked up to his uncle Tull for breaking with tradition and chasing his own ambitions rather than accepting the fate handed down to him by his father. But even Tull seemed every bit as nervous as Koda. Would Tull accept the crown if he left for Nashoon? Megan stood at his other side, clearly anxious by the stillness in the air and feeling quite out of place. Then there was the commander of the White Cloaks, Marcus Newsun, attempting to save face after the most monumental failure of his lifetime. Koda sneered.

The noblemen were silent, waiting for the prince to say the words they all waited to hear. Eyes locked on Koda's sleepless face. Athar Moonfall broke the uncomfortable tension, "My Prince, I said the king is dead. We are all awaiting your decision. Will you ascend to the throne or should we begin to discuss another successor?"

Koda sluggishly turned his head toward Athar.

"Yes, I know my father is dead. I was there when he was killed. Where were you again?"

Athar attempted to maintain his composure in the face of such an insult. He spoke, ignoring Koda's question, "We, the Seven, feel that perhaps..."

Koda's heavy eyes narrowed as he replied, "You think I should walk away from all this? My father counted on me to carry on his legacy. There was a time when I fought him every step of the way, but that time is far behind us."

Tull put a gentle hand on his nephew's shoulder, "Koda, it is okay if you wish to take a leave of absence and mourn. You don't need to make such a decision right now."

Athar stood to interject, "Actually adviser Tull, this needs to be decided now. We need a leader now more than ever. The city is in a panic. The Black Rabbits not only killed our king, but laid siege to the hopes and dreams of this city. No one will want to live, trade, or study here anymore. We must act decisively."

"My Prince, I will send for double the amount of White Clo–" Marcus started.

"Are you suggesting, Captain Newsun, that we ought to invest even more time, money, and resources into hiring countless more of your cloaks?" Koda said with a biting charm, "How convenient. They were so worth the money the first go round. No, I do not believe that even more cloaks will solve the problems facing us here today." Koda locked eyes with Commander Newsun, weighed his next words carefully, and spoke, "The White Cloaks, however, have not overstayed their welcome in Lost Dawns. There is a way that we can increase our military might without paying for the quartering of hundreds more cloaks. Instead, we must raise an army of our own, trained by the White Cloaks. We, our people, can stand up against those who would dare rise against us." He stood up and slid back his chair.

The room broke out into a loud murmur of argument between the seven lords, but all were stricken with silence as Koda pounded his good fist on the table.

"The White Cloaks alone can not defend us. We need a standing army of our own!"

The nobles began whispering amongst themselves. The wooden table vibrated as Fendrick Redroot slapped his hand down, "What utter foolishness! Who among us can fight? You, Prince Koda? Do not be so rash."

"Do you have no faith in our people at all, Fendrick? With proper training anyone can fight!"

Fendrick looked back at Koda, considering the boy's words. Koda turned toward Megan, "High Mage Megan, what are your thoughts."

"My Prince," Athar said before Megan could speak, "she is but a mage, she has no say in th–"

Koda silenced him with his hand and beckoned Megan to speak.

"Lord Moonfall, I have seen more war than you, and I can see that the White Cloaks have failed at the most important task put before them. It is clear to me that Long Whisper needs its own army."

"Yes, yes. That is exactly what I have been thinking. The people of Lost Dawns love this city, not because we pay them to do so, but because it is their home. They would take up arms to defend their home—*our home*—from those who would see us perish," Koda spoke with fire in his eyes.

"Even though we are without the warrior tribes, I think he is right. Our people could be trained to battle," Tull agreed.

Koda rose from his chair, "These may be the darkest of days," Koda stared into the faces of the seven nobles before him, "but *I* will lead us out of them."

30

Wiccer groggily woke up. His surroundings were alien to him, but he recognized that he was in an infirmary. His brother lay in an adjacent bed across from him. Elisa sat sleeping in a chair at Avren's bedside. Wiccer slipped out of the sheets and jumped out of bed. It cost him dearly, as his head spurted with a burst of pain and his leg buckled underneath him. He crashed resoundingly to the floor.

Wiccer gingerly inspected a heavy wool bandage wrapped around his head and grasped his throbbing leg. Reaching for a crutch leaning against the wall, Wiccer hobbled to his brother's bedside.

"Avren, what did they do to you?" Wiccer quaked with heartache as he looked down at his brother. A deep, crimson red seeped through the bandages on his chest. His once ebony features were now deathly pale, his breathing a weak wheezing. Avren slowly motioned his hand up. Wiccer shivered as he grabbed it with both hands, "Avren, you're going to be okay. I'm going to make those Rabbits pay for this!"

Elisa awoke to find Wiccer collapsed in depression and shock, "I'm sorry Wiccer, I truly am."

It was clear that she had been up all night and day by Avren and Wiccer's side.

Wiccer burst out in a depressing chorus of tears, "How can you say that! You're one of them! You've always been one of them!"

Elisa shook her head, tears forming in her eyes. She just wanted to be there with Avren, "I am not one of them! I never could convince you..."

"Then why did you protect them! As far as I'm concerned you did this to Avren. If my brother dies, it will be on your hands!"

Elisa's lips quivered with anguish, "Wiccer please, Avren is...is..."

"What? What is he to you other than someone to lay with?"

Elisa burst into tears, "He is all that I have!" she turned to Avren, gently caressing his face, "...All that I want," she sobbed.

"Wic-Wiccer" Avren's voice was a shriveled husk of what it once was, "Enough. Do...do not be blinded by your hate."

Wiccer shivered in rage, "Do you not hear yourself, Avren?"

Avren attempted to tighten his grip, weakly pulling Wiccer close to him, "E-Elisa is one of us. Y-you need to gr-grow as a leader. K...keep a clear mind," Avren's grip fell loose, his breathing began to slow.

"Avren, please. Don't leave me, not you too!" Wiccer tightly squeezed Avren's limp hand. He bawled into his brother's chest. Elisa did her best to comfort him.

"I-I love you little..." Avren's rasped with his final words to his younger brother.

31

Elucard leaned on Inle. The patch job done to his wounds was wearing away as the trio made their way through the woods. The cold rain washed away any chance that they could be tracked, but the heavy water pounded upon their weary shoulders, weighing down their clothes. They had traveled all day and all night, but were still another night's travel away from home.

"I hope Jetta finds some shelter soon," said Elucard. His cold breath wisped in the air. He struggled each step of the way, both physically and mentally. His mind was fractured like glass scattered all over the ground. Jetta's words pierced him like a lance.

Jetta...He still saw her as the child he remembered – innocent, pure...naive. His life as a Black Rabbit wasn't easy, but it was simple. He merely took orders and would someday die by the blade. He was growing into this life. However, this all changed the day that Jetta came back into the picture. His promise to her bubbled to the surface and complicated his once simple life. She spoke a truth that he once would have lived by. It was not the code of the Rabbit, but the law of the rest of the world. It did not comply, but it made sense. But she could not possibly understand the sacrifices he had made. She saw him as who he had been, not who he was in the present. What did he see himself as? Who he was? Who he is? Who he could be?

Damn her!

"Master, I'm proud of what you accomplished back there," Inle said, breaking Elucard's train of thought, "You are a legend now, both famous among our people and infamous among everyone else."

"Infamous for the wrong reasons," Elucard whispered in a daze.

There was a silence between the two. Inle felt the sting of his master's words. He stopped, the rain still pouring on their heads and shoulders. Inle lifted his mask. His cool and tired silver eyes locked onto Elucard's tired magenta ones.

"Elucard, my master, listen to me. Whatever doubts you have in your life, your actions are praised by the true people that care for you...and love you," Inle said.

Elucard stared down at his muddy feet, slightly light headed from his loss of blood. He raised this student on the philosophies of his master, Legion; the same philosophies that turned him into to the efficient assassin that slew a king. Inle was the prime example of a perfect Rabbit.

"Inle, if you were asked to, would you kill the person you were closest to?"

Inle smiled weakly. Closest to him? His family was long gone and the only person he felt true affection for was the person he was holding in the downpour. He loved Elucard more than just as a brother. He saw the Black Rabbits in a light of chivalry and servitude. He yearned for a way to mix his love for Elucard with his love for his clan; a sentiment, it seemed, that Jetta did not share.

"Elucard, a blade is only as sharp as the Rabbit wielding it. You taught me this, Master. Do not let the heart lead where the mind will not follow." Inle put a gentle hand upon his master's cool, wet cheek. He slowly moved his unmasked face closer to Elucard's, "Unless that heart leads you to me," Inle whispered, raindrops bouncing off his nose.

Elucard was exhausted, locked within Inle's hypnotic charm. He had feelings for his student, but could not requite the feelings Inle had for him, "Inle, I can't..."

Inle moved slowly until he could feel Elucard's breath. With his other hand he removed Elucard's soaked through hood.

"Inle..." Elucard's worn eyes sunk within the shadow elf's. A moment in time froze for the two men.

"Guys, over here, I made a fire!" Jetta called from a short distance to the east, "Let's replace those bandages, Elucard!"

Inle quickly moved away from Elucard, clearly annoyed by Jetta's ill-timed interruption. He refastened his mask and whispered into Elucard's ear, "I will wait for you."

***

Under a thick canopy of branches and leaves, the fire blazed. Elucard slept peacefully by its warmth. Fresh bandages hugged his ribs. Inle watched the elf with a sense of fondness as Jetta cleaned his wounds.

"I can tell that you care for him very much," Jetta said, gesturing over to her best friend.

Inle grimaced from a rush of pain as an alcohol soaked cloth burned a tender gash in his arm, "More than you'll ever understand," Inle responded with a slight chill.

Jetta was briefly silent, taken aback by the insult, "I've known Elucard since we were children. He's my best friend. He's like an older brother to me. I think I'd understand."

Inle turned to face her fiercely, "Then why do you torture him so? Why won't leave him be?"

"What are you talking about? I would never hurt Elucard!"

"You play with his heart and mind with your heresy. You think I can't see the turmoil he's in?" Inle snapped.

Jetta bit her lip, her heart rising in her throat, "I'm sorry. I didn't know I was hurting him. I only want to help him."

Inle sighed heavily, "Jetta, I don't know what Elucard was like as a child, but he's a Rabbit now. It's one of his greatest achievements, and when we return he'll be honored as our First Blade. But he won't be able to function if you keep twisting his conscience with these thoughts."

"Twisting? I'm trying to be rational. I want Elucard to–"

"I suggest you keep your ideas and philosophies to yourself...for Elucard's sake and for yours," Inle said, interrupting her.

A silence cut deeply between the two. Only the soft pattering of the rain bouncing off the leaves could be heard. Jetta had only wanted to help Elucard. It had never crossed her mind that she was 'torturing' him. No, she could not be torturing him. She was purging the infection from his mind. Elucard still saw the good in her words, but it was clear that arguing with Inle would get her nowhere. She needed to keep her path steady and illuminated, for Inle was like the rest of the Black Rabbits, an obstacle that would keep her from moving forward.

"Get some rest, Jetta. We have a long road ahead of us," Inle said.

Jetta finished tying off the bandage around his arm and lightly smiled at Inle. *I must stay strong for Elucard. I must.*

***

The clan roared in celebration as the three returning victors entered the retreat. Elucard made his way to Legion, his High Blade, and knelt in respect, "Master, it is done."

"What did you feel, Elucard?"

The clan went silent and awaited his response. Elucard paused. He was reminded of the last time he stood here. He was asked the same question before. The proper response would be the same as before. *Satisfaction.*

But this was not what he felt. This was the biggest mission of his life, a kill that would raise the bar for all Rabbits. This was 'it.' The moment in his life he had worked toward. To be respected, praised, loved. And yet he didn't want this.

Did Jetta's words have so much weight in them? He tried to reflect on Inle's words instead. His student, a brother in arms, the friend he could always count on. Inle understood everything that he was going through. They fought and bled for the same cause. Everything he built, Inle strived for and supported. Inle's words were what really should have held the most weight in his heart. Then why were Jetta's more important to him?

"Elucard, we're all waiting," Legion said, breaking through the awkward silence.

"Satisfaction," Elucard said, rather mechanically.

Jetta hid an annoyed sigh, while Inle started a cheer for Elucard. The compound erupted again. Elucard stood, admittedly pleased with the excitement, Legion leaned into his ear, "We have much to discuss about your future."

"Yes, but first there is some business that must be dealt with," Elucard nodded before scanning the many faces of the clan.

Elucard snaked through the crowd until he was standing opposite of Malady. Malady was leaning against a pillar. He begrudgingly smiled, "Welcome home, Elucard. It is good to see you alive and well."

Elucard lifted his chin in displeasure, "No thanks to you."

Malady scoffed, "What do you mean? We all wished you a fortunate mission and a safe return."

"Enough with the lies and the scheming! You sent your apprentice ahead to tell the king of our mission and laid a trap for us!" Elucard shouted furiously.

A resounding gasp fell over the onlooking crowd. Legion pushed forward, "Elucard, is this true?"

"It is," Elucard said sternly, crossing his arms.

Malady sneered, "Quite an allegation!"

Elucard pulled a bloody magenta scarf from his garb and dropped it on the ground, "I took this from your traitor of a student after I spilled her guts."

Malady scowled at the sight of Tesha's scarf, but gathered his composure, "Clearly Tesha sought to sabotage you out of jealousy of your success. Either way, I had nothing to do with it."

"Liar!" Elucard yelled aggressively.

Legion got between the two quickly, "Elucard, enough." Legion turned to Malady, "Your petty rivalry is tearing this clan apart."

160

"Rivalry? Rivals are equal, you're just some stooge my mother chose to be my sparring partner," growled Malady.

"Leandra didn't choose you because you would have made a weak leader! You see that, don't you? You hold onto your childish grudges and let them taint your future!" Legion spat. His frustration with his Blade Brother flared into anger.

"Don't you dare mention her! You want us to end this? I would challenge you to a final duel, but how would that look dueling the High Blade? However, I will challenge Elucard instead."

Elucard's eyes widened in fear.

Legion, pushed Elucard behind him, "No, not Elucard."

Malady flashed his teeth, "You don't want to end this rivalry?"

Legion glanced over to see Ryjin standing by his quarters. The Silent Master made a small nod as if approving Legion's future actions. Legion unsheathed his massive blade and thrust it into the stone ground, "I am your Blade Brother before I am your High Blade. It is my duty to end this before anymore needless blood is shed. In two days, we fight in front of everyone, to the death."

Malady drew a sword from his back and thrust it in the ground, inches from Legion's, "Accepted."

32

Koda sat among the vast collection of tomes and scrolls in the library of the Verdant Academy. Books of ancient histories, lore, and magical theories piled up like a miniature fortress around the young elven prince. His familiar slept peacefully at his feet. His once broken hand had nearly fully healed. Koda noted that this must have been a side effect of working with the Magi.

"You know, there isn't really anything about the origins of the Mage Council here, Wildeye," Koda whispered to the wolf, not really expecting a response of any sort from her. He continued his train of thought all the same, "I mean, there is a vague description here and there of how the council was formed, but most of these stories are just accounts of the Arcana War that discuss the council's role in it. All of it is also clearly biased towards the mages." Wildeye opened a single eyelid and arched her brow, clearly a little annoyed by the interruption from her afternoon nap, "But there isn't really anything here that tells me who the first mages were or how they gained access to the Magi."

"That is because they don't want to teach that the first mages stole from Nashoon!" a familiar voice cut through the solitude of the library.

Xile hobbled into the massive gallery of tomes, gripping his gnarled staff tightly. He looked around at the thousands of ancient books, with disgust scrawled across his aged face. He had always reviled the notion of confining knowledge to boring books and delicate scrolls. The forest was where all knowledge was meant to be kept, not some man-made structure.

"Grandchild, Tull told me this is where I would find you," Xile spoke with a heavy rasp. He was growing older and any youthful energy he managed to hold on to was fleeting.

"Grandfather! This is a most welcome surprise! What are you doing here?" Koda asked, pushing the stacks of books out of his way. Wildeye sprung to life and leapt up to lick the elder.

Xile patted the wolf on the head, whispering in an ancient wolven tongue to calm her down, "My son is dead. Nashoon's forest may be timeless, but alas, the world around it still withers. I've come to pay my respects and to take you back home."

Koda sighed with a grim expression on his face, "I can't."

Wildeye circled around Xile, and whined at Koda.

"Your wolf knows it's time to leave this place behind. Come, we will mourn your father and continue your training together. We've lost far too much time."

Koda lowered his head. Being the Arcane Guardian had always been his future, his destiny. However, ever since he left the safety of the forest and came to be a part of his father's world, life had made new plans for him. He was becoming a mage, and more importantly, he was to be a king, "I can't go with you."

Xile limped closer to his grandchild. He fidgeted with the fine threads of Koda's green mage robes. He pursed his lips, eying Koda with disappointment, "You can't or you won't?"

Koda lifted his head to meet his grandfather's gaze, "I am to become the mage king of Long Whisper. My people need me here. I won't..."

Xile sneered, "A mage! Such a vile thing to be; mages are the complete opposite of everything I raised you to be. How can you do this to me, Koda? And a king? King of what? These elves do not need a king, they need no leader. They need the forest and their traditions. You are lost, my grandchild, but I am here to lead you back to Nashoon. Now forget these foolish and childish dreams and come home!"

"The mages are good for this world. They have taught me the things you refused to teach me! The Magi needs to be explored and used for the good of the people. It needs to be shared, not hidden!"

Xile shook his head and scowled, "You need to be retaught, Grandchild. Those mages have corrupted you. Now come, child, enough with your silly games."

"Everyone wants me to be pulled their way, but never had I realized the responsibilities that were truly put before me. Grandfather, more than ever, the people of this land look for a leader. They willingly chose to leave the old ways behind because as you said, the outside world isn't timeless. Everything changes. This includes the Magi. I chose to become a mage to learn how to better protect my people, and I will become their king to better lead them.

My parents sought to create more than a new legacy. They had a vision of the united tribes. One banner for one united people. My father died a martyr for this cause and I will not allow his sacrifice to be in vain," Koda knelt to hug Wildeye, "I'm sorry girl, but our fates are no longer intertwined."

Xile looked baffled, "What of your responsibilities as Arcane Guardian? Who is to take my place?"

Koda shook his head and spread his arms out, spinning around, "Grandfather, you already left Nashoon. Travel the lands. There is more to the world than just Dawnedge."

Xile turned and walked away in complete frustration. Once at the doorway he called for Wildeye, "Come, Wildeye. Your pack will be overjoyed to see you again."

Wildeye slowly walked forth, but halted to look at Koda. Her eye flared before she trotted back to the side of her companion.

Xile nodded in approval, "Take care of him. He makes foolish decisions, so he'll need you to protect him."

***

Within the court of Lost Dawns gathered all the nobles of the eight tribes dressed in their finest clothes. They lined up in two columns lowering their heads in elegant bows to their prince as he walked slowly by. His blue furred familiar strode by his side, decorated with fine jewelry. Wildeye had a bracelet on her right leg, and a gold and silver linked collar draped around her neck.

Koda wore finely threaded deep purple and green robes. A golden silk cape hung from his left shoulder. He bore the amulet of his late father that marked him as Dawnedge royalty. On his back was sheathed an ornate sword, encrusted with various rare gems.

As Koda reached the throne, he sat down and placed the sword across his lap. Tull delicately picked up the ornate wooden crown from the throne and hovered it like a halo just above Koda's head. It was carved from the Elder Tree. High priests had inscribed an ancient angelic prayer in the wood with golden runes that read:

Eternally I will serve my kingdom,
Eternally I am a student of life,
Eternally I will seek your wisdom,
Eternally I will avoid all strife,

Koda closed his eyes, grasping at a fleeting memory of himself on the bank of a pond reading a book of ancient tales with his wolf lying beside him. He opened his eyes to recite his oath.

"Ruens be my witness as I wear this crown,
Protecting the smallest farm to the largest town,
Bestow upon me your perception and foresight,

And forever I will represent the Lost Dawn's light."

An ovation swept the room as Tull placed the crown of Long Whisper on Koda's head. A new king had risen.

***

King Koda paced in his study, listening to a new report on his fledgling project.

"My King, as predicted, the people have signed up in droves for your new military. The people are tired of being victims and wish to take a more active role in protecting the land that they love."

"What of the White Cloaks?" Koda asked frankly.

Tull unfolded a letter from Marcus, "The Long Whisper division of the Guard of the White Cloaks will be dissolved. Only a few White Cloaks will remain to act as drill instructors for the new military. Guild Master Marcus Newsun will personally lend his skills and knowledge as both a military adviser and lead instructor."

Koda nodded, pacing the around the tribal council table, "Any news of the Black Rabbits, particularly the ones responsible for my father's murder?"

"Our wolf riders haven't returned, no doubt they were slain or have lost the trail," Tull said, with a low voice.

Koda nodded, slightly vexed by the lack of information, "Tull, how do they get their recruits?"

"According to our Black Rabbit informant, they recruit from small towns and villages in exchange for protecting those towns. We never had enough White Cloaks to protect those areas, so they have had an easy time recruiting."

"Make sure to send our newest soldiers to protect any community from which the Black Rabbits might pull recruits. I hate to sound cruel, but if we can't catch them, we'll starve them." Koda said, disgusted by the image of starving an animal.

Tull nodded and grinned, "As you say, my King."

33

The first snow began to fall during Avren's funeral. The White Cloaks drove ceremonial daggers into their fallen commander's coffin one by one making echoing thunks as each Cloak stabbed the wooden box and paid their respects. Wiccer winced at each the piercing sound of each *thud*. Then it was his turn. Wiccer limped over, supporting his weight on a cane. The silver trim of his white tunic shimmered from small shafts of light that pierced the dreary clouds.

Before driving the blade into the coffin, he held still. Light flurries danced around him as he whispered his final goodbye, "Farewell, my Captain, my friend, my brother." He struggled with the words and fought with everything in him to keep from collapsing on the coffin, if only to cling to his brother one last time. Keeping his composure, he slammed the dagger and slowly limped to his place alongside his father. As the coffin was lowered into the ground, the White Cloaks drew their swords to salute a hero.

***

The Mystic Fang tavern was a popular destination in Lost Dawns for the White Cloaks. Its location was a short walk from their headquarters. It opened early and closed late. The bartender often gave Cloaks a discount and today was no different. Cold drinks were passed around as the Cloaks told very tall tales of Avren's exploits and embarrassing deeds. Those who knew and loved him celebrated his life with a long night of stories, laughing, and drinking. Surely his spirit lived on in their revelry.

Marcus drank silently, not looking up to make eye contact with his only remaining son. Wiccer did the same. They may has well have been complete strangers. Were it not for their similar features and the blood that bound them, they would have been.

Wiccer moved to break the uncomfortable silence, but was unexpectedly interrupted.

"I hear that you fought hard," said Marcus, still not looking up from the untouched foam head on his ale.

Wiccer opened his mouth to speak but nothing came out. Moments passed before he was able to say anything, "Not hard enough, apparently."

"I guess not," Marcus shrugged. Wiccer had trouble reading him, he wasn't depressed, just disappointed.

"Next time father–" Wiccer started, but all that was on his mind was his own failure and his hatred for Elucard. The elven assassin was directly linked to his biggest failures in life. All he wanted was to watch the Black Rabbit clan burn. His heart and soul were consumed by visions of Elucard's lifeless corpse swinging quietly from the gallows. But it was not merely vengeance he sought in this, but his own redemption.

"There won't be a next time," Marcus spat before rising from his seat, he clanged the iron stein a few times with a fork from the table. The bar quickly settled down until it was dead silent. Marcus looked around before making his announcement, "I have something to tell you all, lads. This seems like hard news to say on top of an already somber day, but I've been informed that King Koda will be releasing us from our duties."

A mixture of worries and questions erupted in the Mystic Fang. Marcus clarified, "Long Whisper is putting together their own military. I'll be personally overseeing the training of this army, alongside a select few of you. We are to act as drill instructors, but we will no longer be needed for protection." Marcus eyed his son's distraught face, "Protection… We failed miserably in that regard and Lost Dawns has taken note of that."

Wiccer clenched his teeth in anger, "Father, I volunteer to instruct the elves!"

Marcus ignored his son, "The rest of you will be reassigned to other countries. This division has been disbanded. Finish your drinks. You will be contacted if you will be needed to train the future soldiers of Lost Dawns." Marcus placed his drink on the table and walked out of the tavern with Wiccer limping after him.

"Father, I said I volunteer to be a drill instructor," Wiccer shouted at his back.

Marcus stopped abruptly and stood still. Snow crept down slowly from the sky and bathed in the glow of the street lamps, "No, you're going home to our cabin in Long Whisper."

"Father my leg will heal, and I'll be able to perform any–" Wiccer begged his father for another chance to prove to himself that he was worth the effort put into him, but his cries fell on deaf ears.

"No!" Marcus interrupted, raising his voice, "I'm retiring you."

Wiccer was taken aback, tears formed in his eyes. He hung his head low, choking out his words, "Why? Why do you hate me? I already know it's my fault Avren is dead. If I trained harder, I could have have saved him. If I listened to his lessons I could have saved the king. Please give me another chance to make up for all my failures. Please, I need this!"

Marcus walked away calling back to Wiccer in low voice, "Pack up and go home. You're dismissed."

Wiccer slammed the side of his fist on the tavern wall. Everything he had ever worked for and loved was gone.

34

Thirty years ago Ryjin Leafsong failed at his attempt to assassinate Jaelyn Dawnedge. Ryjin was spared, but was exiled from Long Whisper, never to be heard from again.

Ten years passed before Ryjin formed an alliance with three elves from the renowned warrior clans who had refused to join Jaelyn's new kingdom. They were Kilid Windspear, Ronos Pathrunner, and Leandra Nighthunter. Together with the newly named Silent Master, these four elves created the shadowy Black Rabbit Clan. These assassins would wreak havoc on Long Whisper and slowly grew in number.

Kilid, Ronos, and Leandra admired Ryjin for his ideals and boldness. Over time, Leandra fell madly in love with him. Her passion for him flourished, and although Ryjin returned no emotion, he still sired a child with her all the same. Malady was born.

Years passed and Kilid and Ronos left the clan to pursue their own ambitions elsewhere in the world. Ryjin saw this as an unforgivable betrayal. With the loss of two of his most trusted friends and advisers, Ryjin grew paranoid of whom he could trust. He created two new ranks for him to oversee that would serve to enforce his laws – the High Blade and First Blade.

***

A young Malady, about the age of thirteen, sweated profusely as his raw knuckles beat into the tree. He knew he needed to train hard to impress his mother and even harder to impress his father. His skill as a fighter came naturally, but it was the praise of his parents he really worked for.

A familiar voice called from the woods, "Malady, where are you? I have excellent news for you!"

Malady smirked. His mother had the news he had been waiting to hear since he had been told of the Silent Master's new ranks. Finally his mother would bestow upon him his birthright and he would finally sit at his father's side, lording over the clan.

"I'm here Mother. You wish to see me?"

Leandra was a toned elf. She wore a black leather tunic with violet belt straps crossing her chest. On her back were two claymores. She had the strength and skill to wield both in each hand, a feat that most men would only dream of.

By her side was a small child, a bit younger than Malady. His frame was small for his age, even for a new recruit. He was an elf like himself. He had light silver hair that had been cut short and his eyes were a deep red.

"Mother, who is this recruit with you?" Malady asked, confusion plastered on his face.

"Malady, this is Legion. He is to be your sparring partner," Leandra said, pushing forth the small Legion.

"Sparring partner? I don't need a sparring partner. My skill is nearly perfect!" Malady scoffed.

"Well, I think it could use some work. Also, Legion could learn a thing or two from you. Being able to teach is an aspect of leadership you'll need to have if you plan on being High Blade." Leandra placed a sheathed sword into the arms of Legion before stepping away.

Legion held a blank stare on his face, not knowing what he was in for.

"Well, what's your story kid? Where do you come from?" Malady asked, trying to make the best out of his situation.

Legion stared at his sword, hesitant to speak at first, "My father gave me up to pay off his gambling debt."

"Your Father sounds like a bastard," Malady said with a disgusted smile, "But you'll be missing him once we get started. Draw your blade, kid."

"My name is Legion," the young boy sneered.

Malady rushed at his sparring partner, swinging his blade, disarming Legion and leg sweeping under his feet. Legion crashed to the ground and Malady pointed his sword under Legion's chin, "Learn to hold your blade right, then we'll see about you earning your name."

***

Years passed and Malady grew strong. Legion grew stronger. Malady was no longer in a position to teach Legion. Now they were truly equals.

Far away from the Black Rabbit retreat, the soft glow of a campfire blazed under a starry night. Malady and Legion sat together. Across from them stood Leandra Nighthunter regaling them with tales of how

170

the Black Rabbits came to be and how the warrior tribes once lived wild in the forests of the land.

She sat down cross legged by the fire. Opening a large leather bag, she took out a set of swords wrapped in animal pelts. One was much longer than the others.

"You two have grown in these last few years. My son has proven himself a natural teacher, while Legion, you have proven to me that you are worthy to be called a son of my own. You are brothers now. Not only in arms, but like the old ways, I wish to make you Blade Brothers."

"Blade Brothers?" Malady asked, a look of whimsy in his eyes.

"When one of you succeeds, both of you succeed. When one of you fails, you both fail. You will be brothers in skill and in soul. You will become one."

Legion grinned widely as Malady nodded with approval at his new Blade Brother.

Leandra unwrapped the swords, giving the long sword to Legion, while Malady received a set of five arming swords, "Legion I want to train you in the form of the Giant's Blade. You were weak once, barely able to wield your sword, now I will teach you to use a claymore, the choice weapon of the Nighthunters."

"I will use it well, Leandra," Legion said, stoically.

She turned to Malady, passing the five blades to him, "You have always shown a prowess for blade skills. Now I shall test you with the form of the Many Blade. Using each blade quickly and precisely will throw off your opponents and give you an edge in the heat of battle."

"Mother, I am honored," Malady said, bowing his head.

"My sons, you are both on the path to greatness."

***

Malady led Legion through the shadowy woods. They dashed from branch to branch, surrounded by a sea of leaves that reflected the moonlight from the rain that came before. Both were dressed in dark leathers, their deep purple cloaks dancing behind them.

"Malady, when will you tell me where you are taking me?" Legion called ahead.

"Brother, tonight you will become a true Black Rabbit. I am to oversee this," Malady shouted back, a smile strewn wide across his face.

Legion had been training for years, but had never been regarded a true Black Rabbit by his peers and teachers, despite his great skill and potential. Malady stopped just shy of a small tavern on the outreaches of a small farming village. The tavern was a shoddy building. Its walls were made of wood that was splintered and rotting. Its thatch roof had holes poked through to let plumes of smoke billow out. The lights shown through the window lit up the silhouettes of patrons having a good time inside.

"Malady, are we on a mission?" Legion asked as he tried to find a reason of them to be there.

Malady grinned, "Come, Brother, follow my lead."

Once inside, the two assassins found the pub full of life. Whores and drunks danced and drank and made merry. But the two were more interested in an older man who sat a deep stupor. His face had a patchy peppered beard and his eyes were tired and half closed. His tunic was filthy and his vest had splotches of food stains on it. He looked up and burped loudly as Legion and Malady moved toward him.

"This is him. Grab him and bring him outside around back," Malady told Legion.

"Who is he?" Legion inquired.

"A weed," Malady said, "Quickly".

***

Behind the tavern, Legion threw the old drunk to the ground. Malady massaged Legion's shoulders, "Are you ready for your first kill, Brother?"

Legion shot a wild glance at Malady, "What? Kill him? Why?"

"The man is a stain on society, much like the stains on his vest."

"Who is he?" Legion asked, watching the man stumble around before falling on his bottom.

"Legion, you don't recognize him? Has it been that long for you?"

Legion gave Malady a curious look. His Blade Brother motioned for Legion to study the man. Legion crouched down to examine the features of the worn and weathered elven man. Slowly it began to dawn on Legion who he had been sent to assassinate.

"This...This is my father!" Legion exclaimed, slack jawed.

"Yes, my brother. It seemed only right that you were to be the one to kill him."

Legion backed away, shaking his head, "I-I can't do this, I can't kill my own father!"

Malady pulled Legion back, keeping an arm around his shoulder, "Legion, he stopped being your father when he gave you up. He sold you to settle his gambling debts. This man is a leech. He is worth *nothing*. He is good for *nothing*." Malady kicked the drunkard backwards before asking him, "Do you know who we are? Do you know who he is?" Malady pointed at Legion.

The man hiccuped as he wobbly looked Legion over, "Should I?"

Legion pulled down the mask that covered his mouth and pushed his face into his father's, "Look at me! Really look! Do you know who I am?"

The man shook his head.

Malady drew a sword and put it to the throat of the man, "Do you recall now?"

The man's eyes widened as he felt the gravity of the situation, "I don't know him! I don't know him!"

Legion grabbed the man by the shirt and lifted him into the air, bringing his face so close to his that he could smell the rancid odor of booze on his breath.

"You drove my mother away, you sold me to settle your gambling debts, you drank your way into a bottle, and your whole life is nothing but a failure. I always wondered what I did to deserve to the life you forced me into! I was ten! Ten when you sold me to a clan of assassins. Six when you beat my mother half to death because you lost our house in a game of cards!"

The man began to sob, "I'm sorry! I'm so sorry!"

"Who am I?" Legion shouted, enraged by the memories that boiled in his mind.

"You're my son! Legion!"

Legion dropped his father to his knees before swiftly drawing his blade, "No, now I'm the man who is going to kill you!" Legion said before viciously parting his father's head from his body.

Malady watched as Legion still shivered with raw anger, "Brother, how does it feel? Do you have retribution?"

Legion was breathing heavily as he turned to look at Malady, "Alanna has given me purpose," Legion cleaned and sheathed his blade, "And now she has given me vindication."

Malady nodded, "A night to remember, brother."

***

As Legion and Malady became adults, it grew clear to Leandra that Legion was surpassing Malady. Not only she, but the Silent Master saw this as well. In time, no matter how hard Malady pushed himself, he could not garner the same praise that Legion was showered with by his parents.

When the time came to choose a High Blade, the two Blade Brothers knelt in the shadowy presence of the reclusive Silent Master. Leandra stood by his side.

"Leandra, you have shown much attention to these two elves. Is one to be our High Blade?" Ryjin's thick voice growled in the darkness.

Leandra pursed her lips, pacing before her two sons, "My Master, one was born with promise but has not shown that he can live up to his own potential."

Malady's head shot up in surprise, a baffled look on his face.

Leandra continued, "While the other started with absolutely nothing, but clawed his way to greatness."

"Mother! You would choose Legion over me? I am the son of Ryjin Leafsong! I am entitled to the title of High Blade! It is my birthright!" Malady blurted out. He was completely livid by his mothers apparent betrayal.

"Birthrights are a fool's delusion!" barked Ryjin, his voice cracked through Malady's gripes.

Leandra helped Legion rise to his feet, "I choose you to be High Blade, Legion."

Legion backed away, shaking his head, "Please, Leandra, Silent Master, I do not want this. My bond with my brother is too sacred to me to soil it by taking something from him that I know he has wanted since he was a child. Please choose someone else." Legion bowed before them.

Leandra looked crestfallen, "You are perfect for this role Legion. It is you that we want."

Legion refused once more, "I can not accept this title."

The Silent Master looked up to Leandra, "Who else?"

"There are two humans – Blade Sisters. They show much promise. They are younger than Legion and Malady, but in time will be as strong. Avalon shows slightly more initiative. Vada, the other, is fiercely loyal to her. I recommend Avalon to be High Blade, with Vada as First Blade."

The Silent Master nodded before leering at Malady, "Leave my sight. You disappoint me, my son. You couldn't share a moment's glory for your own Blade Brother? Pathetic."

Malady ground his teeth and balled his fists. He sprouted up and grabbed Legion by the collar of his tunic, "You have embarrassed me! I challenge you to a duel. Only blood will make this right!"

"Malady, brother, please. I never meant to hurt you," Legion cried out, anguish quivered in his voice.

Malady bared his teeth, "You will duel me. You owe me this!"

Leandra pulled the two apart, "Legion, duel Malady, end this pettiness. It defiles the title of Blade Brother."

"As you wish, Leandra." Legion sighed.

***

In the opening in the forest where the two boys first sparred, the two blade brothers stood facing one another. Off to the side, Leandra stood next to the newly appointed High Blade and First Blade.

Avalon stepped forward, "May this duel, no matter its results, end this quarrel. You may begin!"

Malady drew two blades and lunged forward, unleashing a series of slashes aimed at Legion. Legion side stepped and circled around, landing a clean kick into Malady's back that sent him rolling to the ground. Legion had not even drawn his blade yet.

Malady scrambled to his feet and reached for another set of swords. He twirled them in a skillful fashion then thrust them both forward at Legion. Legion dodged and responded with a quick elbow to his Blade Brother's throat.

Malady fell to his knees choking for air. The sound of steel being slowly released from its scabbard rang out through the silence of the battlefield. Legion had finally drawn his blade.

"You know I'm stronger than you. Please submit, Brother. There is no need for this to go any further."

Infuriated, Malady dove at Legion, swiping his swords, but striking only air. Legion lifted his sword as if it had the weight of a feather and gracefully slashed into Malady's left thigh. Legion quickly brought down another strike that sank deep into Malady's right thigh.

Malady collapsed onto the grass, unable to stand. He screamed with a primal rage.

"Submit! Let this be over. Let us put this foolishness behind us, Brother," Legion repeated.

"I have no father, no mother, and now I have no brother. Kill me," Malady sneered as he threw his blades to the ground and lowered his head.

Legion's hand shook as the edge of his blade hovered over Malady's neck. Now his sword was too heavy to lift, much like his heart.

With a single swipe, Legion sliced a gash across Malady's eye and walked away.

"I am sorry, Brother, but I can't."

35

Elucard winced as Jetta slowly removed the blood soaked bandages from his side. Dried blood stretched and broke as it was peeled from the surface of his skin.

"I swear to Alue, Elucard, if you break your stitches one more time, I'll kill you myself!" Jetta said as she examined the slowly healing wound.

Elucard gave her a wry look, "Alue?"

Jetta glanced around quickly before attempting to cover up her misstep, "Alanna... I meant Alanna."

Elucard prodded her curiously, "Your medical instructor told me you can speak the angel language fluently. My master taught me a bit but I doubt I could speak it so freely. Where did you learn such a skill?"

Jetta sighed, remembering the old priest of Alue that passed through Ravenshore. He was an elderly man, not dressed in fanciful religious garb, but in beggar's rags. Had it not been for her kind ways to offer the man a free meal, she would never have learned of his true nature, "I found a teacher in a kind old man." She paused and a reminiscent wonder filled her eyes, "Ambrose of the Wandering Winds, a nomad of the cloth. He passed through Ravenshore one rainy autumn's eve and I had the good fortune of offering him what small comforts I could."

Elucard was captivated by the idea of such a stranger, "He took you as an apprentice?"

Jetta tightened the bandages around Elucard's wounds, "Aye. He preached kindness, compassion, and forgiveness. He passed onto me Alue's words and her lore. Through him I learned to speak Angelic," Jetta trailed off, lost in a gentler time, "...all useless to me now. The Angel of Mercy is but a weakness in the eyes of the Angel of Death."

Elucard lifted up her chin to expose her eyes swelling with tears, "Hush now, Jetta. It is your job to show strength to those that need it most. Alanna values that in her Rabbits."

"Trev Alan'Na zsesh A'leu o'blivis," Jetta whispered in Angelic. Her words went unnoticed by Elucard as he limped away.

'Even Death will seek mercy in the end.'

***

Elucard knelt before Legion and Ryjin within the quarters of the Silent Master. Elucard was still covered in bandages, and despite his weariness, he was more than excited for this moment.

"Elucard, as you know, Vada has yet to return. She is either dead or has joined her traitorous Blade Sister. Either way, a new First Blade must be named," Legion said, turning to the Silent Master who nodded approvingly from the shadows, "You have shown tremendous growth, prowess, finesse, wisdom, and patience. All of which are required of a First Blade." Legion took out his own blade and passed it to Elucard, "Rabbit, will you be my First Blade?"

Elucard gazed into his master's eyes. He cut his hand on Legion's sword and smeared the blood on his own blade, "I accept, my High Blade."

***

The clan gathered around the two combatants in the center of the compound. The sun was setting, sundering the azure sky. Elucard stood beside Ryjin, anxious to see his master display the legendary skills he had always known him to have. Even so, a small part of him was afraid that Malady's malice would give him an advantage in this particular bout. Skill versus drive. It could go either way, and Elucard knew that.

Ryjin held a hand to quiet the clan's collective chatter, "Legion and Malady. This rivalry has corrupted the unison of this clan. It must cease, for the sake of the Black Rabbits' future."

Legion nodded, unsheathing his long sword.

Malady turned and shot a grim smile at his Silent Master, "You were my father, but you never treated me as a son. No, that honor was given to him! Well, Father, I will destroy everything that you love. I will crush him beneath my feet, and when he begs for forgiveness, I will cut out his heart and give it to you!"

Legion shook his head in disbelief at the statement, "You never understood, Brother."

Malady drew two swords from his back, "You dare speak to me as if I don't understand, Legion? I watched as you snaked your way into my life and into my family! I let it happen. I was a fool! But I shall correct my mistakes!"

"No, it is my mistake to correct. I should have killed you when you begged me to!" Legion roared as he ran at Malady, dragging his edge along the stone ground.

A lighting fast swing connected with the dual swords in a deafening clatter of steel, Legion recoiled, swinging another hefty blow at Malady's side. Malady parried, countering with his own attempt for Legion's left shoulder.

Legion leapt backwards and hacked savagely into the ground, creating a thunderous shock wave of air that drove straight for Malady.

Malady rolled to the right as the wave collided into a crowd of dodging assassins. Malady snorted with anger as he lunged towards his opponent, spinning his swords like whirling buzz saws.

The deadly attacks ripped at Legion, catching him in his upper arm. Legion backed away, lowering his blade to examine his wound. Sneering, he charged forth with a flurry of excessive swings, each deflected by Malady's incredibly fast rotating weapons.

Legion saw an opening as his claymore clanged off a deflection. Thrusting his sword into the ground, Legion heaved himself up and over the blade's guard and landed a solid kick that sent Malady flying onto the ground.

Recovering his blade, Legion swept his sword, knocking his Blade Brother's dual swords out of reach. Malady windmilled his legs, spinning himself back to his feet before sliding three new swords into his hands.

"You haven't lost a step, Legion," Malady said, admittedly impressed with his Blade Brother's prowess.

Legion rested his gigantic long sword on a shoulder, "As well with you, Brother. In fact, you've greatly improved."

Malady grinned ruthlessly before taking off and twisting a series of slices with his three blades. Each sparked as they clashed against Legion's sword.

Legion deftly swiped upwards with his sword and then combined it with a piercing thrust. Malady side stepped and parried the attack before spin kicking into the small of Legion's back.

The High Blade collided into the ground, but tumbled to recover, kneeling as he caught his breath, "This ends now, Malady!"

Malady dashed forth, mustering his energy to increase his speed. Legion lifted his blade to counter the reckless attack, but Malady knocked Legion's sword downward with flat of his own blade. With all of his might, Malady drove two of his blades into Legion's shoulders and laughed wickedly.

Legion gasped in complete agony as he struggled with the pain. Malady twisted both the impaling blades as Legion screamed. Clasping his hands around Legion's throat, Malady smiled viciously. Legion grunted as he grabbed a dagger from his opponent's belt and drove into Malady's side. Malady collapsed backwards, clutching his new wound. Both men sat on the blood splattered ground heaving, staring at each other.

"I took you under my wing. I took you in as my friend, my brother! I am the reason why you are so great! Me!" Malady hissed, too exhausted to raise his voice.

Legion swayed as he struggled to stand. He stumbled as he walked over to Malady and grabbed him by the collar, "Everything I achieved…" He huffed as he began to punch Malady, sluggishly in the face, "Was because of you. You pushed me. You drove me. You were my ambition, you were my sword." Legion increased his speed as blood sloshed from the raw facial wounds his fists left on Malady's face, "You are my heart! You are my soul!"

Legion released a half conscious Malady into a pool of his own blood, "You are my Blade Brother."

Quelled by the emotion, Malady flashed back to the days of meeting Legion, his training with him, laughing, friendship, brotherly love, "W-Where did it go all so wrong…my brother?"

Legion stood over the defeated Malady, "When you held your ego over the love we had."

"I betrayed my clan. I betrayed you, all for my envy. I am deeply sorry, my brother. Forgive me."

"Malady, I can forgive you, but this clan can not."

Malady choked up bubbles of crimson liquid, "Leave me to die. It's all I deserve now."

Legion removed the two blades from his shoulder, grimacing greatly. He scanned over the eyes of his kin before finally resting his sight on the Silent Master. Turning back to the surrendered Malady, Legion sheathed his claymore, "This clan has seen too much bloodshed between Rabbits in these last few days. Malady, you will leave the Black Rabbits and this land. You are exiled for all eternity."

Malady closed his eyes "Do you remember when I took you to kill your father?"

Legion listened to the wind whistling past his ear, "Always."

Malady turned his head on its side, coughing and wheezing greatly, "You said Alanna gave you a purpose and vindication. What does she give you now?"

"Clemency."
Even Death will seek mercy in the end.

36

The wood cracked as it split in two. Wiccer tossed the pieces into a small woodpile. Spring was settling into the void left by the dreary winter. However, the wind was still cold, and unlike his shivering body, his heavy heart and bitter thoughts didn't need a warm hearth to melt away the lingering of the past season.

A set of footsteps crunched the dead leaves. Wiccer paid the new presence no heed. He was neither a stranger nor a welcomed guest.

"It's been a while, my son," Marcus said. His voice broke the long silence between the two.

Wiccer ignored him, grabbing a handful of logs, as he headed for the cabin. Marcus struggled with the awkward silence, "Let me help you with those."

"Do as you wish," Wiccer spoke flatly, with much disdain in his voice.

Marcus grabbed the young man's shoulder, forcing Wiccer to face him, "Listen, there is no need to make this harder for me than it already is."

Wiccer dropped the logs down on the ground, outraged, "Harder for you? Do you even remember how you left me?"

Marcus bit his lip as he stressfully combed his hair with his fingers, "Wiccer, son, I did what needed to be done. I di–"

"You did 'what needed to be done'?" Wiccer blurted out the words angrily, "Do you have any idea how that affected me? You not only shut me out of my closure, but you destroyed any way for me to cope with my pain! My pain, Father! My mother is dead, my brother is dead, and the only thing that kept me going was the White Cloaks. And you took it all away! You did what needed to be done? Can you even grasp how that sounds to me?"

Marcus was silent.

Wiccer's eyes showed an edge of fury and sadness, "Answer me!"

"I – I didn't want to lose the last member of my family. Vivian...your mother, wouldn't forgive me if I lost both of you. I just wanted to protect you, I didn't know how to act, how to cope with losing Avren. I didn't want to lose you as well." Marcus choked with the last words, "Wiccer, I'm so sorry that I caused you so much pain."

Wiccer's scowl turned to a weak smile as he went to hug his father, "We're all that's left, but were not alone. They watch over us in spirit. Can't you feel them?"

Marcus tightened his squeeze, "Every day, my son. Every day."

***

Wiccer placed a cup of strong coffee in front of his father. He himself drank it light with cinnamon and a single teaspoon of sugar, which was how the men of Scorch usually took their coffee, but his father was a breed of hardened souls and drank it black. Wiccer sat at the old oak table wondering what really brought the former guild leader to the cabin.

"How goes the training of the troops? Do the elves learn fast? How strong are Long Whisper's forces becoming?"

Marcus gulped a large swig of his coffee taking little notice of the scalding temperature, "The people of Long Whisper are done being the victims, they grow fast and strong. Many new soldiers have been placed among each village and town in the country. There haven't been reports of Black Rabbit sightings yet, but it's been three months, no doubt they'll be recruiting soon, now that the roads have been cleared of the winter's snow." Marcus paused, eyeing his son, waiting for the right moment to tell him the other set of news, "Elisa–"

"What about the Rabbit?" Wiccer sneered, still clearly upset with her and her lack of cooperation.

"Elisa has agreed to be a spy for Long Whisper. She says she heard that there was a new First Blade but didn't know who. She wants to help us bring down the Rabbits...for Avren."

Wiccer was silent. Perhaps Elisa did care for Avren. Perhaps he was too stubborn to see that, "That is good. What of leading you to the compound?"

"I told her that we'd hold off on that until we had a more elite squad of soldiers. Despite our leadership, these elves are not ready for real combat. The Rabbits would decimate any soldiers we bring and, no doubt, escape and set up somewhere different."

Wiccer rubbed his chin, "Are you planning on training an elite unit?"

"Truthfully, I was hoping Elisa would train a unit of troops in the ways of the Black Rabbit; use their own techniques against them. Have our troops think like a Rabbit to flush out a Rabbit."

"What did she say?"

Marcus took another sip of coffee, "She'd rather help as a spy, but did mention it was a good idea."

Wiccer nodded, "It is an interesting idea… an anti-rogue op."

"Just a thought, until Elisa changes her mind, that's what it'll stay." Marcus stood up to pour himself another cup of coffee, "Wiccer, strife in Varis and Estinia grows in the south. There may be a war coming. Long Whisper may want to stay out of this with its army still so small."

"What does that mean for you?"

"The majority of the White Cloaks take residence in Varis. Guild Master Petrove wishes me to enlist as an officer in the Varis army if war does break out."

"What of King Koda's army? Who will you send in your stead? Danica? Maxwell?" Wiccer asked, his curiosity piquing.

"You, actually," Marcus smiled.

Wiccer raised an eyebrow, "But you retired me? And I was only ever a sergeant!"

"Wiccer, I trust you most to keep a level head and to be the eyes and ears of the elven forces. They will need a leader who is well trained and who is honest and hard working. I want you to enlist in King Koda's fledgling army. You have the experience that is desperately needed."

Wiccer's heart skipped a beat. He thought he wanted this, but he didn't know if he actually wanted it or still needed it for closure.

Marcus chuckled, patting Wiccer's hand, "You need some time to decide. It's bigger news than you could have hoped for. I'm home for the next week on leave. If you say yes, come back to Lost Dawns with me. If not, I'll understand."

Wiccer, nodded. He would need those days to think.

37

The horse trotted down the puddle-spotted path toward Ravenshore. At its rear, it pulled a cart used to haul newly gathered recruits for the Black Rabbits.

Inle balanced a knife on his fingertip before spinning it into the air and catching it. He did this repeatedly when he was bored. Elucard had pointed this out on several occasions. Jetta took inventory of her herbs, medical supplies, and instruments. Elucard, taking hold of the reigns, smiled pleasantly in the cool spring day.

It was his turn to head into a village to recruit potential Rabbits. This was a task that a First Blade had to be familiar with. He was excited at the responsibility, but also at the prospect of returning to Ravenshore. It had been six years since he was a useless kid destined to be a fisherman. If it were not for the Black Rabbits, life as he knew it would have been drastically different and far more boring.

A large wooden wall with a pair of armored guards posted outside came into sight. Elucard, bewildered by this unfamiliar sight, halted the cart.

"Master is this Ravenshore?" Inle asked, lifting his head just above the rim of the cart.

"Elucard, why is there a wall around our village? Who are those men? They don't look like White Cloaks," Jetta spoke with a mixture of curiosity and surprise in her tone.

Elucard scanned the perimeter. Several men in polished bronze armor adorned with the Dawnedge insignia marched back and forth along a tall wooden wall. This was very discomforting to the new First Blade.

"Inle, Jetta, throw on your traveler's cloaks," Elucard ordered. Jetta was right, these men were not White Cloaks. They were different.

"Are we still recruiting?" Inle asked as he pulled up his hood and removed his mask.

"No. We are on a new mission now." Elucard's eyes remained fixed on the armored sentinels as he spoke, "We're investigating the changes made to Ravenshore. Find out who these men are, when they got here, and how long they are staying. Jetta, you and I are going to ask our families. Try to find out as much as you can. Meet up at the local tavern called the Rusty Hook."

The two team mates nodded with understanding.

***

The old docks creaked under the Elucard's feet as the salted air pelted his eyes and nostrils. Spotting the rickety old fishing vessel, Elucard watched motionless as he saw his father tying a heavy rope onto a post. The grizzled elf hadn't changed one bit. His crimson beard covered his sea worn features. A heavy woolen coat hung on his body as he hopped past Elucard.

His father didn't bat an eye at the man staring at him, but he ordered him around nonetheless, "You going to stand around looking useless all day, or are you going to grab that batch of fish? Your mother is making a stew and she's going to need something to put in it."

Elucard snapped out of his nostalgic daze, "Pa?"

"You better hurry it up. I ain't going to wait all day," his father said, gruffly.

Elucard, still confused, shouldered a string of fish and followed the old man to his former home.

***

Elucard followed River into the small cottage. The familiar smell of his mother's cooking floated through the air and a fog of memories clouded Elucard's head.

"It's been awhile, hasn't it, Elucard?" River asked in a low voice before calling to his wife, "Salene, set a third plate, we have a visitor."

A sing-song voice chimed from the kitchen, "Is Lyra Breezelark paying us another visit?" Salene walked around the corner, cleaning her hands with a dish towel. When her eyes locked onto him she dropped the towel and stood frozen in the doorway.

Elucard was similarly afflicted. He slowly lowered his hood and attempted to find the words to say. In a moment such as this, they did not come easily, "...Ma...I'm home," he managed.

Tears bubbled in Salene's eyes as she ran to her lost son and embraced him in a tight hug, "Elucard, you're here! You're really here!"

River put a rough and heavy hand on Elucard's shoulder, hiding his emotional urge to never let go of his only son again, "Welcome back home, Elucard."

186

Elucard, careful not to get too attached to this moment, spoke in quickly, "Ma, Pa, I'm not here because I'm on leave. I need information on Ravenshore."

River tried not to rush the fleeting time that Elucard had, "First we eat, then we'll discuss your Black Rabbit business."

***

Dinner was quiet for a time. The only sounds in the air were of spoons clanking on wooden bowls and teeth chewing the potato and fish stew. Finally River had to ask the question that burned in him since he heard the rumors, "Were you responsible for the assassination of Jaelyn, Son?"

Salene thrust him an ice cold stare, "River, we promised we wouldn't talk about that," she turned and smiled at Elucard, "We're just happy you came back home."

Elucard shot him glance. How could he tell his parents that he was the one that killed their king? He was celebrated among his peers, but reviled by the rest of the world.

River egged on further, "It's true though, isn't it?" River searched his son's dark eyes for an answer, but what he found sunk his heart, "More than that. You killed him, didn't you?"

"What if I had?" Elucard blurted, dropping his silverware onto the table.

"How can someone from Ravenshore—our *son*—become the most infamous criminal in all of Long Whisper?"

Elucard stopped chewing. He glared at the man that used to be his father, before Legion came into his life. It was in another lifetime in the distant past that he had lived in this household. Now he was one of the most notorious assassins to ever bear the name "Black Rabbit." He was the First Blade now. He was the monster every child feared was hiding under their bed. He relished in it all.

"Criminals break the law, Rabbits don't live by the same law that civilians do. Our code allows us to carry on the work of Alanna; to balance the scales when they tip over. We are the wildfire that purges the overgrown forest. Father, my assassination was a necessity."

River was irked by the statement, "So you are an outlaw? And do you really believe everything you just said? Not even Alanna herself would stand for such blatant madness."

Elucard turned to face away from his father, "I would never expect a fisherman to understand my duties. It takes an evolved individual to

187

become a Black Rabbit. Not like those other three that came from Raven..." Elucard let his voice trail off before finishing.

River stood up, "What of them? The blacksmith's apprentice, the stable boy? What happened to them?"

A darkness shrouded Elucard's mind as he thought about his past actions, "They didn't evolve," he said coldly.

 River moved around the table and lifted Elucard up by the cowl to face him "No remorse. What happened to you Elucard? Do you see what you've become?"

"I've become a Rabbit," though, he wasn't completely sure what he'd become. He spoke the words he was trained to say, but they became hollow. They were just words that no longer carried the weight they once had. He had everything that every Black Rabbit dreamed about, that he dreamed about. But now that he had it all in his grasp, he was unsure if he was happy with it at all.

Salene rocked the table by slamming her hand on top of it, "Enough! Both of you! We're together. Maybe not for long, maybe not for the right reasons, but isn't being together enough?" She began to weep in her hands, "I've wanted this more than anything, and now that I have it, I don't want it anymore."

River went to comfort his wife, "I'm sorry Salene, I really am." He turned to Elucard, "Aren't you happy you're home? Tell your mother how much you missed her."

Elucard sat motionless. The cold realization dawned on him there. He hadn't missed either of them. He had to get out now. It was not fair or right to stay and lead them to a false hope that he knew was as hollow as he had become, "I have to go," he said, coldly.

River snapped a growl at him, "Leave then! Go back to your Black Rabbits. I hope you find happiness in your pitiful life, because there's nothing left for you here!"

"You're right," Elucard said before walking out the door.

***

The Rusty Hook was formerly a bar for the fisherman and traveling merchants that docked their ships in Ravenshore's port. However, with the influx of soldiers, it had became the hangout of guards looking to get a drink and a bite to eat after a long day of keeping the fishing village safe.

Inle, Jetta, and Elucard sat at a corner table, their hoods shadowing their faces as they spoke in secretive whispers too low for anyone but them to hear.

"The wall was raised a month ago when the guards were assigned to Ravenshore and its neighboring villages," Inle recounted his information.

"The new king, Koda of the Dawnedge, has raised an army. They are being trained by the former Long Whisper division of White Cloaks," Jetta added.

"They are attempting to block us from recruiting. We must tell Legion at once," Elucard said, sneering at the sight of the guards walking about the bar.

"Ungrateful fools," Inle spat, "It's an honor to be recruited by the Rabbits! We do good work for this nation"

"This is what the people want. For years the Black Rabbits have kidnapped the children of these villages and turned them loose against their own country. How can you blame them for standing up for themselves?" Jetta retorted, leering at Inle.

Inle scowled at her, "You never believed in our cause. You would betray us the first chance you got. Now's your chance, Jetta. Turn us in! Save your own cowardly skin. Forsake the Black Rabbits. Forsake Alanna!"

"Enough, Inle!" The argument with his father had almost completely eroded his patience. A fresh outburst from the everlasting feud between the two teammates was the last thing he needed.

Inle drove a knife into the table, turning some of the guards' heads, "Elucard, why do you protect her? She brings nothing but venom to our clan. I've seen her medallion, a mark of Alue, not Alanna. She wears a mask to hide her two faces. She needs to be dealt with, as any traitor to the clan would be!"

Jetta stood fast, clenching her teeth in anger. She hated the clan, but was fiercely loyal to Elucard. Nonetheless, she could hold back her fury no longer, "Betray the clan? The clan is a blight on this land. You speak of purging and reaping the weeds that keep the world from flourishing. The Black Rabbits *are* the real weeds in the garden!"

Inle crashed the table away from him, shaking with unquenchable rage. He grabbed Jetta's collar and slammed her against the wall. A knife gripped tightly in his fist, pressed against Jetta's neck, "You bitch! I will gut you right here in front of everyone, and we'll see that you bleed black like the color of your heart. All you do is twist Elucard's mind! No more, I won't let you do anymore harm to him or my clan!"

189

Jetta spat a slimy wad of mucus into Inle's face, "Water for your garden!"

Inle's silver eyes widened with animosity, unleashing a backhanded blow to Jetta's cheek. Without hesitation Elucard pulled his student off of her and caught him in the gut with a heavy punch. Inle fell to his knees groaning in pain. Elucard's blade sheened under his student's neck.

"I said enough, Inle."

Inle sneered at Jetta, trying to calm himself in the shadow of his master, "Master," he lowered his voice, fury still under his breath, "You can't protect her. She speaks blasphemy."

Elucard tensely looked around at the growing crowd of soldiers and sailors edging closer to their incident. He sheathed his sword and dragged Inle to his feet, whispering in his ear, "Our enemies are too close to be dealing with your feud against Jetta."

"But Master–" Inle whispered back.

"Drop it, Inle. This is not your call!" Elucard hissed.

Jetta gathered her composure and addressed the gathering crowd, "My friend has just had one too many beers. Excuse us, we were just leaving."

Elucard slapped a few gold trit onto the counter, "Sorry to sour the mood. Drinks are on me."

A wave of gleeful cheers erupted from the patrons of the tavern. Elucard put a sincere arm around Jetta, comforting her. Inle shot them both an irritated glare. *Elucard, I will save you from the witch's clutches.*

38

"He is a crooked nail. Nothing but a defective tool in this state. Completely ineffective to us," The Silent Master's low growl of a voice passed through the dark quarters. Legion knelt before him, Inle stood off to the side, enamored by the presence of the legendary High Blade and the Silent Master.

"Blinded by the words of the girl, my Silent Master. She is a fragment of his past with great influence over him. Moreover, she has defied our teachings, giving her even more control over his mind. Elucard is just the symptom, Jetta is the virus," Legion spoke frankly.

The Silent Master turned to Inle, "You have seen this venom affect our First Blade? How can I be sure you are not merely jealous of his affection for her?"

Inle chuckled at the concept of being jealous of Jetta, but bowed his head reverently, "Jetta was, at first, a harmless comfort to Elucard. But over time I have have watched as she rotted away at his mind with one blasphemy after another." A look of disgust spread across his face, "The longer you allow people like Jetta to fester within our clan, the further away our Elucard will become."

"Legion, he is your apprentice, so it falls to you to deal with this problem. Kill the girl." The words left Silent Master without emotion or pity.

Legion's eyes widened, knowing full-well what an act would do to his relationship with Elucard, "Master, Jetta's loss to Elucard may do more harm than good. Allow me to banish Jetta. Within time, Elucard will forget about her as he once did, but if I kill her, Elucard will lash out. He will lash at m–"

"No!" interjected Ryjin. He was disgusted by Legion's weakness, "I allowed you to spare a life once before. The life of scum who directly worked against me—against our clan! No, I will not allow you to show mercy once more. You will kill this girl and make an example out of her. We will not have another…another Avalon!"

"I will do this task, my master, but Elucard must not know it was me. If he does, it will tarnish…" Legion knew that killing Jetta would shatter any trust or love Elucard ever had for him. He was like a son to him.

191

Destroying that relationship would be the end of Legion. He would need to keep this secret, even if it killed him to do so. The Silent Master was right, he showed great weakness when he spared Malady. He would need to keep his reputation intact or he feared he would be the next target in Ryjin's sights, "…my influence over him."

The Silent Master rubbed his chin, "The boy will overcome whatever pitiful affection he has for the girl, but your secrets are yours to keep. He will not to find out from me who killed her. Legion, send Elucard and Inle on a mission. Have it be an evaluation of Inle's accumulated skills. When they return, the deed shall be done."

Inle and Legion bowed.

***

Elucard and Inle perched in the shadows looking down at Galdo's butcher shack. Galdo was a mercenary that had a knack for poaching jobs from the Black Rabbits—an action the clan had taken notice of.

"Listen up Inle, Legion has seen fit to have you complete this mission as a final test to ascend from being my student, to my colleague."

"Yes, Master," Inle said, nodding intently. A wild ball of several emotions hung in the back of his mind. This was the night that Jetta was to be taken out of the picture. His master would be set free of such a twisting weight. Inle was free as well…to be with him.

"This Galdo is not to be taken lightly. What he lacks in speed and agility, he makes up ten-fold in power and resilience," Elucard continued.

"Yes, Master" Inle replied as he fingered through his satchel full of tools and weaponry.

"Stay light on your feet and keep moving. We'll tire him and take him down before he has a chance to fight back," Elucard said, taking a mental note of a large gathering of clouds moving in from the east.

"Master," Inle pointed at the door to the shack, "Movement. This could be our opening."

"Aye, well spotted, Inle," Elucard whispered, quickly turning his attention back on the cabin.

Moments later, a towering man with thick, muscular arms covered in matching dragon and demon tattoos exited the shack. Hoisted over his shoulder was a massive chunk of steel, shaped into a jagged sword.

Elucard signaled Inle to drop from their hiding spots and follow his lead. Their feet strode along the grass as if gliding in the shadows.

Elucard silently drew his blade and drove it straight into Galdo's back. Inle appeared in front of the giant man and struck into his lower chest.

Galdo cried out in pain before swinging his thick sword in a wide arc at the two assassins. Blades in hand, they nimbly dodged the attack, regrouping some feet away.

Low to the ground, Elucard gestured to Inle. The shadow elf complied and dashed forward, slashing at Galdo's legs, spraying blood from long cuts. Galdo roared ferociously and caught Inle by the throat with a titan's grip.

Inle gasped for breath and clawed desperately at the giant's arms. Galdo mercilessly slammed Inle into the ground. Elucard made his move, jumping and slashing downwards Galdo's right shoulder. Galdo barely flinched as he backhanded Elucard away, sending the elf flying into a large tree.

Galdo raised his sword over his head and brought it crashing down toward Inle's crumpled body. At the last moment, the Rabbit shoulder rolled away. Recovering, Inle slid behind the man and cut through his tendons, bringing the incredibly large man down to his knees with a thundering crash.

Elucard shook off the daze and lunged at the fallen mercenary with a series of muscle slicing swipes aimed at the behemoth's chest and arms. Galdo grunted as he tried to stand, but fell back down as Inle skewered him in the back.

Galdo fell to his hands scowling at the two Black Rabbits. Elucard sheathed his blade, bowing to Inle, "Do the honors."

Inle nodded, dropping his blade in a savage arc, cleaving Galdo's neck almost entirely free of his body. The giant's head hung by what few threads of muscle fibers, tendons, and veins tethered it to his mutilated body.

39

"Are you sure you don't want me to come? You two might get hurt," Jetta said. Her medical satchel was packed up and slung around her shoulder. She stood in the First Blade's quarters already prepared for another mission.

Elucard placed his hands on her shoulders and gazed into her enthusiastic eyes. Inle stood in the archway leaning against the frame. Elucard removed her satchel and placed it on the ground, "Not this time, Jetta. Master Legion told me this is to be a special test for Inle. He'll need to be able to take on this mark with little assistance from even me," Elucard smirked as he watched Jetta's disappointing eyes lower, "Cheer up Jetta, we three will still have plenty of missions together."

Jetta watched as the two boys walked out of the quarters, she waved them goodbye, "May Alue watch over you, Elucard," she whispered.

***

Jetta carefully dug into the ground with a small spade to extract the delicate feverroot from the cool soil. Clipping the thin tendrils off the root with her shears, she put what she gathered into her bag. She brushed off the dirt the best she could from her trousers. She then pulled out her waterskin and poured a small amount of water onto her dirty hands to wash them.

She looked around the quiet forest and shivered in the brisk evening air. A cluttered sound in the trees directed her attention. She peered into the tall pines to see a large crow cawing at her. The oily black feathers sheened in the rapidly falling sunset. Two more crows sailed into the tree to join the first. Each cackled at her before moving closer to another tree near Jetta.

"Oh bugger off, I'm leaving," Jetta muttered. Jetta took account of what she was able to gather up, slightly disappointed that she was unable to find any emberwart to make new blistercloth, but the several bushels of feverroot was a lucky harvest.

Jetta walked through the woods as the shadows grew longer and the air grew crisper. She picked up her pace to make her curfew, knowing full well a Rabbit unaccounted for would be a punished Rabbit.

However, she slowed down to a slow walk as she approached the small bridge that went over a creek. This bridge was where she first reunited with Elucard. It was where she vowed to be a stronger person for him; for her friend. She rested on the banister and lazily watched as a leaf moved chaotically around the rocks and into slower waters.

It was how she felt these days. She struggled with the Black Rabbits, trying to fight back against the current, but anytime she was with Elucard, she knew he and her would someday find their slower waters. That one day they would find peace.

"You're out late."

Jetta quickly looked to her side, startled by the sudden appearance of Legion. She always liked Legion. They didn't know each other well, but Elucard always spoke with admiration about his Master.

"Forgive me, my High Blade, I was–" Jetta clumsily hobbled over her own words, knowing it was nearly past the curfew.

"No need to apologize. I know you were out gathering medical supplies," Legion walked closer, smiling faintly. He leaned over the same banister and mused over the gentle stream, "I come here when I want to think about what weighs the most on me."

Jetta turned back to watch the stream, "The thing that weighs the most on me... I often think about that as well."

Legion glanced at the young elf, "What burdens you now, young one?"

Jetta furrowed her brow as tears slowly swelled in her eyes. She rubbed her eyes with her sleeve, "High Blade, I was never meant for such a life, and even its goddess rejects me. I feel like I am a leaf caught in a storm, endless floating lost and alone. I seek my tree."

Legion nodded, 'her tree.' Her tree was Elucard. He let out a heavy sigh and put an arm around the grieving elf, "Jetta, Elucard is but a leaf in the storm too. Do you know why he flourishes though?"

Jetta looked up at the scarred man, "Why?"

"Elucard does not seek an end to the storm, because he knows that as a leaf, he does not matter. Some day he will fall to the ground and wither into the soil like any other leaf."

Jetta looked away, a metaphor she couldn't have articulated better herself. Elucard was at the mercy of the Black Rabbit storm.

"Jetta, the storm will always blow, no matter if you are trapped in it or not. What you must realize is that just because we are in it, doesn't mean we are 'trapped.'" Legion grasped Jetta in a long hug, "I am sorry if you always felt trapped. I am sorry you were always so aimless, that you couldn't find your peace or happiness." He slowly unsheathed a dagger.

Jetta clenched her eyes shut, tears dropped over and down her cheeks, "Please…please let Elucard go. He deserves to be free from your storm. I'll stay in his place," her words were a raspy whisper now. She tightened her grip on Legion's cloak as she pleaded.

Legion pushed Jetta off of him, the dagger brandished in his hand, "Jetta…" he spoke shaking. Of all the lives he was ordered to take, this was the one he regretted before taking. Even when he killed his own father, he had no remorse. However, staring into the eyes of this young woman, he knew this death would set a chain reaction of events that would bury him in sorrow for the rest of his life, "Jetta, someday I'll save Elucard for you. Someday he'll be set free, but he will have to be in this storm without his tree… without you to be his beacon… without you to show him his way home."

Jetta stumbled backwards, but then stood still. She knew the Rabbits would one day try to separate her from from Elucard. She lifted her chin not in submission, but in defiance, "I'll pray for you, Legion."

Legion swiped cleanly across her throat and threw the knife into the wooden planks in anguish. Jetta gurgled trying to breathe as blood gushed from her wound. She fell to her knees but kept her chin up, tears streaming from her eyes. She shakily held her hands in contrition.

Alue can you hear me?

Jetta collapsed at Legion's feet. His head bowed in depression. He crushed Elucard's last breath of hope. His last tether to his past. His last piece of himself. Crushed beneath the feet of the Black Rabbit. He would either rise to be the soulless assassin the Silent Master would want him to be, or he would become the withered leaf on the ground. Either way he would be lost without guidance.

Alue I want to go home.

40

The clouds rolled in, setting a grim shadow upon the Black Rabbit compound. Elucard stood quivering. The entire clan knelt around a bridge that ran over a creek. Ryjin stood cold and still, his hands folded across his chest. Jetta's lifeless body lay strewn on the stone ground. Her clothes were soaked through from a gaping opening in her throat. Her eyes, stricken open from witnessing her own traumatic demise, stared blankly at Elucard...

His nails dug into his palms as his fist tightly closed, turning his skin a ghostly white. His body trembled as he struggled to stand, "J-Jetta..."

A silence blanketed the retreat.

Elucard's face wrinkled in complete anguish as he began to bawl uncontrollably. He fell to her body, cradling her in his arms. Her blood seeped into his clothes as he held her tightly in his embrace. He felt that if he held her tighter, he might rouse her from her bloody slumber.

"I wasn't there... I wasn't there to protect you. I'm sorry! Please don't do this. I'm so sorry."

Inle slowly moved forward, crouching down beside his grieving friend, "Elucard, it was for the best. Now you can move on without conflict or confusion."

Elucard clenched his eyes shut, he sucked in lungs of air, and stopped his crying before exhaling a single question, "Inle, what do you mean?"

Elucard turned and stared at his masked pupil with eyes hot from tears.

Inle placed a hand on Elucard's shoulder, "Elucard, you knew this day was coming. You knew she needed to be dealt with. She was corrupting your mind. You couldn't think clearly with her around. A blade is only as sharp as the Rabbit wielding it."

Confusion scried over the elf's face. Elucard spoke quietly, "Inle, did you know about this?"

Inle shook his head, "It doesn't matter who was involved, Elucard. You need to let her go. With the king's soldi–"

"Who did this?" Elucard asked with a biting chill.

"It doesn't matter, Elucard," Inle said again.

"Who did this?! Who killed Jetta?!" Elucard shouted at the top of his lungs. Elucard snapped his head, searching for any Rabbit brave enough to come forth with the truth. Finally, his eyes rested on Ryjin.

Elucard softly laid down Jetta's body and made his way toward the Silent Master, "Tell me. Who did this?"

Ryjin slightly raised his chin, "Take her body and bury her. Put her to rest and beg Alanna to take pity on her traitorous soul. Mourn for however long you must, and then put it behind you. That is what I expect—no, *command* of my First Blade."

Elucard's eyes shifted from a tormented sadness to a deathly coolness as thoughts raced through his head, "Ryjin. Who killed Jetta."

The Silent Master replied slowly with a dangerous edge in his voice, "Bury her, and bury your hatred with her. I will not tell you again."

Elucard gently picked up the lifeless body of his childhood friend and walked toward the woods. Calling back to the assassins watching, "Pray to Alanna I never find the Rabbit who did this."

41

"You saw stars in even the cloudiest of nights, Jetta. I don't know how you did it, but you never gave in. You never surrendered and they tried to extinguish the flame that burned inside of you. And here we are," Elucard chuckled as he stood over the makeshift grave marker. Her blood stained his garbs and gloves. He had no more tears to shed for his fallen friend, "I made a promise to protect you, and in the end, it was you who protected me. You know, my father and you might have been right all along, but, I don't know if any of that matters now."

Elucard quickly drew his sword. He wasn't alone anymore, "Have you come to pay your respects?"

Inle had a hand resting on his blade's handle and stepped cautiously from the shadows. He knelt in front of the grave and said a silent prayer to Alanna, "You should have played your cards better, Jetta. In another lifetime, perhaps."

Elucard turned to Inle, "I never told you about what I did to become a Rabbit, Inle."

"I've heard rumors..." Inle said quietly, not sure of the purpose of the conversation.

"Three of my friends from Ravenshore – we survived the Blood Forest together. They ran away from the Rabbits, hoping to start a new life away from it all. I had the chance to join them, but I killed them instead."

Inle nodded, "You did the right thing, Master."

"I don't know that I did. I don't know that anything I do is the right thing anymore," Elucard said. Exhaustion and confusion set in as he buried his face in his palms.

"Master, that's Jetta talking. Do not listen to her, remember your lessons, remember who your family is."

"My family... my family is in Ravenshore wondering how their son became so lost. My family is in the ground before our feet. My family would never have me kill my king or my friends. My family is who I promised to protect!" Elucard spat as he turned his head to face the shadow elf, "My family is not the Black Rabbits!"

Inle stepped backwards, a hand still on his sword handle, "Elucard, please, I don't want to harm you. No blood has to be shed tonight."

"You forget so soon? Blood has already been shed," Elucard sneered, sliding his blade from its sheath, "Stand aside, Inle. This clan has manipulated me long enough. It is time I dealt retribution."

Inle drew his blade, "The Silent Master was right, you are a defective tool. That bitch has twisted you too much. Her death was supposed to put her mind games to rest. I wish I cut her throat myself!"

Elucard roared, tears flowing from his eyes as he rushed his former student, "The Rabbits have poisoned every aspect of my life. They strip away the potential you have and replace it with the drive to murder, and for what?" Elucard yelled as he savagely swung his blade.

Inle parried and unleashed a ruthless backhand, swiveling Elucard's head, "The drive to murder? Have you forgotten our divine purpose in life? There is no greater honor than to live and die by the Black Rabbit's blade!"

Elucard snapped his head back fast enough to dodge a series of thrusts from Inle's sword, "How can you think Alanna would want us to slay the innocent for coin? Inle, they feed us lies! I saw the prince's eyes when I took away his father from him. I was a fool to think that a man uniting his people deserved to die! It brought me no closer to the glory the Rabbits promised! How is a society supposed to function if there are individuals that live outside the law?"

Inle jumped, spinning into a roundhouse kick that sent Elucard sliding backwards, "You spew the same bile as Jetta. It pains me to see you as an enemy. I loved you!"

Elucard took out a fan of shurikens, "Rabbits are incapable of love, Inle."

Even before the shurikens plunged into his chest, it was as if Elucard clenched and crushed Inle's heart. Wide eyed and speechless, Inle stood entranced as he took a flying kick to the head and crashed to the ground. He slowly recovered to his feet, his head lowered, his mask veiled in the shadows.

Elucard readied his blade before charging once more into the fray. Inle broke from his daze and fired several mad swipes with his blade, slicing gruesomely into Elucard's side and right shoulder.

Elucard ignored the sharp pain and unleashed a flurry of slashes. Several connected, spraying blood from the grievous wounds. Elucard finished with a heavy kick to Inle's chest, making him reel backwards.

Inle slid, catching himself with an arm and knee as he fell to the ground. Lifting his sword, Inle leaped at his former Master, cutting deeper into Elucard's side. The clown-assassin spun neatly, attempting to lop off Elucard's head, but the elf from Ravenshore was quick to raise his sword behind and block.

Both blades were locked in a struggle. Inle's energy and rage slowly rose, "I did it all for you! For you, Elucard!"

Elucard slowly lifted Inle's blade away from his exposed neck. With the flick of his wrist, he was able to fling it out of Inle's grip, sending it deep into a tree, "Don't let your sick delusions fool you, Inle! You did it all for yourself!"

Inle slid a pair of small daggers into his hands and threw them at his enemy. Elucard back flipped several feet, dodging them with grace.

Elucard landed, breathing hard. The gaping wound in his side poured blood onto the grassy forest floor. Inle frantically ran to his sword, which was still stuck in the tree. Elucard snapped a shuriken through the air, catching Inle's palm as he reached for his weapon.

Inle growled in pain, giving Elucard enough time to dropkick Inle onto his back. While kneeling on top of him, Elucard heaved his sword, face down, over Inle's chest and stabbed downward. Elucard stopped just short of the shadow elf's chest, "Pull off your mask, Inle!"

Inle slowly complied, removing his mask, eyes wide in fear.

"You won't die tonight, not you." Elucard hissed, thunder bellowed across the heavy night skies.

"No one will ever love you the way I did!" Inle whispered, his eyes now flared with passion.

The rain came down fast and hard. Blood seeped into the pores of the wet ground. Elucard stood, towering over his apprentice, his sword still pointed at Inle's cut up chest, "I want you to understand this, Inle. I want you to watch this clan burn. I want you to have it all come down around you. And when you have suffered as much as me, then I will kill you."

"Elu–" Inle started.

A hefty kick across Inle's face rendered him out cold.

42

The winds howled as Elucard entered the compound. The rain was relentless. It pounded on his shoulders and the wind bid him to turn around. But his hatred possessed him and so onward he marched.

Staggering into the familiar center of the Black Rabbit compound, Elucard hunched over, leaning slightly on his and Inle's swords, as if they were canes. Elucard lifted his head and sneered at Ryjin, who seemed unmoved by his dramatic reappearance.

"The Black Rabbits have tipped the scales…" Elucard could hardly speak, faint with the loss of blood.

Ryjin snapped his fingers, signaling for all the assassins to draw their weapons and move closer to Elucard, "You are nothing but a rabid dog. You must to be put down."

Blood dripped down both sides of his mouth as Elucard responded, "Will you put me down, Ryjin, or will one of your other dogs do it for you?"

Ryjin smirked, "Kill him."

The Rabbits roared as nearly a hundred bodies leapt into the night to strike Elucard down. Elucard spun wildly, parrying and deflecting steel with his two swords. Taking well placed strikes, Elucard moved his way through the crowd, decimating and maiming his former clan mates. Bodies dropped into a bloody heap behind him. However, Elucard moved slower and slower as swords, sais, and daggers shredded and punctured his body. The closer he moved to Ryjin, the weaker and more sluggish he became.

Elucard fell to his knees at the feet of the Silent Master, blood and rain soaking through his clothes. He could no longer lift his arms nor his head.

"Who k-killed J-Jetta?" he murmured, barely aware of his surroundings.

Ryjin grabbed the weary Elucard by the throat, lifting him up so that they were eye to eye, "You'll die, never knowing," the Silent Master whispered in his ear.

With adrenaline pumping through Elucard's body, he let out a soul shattering scream as he lifted both his swords and cross cut the hand that choked him. Ryjin reeled his head back in pain as his handless wrist gushed and sprayed blood across Elucard's face.

Ryjin sneered, gritting his teeth as he landed a savage blow to Elucard's chest with his remaining fist. Elucard's chest compressed as his heart rattled. Landing hard, several feet away, Elucard lay sprawled on his back, drifting dangerously close to death.

The rain patted down on Elucard's sleepy face, "Jetta, wait for me. Wait for me at the old willow tree."

Elucard heaved in a great whiff of breath as he rolled over. Sputtering up the iron taste of blood, he used his last bit of new found energy to stand. Rabbits to either side of him cautiously shuffled forward, over their fellow clansmen that blanketed the ground. Ryjin seethed pure anger, shivering in pain while grasping his bloody stump.

It was as if all time paused in a brief moment of solace. Elucard reached into a pouch and exploded a smoke pellet on the ground, concealing a last ditch effort to escape the dire situation.

"After him!" Ryjin shouted over and over as the pursuing assassins pierced through the smoky cover.

***

Elucard ran as fast as his battered body could take him, but collapsed at the cliff face of a waterfall. The waters rushed, more powerful from the stormy weather. Elucard gripped his swords with a slippery, blood-soaked grip, waiting for any assassin to catch up to him. Legion moved into the moonlight from the shadows.

Elucard surrendered his blades to the feet of his friend and mentor, "So it ends here?"

Legion kicked the swords aside in a clatter. He lifted up his student's bloody heap of a body, "Elucard, do you remember when you asked me if I kept any humanity?"

"Yes, Master," Elucard sputtered.

"You are my humanity, Elucard," Legion kissed the forehead of the dying elf, before dropping him over the waterfall.

Several assassins approached Legion, "Where is he?"

Legion passed them heading back to the compound, "It is done."

43

"Let's see what you've learned," Megan said. She stood on the opposite end of the underground arena, surrounded by enchanted trees.

Koda nodded and bowed his head before jumping into the air and landing with a heavy impact that shook the ground. The crackling and tightening sounds of roots exploded from beneath Megan, attempting to bind and encase her. However she was quick and rolled out of harm's way, only to find Koda manifesting several leaves with serrated edges to soar in her direction.

Megan roared as her skin transformed into a hard bark. The leaves bounced off of her armored skin and Megan answered back by transforming her hand into an outstretching vine laden with thorns, whipping and slapping at the ground, trying to catch the elf as he nimbly dodged out of the way of each attack.

Koda tumbled toward Megan's right flank and mustered his courage to grab the next attack. He winced as the thorny vine wrapped around his arm, and used the entanglement to yank Megan into close range. With trained reflexes and cunning, Koda conjured a small pile of dust into his hand, and blew it into Megan's face.

She sneezed before falling sleepily to the ground. Drowsily, she tied the thorny whip around her hand. The sharp pain kept her from falling asleep. A massive trunk rose beneath her feet, bringing her into the air, "Your clever tricks won't win the battle against me, your grace! Show me what you have really learned!"

Koda smirked, knowing well what she meant. Thrusting his hand into the air, he began mustering his focus into his palm. Light flashed around him as a brilliant blue aura enveloped him. His hand quivered as it lit up with bright light.

Megan smiled, but her face quickly turned to dread as she was slowly lifted from her tree. Her arms fell to her sides as if she was bound by an unknown force. She struggled against the alien power but to no avail.

Koda's thoughts raced wildly and his vision became blurry. Sweat dripped from his forehead and his face went pale. The strain overcame him as he swung his arm downward, crashing his teacher to the ground.

Megan dazedly stumbled as she tried to stand. A laceration bled from the side of her head, "The power to control life itself. That is just the surface of the Magi's power. We must learn more."

Koda collapsed to the ground, heaving, "W-we will. W-e must to protect my people."

Megan grinned, "You have done well, Koda."

***

Koda stood before the council of teachers once again; now older, now wiser, and now a mage in his own right. Megan bowed as she presented him with the official robes of a graduated Vernal Mage, "You've earned the right to wear these robes more than most, Koda. You have untapped potential that needs molding. In the future, you will find that you will be challenged physically, mentally, and spiritually. May you remember what this school has taught you and may success follow you wherever you go."

Koda bowed and accepted the robes from his master. He proudly donned the ornate threads and tied the green sash around his waist tightly. Pride swelled in his heart, "I will apply what you have taught me. You will see."

"I have seen, already," Megan said, smiling.

***

Koda sat, holding his goblet aloft. Wine sloshed around the rim as he rose to his feet. Large quantities of smoked meats and roasted vegetables laid across the long banquet table. On either side of him, lords and their advisers sat enjoying the feast put on by the royal family. The noise that echoed in the large dining room quieted as the elves turned to see what their young king had to say.

"Friends, I gather you all to feast in a period of new found peace. Our army grows in power each day. It has been a mere three months since we began training up our own forces, and yet we have received numerous reports from several towns across the country. The Black Rabbits have not dared to make any appearances. It is safe to say that their numbers are dwindling. Our city flourishes and our people are no longer living in fear. I raise to you all, a toast to Long Whisper. May we continue in our prosperity!"

All but one noble raised their drink. Athar stood, unimpressed, "What of the inevitable war in the south? King Dallin of Varis and King Aric of Estinia have failed to reach a treaty. Aric will no doubt invade Varis and attempt to conquer and enslave the people there."

Eyes turned and locked onto a nervous Koda, "I was unaware of such a conflict."

Athar laughed with a mocking tone, "Here we have a green king, completely oblivious of his own borders. My lords, this is our leader!"

Koda began to sweat, unable to handle this level of criticism, "What news have you heard from Varis?"

"Elven refugees afraid of an oncoming war are flocking to our lands. Varis supported your father's rise to the crown, no doubt we should support Varis in their time of need," Cass Baneberry suggested.

"Our army may be growing, but they have never seen a real battle. Our forces would be crushed in actual combat," Fendrick Redroot said flatly.

"We can't just ignore Varis!" Aisling said, raising her voice over the shouts from the various noblemen.

Tull leaned into Koda's ear, "My King, you must take control of this situation and make a decision."

"But Tull, what if I make the wrong choice?" Koda asked, afraid of such a decision and what devastation it could do to the nation's fledgling peace.

Tull patted him on the shoulder reassuringly, "Koda, any decision is better than no decision. Show them that you can lead a nation, not just in time of peace, but in a time of need as well."

Koda, raised his hands, simmering down the arguing, "My lords, we must raise the shield of courage for our people and for those seeking our protection. Estinia wishes to burn Varis, so who is to say they will stop there? We must stand beside our allies and quell this threat!" Koda said. The confidence he gained from becoming a mage resonated in his voice.

"Well said, young King. You will be remembered as the hero that led Long Whisper to victory!" Athar Moonfall cheered, smiling and clapping.

The nobles rose from their seats clapping in awe, inspired by the bravado of Koda.

***

Cast in the weak lighting of the rose garden, Athar Moonfall whispered angrily with his most trusted adviser, "Silva, you pea-brained rat! That's the second time you were wrong about Koda!"

"My Lord, my eyes are everywhere in this city, I swear the information I had was to be trusted!"

"The same eyes that assured you he would not take the crown?" Athar spat, mockingly.

Silva nodded anxiously.

"I'm trying to orchestrate the fall of the Dawnedge house, and yet with each blow I strike them with, they recover with double the force. This war, however, could provide an opportunity for Koda to—for lack of a better word—*perish* in combat, and I, myself to rise a hero." Athar Moonfall grinned delightfully at the thought.

"My eyes tell me that the Rabbits have trouble in their warren. Perhaps we should wait for them to get reorganized before making our next move," Silva whispered, looking around as if the Black Rabbits were watching her every move.

"Tell me, who are these 'eyes?' I must know this."

Silva shook her head, "If identities were revealed, My 'eyes' may go blind."

"Very well. Keep your secrets, Silva, but fail me again and your 'eyes' will be the least of your worries," Athar warned.

44

Marcus sat by the river bank with a fishing rod resting in his hands and a long blade of grass fixed between his teeth. He turned to watch as his son sat beside him with heavy bags beneath his eyes. Marcus moved to shield him from the glare from the morning sun.

"Not used to waking up at dawn anymore?" Marcus chuckled, passing him a mug of coffee.

"What makes you think the fish aren't still sleeping?" Wiccer said, taking a sip from the mug and frowning from the lack of cinnamon and sugar.

"Believe it or not, it was your mother that got me into fishing. Your great grandfather taught her the secret of fishing at daybreak. She fished every morning. Even when she got sick, she still fished," Marcus grew silent, remembering Vivian.

Wiccer let a moment pass between them, taking in the silence, before speaking again, "I was too young at the time, but how did you deal with losing her?"

"I never did. Avren took care of me. He became the man of the house while I wallowed in depression and self pity. I had to shut out all the love I had for your mother to move on. I don't...I don't take death very well." Marcus let out a sigh, "I know you see me as this great commander and strong figure, but when your mother died, when the baneblood sickness wilted her body to a shell, I just couldn't handle it."

"Father..."

Marcus choked, closing his eyes tightly, "When Avren fell, I shut you out. I reverted to the same weak-minded man I once was. Wiccer, in many ways you're a stronger man than I am."

Wiccer paused, but tried to lighten the tension that hung in the air, "I've decided to take your offer. I want to join Long Whisper's ranks. Avren wanted me to not be blinded by hatred. He wanted me to be a stronger leader." Wiccer nodded to his own words, "I want to be that leader."

Marcus grinned as a low laugh escaped him, "Well, for your first duty, why don't you brew me another cup of coffee."

Wiccer laughed, taking the mug and walking across the field back to the cabin.

Marcus turned back to his fishing line. From the corner of his eye, he saw a large object floating downstream. At first he could not make out what it was. A villager's laundry gone rogue? Perhaps a river-trader's boat had lost some small cargo? As it drew closer his eyes widened. It was a body. Lifeless and bobbing with the ebb and flow of the river. Marcus tossed his fishing rod aside and leapt into the water. He pulled the battered body to the shore, "Wiccer, hurry! Come back!"

Wiccer ran to his father's side as Marcus felt for any signs of life.

"Wiccer, fetch the medical supplies, this elf is still alive! Wiccer?"

Wiccer stood utterly frozen as he looked down upon the broken body of the elf that had caused him so much misery and strife.

"Wiccer?!" Marcus yelled, hoping to snap Wiccer out of the trance he was in, "Son?"

"Let him die," Wiccer said, with no hint of emotion or pity.

PART TWO

VENDETTA'S EDGE

45

Elucard gazed at the old willow tree. The dry, leathery bark had moss sparsely growing on its north side. Its leaves drooped, providing a small shelter from the blistering sun. The water from the small fishing pond gently caressed its roots.

Jetta sat on a low hanging bough, beckoning Elucard to sit by her. Her blue summer dress waved in the breezy air. White lace hemmed the end of her seams. Her auburn hair was tied into a loose ponytail, complete with an adorable yellow ribbon.

"Elucard, come sit with me. It's a beautiful day, don't you think?"

Elucard cautiously stepped closer but stopped just short of his lifelong friend. She called out to him again, her voice softer, almost a whisper.

"Elucard, come sit with me. It's a beautiful day, don't you think?"

Her voice was scratchy and labored as she spoke again. It was as though only some of her words were vocalized, while others were nothing more than gargled chokes.

"Elu – come – with. Beautiful day – think?"

Elucard gasped in horror and stumbled backwards as a thin red line spread across Jetta's throat. Blood seeped from the thin wound slowly at first, but soon the blood was gushing forth, tearing the pulsing wound wide open. Her eyes grew wide and she teared up, reaching forward—yearning for her friend.

"I'm sorry Jetta! Please, stay with me!" Elucard shouted as he ran to catch her falling body from the tree branch. However, when she collapsed into a heap in his arms, her lifeless corpse wilted like a flower and turned to ash, sending fragments of her broken body floating in the air like a fine smoke.

Elucard choked up as hot tears bubbled in his eyes. His hands tightened into fists. An unfamiliar voice echoed within his scattering, dreary thoughts.

"His fever is spiking."

Marcus lifted his hand off of Elucard's clammy forehead. Moans shakily escaped the dying elf. Wiccer hurried to give his father a washcloth, freshly drenched in ice water. He sneered at the battered elf's body, squirming about in the bed.

"Father, we should just let him die. He doesn't deserve our help!"

"Wiccer, we talked about this. We are not executioners, we are men of law. By Jedeo's blade, we shall not let him die until we have healed him and brought him to justice."

"He assassinated King Jaelyn! He had Avren killed! My brother! Your own damn son!"

Marcus snapped his head at Wiccer, his eyes flaring, "You think I need you to remind me of that? You think I don't want to break this elf's neck?"

"No," Wiccer spoke quietly, avoiding his father's gaze.

"Louder!" Marcus commanded.

"No!" Wiccer shouted instinctively as if he was a White Cloak once more.

Marcus let out a labored sigh. He, too, had fought the urge to let Elucard die. But he knew that this could be the opportunity he had been waiting for – a chance for Long Whisper to be rid of the Black Rabbit menace, once and for all. To that end, Elucard could yet prove to be an invaluable ally.

"Wiccer, the truth is…" He began. He knew that telling Wiccer his plan would not go over well. He knew that it was taking every fiber in Wiccer's body to restrain him from killing Elucard, but he also knew that his son trusted him above all else, "The truth is, I have plans for Elucard beyond bringing him to justice."

Wiccer shook his head. He had suspected as much.

"Wiccer, the elf's been ripped apart for a reason. Maybe the Rabbits turned on him. Perhaps he could be convinced to side with us. He owes us his life," Marcus said, mostly attempting to persuade his son to join his cause, and partly to convince himself that he had not lost his mind.

"I can't believe you. I can't – I can't even talk to you right now!" Wiccer began to pace around the tiny bedroom. His brother was dead, his cloak stripped from him, and his life was in shambles all because of Elucard. Now his father was telling him that they – no, *he*, had to save Elucard.

"We're out of Sunwart Root. We could also use some more bandages," Marcus spoke quietly, as if ignoring Wiccer's anger, "Head to the old guild hall. It's a military outpost these days. Tell them that you're my son. Get Sunwart Root for his fever, bandages, and try to scrounge up some dullweed for his pain."

"Yeah, wouldn't want him to suffer..." Wiccer mumbled under his breath. His father didn't seem to catch the comment.

"We went through a week's worth of medical supplies in three days, make sure to pick up double. Take the cart, but do not tell them who we are treating!"

Wiccer curled his lip defiantly at first, but then nodded when he met his father's stern gaze.

"Make haste, boy."

***

The old guild hall was once a common destination for weary travelers on the roads of Long Whisper. The White Cloaks often shared their lavish feasts with those in need. From the winter's moon to the summer solstice, the guild hall was always ready to accommodate anyone with tired feet who had time to hear stories of challenge and triumph.

These days, the banners that once hung from its stone walls had long since fallen. The once welcoming doors were now hidden by a crude wooden palisade wall. The aroma of fine baked goods was now the rancid stench of burning mystery meat.

Wiccer stopped his cart just outside the gates of the crudely constructed walls. A guard inspected the empty cart before prying a few answers from a tired Wiccer.

"What brings you to Outpost Wolfcry?"

Wiccer looked up at the weathered guild hall, remembering the time he had spent safe within its walls. Calling it Outpost Wolfcry salted a still open wound. The wound that he was no longer a White Cloak, and that the building no longer belonged to his White Cloak family.

"Is that what it's called, these days?" huffed Wiccer.

"Are you from around here?"

Wiccer nodded, "I live a night's travel north of here. My family has run out of medical supplies, and we are in need of them."

The guard looked Wiccer up and down. Not only was he no elf, but he was clearly a foreigner, "Are you sure you are from here?"

"I don't have time for these games. I am in urgent need of medical supplies! General Marcus Newsun sent me!"

The guard snapped to attention, as if Marcus himself were sitting at Wiccer's side, "General Newsun sent you?"

"I'm his son," Wiccer said flatly.

The guard called for the wooden gates to open up before hastily turning back to Wiccer, "Sorry for the trouble, sir."

Wiccer shook his head. Why did this task bother him so much? Perhaps it had less to do with fetching supplies for someone that he wanted to let die and more to do with the lack of notoriety he had with these new soldiers. He was once a sergeant in the Guard of the White Cloaks. His very presence demanded respect. Now... now he commanded nothing.

As he steered the cart next to the quartermaster, he gawked at the amount of travelers and children that crowded the inner outpost. A staggering line of elves in ragged attire waited for a large iron cauldron of boiling beef stew. The quartermaster was busy too. Wiccer stood in the crowd, waiting as soldiers passed out fresh clothes and blankets to the travel-worn elves.

Wiccer caught the attention of a passing guard, "Who are all these people?"

"Refugees from Varis. They are traveling north from Sparrow Port."

Wiccer mapped out Long Whisper in his head. Sparrow Port was a large coastal city to the south that bordered the Serpent Sea.

"Long Whisper is gearing up to go to war alongside Varis. That is one reason why the refugees are heading north instead of taking up residence in Sparrow Port. If Estinia breaks through Varis, Sparrow Port will be the first to be razed," the guard said.

"King Koda is going to war?" Wiccer asked. He was wide-eyed in disbelief. The Long Whisper army was in no condition to go to war yet. It was true that recruitment had spiked since the country learned of the Varis-Estinia conflict, but the soldiers were still green.

"You, there, what supplies do you need?" shouted the quartermaster, trying to capture Wiccer's attention.

Wiccer snapped out of his daze, "Medical supplies. Two weeks' worth. Sunwart Root and bandages mainly. Dullweed if you can spare some."

Wiccer found himself drifting back into his thoughts as the quartermaster had a few men load up the cart. Wiccer was so wrapped up with Elucard, that he'd had forgotten that his father was going to war and that he would soon be training Long Whisper's recruits. Whatever qualms he had with Elucard seemed somewhat petty in comparison now.

***

"Father, I'm back!" Wiccer called as he stepped back inside his house. In his arms he carried a crate of medical supplies.

Marcus emerged from the bedroom where Elucard was still being cared for. His hands were crusted with dried blood. His eyes drooped with dark, heavy bags under them, brushing the sides of his nose. Wiccer could tell he had not slept much in the two days that it had taken him to make the supply run.

Wiccer rested the crate on a nearby table, and led Marcus to his own room, "You need to sleep, father. I'll watch over the elf. Get some rest."

Marcus made no attempt to protest, "He needs his bandages changed. I found a small amount of Sunwart by the river, but he could use some more. The elf is fighting a battle in those dreams of his," muttered Marcus in between a long yawn.

Wiccer laid his father down, removing his leather boots. He pulled a wool quilt over him as he reassured Marcus, "I will take care of him. I promise. Now go to sleep before you keel over and die."

Wiccer quietly moved across the cabin, making sure to grab the crate before entering the room where Elucard feverishly thrashed and wailed. Slicing into the root with a small knife, Wiccer held Elucard's mouth open to let the juice drizzle in. Taking out a mortar and pestle, Wiccer ground the Dullweed and remaining Sunwart juice into a fine paste. He gently removed the soaked bandages and applied the salve to the elf's wounds before replacing the used bandages with fresh ones.

"I didn't kill him."

Wiccer looked up from his task after hearing the hoarse voice. He dismissed it, thinking it was another fever dream of Elucard's.

"Your brother, I didn't kill him."

Wiccer listened quietly this time. He glanced down at Elucard to see if he was addressing him, or not.

"I'm sorry that you lost your brother."

"How did you know he was my brother?" Wiccer asked, now realizing Elucard was speaking to him.

Elucard gingerly opened his eyes. The morning light intensified his headache, "I heard you speak of him and how I was responsible for his death."

"You are responsible!" Wiccer snarled.

"I am. But my hand did not slay him. We have the same enemy, you and I," Elucard coughed. The Sunwart juice had a sharp taste, like a fire blazing in his throat.

"Enemy? Was he not your ally that night?" Wiccer looked befuddled by Elucard's comment.

"At the time I would have gladly served at his side, fought along with anyone in my clan. Not anymore. I tell you this because we clearly share a common foe now."

"My goal is to see you hang!" Wiccer growled as he shook his fist in the face of the half-awake elf.

"I am guilty of my crimes, I know that. But vengeance is a stronger form of justice. Don't tell me you feel otherwise."

Wiccer leaned in close. He remembered the night of the battle with Elucard and his squad vividly. He remembered the elf that fought his brother, but he did not recall his name, nor did he know his true face, as it was covered by a clown mask, "Who killed my brother?"

"His name is Inle Ebonpath. Like you, I wish death upon him...and the rest of my clan."

"Your clan did this to you? What did you do?" Wiccer asked astonished by the ruthlessness of what Elucard's clan could do. Ghastly wounds covered Elucard's body. He was bruised from broken ribs and pale from the intense amount of lost blood. He clung to life by his sheer willpower and thirst for revenge alone. Wiccer saw this and wondered what his clan could have done to warrant such an unquenchable hatred.

Elucard felt light headed as he tried to produce images of that night. Flashes of violence screamed through his mind like a diving falcon swooping in for a field mouse. He grit his teeth as his head began to burn up. His body pulsed with great pain, curling his back.

Wiccer placed a firm hand on Elucard's bare chest. He dabbed a cold wet cloth onto his patient's face, "Rest up, it seems we still have much to discuss."

46

The fog roamed from the river to the Newsun cottage. The clouds rolled and churned ever so slightly as the morning sun's shafts barely penetrated the mist to light the room where Elucard woke.

At first his eyes cracked open slightly to examine the bedroom where he stayed. The grainy wooden walls were a dark tint of red. A silver chain bearing the silver emblem of Jedeo hung from the banister of the headboard. A platter with a glass of water and an untouched sandwich sat atop an old wooden nightstand. On the opposite side of the room, Elucard saw himself in a mirror above an oak dresser.

Elucard reached for the banister to support himself as he slowly attempted to get up. He grunted as he accomplished his goal, but now that he was sitting up, the next feat would be to stand and walk. Feebly, he rose to his feet, but collapsed onto the nightstand, knocking over the platter of food.

Wiccer and Marcus rushed into the room at the sound of the clatter. Elucard leaned onto the bed, breathing heavily through the pain and stiffness in his legs.

"You've been out for a week. You'll need to practice walking to get the blood flowing through your muscles again. Give it time, you have plenty of that," Marcus said, helping Elucard back into the bed.

"What is your game here? Why haven't you killed me yet?" Elucard said, grimacing from the numbness in his feet. It was as if a hundred tiny daggers were poking the flat of his feet.

Marcus turned to his son, "Wiccer, fetch Elucard a glass of water, be quick, I'd like you here when I present this proposal."

Taking the glass from Wiccer, Elucard gulped down the water like a fish that had just been released. He gave his thanks before setting the glass aside.

"Well, I'm interested in your plans. So let's hear them," Elucard said. For all the crimes against Long Whisper and the strife he had personally caused Wiccer's family, finding why they kept him alive was a point of great curiosity for him.

"Elucard, my name is Marcus Newsun. I am a general in the Guard of the White Cloaks, and up until recently I served as a military adviser for the fledgling Long Whisper army. It is true you were once a great enemy of mine and my family. You are certainly still an enemy of Long Whisper for… obvious reasons."

Elucard lowered his head.

"But, I believe in redemption. I do not believe that even you are so far gone that you cannot atone for your crimes and serve a higher purpose," finished Marcus.

Elucard looked at Wiccer, who quickly looked away.

"A higher purpose?" Elucard seemed confused still.

"Elucard, my son tells me you are an enemy to your clan now. I understand that it was them who left you in such a mess?" Marcus inquired knowingly.

Elucard nodded, not yet ready to retread on that subject.

"The Black Rabbits are still a great threat to Long Whisper. And despite the hindrance that the ever-present soldiers pose, I believe that they are ill-equipped to actually bring down the assassins. Would you agree?"

Elucard thought back on his training. How he was practically reborn in order to become a Black Rabbit. He had been bred to kill at even the slightest provocation. He was sure that even the strongest soldier in Long Whisper was no match for even the weakest Rabbit.

"No, I don't believe your soldiers could survive an encounter with the Black Rabbits."

"I didn't think so. They would need specialized training. Training tailored specifically to combat a Rabbit." Marcus looked over at Wiccer.

"An anti-rogue operative? Father, do you really want to go through with this?"

Marcus turned to Elucard, "Would you be able to teach a select group of soldiers to become Rabbit hunters?"

Elucard looked at Wiccer. His scowl now replaced with a look of intense interest. They were serious. They wanted Elucard to teach Black Rabbit secrets to soldiers, to go to war with his clan. This is why they kept him alive and tended to his wounds.

A higher purpose.

This would give his life a whole new meaning. A better use of his skills than having them waste away in a cell, "I am willing to do this."

Marcus rubbed his hands in excitement, "Good! Redemption is within your reach, Elucard. This is merely the first step."

Wiccer looked excited as well but then frowned as a large hurdle came up in his mind, "Father, what of the king?"

"Ah, my son. That would be the next step!" Marcus grinned.

47

"You were taught speed, prowess, cunning, and strength. All things in which you have become adept. In our most dire of times, you proved your loyalty. Where Elucard failed, you will succeed. Inle Ebonpath, will you be my First Blade?"

Inle knelt before Legion and Ryjin. This was the proudest moment of his life—to become the successor of his master, Elucard. However, this day could only have been better if Elucard were there to see him. He raised his face, covered by the battle-scarred clown mask, and spoke four simple words, "Yes, my High Blade."

Legion's eyes were emotionless. Without Elucard, he no longer had the same passion for life that he once had. He failed as a teacher and he failed as a father. His son had turned against him and had attempted to destroy everything that he held dear. The philosophies that he thought Elucard lived by were spat upon and disregarded. A betrayal he knew was inevitable after Jetta's death. He once wondered how a single push could be enough to corrupt a mind. Presumably the same way that a single pull could save a mind. Legion shook away his thoughts.

"Then arise, Inle, and stand by my side," Legion said, nodding to the shadow elf.

"This is a great honor. I shall not let my clan down!"

Ryjin stood and walked over to the new First Blade, "Look at you, Inle. Be proud of yourself. Many would give anything to experience even a fragment of a moment such as this, child. Do not let those who would frown upon your accomplishment burden you."

"My Silent Master, why would they frown?" Inle asked, a hint of sadness and confusion mixed in his voice.

"Inle, you were the student of the traitorous Elucard. Despite your former master's death, his mark was left on the clan. Eight died that night, twelve more injured. He took my hand. All because we tried to free him. And how did he repay us? How did he repay you?"

Inle felt the scars over his body flare as he remembered how Elucard looked at him with sheer spite. How he chewed up Inle's love confession and spat it into the dirt. He stomped on his heart, on his friendship, and on the bond they had.

"I am not Elucard," Inle sneered.

"No, you are not, but the clan does not fully trust you," Ryjin croaked, "They don't know you like I do, Inle. They do not yet see your dedication."

"How can I prove my loyalty?"

Ryjin smiled, "I am sending you to Lost Dawns. You are to find King Koda and take his royal signet. Be sure to confront him and send a message. Do not kill him, just send a message."

Inle nodded at the directions, "What will be the message, my master?"

"The Black Rabbits still control Long Whisper."

***

Elisa waited outside the Silent Master's quarters, straining to pick up any information that she could. However, she only caught bits and pieces, nothing of any use. She had been back with the Black Rabbits for two weeks now, flabbergasted by how much everything had changed. Any friend that she once had was either gone, dead, or saw her as no more than a stranger. Even the Rabbits she had recruited no longer acknowledged her as a Rabbit. She had spent too much time away from her clan to be of any use to the White Cloaks.

The quarters opened up and Inle walked out. From what she heard, he was the one who killed Avren. A feat that, although she despised him for, was actually a badge of honor amongst her clan.

She bowed to him, but he did not seem to take notice of her.

"Typical. Even the clown sees me as a ghost," mumbled Elisa.

"How are you adjusting to life back in the clan, Elisa?" a voice called out to her.

Elisa looked up to find Legion standing in front of her. Legion had always been the quiet sort. She never worked with him, but he respected her all the same.

"It goes slowly, High Blade," she muttered truthfully.

"You were a prisoner of the White Cloaks for years, I'm surprised they didn't hang you. You were tasked with infiltrating Lost Dawns. Had it not been for your relationship with Vada, we'd have sent a Rabbit to assassinate you."

Vada, just another friend lost to the winds. She was once Elisa's best friend in the clan. She personally recommended Elisa for the job in Long Whisper.

"I never broke. They must have admired that," Elisa replied, trying to sound as convincing as possible.

"And Koda just let you go?"

"Well…" Elisa had not think this far into her lie, "When the White Cloaks dissolved, the soldiers that took over were going to hang me, but I managed to escape. The guards that the fools stuck me with had a drinking problem. Not to mention I had *other* tools at the ready." Elisa slowly ran her hand from her inner thigh, up along her exposed stomach, before resting it sensually in the cleft of her breasts.

Legion was somewhat taken aback, "I see. It's good to have you back. We'll try to find some work suited for a veteran such as yourself."

Elisa held a weird and wiry smile until Legion left. She exhaled a long breath, sinking into the shadows. It seemed the difficult task of regaining the trust of the clan was yet before her.

48

The enormous cathedral of Jedeo had been built as a centerpiece in the mountainside city of Jedeoheim. The city itself was a triumph of engineering, with its Gothic structures, towering granite statues, and enormous walls carved with the history of Jedeo during the Night Wars. It was a black stone building, adorned with watchful gargoyles and decorated with intricate stained glass windows, depicting the heroes of Jedeo's lore.

Avalon walked down the long hallway, banners of the Silent Ones draping the walls to either side of her. A depiction of a sun with a downward blade in the foreground adorned each banner with its white and gold colors. The arched buttresses webbed all around her. Keystones etched with incantations were inlaid on each doorway she walked through.

Avalon's white and black trimmed coat billowed as she raised her hood. Her sword was sheathed on the small of her back. She bowed to each monk she passed. She had found her calling as a Silent One, a holy warrior dedicated to serving the divine light of Jedeo.

It had been nearly five years ago to the day that she first stood in front of the massive golden oak doors of this very cathedral.

Avalon grabbed the cast-iron knocker and pounded it on the door for a third time before it slowly creaked open. Before her stood a rotund old man with a white wool habit. He looked the travel-worn Avalon up and down. She reeked something fierce and was wrapped in a stained tan cloak. Her face was covered by a large scarf so that the monk could only see her fierce eyes.

"You girl, what is it that you want?"

Avalon undid her scarf, "Please sir, I've been traveling for years to reach this sacred place. I have heard countless tales that this is the citadel of the Silent Ones. I have killed many to reach this place. I beg of you, please teach me!"

The man stood silent, muttering unintelligibly, before walking back inside, slamming the door behind him. Avalon was motionless. Before she could knock again the door opened. This time a woman in a long white coat with a silver trim, appeared before Avalon.

"You girl, what is it that you want?"

Avalon was silent with annoyance. She had just told the monk why she was here, and she did not care much for having to repeat herself.

"Speak up," the woman said sharply.

"I am here to become a Silent One."

"Is that all?" said the woman, clearly unimpressed, "Why should we make you a Silent One?" she asked, lifting up the ragged cloaks that Avalon was wearing in disgust.

"I have traveled very far–" Avalon started.

"So have many before you."

"And I have killed many–"

"So have many before you."

"I seek redemption!" Avalon blurted out, fearing she would be interrupted again.

The woman sized her up before arching her brow, "It is true, you have seen your share of scraps. The life of a Silent One is not for the faint of heart. Do you have the patience and discipline required of a Silent One?"

Avalon nodded, "I do. Just give me a chance!"

The woman rubbed her chin, "I don't think you do."

Avalon steepled her fingers, "Let me prove myself!"

The Silent One walked back into the cathedral, slamming the door behind her.

Avalon stood at the door, waiting, wanting. For days she stood without sleep, without food. Even through the pouring rain and the deathly chill night she waited.

Days passed, and finally the door opened once more. The same woman as before gracefully stepped out. She looked at the shivering girl before her and spoke firmly, "Walk away now and I will see that you are given shelter and food, perhaps new clothes and a warm bath. Just admit you are not ready to become a Silent One."

Avalon closed her eyes, her tears were cold to the touch. Walking away would have been an easier choice for a lesser woman, but she was not ready to give up herself.

"I will become a Silent One," Avalon stated, her diligent attitude rung in her voice.

"We shall see," The woman said slamming the door in Avalon's face once more.

Three more days passed. Avalon shivered in the cold seaside air. Her tired body was giving up on her as she stood swaying back and forth in utter exhaustion. The thought of the door opening was the only thing that kept her going. She could not quit now. She had survived becoming a Rabbit, so surely she could survive becoming a Silent One.

As she was reaching the bitter end of what she could handle, the rotund monk came out with a heavy quilt and bowl of steaming porridge, "For you, ma'am," he said, trying to hand it off to the nearly non-responsive Avalon.

Her hands trembled as she went to take the quilt and food, but stopped short. Her face was gaunt, her lips were parched and cracked, and her body shook from the cold that lay deep in her bones.

"I will become a Silent One," she said with a weak, shaky voice.

"You would rather die than quit?"

"I would rather die than live another life as the criminal that I am."

The man nodded and quickly slammed the door. However, Avalon did not have to wait much longer to see the familiar woman again.

"I have seen that you have patience and discipline, but so have many that came before you."

Avalon lowered her head, readying herself for another few nights of mental and physical torture.

"But, unlike many that have come before you, you show determination. A trait that we seek in all of our Silent Ones. You, girl, are ready to join us."

Avalon's head shot up, her eyes wide with joy.

"Quickly, come inside. You must be freezing."

Avalon smirked. The trial that she went through was much harder than the training, moreso because she was already finely tuned in her Rabbit training. A Silent One could fight hard, but she knew that a Rabbit would fight harder. Perhaps this was the reason why she rose through the ranks so quickly. Perhaps this was the reason why the Red Wing wished to see her.

Avalon knocked on the wooden door to the study of with a quick rap. Instantly, she was beckoned to enter.

The Red Wing's study was nothing more than a prayer mat and a shrine to Jedeo. Several swords were displayed on the walls. The Red Wing herself had her Silencer sword placed on the shrine, which she prayed to.

"Iron Wing Avalon, remove your Silencer in the presence of your Red Wing. Have you been taught nothing?"

Avalon bowed quickly and unbuckled her belt and scabbard, placing her sword on the ground, "Forgive me, Master. I forget who I am, sometimes."

The Red Wing turned to face her, an eyebrow raised, "It seems you forgot again. I am your Red Wing, not your master."

"Red Wing Sa'veen, I am truly sorry," Avalon apologized, bowing several times before Sa'veen motioned for her to stop.

"Avalon, do you have any idea why you've been summoned here?"

"No, my Red Wing."

"How well-versed are you with Jedean lore?"

Avalon pondered, she was keen with combat and meditation. She reveled in the history of Silent One battles, especially battles involving Jedeo, but in the lore itself, she was no scholar.

"I… know enough to get by," She admitted.

Sa'veen smiled, "Why are we called the 'Silent Ones?"

Avalon knew this one. It was the same question she first asked her instructor, "My Red Wing, we are called 'Silent Ones because we silence the Night."

"What is our Silencer?"

"Our sword, imbued with a sliver from Jedeo's own blade."

"Who was the first of our kind?"

Avalon stopped short of this. She always assumed that Jedeo was the first Silent One, but she was not, "Autumn, sister of Jedeo."

"When Autumn created the first order, she took a vow of silence. Why?"

Avalon was not sure of this one either. This was getting into the deeper and more obscure parts of Jedean lore. She also wondered the purpose behind the quiz? Was this all a final test? She knew she had to make a guess, "Because…Jedeo was mute."

"Yes, partially right. Do you remember how Jedeo's voice was lost when her throat was cut during an attempt on her life? Autumn established the first order on the anniversary of that day. In homage, Autumn took a vow of silence. Another reason why we are called 'Silent Ones'," Sa'veen stood, taking her blade from the shrine, "Avalon, you have proved to be a most valued Silent One. It is time that you take on more duties. I wish to make you Silver Wing."

"I'm skipping a rank?" Avalon gasped.

"Not just that, I wish to send you to Lost Dawns in Cypress to start a temple there. You'll need that extra rank to start training Silent Ones," Sa'veen said seriously.

Cypress, Avalon's old home. She knew that one day her past would catch up with her, but she was not sure she was prepared for such a day.

"Silver Wing Avalon, what do you say."

"When do I leave?"

"In the morning, I've prepared a platoon of thirty Silent Ones to assist you, as well as a Bronze Wing to serve as a lieutenant."

Avalon gawked at the news, "Thirty Silent Ones? Why so many?"

Sa'veen snapped her fingers, "Ah yes, I did forget to mention that Long Whisper is going to war with Estinia alongside Varis. You will be joining the young king."

Avalon raised an eyebrow. The news got wilder and wilder, "Why would we be getting involved in such a conflict?"

"With the Silent Ones establishing a presence in Long Whisper and Varis, it shows good faith to assist those countries in times of great need. Are you prepared to assist in such a task?"

Avalon had seen combat all her life. All she knew was how to take lives. Whether it was under the banner of the Black Rabbits, Silent Ones, or anyone else, it was all the same to her.

"Jedeo will grant me strength," Avalon said, holding her fist to her heart and bowing her head.

"Amen."

49

Elucard poked his head out of the covered wagon. Marcus sat quietly at the reins, scanning the path ahead. Elucard had not been in Lost Dawns since he slew King Jaelyn. Now, the city was more alive than ever. He had never seen a place as loud and crowded as this. When last he came, everything was so calm. It was as if the city itself was already mourning the king it had yet to lose. But now, the city was bustling and alive with the sound of joy. As the wagon approached the city's center, Elucard could not help but be amazed by the sight of the elder tree. Its enormous branches stretched far and wide, reaching toward the heavens, and its roots twisted and burrowed along the lowest depths of the city.

Once they arrived, Marcus led Wiccer and Elucard through the castle halls toward the throne room. Elucard was appropriately shackled between them as a precaution. The three pushed through the large ebonwood doors and were met by a gasping court filled with nobles from the seven noble tribes and the countless advisers Koda had in his service.

Upon the sight of the chained assassin, several guards unsheathed their blades and rushed at Elucard. Elucard did not flinch, but held his neck exposed as if greeting his certain fate.

"At ease, men," Marcus commanded.

Koda raised himself from his throne, his wolf growling with exposed fangs. Koda watched the nobles as they whispered amongst themselves. However, this time Koda was not the child he once was. No longer was he helpless and scared.

Fury set into his face as he raised Elucard into the air with the Magi. Koda walked forward as Elucard struggled with his new situation. With one hand holding the assassin in place, he morphed the other into a frightening mass of tangled thorns. He kept his grip stern so that he could impale Elucard in a single thrust.

"You have a mere moment to explain yourself, Marcus Newsun. I will grant you that much because of the respect I have for you," Koda said in an angry and impatient tone.

"Father, this isn't going to work, let's cut our losses short and just hand him over!" Wiccer lowly said in Marcus's ear.

"Have faith," Marcus replied.

Marcus moved Elucard behind him, away from the glaring king and cautiously approached the steps of the throne.

"My king, I bring not a Rabbit, but an ex-Rabbit. He wishes to serve you by hunting down his former clan."

"Rabbit or not, the kingslayer himself stands shackled and bound behind you. You will hand him over, and he will hang for his crimes!" His voice was sterner and louder. He exuded authority and his words resounded in the great hall, snuffing out the whispers of the noblemen.

"My king, the Black Rabbits have not simply disbanded. They will find an alternative way to increase their numbers, and when they do, they will continue to hold this nation hostage," Marcus retorted.

Koda approached closer, and although Marcus' large frame towered over him, he was still the one in control. Wildeye followed closely at his side.

"In which case the soldiers you are to be training will cut down any Black rabbit threat," Koda spat harshly.

"Your soldiers can not defeat a Black Rabbit. I do not know how to counter their training," Marcus said flatly.

Koda was silent but furious. The new army was his only answer to the Black Rabbits and here the great Marcus Newsun was telling him that they were not enough to defeat his foe. He looked down at his familiar, as if looking for advice. After a moment, he walked back to his throne and sat down.

"Tell me what this ex-Rabbit is here for, then," Koda said with defeat in his voice.

"My king, my lords, I propose that we use a former Rabbit to kill Rabbits. Elucard may, at one point, have been your most dangerous fugitive... but now he can be your most dangerous asset. He, under the watchful eye of my son, will train a squad of soldiers to become assassins that will have the knowledge and training to hunt assassins. They will be the ARO, Anti-Rogue Operatives," Marcus explained, as if he had rehearsed this pitch many times, before.

A Leafsong princess looked eyed the mysterious Elucard with great interest, "I am curious, Marcus, does this criminal really possess the skill to defeat one of our soldiers with such ease?"

Marcus grinned. He had captivated the nobles, and convincing the nobles of this crazy plan was half the work. He winked at Elucard, who was both bored and insulted by the question that the princess had asked.

"My dear, this Black Rabbit would not bother showcasing his skill unless he was fighting at least three men." Marcus waited as the nobles gawked in shock and excitement before continuing, "And he'll do it whilst still shackled!"

Elucard did not know how to feel about being on display like some circus animal. He knew Marcus meant well, but he seemed to be enjoying himself a bit too much. It was true, he could take out three soldiers, even while chained, but his skills were never meant for showing off.

Three guards ushered close to Elucard, their swords poised to strike. Elucard stood completely still, his hands, heavy with the iron chains, hung in front of him. The assassin watched as each man got into position, forming a half circle around him, before one man charged, slashing down with his weapon.

Elucard moved quickly, dashing into the swing of the man on his right, thrusting a pin-point strike into the under-arm of his assailant. The attack stiffened the man's arm, dropping his weapon. Instantly afterwards, Elucard swung the guard in a shoulder throw into the man that was on his left. Both barreled to the ground.

The remaining soldier cleaved horizontally into Elucard. With swift thinking, Elucard tightened his chain straight, blocking the swing. Elucard then flipped over the man and used his chain as a garrote to choke him.

"Elucard, enough!" Marcus broke out, halting the fight.

Elucard kicked the gagging man away from him and bowed to Koda.

Marcus nodded to Elucard, as if silently thanking him before turning to Koda, "Elucard is aptly trained. He told me that before becoming an enemy to his clan, he was of a high rank. All the same, a lesser skilled Rabbit is still capable of defeating our men."

Koda held his words, watching his nobles discuss what they had just seen. They gobbled up the excitement of such savagery and chirped with thrill. They were like a flock of chickens clucking ceaselessly in a coop. He studied Elucard, and then Wiccer, who seemed to be avoiding eye contact with anyone, caught his eye.

"Wiccer. You have as much justification to despise this elf as I do. I wish for your opinion to weigh in. Can I trust such a person?" Koda asked.

Wiccer, who was leaning against a pillar with his arms folded, walked forward. He jeered at Elucard, before letting out a heavy sigh, "This is beyond a matter of trust, my king. It is a matter of necessity."

Koda slowly nodded, "What of the other Rabbit? Wouldn't she suffice?"

Wiccer knew Koda spoke of Elisa. While she could train the soldiers to an extent, Wiccer knew that she would not be as willing or as adept at it. It was true that she was a formidable opponent, but she was not the same as Elucard. Elucard was ARO's best hope of becoming everything his father wanted it to become.

"My king, Elucard is the only one who can train our soldiers to be strong and brutal enough to defeat the Rabbits for good."

Koda looked at the wave of interested noble faces that surrounded him. They had bought into this little performance, but he had not. However, it was difficult to argue with such results displayed by Elucard.

"I will need time to make a decision. Until then, Elucard will be held in a cell," said Koda.

Elucard nodded, allowing himself to be taken into custody.

***

Koda sat with Wiccer for a late dinner in the dining hall. Wildeye curled up against Koda's leg. Marcus had called it an early night, and was slumbering peacefully in a guest room.

Koda sipped the smoothing honey mint tea, taking in the sweet aroma. Wiccer likewise enjoyed his tea. Their conversation was an echo of the one earlier in the throne room.

"You can't sit there and tell me that it is not a matter of trust," Koda said, in between sips.

"Trust could play a small part, my king, but not as much as you might think," Wiccer strained.

"What's keeping him from turning around and stabbing me in the back?"

Wiccer bit his lip. He did not trust Elucard either, but he did seem sure he could be trusted enough not to harm the king.

"His vendetta keeps him on our side."

"Vendetta?" Koda asked, not knowing what brought Elucard to their custody in the first place.

"His clan must have turned on him violently. They left him for dead and now he wants their throats. As far as he is concerned, he would go

230

to any means necessary if it meant it would take down the Black Rabbits."

Koda tried to imagine what could have pushed a loyalist such as Elucard to the point of no return.

"This vengeance…It will keep him on our side?

"We can only h–"

"Hold on!" Koda said sharply, cutting Wiccer off.

Wildeye snarled viscously. Koda received images flashing in his head of a shadow in the rafters. Everything in his mind screamed danger. Where was this premonition coming from? Was it from Wildeye? His train of thought was interrupted by the clatter of a figure landing on their table. The figure was draped in a deep purple cloak. He was dressed in black and gray assassin's garbs. Belts fastened around his waist and legs held knives and utility pouches. His long hair was a vibrant purple, a color similar to Elisa's. A silver steel clown mask covered his face. In one hand he pointed a sword at Koda.

Wiccer knew exactly who it was, "You!" he roared.

"You are a difficult one to find, my king. Nevertheless, here you are." Inle's voice was low, but sounded amused.

"Guards!" Koda shouted at the top of his lungs. Several soldiers with long halberds thundered through the doors to come to their king's aid.

Inle chuckled, hopping joyfully off of the table. After a sudden flash of blades, he stood atop the table once more, wiping his blade from the collapsing guards' blood.

Wiccer unsheathed his sword, moving between Inle and Koda, "I do not know why you are here, but I will have my vengeance all the same."

Inle cocked his head, and snickered, "Yes, yes, you do look familiar. I'm guessing your superior did not survive his wounds that night."

Wiccer clenched his teeth, his anger overriding his collective discipline, "He was my brother!"

Inle bowed, "I will then take credit for that deed. However, we'll have to play this little game later. I'm on Black Rabbit business here."

Wiccer rushed him in a fit of rage, "This is no game!"

Wiccer swept downward but missed as Inle side-stepped him and ran forward toward Koda. Wiccer rotated to his right and swung at the passing assassin. Inle dropped to his knees to slide under the attack.

Between Inle and Koda, Wildeye leaped at the assassin, bearing her fangs. Inle ducked and continued his advance toward the king. Koda jumped backward and manipulated Wiccer's wooden chair to grow rapidly and knock the attacker sideways. Inle, taken off-guard, spun violently, crashing onto the table. Wiccer did not hesitate as he brought his sword down on Inle. Inle rolled to the left and pushed himself back onto his feet.

"It seems this king has more fight in him than the former one," Inle said, devilishly.

Koda hovered the chair in front of him, while Wiccer circled behind Inle. The shadow elf put his second hand on his sword, now putting more effort in his advances. Before Inle could attack, Wiccer and Koda advanced first.

Wiccer slashed for Inle's head, but was parried by the Rabbit's blade. At that same moment, Koda rushed an overgrown mess of roots from the chair, hurdling at Inle. Always a step ahead, Inle jumped and ran along the roots towards Koda. The king moved backwards, manipulating twisting branches from the neighboring chairs and table, but Inle tumbled and dodged each wild attack.

Inle landed beside Koda and caught him with a side kick, knocking him across the dining table. Wildeye slid into Inle's peripheral vision, lunging for the shadow elf's throat, but caught Inle's forearm as he went to intercept the deadly attack. Wiccer leapt forward with a series of steel flurries. Despite his other hand being held by the wolf, Inle worked overtime to block the majority of attacks, before parrying the last into Wildeye.

Wildeye yelped as she released her grasp on Inle. Inle spotted Koda wincing from an unseen wound before the Rabbit cartwheeled over the table to go after the king.

Wiccer jumped over to follow but was met with a combination of kicks and punches rendering him dazed. Inle grabbed Wiccer by the throat, laying him splayed out on the cold ground.

Recovering quickly, Koda attempted to cast another spell, but a trio of well placed daggers lodged into the king's hands and arms. Koda hissed in pain as he stumbled backward in fear. Inle dropped down and swept his foot, tripping Koda's legs. Spinning with the grace that only a Rabbit could have, Inle flourished his blade into Koda's face.

"Don't fret, my king. I am only here to bring you a message," Inle said, grinning wickedly under his mask.

Koda swallowed hard, still frightened by the figure towering over him.

"Know this. We Black Rabbits are not threatened by your attempts to quell us. We still control your roads. We still control your villages. We still control you!" Inle's emphasis on the word "you" lingered in Koda's mind as he grabbed the king's hand. With a vice-like grip, Inle squeezed his finger and removed a golden ring.

"Use this knowledge well, my king, and have pleasant night," Inle said as he bowed and vanished into the shadows.

After he was convinced Wildeye's wound was non-threatening, Koda scrambled to Wiccer, who was just coming to, "You were right."

Wiccer eyed him fuzzily, his head still foggy, "Huh?"

"Bring me Elucard."

50

The sands whipped in the hot winds as the dry earth cracked underneath the weight of her feet. All around her the crowds cheered.

"Night Whisper!"

"Night Whisper!"

"Night Whisper!"

It was all she'd known for years. Her other name was like dust. It took no form or shape. It had no meaning. All that existed now was that of "Night Whisper."

Sweat dribbled down the side of her face. Blood blotched across her hands and armor. The sun above was unforgiving; a blessing for a cold desert night, but a curse on a day such as this.

Across from her was a mountain of a man. He dwarfed her small frame. From his shoulders to his waist were intricate tattoos; each represented a horde he fought for. His veins bulged over his ripped muscles. His jawline was hard and chiseled. His brow pushed forward leaving his white eyes in a layer of shadow. He needed no weapon, for the bones in his hands had become rock solid over the many years of breaking them over others' bodies and faces.

Although the crowd cheered her name, she was the underdog. It was Uther Ironsoul that she could never defeat. Today would be no different.

Night Whisper dashed forward thrusting her short gladius into Uther's abdomen. The giant man grinned with an arched upper lip. He showed that the pain was but another pleasure in his life, akin to the naked body of a helpless woman. With a heavy fist, he backhanded Night Whisper away, having her body slam backwards at least six feet.

Dazed, Night Whisper found a spear at her side and flung it keenly into his shoulder. Uther took little notice of the protruding shaft as he rushed forward. Night Whisper stepped to the right and landed a series of jabs to his side, ending with a sturdy kick that would have splintered the ribs of a lesser man. Not Uther though. Grabbing her by the throat, he lifted her up in the air and brought her smashing into the ground on her back.

Night Whisper's vision blacked for a brief second, hearing the jeers and gasps of the arena audience. Struggling to stay conscious, she came to at the same time a large foot came crashing down onto her.

Screaming, Avalon woke up from her nightmare. Her breathing was a labored pant, her eyes wide with fear from a long past of trauma. She slid to the side of her bed and inhaled deeply, slowly trying to calm herself. It was only a dream. She looked around her cabin, calmly feeling the gently rocking of the boat. She tightly gripped her blanket as she swallowed the nightmare to the back of her mind.

Her cabin door swung violently open.

"Silver Wing Avalon, are you alright?" said the Silent One approaching the room. She inspected the cabin, sword in hand. Satisfied that they were alone, she sheathed the long sword onto her side and quickly tried to inspect Avalon for any signs of an attack.

"I'm alright...what is your name?" Avalon swatted the Silent One's attempts to check on her.

"Bronze Wing Adema. I'll be leading your platoon in your stead."

Avalon had to struggle to keep from staring at Adema's strange features. Avalon had seen several types of elves in her travels. Mist elves, dune elves, shadow elves, but this elf had long black veins that seemed to carve cracks into her face. Her eyes were amber, and her hair was a pale white. Avalon brushed past Adema and made her way to the deck of the ship. The waters swayed the transport boat in a soothing fashion. It seemed her nightmare only awoke Adema, for the rest of the ship was quiet.

"So you are my 'First Blade'," Avalon said, amused with the idea that Silent Ones might use Black Rabbit ranks.

"I don't follow, my Silver Wing," Adema followed her out, still unaware of the reason behind Avalon's terrified scream.

Avalon walked out of her cabin and onto the deck of the ship. The night was cool after a light rain. She leaned against the railing, still visibly shaken from the nightmare. Adema rested her hand on her Silencer's pommel and attempted to prod the issue, "That must have been some nightmare. Do you need to talk?"

Avalon lowered her head and was silent for a long stretch of time, "I left my past behind to stop the needless killing—to stop my needless suffering. However, before I reached my sanctuary, I was sold into slavery as a gladiatrix. With the Black Rabbits, they give you a purpose. It might be a false sense of purpose, but you truly believe you kill for a purpose greater than yourself. Do you understand, Adema?"

"I admit, my Silver Wing, I could never understand the road you walked without walking it myself. I was trained to become a Silent One as a small youth. It is the only life I have known."

Avalon smiled, "You and I, we may have grown up on opposite ends of the sword, but we are much alike. The Black Rabbits gave me a false purpose, but it was something I could hold onto. When I became a gladiatrix, killing was a means to survive. There was nothing noble in it. I admit I was good, but..."

Avalon gently touched her face, softly running the back of her hand over the several scars that riddled her face. In her years in the slave pits, she had been beaten to near death over and over. However, like bones that broke, she healed and grew stronger. Avalon was reborn over and over, harder and stronger than before.

"He was better than me. He could take more punishment and he was stronger. I had speed, I had skill, but I still lost. I lost every time. And every time I recovered, I became more determined to end his life. I had never felt as much bloodlust in my entire life than I did when I fought him."

Adema grew tense as she saw the look of murderous intent creep up on Avalon's face. She watched as Avalon's hands trembled. It wasn't fear that caused the shaking, but excitement.

"Avalon?"

Avalon stopped as a flood of adrenaline flushed from her body. She noticed her hands were tightly clawing into the railing.

"Get some rest, Adema."

51

Vada kneeled before her Silent Master, weary and defeated. Her once crisp Black Rabbit clothes were now old and tattered. Her sagging eyes were a testament to the fact that she had gotten little or no sleep in the years that she spent hunting her former blade sister. She held quiet as Ryjin studied her.

Finally she broke the silence, "Master I–"

"Is she dead?" Ryjin said, not letting Vada finish.

Vada lowered her head. She did not have a real answer for that question. Her mission was to find and kill Avalon. Neither of which she was sure she did. All she knew was that after hunting her down for over three years, she was tired and wanted to go home.

"Master I tracked Avalon to the desert realm of Scorch. There I learned she was captured and sold as a slave to be thrown into the arena pits. I heard rumors of one called "Night Whisper." I could never get close enough to this gladiatrix to see if she was Avalon, but she fought like her."

"Is she dead?" Ryun asked once more.

"If she is Night Whisper, she will die a gladiatrix or die serving as a slave," Vada replied, her head still lowered as Ryjin glowered over her.

"Vada you have been gone for too long. I welcome you home. However you should know that in the time you were gone, you were replaced as the First Blade."

Vada bowed. She knew that with her absence, the clan would have a new High and First Blade. She was no fool. It just meant she would have to prove herself all over again—a task she was ready for.

"My Silent–" Legion appeared in the entrance, Inle by his side. A look of surprise covered his face when he saw that Vada had returned. He stepped further in the quarters, ushering Inle to follow.

"My Silent Master, Inle has returned from his mission," he continued, trying to keep from asking questions about Vada and her pursuit of Avalon.

Vada looked up, eager once more to be apart of the inner workings of her clan. She studied Legion, but found him hard to read. He seemed to have love, loss, regret, and confusion swirled together in an emotional mess deep within his eyes. Vada was unsure what to make of it, but it was clear that she had missed more than she knew.

The Silent Master nodded toward Vada, "You may leave us."

Legion quickly caught her arm and objected, "My Master. This is Vada, she was the former First Blade. I must insist that she stays. Not only does she need to get caught up on the status of our clan, but I value her opinion."

Inle's eyes lit up at the idea of being in the presence of some type of legendary former First Blade.

"Very well; Vada you may stay," Ryjin said quietly.

Vada nodded, showing her thanks. Legion gave Vada a quick summary of what she had missed before having Inle give his report.

"I have returned from Lost Dawns to say that the mission was a success." Inle held up the glinting gold signet as proof, "I defeated the Mage King, his wolf, and a former White Cloak. Showing them that no matter how hard they fight, they will alway be a step down from a Rabbit."

"A daring power play, Inle. It is true, this will show King Koda that the Rabbits still hold power over Long Whisper, but we must do something about our recruitment situation," grinned the Silent Master.

"If I may," Vada started, "I heard through my travels that King Dallin of Varis and King Aric of Estinia are going to war with each other and that King Koda is already gearing up to aid Dallin. Perhaps we can use this knowledge to our advantage."

Legion nodded as if forming an idea, "What we need is to do is form an allegiance with Estinia. Find a way to sell our services and, in exchange, gain recruits from their soldiers."

"Master, I will travel to Estinia and put this plan into motion with your permission," Inle said quickly, eager to prove himself once again.

Ryjin nodded in approval of Inle's request.

"Master, I seek permission to join him!" Vada pleaded, not willing to let her chance to prove herself anew pass.

"Very well. The both of you must prepare to leave at tomorrow's first light," Ryjin said dismissing them.

***

"You just got back today, and now you're leaving?" Elisa whined as she plopped backwards on Vada's cot. She was thrilled to have her best and only friend in the clan back. But Vada was about to disappear just as suddenly as she had reappeared.

"Elisa, I need to do whatever it takes to get in the good graces of the Silent Master again," Vada said as she packed a large bag.

Elisa strolled over and swiped the bag over her head, "At least tell me about this mission that's so important."

"You know I can't tell you that, now give me back my bag!" Vada frowned as she reached to snatch back her belongings from her persistent friend.

Elisa began tossing the contents out in a successful effort to annoy her friend, "Can't or won't?"

Vada grabbed her bag back, her reach as a human was longer than that of her shadow elf friend, but the damage was done, she had to repack, "Both."

Elisa stole the bag back and jumped onto the cot, holding the bag high in the air, "Well, I'm going to make sure you can't pack until you tell me something! You forget I held Lost Dawns in terror for a year, this will be nothing!" she said, giving a smarmy grin.

"Elisa Moonshard, you are insufferable! Alright, you broke me. Inle and I are traveling to Estinia to strike an alliance and gather Rabbit recruits from its army. I'll probably be gone for awhile, so you'll have to hold down the fort. Now give me back that bag!"

Elisa's eyes widened with the news. This was exactly the type of thing Wiccer needed to hear. The sound of the door sliding open shook her back to reality. Inle stood at the entrance.

"Vada, Legion wishes to see you."

Vada nodded, walking out. Inle slowly walked into the quarters, approaching Elisa, "I spent a bit of time at your former home."

"My home?" Elisa asked, unsure of Inle's intentions.

"You spent a good of time with the White Cloaks," Inle said as he backed Elisa into a wall

"I was their prisoner, if that's what you mean."

"That must have been a terrible time for you," Inle came in close so that she could see his bright silver eyes underneath his mask.

"I managed," Elisa squirmed trying to get past Inle

Inle thrusted his hands against the wall, trapping Elisa, "I think you and I both know how you managed."

"I've got to go," Elisa said trying to push Inle away from her.

Inle smiled fiercely under his mask, letting Elisa quickly walk away from him, "Don't go too far, shadow kin."

52

"Atten-tion!" Wiccer's voice rang out across the large squad of young soldiers out on the parade field. Each elf snapped straight, their heels clicked together, and their arms fell flat against their sides.

"Listen up, men! I'm Sergeant Wiccer Newsun. A former White Cloak and current instructor of you Long Whisper lot!" Wiccer walked slowly, but intimidatingly, in front of each soldier before falling back next to Elucard.

"This is Elucard Freewind. He'll be instructing those of you who decide to join us." Wiccer finished by motioning to Elucard to take over.

Elucard was quiet for a moment. He walked up to each soldier, inspecting their arms, testing out their balance, and checking the strength of their backs. He was pleased. These elves would prove to be excellent recruits. Marcus did promise that he would find the best recruits for them. Sadly, Marcus would not be able to see his idea come to fruition from his outpost in Varis.

"Sergeant, permission to ask a question!" shouted out a soldier on the far end. He waited for Wiccer to nod before continuing, "Sergeant, we were told that you would be putting together a special unit that was specifically designed to combat the Black Rabbits."

"That's correct," Wiccer replied. He could already tell where this line of questioning was going.

"Sergeant, this soldier's question is: Who is this elf that is inspecting us and what are his qualifications?"

Wiccer smirked, these soldiers were, indeed, well trained, "Men, Elucard Freewind is not some random mercenary we picked up off the road. He is a high ranking Ex-Black Rabbit."

A wave of sneers crashed over the squad, another soldier piped up, "Sergeant, permission to speak freely?"

"Speak freely, Private," replied Wiccer.

"You expect us to take orders from a Black Rabbit? The scum of Cypress? He's probably killed more of our people than we've killed of his kind! What if he was related to the killing of Jaelyn?"

Several members of the squad rumbled in agreement.

Elucard walked up to him, staring him dead in the eyes, "You will listen to me, because I am the only one that can teach you to kill those like me!"

"We'll never take orders from you," the soldier jeered, walking away. All but one followed him.

"Well, damn," Wiccer cursed, "I guess that went over better than I thought it would."

Elucard glanced at the one remaining soldier. He was a thin elf. He had messy platinum hair, vibrant sky blue eyes, and a slightly pointed nose. He grinned, showing off his pearly white teeth.

"Do you actually know the Rabbit who killed Jaelyn?" the lone soldier asked.

"I killed Jaelyn," Elucard said flatly, giving him his full attention now.

"Well, then I would like to join your unit. Training under a Rabbit isn't as interesting as training under *the* Rabbit."

Wiccer waved him away, "There isn't going to be a unit."

The soldier raised an eyebrow, "I'm guessing you need a few more bodies. Perhaps I can be of service."

Wiccer looked at Elucard, then back at the soldier, "What is your name, Private?"

"I am Calsoon. I will lead you to your new squad."

***

Calsoon led Wiccer and Elucard into the deepest reaches of the Roots to find his first recruit. Keeping one hand on his coin purse and the other on his sword hilt, Wiccer thought back to his last venture into the Roots. The Roots seemed have decayed even more and more as the years passed by. Elucard looked unfazed by the state of the city, but all the same, he kept his wits about him as he followed their guide.

They stopped at a dilapidated tavern. Several apartments were stacked on top of it in a precarious manner. A maze of fire escapes and gutters framed the structure. Calsoon rapped on the front door. A peephole opened up before a gruff voice called out behind the heavy door.

"Password."

"Shadows in the wind weep silently," Calsoon whispered.

The peep hole closed and a sound of chains sliding and locks turning clattered from behind the door. Soon the door opened, and a large black furred Kanis stepped aside. His arms were folded across his chest as he eyed Wiccer and Elucard suspiciously.

"What is this place, Calsoon?" Wiccer asked with worry blanketed on his face.

"Welcome to the Drain. Try not to make direct eye contact with anyone. It's seen as a threat," Calsoon said with a cheerful tune.

Inside the Drain, the air was heavy with a musky smell that was mixed with the thick smell of burning tobacco. The window had a film of grime letting only sparse light through. The tavern was loud with the sounds of patrons throttling each other in harsh scuffles and cat calling of the bar wenches for a refill of ale. Calsoon, Wiccer, and Elucard had to watch their step as they avoided broken glass and puddles of vomit still dripping over the tables from collapsed drunks.

"I thought you were leading us to new recruits. Why are we here?" Wiccer asked, his frustration slowly getting the best of him.

"How much money do you have on you, sergeant?" Calsoon asked as he led the two to the back of the pub.

"Thirty dawn-face. Why?" Wiccer asked as he grew more and more anxious. The patrons of the Drain leered at his clean, pressed clothes and straight, trimmed hair.

Calsoon stopped at another wolf-folk bouncer, "We're here to see Basilisk."

The bouncer moved aside and Calsoon beckoned for Wiccer and Elucard to follow him into a small room that served as an office. There, sitting behind a desk was a sharply dressed, rather heavy set human. He had olive skin and was balding. He was dressed in red nobleman's attire. A teal kerchief sat in his front pocket. He smiled once he saw Calsoon, standing up with his stomach slightly pushing his desk away.

"Calsoon, my favorite runner. Do you have my fifty-seven trit?"

"Ah, Basilisk, afraid I could only rummage up thirty," Calsoon said while bowing down graciously.

"What do you suppose you are to do about the twenty-seven trit you owe me?"

Calsoon grabbed Wiccer's sword and tossed it onto the desk, "A finely crafted sword is at least worth another forty knotted-leaves, consider the extra a bonus for your patience."

Wiccer snatched his sword back and sheathed it, now livid, "Calsoon, I order you to tell me who this man is and what we are doing here."

Calsoon smiled and bowed, "Of course, of course. You see our mutual friend Blayvaar has a small debt to pay Mr. Basilisk here. If I can't find the money to pay it, he will take Blayvaar's hands as payment. Blayvaar would be a tad bit useless to us if he were to lose his hands."

"Who is Blayvaar?" Wiccer roared, still fuming.

"He is your soon to be recruit. A skilled thief and master of the throwing knife."

Elucard tossed a sizable purse of silver trit onto the desk, coins spilling off onto the floor.

Wiccer leaned over to Elucard's ear and whispered, "Where did you find that money?"

Elucard spoke from the side of his mouth, "When Calsoon asked you how much money you had, I assumed having some would be important. So I swiped some from a drunk."

Basilisk finished counting, looking quite pleased, "This will do nicely," he said, snapping his fingers. A door opened up behind him and two goons tossed a wily looking elf onto the ground. His hands were tied and he was gagged with a dirty rag.

Calsoon helped him up, brushed him off, and removed his gag, "Blayvaar, my friend. I think it would be best if we made our exit."

Outside on the streets, Blayvaar vigorously shook Calsoon's hand, "I can't thank you enough Calsoon! I owe you my life!"

"My friend, as much as I'd love for you to owe me your life, it was these fine gentleman that deserve your thanks. And they don't need your life…well, not entirely," Calsoon quipped as he slipped his hand free from the vice-grip of the ever grateful Blayvaar.

Blayvaar blinked at Elucard and Wiccer, "How can I thank you two?"

Wiccer looked at Elucard, who nodded, before looking back at Blayvaar, "We would like to recruit you to use your services to hunt Black Rabbits."

Blayvaar smirked, "Not my usual thing, but I'll join you."

***

Trek knelt down to study the the mud and stones on the path. His brother stood over him, blocking out what little light Trek had in the thicket.

"Which way?" Rulan said, clearly impatient.

Trek brushed his fingers over the wet mud while muttering to himself.

"I think you're distracting him, Rulan," A smaller elf said. Like her two brothers, her hair was a dark shade of red. She wore it tied up in a twisted bun. She sat down with one leg curled under the other on a boulder while inspecting the medicinal supplies in her haversack.

"Well I think some of that mud is stuffed in his ear. I said, 'Which way?'" Rulan flicked the tip of his brother's elven ear.

"Hey, quit it! He went this way," Trek shouted, "Essie, maybe you should stitch Rulan's mouth shut so I can concentrate better."

Trek and Rulan dashed down the path and across the brook. As the triplets darted through the woods, Trek stopped suddenly. Rulan and Essie bumped into the back of their halted brother, nearly toppling him over.

"Trek, what is it this time? We're going to be the last ones to finish!" Rulan huffed.

Trek stared into the deep brush, squinting his eyes and going over various details in his mind, "There something amiss. We're being watched."

Essie peered at the direction Trek was looking in, "I don't see anything."

"Guys, the finish line is just over there, I can hear everyone. We're going to be the laughingstock of the scouts if we're last again!"

Trek turned to look beyond the forest border. He listened to the cheers of celebration as another team of scouts passed the finish line. He turned back to the brush, but the feeling that he was being watched had subsided, "Let's go."

Trek, Rulan, and Essie reached the finish line with their peers chuckling at them.

"Well, well. The Windfoot Triplets are the last ones again," chided their platoon leader. He turned to a group of men, "Sergeant Wiccer, you've seen them work. Any scouts catch your fancy?"

Wiccer turned to Calsoon, "You're sure we want the Windfoot siblings? They performed the worst."

Calsoon grinned delightfully as he watched Elucard emerge from the woods.

"They were the only ones that knew I was watching," Elucard said as he walked up to Trek, "You knew I was there. How?"

Trek blushed, not used to receiving compliments, "There were two set of tracks. The first was from our platoon leader. The other was there, but it was very faint; I'm guessing you wanted to be tracked, but only by a scout with true skill."

"You have that skill," Elucard said simply.

"I – I suppose," Trek said modestly.

Wiccer turned to the platoon leader who was surprised by Trek's skills, "We'll take the triplets."

***

Lear laid about sluggishly on a swinging hammock. The sun was setting and a nice breeze rushed through his shady retreat by the creek. He gnawed on a long blade of grass between his teeth. His long whiskers bounced slightly as a gnat buzzed on top of them. His long tail swayed back and forth, dangling off of the hammock. His ears twitched as he noticed a small group of people gathering around him.

"A cat folk? In Lost Dawns?" Wiccer asked befuddled.

Lear opened one eye and retorted with the grass still clenched in his teeth, "This yikahti doesn't like to be called 'cat folk'!"

Calsoon bowed to Lear, "Forgive Wiccer. Despite his own origins, he is not used to the more exotic visitors of Lost Dawns."

Lear rested his eyes once more, "This yikahti is forgiving. Be on your way."

Calsoon bowed again, "Actually, my friend, they are here to see you. To test your talent and perhaps offer you something you've always wished for."

Lear snapped his eyes open and leaped out of the hammock, drawing his saber, "Who wishes to test This yikahti's talent? He who dares test the talent of Lear Crescenteye better bring his own."

Calsoon smiled smugly at Wiccer, "Go ahead, Sergeant, test his talent."

"He wants to duel me?" Wiccer asked, slowly drawing his own sword.

"Isn't that why you are here?" Lear growled, annoyed by his challenger's hesitance, "Perhaps you are not worth This yikahti's time."

"My dear Lear, haven't you always wished that a true challenge would present itself to you in Lost Dawns? You once heard of the great warrior clans of Long Whisper. Did you not wish that they would accept you as one of their own? Well, you may know that they are gone, but instead there is an army," Calsoon explained.

"Bah, this army is full of talentless hacks," Lear said as he leapt back into his hammock. He waved Wiccer off and ignored him.

"You just haven't been looking in the right places. Duel me and I will show you that my talent is greater. When I defeat you, you will have a chance to fight for us and find the challenges you seek," Wiccer stepped in, seeing where Calsoon was leading Lear.

245

Lear twirled his saber in an expert display of swordsmanship before pointing his blade in Wiccer's face, "You say you have more talent than This yikahti? Then show us!" he demanded as he moved once more out of his hammock.

Wiccer thwacked the blade away and dashed in close, slashing diagonally upwards. Lear back flipped on top of the hammock, balancing himself effortlessly. He smiled cockily, then somersaulted over Wiccer, smacking the back of his head.

Wiccer waited for him to land before lunging at him with a thrusting advance. Lear attempted to parry, but Wiccer anticipated the technique and spun, countering with a skillful disarm of Lear's saber. The blade clattered on the ground. Wiccer pressed his sword on the yikahti's chest.

"Such talent!" Lear said in awe.

"The Black Rabbits possess more talent than I. If you join us, we will teach you to combat that talent and you will win," Wiccer said, sheathing his weapon.

Lear grinned a wide and toothy grin, "You have a recruit. This yikahti shall join you."

***

Wiccer and Elucard stood in the tall grass of a wide field. A single wooden silhouette of an upper torso stood above the grass next to them. Calsoon wore his typical silly grin that the two men had become accustomed to.

"I'll bite first. Calsoon, what are we out here for?" Elucard spoke up.

"Wait for it," Calsoon said quietly.

"For wha–" Elucard started, but ducked as an arrow whizzed past him and stuck into the wooden target with a loud 'thunk'"

Wiccer dropped down for cover, "Calsoon, what's going on here!?"

"Your unit could use a crafty marksman. I'm here to get you one."

Elucard poked his head above the grass, another arrow whipped through the air, landing with another solid 'thunk' into the target.

"I think you convinced them enough, Timber. Why don't you come over here and join us?" Calsoon called across the field.

Wiccer and Elucard watched, stunned as the grass slowly grew and morphed into a standing mound. Tossing off the grassy gillie suit, a black cloaked, golden furred Kanis made her way to the small group. She brushed a long fur braid that was slung over her shoulder to her back. Her thin smile wiped away when she grew closer.

246

"This is Timber. She is one of the better archers you will find in this army," Calsoon said introducing her to Wiccer and Elucard.

"Calsoon tells me you two are putting together a special unit to deal with the Black Rabbits," Timber said. Her voice was smooth and quiet, like a whisper.

"Welcome to our team," Elucard said, still shaky from his recent encounter with her deadly aim.

"The pleasure is all mine."

***

The new squad lined up on the parade field. Wiccer moved in front of the squad, doing his best to instruct them how to stand at attention before addressing them.

"You seven are the first of a new unit called the Anti-Rogue Operatives, or 'ARO.' You will be trained to think and fight like a Black Rabbit in order to better combat and counter a Black Rabbit! Your training will be tough! You might not like it, but you will like what you become! You will enter a soldier and emerge a new type of hunter! Are you prepared for this transformation?"

"Yes, sir!" the squad shouted in unison.

"Anything else, Elucard?" Wiccer said, pleased with the new squad.

"Yes, fall in, Wiccer," Elucard said sternly, his arms folded against his chest.

Wiccer looked at him baffled.

"You were always our first recruit," explained Elucard.

Wiccer smirked and fell into the formation.

"Recruits, let's get to work!" Elucard commanded.

53

Imperious City was a dark metropolis. Ominous black-stone walls spanned the city's perimeter. They loomed over the shadowy city, standing one hundred feet tall. Hardened stone and mortar reinforced the walls and blades guarded them from any who would dare attempt to breach them. If the sun were in reach, no doubt this city would have blocked that out as well.

The city itself bloomed from the center outward. The fine architecture of noble establishments could be found closest to the center, forming a gradient of deteriorating buildings and poverty that reached toward the shadow of the walls. The Estinian castle was the centerpiece of it all.

Inle and Vada found themselves moving through the city streets with a personal escort. The soldiers made sure no one came close to their carriage, going so far as to brutally beat any civilian that dared come within an arm's length of it.

"You look nervous, dear Vada. Have you never been to a city such as this before?" Inle asked half-mockingly. His knees were crossed, and he seemed to be enjoying the ride as best he could. But no matter how much of a front he put on for Vada and the Estinian soldiers, it was merely a mask that covered his true thoughts. On the boat trip to Estinia he had heard horror stories of the king and queen. One admittedly drunken sailor told of how the king had ordered a peasant to be publicly disemboweled for having the audacity to criticize a lesser nobleman. Others sang the praises of the monarchs. Inle surmised that the truth must lie somewhere in between, but was nevertheless grotesque. However, his training as a performer allowed him to swallow his unease and move forward. After all, he had performed in front of much tougher crowds than this.

"I have done my fair share of traveling," Vada calmly replied, "I have seen many cultures, but none such as this. If we do not watch our step, we may trip into a cell." Vada kept a keen eye on their escorts who marched alongside the carriage just beyond the window.

"You traveled as far as the deserts of Scorch, yes? My troupe never made it out there. What was it like?"

Vada took her attention off of a soldier and his blackened, imposing armor to face her shadow elf companion, "Lawless," she simply said before turning to look back out the window.

"I see," said Inle, smirking under his steel clown mask.

The carriage passed over several bridges before entering a smaller inner wall, but stopped just outside the castle itself. Its looming towers sent a chill down Vada's spine as she exited the carriage. The entire city, including the Gothic castle, was a far cry from Lost Dawns. She was in awe of the city. It was a different kind of impressive. The very architecture of the buildings around her sent chills scrambling down her spine. Imperious City commanded respect, and few would dare to refuse.

As Inle stepped out of the carriage, a tall, thin man stepped before him. He was flanked on either side by a squad of men in shining black armor. Each stood as tall as a bear. Their armor was decorated with etchings of ravens. Their left pauldrons looked liked outstretched wings, with each feather denoting their different ranks in the metallic colors of gold, silver, and bronze.

The man in the middle was unarmored, instead wearing regal noble clothing of reds and silvers. His sniveling face and slicked-back, black hair gave him the appearance of a rat. He spoke with an air of boredom and bowed in an exotic over-exaggerated manner. His thick Estinian accent would have been difficult to understand if it were not for the extensive traveling that both Inle and Vada had done in the past.

"Velcome to de home of de Div'Rah. Bow to Osalin."

"Div'Rah. That is the title they have given their king. It means 'God-King'," Inle explained. Although the Ebonpaths had never traveled to Estinia, he had heard countless stories from merchants of the Div'Rah and his great army.

Vada nodded before whispering back, "Who is Osalin?"

"He is, I assume," Inle replied, nodding toward the rat-faced man standing before them.

They both looked blankly at Osalin before taking a deep bow before the strange man. He let out a wide grin.

"Rabbits show respect, but de Div'Rah des not trust you, yit." Osalin snapped his fingers and the guards marched forward, pulling out chains and shackles, "Chain dem, nice en tight. Squeeze dem of any rebellion dey may hev en dey bodies. Crush bones ef you hev too."

Vada moved to resist, but Inle quickly grabbed her arm, "Let them do as they like, we are guests here. We must make a good impression," Inle said in the silent whisper of the Rabbits.

Osalin waited for his men to restrain the two Rabbits before having them ushered into the castle. As he lead them to the throne room of the Div'Rah he told grandiose tales of how an ancient raven bestowed King Aric and his queen, Natal, with immortality and great power. The raven promised the two powers greater than any other god so long as he helped overthrow the raven's rival gods. With such power Aric had Estinia rise from the ashes of the ancient dragons that Aric had slain with only his voice. Aric let the other civilizations blossom under his shadow and allowed the sun to burn as long as it paid tribute by transforming into the moon each night. In the end it was the raven god that saw Aric as *his god*.

Vada rolled her eyes at such stories, but Inle was thoroughly entertained by the lore, though he was not convinced of it himself. It did allow him a quick study of how King Aric and his queen saw themselves.

Osalin lead them through two darkwood doors before halting in front of twin golden thrones adorned with jewels. Rich patterns of silver filagree intertwined into the gold, engraved images of ravens holding a crown and scepter. Standing before them was an aged man with a pointed beard and moustache. He wore silk threads of silver and reds much like Osalin, but bore a thick golden and silver chain around his neck that clasped onto a beautiful rare stone which gave off a soft glow. His wife was likewise dressed in a long silver and red dress with a cape of woven raven feathers draping down her back and along the floor.

"My Div'Rah. I hev brought you dese Rabbits dat hev traveled from Long Vhisper to seek audience vith you," Osalin said, making a sweeping bow to his king.

"Vhy are dey en chains?" Aric asked, puzzled by the condition of his guests.

"My love, they are from Long Whisper. They clearly can't be trusted," Queen Natal said with her elegant silk-like voice. She did not have an Estinain accent, and her eyes locked into Aric's as she spoke.

"Keep dem in chains, dey can't be trusted," Aric commanded.

"My King, we have come a great distance just to see you. It is an insult to keep us in such a state!" Vada spat. Her tolerance for this circus had come to an end.

"Silence, Rabbit!" the queen roared. Turning her gaze back to her king, she gently rubbed his chest and brushed his cheek, "My king, these Rabbits are wasting your time. They have nothing of value to offer you."

"Dese Rabbits are vasting my time. Take dem away and lock dem en a prison until I've decided vhat to do vith dem," Aric said, motioning to remove Inle and Vada from the throne room.

"My Div'Rah, we can't leave without giving you the gift we brought for you," Inle calmly said, lifting his closed hand to the best of his ability.

"Gift?" Aric asked, blankly.

Inle attempted to step forward, but was met with the clinking of heavy armor. In a moment's notice, several spear heads were pointed at his neck.

"If I may, my Div'Rah," Inle said holding out an extended hand.

Aric moved forward, confident that Inle was no threat to him. He grasped the small object from the masked Rabbit. Upon examination he saw it was a noble's signet, "De Dawnedge Tribe? Dis es a Long Vhisper ring."

"My Div'Rah, I took that from King Koda Dawnedge himself. You have no doubt heard that the Black Rabbits slew the previous king, however..." Inle trailed off.

Aric raised an eyebrow waiting for the elf to finish.

"This new king is quite the nuisance," Inle chuckled, "I removed his signet with ease, but I wish for nothing more than to remove his head as well!" Inle's mask quaked with the laughter that bellowed from the elf.

Aric too erupted in a heavy belly laugh, "Your face es lek a clown, you funny lek one too. Dis one I lek. Unchain em!"

Natal gracefully moved over to Aric to interject, "My love, that is not a wi—"

"Unchain em now!" Aric commanded again.

After the iron shackles and chains were relieved of Inle, the shadow elf bowed graciously, "My Div'Rah, your kindness will be sung from here and back to Long Whisper. I will personally make sure of this." Inle spotted the quivering impatience on Vada's face, "Perhaps onto business, my Div'Rah?"

"Vhat es et you are here for, clown?" asked Aric, sitting down on his throne.

Inle bowed once more before speaking, "The Black Rabbits have sent my colleague and I to offer you aid in your war against Varis. We are aware of your might, but we assure you that the Black Rabbits would be a valuable asset to your forces."

Aric fiddled with the golden signet again, eying its beauty, and caressing the raised crest of the Dawnedge, "Vhy help us? Vhat do de Black Rabbits hope to gain?"

"We wish for recruits. We ask that a fraction of your soldiers be trained under Vada." Inle gestured toward his chained companion. She bowed at the queue.

"Unchain her," Aric told the nearest guard. He turned to his queen, "Vhat do you tink my queen?"

Natal sneered at Inle, she did not like to be undermined by a foreign elf, but it was clear even to her that the Black Rabbits could prove themselves useful in the future, "You should trust them, my love; they are not your enemies."

Aric stood, making a decision, "I trust dese Rabbits. Dey are not my enemy. Clown, vhat is your name?"

"Inle, my Div'Rah."

"You vill personally lead my Black Rabbits ento battle."

"I only ask that my High Blade be at my side," Inle said quickly trying to adjust to the turn of events.

"Dis High Blade, he es your Rabbit leader in Long Vhisper?"

"Yes, my Div'Rah."

"Very vell, dis High Blade vill stand by your side. Come, ve celebrate our new alliance!"

54

Rulan sailed through the air, landing hard on his back to join his brother who was still grimacing from the soreness that throbbed all over his body. Lear and Blayvaar were the next to be sent flying into the air, flipping into a cluttered mess on the summer's grass. Timber and Calsoon both joined forces for an attack but met a similar fate as Elucard tossed them away, sending them rolling into the ever-growing dogpile of recruits.

Elucard shook his head in disappointment. He turned to Essie, who was anxious to come to the defense her fellow recruits. She shrieked as Elucard grabbed her by the tunic and sent her flailing head over heels onto the ground with an abrupt slam.

"Essie, are you a coward or a medic? You waited until your friends were tossed into a bloody heap before you decided to come to their aid. As an ARO medic, you will fight alongside everyone else," Elucard said lecturing the winded medic, "Wiccer, get them into the weighted vests, they're running another mile before we try this again."

A resounding groan came from the recruits as the dread of a fifth mile set into their minds. The ARO recruits had been training for the last few weeks under Elucard's leadership and each day they regretted signing up for such a grueling experience. Although the majority already served in the military, this level of rigorous training was not something they were used to. At times it felt to the recruits that Elucard had a grudge against them.

"Elucard, they could use a break. The men have been running exercises and routines for five hours straight! They can barely walk, never mind run. No one could possibly function under this regiment," Wiccer intervened. Not even his father had him go through such physical abuse.

Elucard looked over the exhausted faces of his men. They were not Rabbits. They did not have the same fear that a new Black Rabbit recruit had, and they did not have the work ethic that he was accustomed to. Maybe he was pushing them too hard.

"Run the mile with the vest, then you can have your break," he commanded.

Wiccer brought Elucard out of earshot of the recruits, "You're pushing them too hard. They're not like us. They haven't been training since childhood. You ca–"

"If you coddle them, they'll never be like us. They need to be ready to fight men that have been trained to kill since they were children. A Rabbit won't hesitate to slit their throats. A Rabbit thinks they've been commanded by the death goddess to bathe in the blood of their enemies. Our men won't stand a chance unless I train them like a Rabbit."

"Elucard, they'll break before they follow you."

Elucard shoved a weighted vest into Wiccer's chest, "A bone grows stronger after it breaks."

***

The seven recruits knelt in a circle on the edge of the tall grassy archery range. The sun had set and the moon was giving Wiccer very little light to go over his plan of attack. Elucard stood in the center of the field, waiting for his ARO recruits to try to take him down using strategy, physical force, and stealth. If they succeeded then the month of gruesome training had paid off. If they failed, then he would double their workload to beat their failure into their bodies.

Wiccer spoke in a low whisper as he surveyed the field, "We can't use weapons in this exercise so we'll have to use our individual skills to our full advantage. So this is how we're going to execute this…"

Elucard stood motionless in the grass, his eyes fixated on a lone shadowy figure walking on the outer edge of the grass.

A decoy.

Elucard watched the figure for a bit longer as the grass began to move unnaturally in his peripheral vision. Keeping his attention on this new distraction, he was taken off-guard as both Rulan and Trek dove at him from behind.

Two decoys, clever.

Elucard threw Trek over his shoulder, quickly stomping on his face, knocking the young elf unconscious. Enraged, Rulan wrapped his upper arm around Elucard's neck and locked his other arm behind Elucard's head in a fortified blood choke.

Elucard did not have much time to react, as Lear, Timber, and Blayvaar soared from the bushes and surrounded him. Assessing the situation using the years of experience at his disposal, Elucard jabbed his elbow sharply into Rulan's ribs, causing him to release the choke. At the same time, Elucard swung himself over Rulan and kicked him in the small of his back, flinging him into Lear.

Blayvaar came in from the side with a leg sweep as Timber jumped into the air for a high kick. Elucard back-flipped into the tall grass, disappearing from sight.

"Don't split up, it's what he wants!" Wiccer barked as he, Calsoon, and Essie came in from the shadows.

"What do we do, sergeant?" asked Essie.

"Stay tight, make a circle, and watch each other's blind spots. Remember what we were taught!"

The recruits corralled up, scanning the tall grass in the blackness of the night. Elucard made no attempt to make a move.

The recruits grew weary as they waited and waited. Slowly their eyes began to droop as the lack of sleep began to finally catch up to them.

"Stay awake, recruits!" Wiccer shouted, trying to keep their morale high.

The moonlight faded as clouds roamed across the sky. All went black, all went quiet. The ARO members peacefully drifted in and out of sleep as the soothing, chilled night calmly wrapped around them.

"He's here, He's her–" the recruits were stirred awake by Blayvaar's screams as a series of painful kicks and swift punches laid everyone out with the exception Wiccer.

Elucard shook his head once again in disappointment, "You think you recruits deserve sleep? Put on your vests, three miles, now!"

"What are we supposed to learn from you running us into the dirt over and over again?! Nothing! I haven't learned a damn thing, except how much I hate you!" growled Rulan.

Rulan helped a groggy Trek to his feet, "Come on guys, who's with me?"

Elucard's memory flashed to Izian making the same stand against Ridge and Baines.

Lear stepped up to Elucard, "You have much talent, Elucard, but This yikahti wants nothing to do with this challenge."

Elucard was stone faced as one by one each recruit began to walk away.

"Give them some time, friend," said Calsoon before hurrying to catch up to the group.

Elucard lowered his head, "You were right, Wiccer."

"I'm afraid I am," said Wiccer, resting a hand on his shoulder.

***

The Merry Wolf was a popular destination for the soldiers in Lost Dawns. Besides an excellent selection of regional brews, excellent food, and a close location to the barracks, it also provided a small discount to those in military uniforms. The tavern was warm in the winters and cool in the summers. It had a rustic interior that harkened back to the small town inns that many soldiers were accustomed to with a stone hearth that had a pot of lamb stew bubbling and ready for its hungry patrons.

The ARO recruits sat at a large oak table. Timber stared meanly at Rulan who swayed sloppily as he slurped the final drops from his empty mug, still in a miserable stupor. Lear balanced his chair on the back two legs, watching the kanis.

"This yikahti thinks you have something you'd like to get off your chest, Timber."

Blayvaar looked up from his lamb stew, "She thinks we should have never left."

Calsoon grinned cooly, "Then why did she leave?"

Blayvaar shrugged as he leaned back, pretending to stretch and catching a small handful of copper trit from a nearby patron.

"I'm a wolf, I stick to the pack, no matter how foolish they are," she muttered.

"I'm with Timber," Trek spoke up, favoring a large bump on the side of his head, "Elucard might be a mad man, but I could feel myself getting stronger. I got stronger under him in one month than I would have from a lifetime under any other instructor."

"Trek, Elucard would end up killing us before he'd be satisfied with our performance," Rulan said as he tried to wave down a server.

"Essie, you've been quiet, what are your thoughts?" Calsoon asked, prodding the issue further.

"I don't know. I agree with Rulan. Elucard's methods would kill any normal soldier."

"Exactly, Essie!" smiled Rulan.

"But, I also think that we weren't meant to be normal soldiers. We were meant to be ARO."

"Did you say 'Elucard'?" A nearby soldier approached the table. The thick stench of ale rose from his breath. He leaned into Essie and asked again, "Did you say Elucard was training you?"

Essie pushed the soldier's face away from her, "Yes, what of it?"

A small group of soldiers gathered around their table as the drunk soldier ushered himself back into Essie's face, "Elucard killed our king.

He's a criminal that should be hanged and any soldier that accepts his teachings should swing beside him when he does. You're all traitors to your kin!" The crowd of soldiers all echoed the drunken soldier's rant.

Rulan stood up to the best of his ability, "That's my sister you are threatening! Make another move and I'll show you what I learned from that *criminal!*"

"Rulan, sit down, you're drunk," Trek pleaded, trying to reason with his brother.

"Sober enough to beat this guy into a bloody pulp!" Rulan pushed his chair away and staggered his way to the other side of the table.

"You mess with the 12th Spearman Division, you mess with all of us!" shouted the drunk. Immediately several more soldiers rose out of their seats, each sporting a 12th Spearman Division unit patch on their coats and tunics. The ARO recruits all stood to support Rulan.

"We are outnumbered seven to twenty-four," Blayvaar estimated.

"The odds are in our favor, we were trained by Elucard," Timber grinned.

"This yikahti admits he likes this challenge!" Lear chimed in as he rubbed his claws together.

The soldiers rushed the recruits grabbing chairs and brandishing bottles. Several of the ARO recruits hopped up on the oak table thrashing kicks at the soldiers, knocking teeth loose and breaking noses. Lear made his way through the crowd slashing his claws left and right, dodging countless heavy punches. With expert footing, he twirled a sent spinning heel kicks into several chins, sending them flying into neighboring tables.

Blayvaar's fast fingers, coupled with his new combat training, allowed him to swipe a belt and use it as a makeshift whip, slapping the leather across faces while still nimbly dodging incoming attacks.

Timber jumped from table to table, making her way to the bar. A pair of soldiers climbed the counter top after her, but were quickly dispatched with a series kicks followed by a shoulder throw that slammed one soldier into the other, sending them both shattering through a window.

The Windfoot triplets somersaulted from the table and landed in front of the first drunk soldier. Trek swept the soldier's feet, tripping him into Rulan's oncoming uppercut. Essie finished the combination with a heavy front kick that sent the soldier crashing into a nearby table.

The tavern door flung open and a troop of city guards marched into the fray to bring much needed order to the scene.

"ARO let's vanish!" Calsoon cried from the shadows of the backroom.

***

The orange sun cracked the skies as it rose, signaling for another morning on the parade field. Elucard and Wiccer stepped onto the field ready to start a new day of recruiting, but were met with a surprising but very welcome sight. Standing at attention in a perfect line were the seven ARO recruits. Their training uniforms were ragged and blood stained, their knuckles were bruised, and their eyes had dark bags under them. It was very clear that they had not seen a night's sleep. Over their tunics were vests strapped full of weights.

Wiccer smiled at Elucard, who nodded for Wiccer to fall into formation. Elucard walked up and inspected his eight recruits as if checking for imperfections. He stopped in front of Rulan, "A bone grows stronger after it breaks."

Rulan looked at his comrades to the left and right of himself before replying, "We're strong, but not broken."

55

Wiccer had spent many years sparring against only his brother. In his younger years he had always been one step behind and one swing too slow to keep up with the older and more skilled Avren. However, Wiccer was a quick learner, and had Avren still been alive, he was sure he would now have the upper hand as he stepped up to face Elucard.

Wiccer moved, furiously rocking on the balls of his feet, leaping backwards, and dashing quickly forwards. He danced and juked about gracefully, knowing that being even a hair off in his timing would lead to a blundering disaster. Everything he had learned as a White Cloak betrayed him when he started to learn the ways of the Rabbits. Wiccer saw this quickly and rectified it just as fast. His once rigid footwork and traditional combat style was being replaced by the erratic footwork and adaptable combat style of a Black Rabbit. The thought of using this vicious training against the very clan that created these techniques electrified him.

Wiccer slid to the side and spun around to slash in a winding attack, but met Elucard's blade. Wiccer smirked. The two had been sparring three hours a day for the last month and he had learned to anticipate Elucard's reactions and favorite defensive maneuvers. Using his freehand, Wiccer grabbed his sparring partner's wrist and locked it into a painful position. Elucard wretched in pain but before he could react, Wiccer sent him sprawling onto the ground with a hefty kick to the chest. Elucard sat up, rubbing his throbbing wrist.

"You're getting better, sergeant," Elucard cheered. The compliment bore a bit of teasing. Wiccer had recently been promoted to captain, skipping a full rank to match the same command that his father had once held in Long Whisper. From the moment they had met up earlier in the morning, Wiccer had been showing off and buffing the new double silver bars on his collar.

"Captain," corrected Wiccer.

"Regardless, you've gotten better. I have to admit that these days. How old are you now?" Elucard asked, still in disbelief at how well Wiccer had been coming along.

"Twenty," Wiccer stated, reaching for his water skin.

"Twenty? And when did you start training?"

Wiccer paused, trying to remember exactly when his training with Avren and his father started, "Twelve, I believe."

"So you have had eight years of the wrong training and bad habits beaten into your head. I didn't know you had that much of a disadvantage compared to the rest of the ARO recruits," Elucard teased. He laughed as he ducked the water skin being flung at his head. Wiccer raised his sword for another round of sparring, "I'll show you who's at a disadvantage, Rabbit!"

Elucard glanced behind Wiccer to see a strangely dressed woman approaching the two. It had been a month since Elucard had seen one, but his eyes weren't playing tricks on him. A Black Rabbit stood before him. Elucard leapt past Wiccer, brandishing his dull training sword. He knew he would not be able to cut her with it, but with enough force he could plunge it into her despicable heart. A Black Rabbit, inside the heart of Lost Dawns? He marveled at her arrogance. Plus, she was smack dab in the heart of the military district. *What was she thinking?*

"Elucard, stop!" Wiccer blurted out.

Elucard halted in his tracks, still bearing his teeth at his sworn enemy. Wiccer hastily ran between the two.

"Elucard, she's one of us."

Elucard was more puzzled than enraged at this point, "One of us?"

Wiccer turned to Elisa, who was wide eyed with fear, as she was not expecting a brush with death. She slowly relaxed her grip on the dagger she held behind her back. She was hesitant to call Elucard an ally, but after spending a month with the Black Rabbits, she was ready for a change.

"Wiccer, I need to talk to you," Elisa said, keeping a close eye on Elucard.

"Elisa, this is Elucard. He was a Black Rabbit once like you," Wiccer said, introducing the two.

Elisa smiled, relaxing to her normal, collected self, "So this is Elucard? All that is on everyone's mind is the Elucard that went mad and turned on the clan. I've heard many things. How you were this cool, devilishly handsome, and cunning elf. You rose to First Blade fast. You were the one that surpassed all. You made the proudest man jealous and the most jealous man fall in love with you.

Elucard Freewind. I don't know whether I should love you, hate you, or fear you."

Elisa's words stirred a stew of disdain and yearning for his former life. It might have all been a farce, but he invested more effort and time into that farce than anything else in his life.

"Is that all they said about me?" Elucard asked, a bit curious.

"No, they also said you were dead," she said in a matter-of-fact manner.

Wiccer smiled smugly, "Well, I suppose we'll have a few surprises for those Rabbits when we see them again!"

"As they will for you as well, I fear, Wiccer," Elisa replied, remembering why she was there.

Wiccer's smile vanished as his attention returned to Elisa, "What have you learned?"

Elisa relayed everything she had heard from Vada. Everything she learned about the Rabbits seeking an alliance with Estinia and joining alongside them in the coming war against Varis in hopes of gaining Estinians as Black Rabbit recruits.

"I wish not to go back, Wiccer. I fear that they suspect me a traitor. They all seem on edge since both Avalon and Elucard left their ranks. Please don't make me go back there!" Elisa pleaded.

Wiccer looked grimly towards Elucard. Then back to Elisa, "You've done well. Avren would have been proud of you. We could use your help in the ARO."

Elisa raised an eyebrow. Marcus did mention an 'Anti-Rogue Operatives' unit to her. He even asked her to help lead it, but she wasn't interested at the time. However it seemed the opportunity to be involved in Marcus's passion project had arisen again. Although she knew no one would stop her from leaving with the freedom she had more than earned, she could not simply leave. It was Avren that she still owed.

"I'll join you. You'll always be able to count on me," said Elisa. Wiccer nodded with a smile before turning to Elucard, "We need to get this information to the king." Wiccer started to walk away, but stopped with a question lingering in his mind, "Is ARO prepared for war?"

"No," Elucard said simply and flatly.

"Then you still have much work to do," Wiccer replied.

56

Avalon and Adema approached the throne where King Koda
Dawnedge sat. They were weary from the long journey across the Omni
Ocean, but there had been no time for rest on such an urgent mission.
War was at Cypress' doorstep and the rest of realm held its breath in
suspense, wondering whether Varis and its allies would be able to
overcome the warmongering nation of Estinia. Avalon's presence
indicated that the order of the Silent Ones had waged their bets on the
fledgling nation of Long Whisper.

"My King," Avalon said with a sweeping bow that seamlessly led
into a kneel, "I am Avalon Bellerose. I have traveled from far beyond
your horizon to offer you our allegiance."

Koda sat still, his back uncomfortably straight against the back of the
wooden throne. At his feet, Wildeye sat vigilantly. Wiccer and Tull
stood on either side of the throne. Wiccer's hand rested on the pommel
of his sword. It had been only two months since Inle infiltrated the
castle and attacked him. Despite the reputation of the Silent Order,
Wiccer took no chances. Even though he was at Koda's right hand
alongside Wildeye, Wiccer was still anxious. Twice Wiccer had failed
Koda. Twice the Black Rabbits had taken Wiccer for a fool. There would
not be a third time.

Koda nodded to his two guests, "My adviser tells me that the Silent
Ones are a guild of warriors that spread the word of Jedeo through
military might. Is this true, Avalon Bellerose?"

Avalon looked pained by the description that Koda gave the Silent
Ones. Adema scoffed as well. Avalon had never seen the Silent Ones as
a military force nor as merely evangelists spreading Jedeo's word.

"I–" Avalon started but Koda interrupted.

"That's why you are sending me a small army. You wish to secure a
temple in Long Whisper. You want Jedeo's word to reach all of Varis.
Perhaps once Estinia is defeated, you will convert the people of that
nation as well. Complete global domination by a single religion? All in
the name of righteousness and piety?" Koda said continuing his assault
on the two Silent Ones' beliefs.

"Young King, how dare you besmirch the name of Jedeo! We will not stand for insults to our Order!" Adema growled.

Avalon rested her hand on her companion's shoulder, "No, Adema, the king is right," Avalon said calmly, "Almost right, at least. King Koda, we are not merely another priesthood that praises our god with fanciful tales of great deeds and heroic acts. Although Jedeo's tale is full of that and had inspired me during some of my lowest points. We are an order of skilled warriors. We do kill in the name of Jedeo, but we protect those that need protection. The people we touch and help are not merely means to our own ends. We do good work for good people. Our Silencers slay the vile creatures of the Night so that the weak may finally be at—" Avalon ended her speech abruptly, looking off into the nearby shadows and slowly drawing her blade.

Koda, taken aback, stared at her bewildered, "What do you think you are doing?"

"Silver Wing, what do you sense?" Adema asked anxiously.

"There's something amiss," Avalon snarled as she let loose a dagger that was sheathed beneath her long, white coat.

The dagger carved through the air and vanished into the shadowy rafters above, but was deflected with a low clatter. Elucard dropped to the ground from the crossbeam he had made his hiding place. He did not draw his sword, but instead raised his arms in a sign of peace. But Avalon would not have it. Lunging fiercely at Elucard, she made several swipes at the elf.

"My King, I have snuffed out a Black Rabbit spy!" Avalon shouted as she continued a barrage of slices at Elucard who somersaulted several times backwards avoiding each of the skillful attacks, "Adema, give no quarter!"

Elucard drew his sword and locked blades with Avalon, "I am no Rabbit, Avalon. I—" Elucard could not get a word in edgewise as Adema launched towards him wielding her Silencer.

Elucard leapt backwards, ducking as Adema swung horizontally and then parried Avalon's ninjato with his own. Avalon stumbled slightly before spin kicking into Elucard's gut. Elucard collapsed to one knee, but tumbled forward as Adema came down hard, hacking at the stone floor.

Elucard dashed forward, rolling on his shoulder before sliding in a half-circle, readying his blade for another advance from the Silent Ones. He spoke again, quicker this time, "I'm no Rabbit! I defected like you, Avalon!"

Avalon, still scowling, hesitated to continue her attack, "Who are you?"

"Elucard Freewind, student of Legion."

"Your exploits have reached far, Elucard. You have slain a king. You expect me to believe you are welcomed in the court of the eight tribes?" leered Avalon.

"It's true, Avalon. As much as I despise his very shadow, I've come to realize his usefulness," Koda said as he stepped down from the throne, his hand raised as he tried to defuse the situation between the two Silent Ones and Elucard, "I must say, I am far more curious as to why you know so much about the Black Rabbits," Koda prodded.

Avalon paused as she tried to come up with a convincing explanation that did not reveal too much about her disgraceful past, "As I said, *word travels*. Elucard's deed was a popular topic in taver—"

"Avalon was was the leader of the Black Rabbits when I was training under my Master," Elucard chimed in.

Avalon stared daggers at Elucard, "I have since renounced and condemned my former clan," she said quickly, hoping to mend any potential damage dealt to her already fragile reputation with the king.

"It seems you started a trend, Avalon," Koda said amusingly, "We have another former Black Rabbit, besides Elucard, in our service.

"Elisa Moonshard," Wiccer said as he inched closer to the relaxed Avalon.

"You said you found a use for Elucard? What usefulness keeps him from swinging from the gallows?" Avalon asked with a mixture of curiosity and contempt.

"I'm teaching Black Rabbit techniques to a squad of Long Whisper soldiers so that they can hunt down the Rabbits," Elucard said, sheathing his sword.

Avalon smirked, "An interesting idea. I should consider training the next generation of Silent Ones like that once I have established a temple in Long Whisper—" she stopped herself and turned, kneeling before Koda once more before finishing her thought, "...with your permission, my king."

Koda nodded, "You and your god are more than welcome here in Lost Dawns if you wish to protect my people. You may open the doors of your temple in our city's abandoned Ruens abbey, provided we survive the war."

57

Wiccer stood side by side with the rest of the ARO recruits. What he assumed would be just another long day of training on that old, familiar parade field quickly turned into something new and exciting. Standing next to Elucard was a Long Whisper soldier. He was an older looking elf. His hair was trimmed neatly short. His straightened gold and green jacket had various emblems denoting his rank as an officer, letting everyone know that he was due a certain amount of respect. His insignia of rank on his lower arm displayed three chevrons balancing on a fulcrum, which meant he was a Staff Sergeant. He was most likely in charge of a platoon. Above it, but below his shoulder, was his unit patch. The patch depicted a true north arrow with an eight pointed star in the background.

'The 2nd Roving Protectors Detachment.' Wiccer's father put together the first three RPD units to patrol each village and city within Long Whisper as well as the borderlands. 'Our vigilance is immeasurable' was the Rovers' creed.

"This is Sergeant Ilaird Jackdaw," Elucard finally said, gesturing a hand to the Rover, "He has agreed to allow you recruits to accompany his patrol to Outpost Wolfcry."

Wiccer knew that outpost well. It once served as his former guild hall and was half a day's travel from his home. It would be a three day's march from Lost Dawns. However, it was not the travel time that concerned him. It was the location of the road leading to the outpost that was so disconcerting. He knew Elucard's reason for picking this particular mission. This route bordered Black Rabbit territory and could be the mission that would make or break the ARO. This was their final test.

"Ilaird's patrol will be escorting a supply convoy to Wolfcry. The road rubs against Black Rabbit territory and though I doubt they will make a move against such a protected train of wagons, you'll be seeing that the convoy makes it to the outpost in one piece," Elucard said, confirming Wiccer's thoughts.

"Will you be leading us, Elucard?" asked Timber. Her voice was unusually shaky from either anxiety or excitement.

"No, Elisa and I will not be joining you. Wiccer will be leading this mission."

Murmurs erupted from the recruits. A chance to confront the Black Rabbits and Elucard was not leading them?

"Succeed in this mission and you'll officially be ARO," said Elucard. He motioned for Wiccer to step in front of the squad, "They're all yours, Captain."

Ilaird nodded to Wiccer, "We'll be waiting outside the gates".

Wiccer stood motionless in front of his waiting soldiers, each wearing worry on their faces. This would be Wiccer's first true mission since his failed attempt at saving Jaelyn, and he was not sure if he was prepared to be responsible for so many lives. His hands shook as he choked on the words within his dry mouth, "M-Move out!"

***

ARO had been trained in escort maneuvers just as Black Rabbits were. Hidden deep in the shadows, a Rabbit can watch without interruption and keep the element of surprise if its objective were to be attacked. Those that would attack would be unaware of the Rabbit and thus lose any upper hand they would have had otherwise. Not only this, but if several Rabbits were escorting, Rabbits could break away and scout ahead or hunt for possible ambushers before a trap was sprung. A Rabbit was at home within the shadows. ARO had been trained to be no different.

Wiccer stalked closely alongside Sergeant Ilaird, using a variety of bird calls that Elucard and Elisa taught him to communicate with his team. This allowed him to be able to coordinate with his men who were too far to whisper to.

"Rulan and Trek, keep alert in the eastern woods," Wiccer signaled with a long coo.

"Roger that, captain," A series of stuttering chirps echoed from the trees on the eastern side of the road.

Lear sprinted up to Wiccer, making sure to stay light on his feet and and incognito. He had had been running about the convoy keeping tabs on all the ARO in their various positions.

"What do you have to report, Lear?" Wiccer whispered lowly.

"This Yakahti reports that Timber spots no one following us. Calsoon–" Lear stopped suddenly as Blayvaar appeared before them, urgency in his eyes.

"What is it Blayvaar?" asked Wiccer, scanning frantically ahead of the convoy.

"A fallen tree lies ahead of us, captain. A single path heads west into the forest. It is very narrow with very little light."

"Did you scout out the path?"

"I did."

"Well, what did you find?" asked Wiccer, growing a bit impatient.

"I heard silent whispers – the kind that Elucard and Elisa taught us. They were saying, 'The caravan is heading this way.' They were Rabbits, I'm sure of it, captain."

Wiccer bit his lip. He knew that Blayvaar was right. '*This is it. This is what we trained for.*' However, a simple ambush was a breezy morning stroll for the Black Rabbits. It was in their blood. '*How would Elucard react?*' He checked his surroundings, hoping that the answer would present itself in some obvious way. And in a sense it did. All at once his training kicked in. '*With precision.*'

"Lear, relay the possibility of an ambush to the Rovers. I'll call to the rest of the team about the situation."

The western path was a thin wooded road that took a longer route to the southwest. It would pour into a large highway that would eventually arrive at Outpost Wolfcry. However, it proved to be a very precarious method of travel for the convoy. The trees were huddled close together and encroached onto the already narrow road. The RPD patrol needed to march single file or else they would bump clumsily into the trees.

Despite it being mid-afternoon, the sun barely breached through the canopy of the arching branches. Had it not been for most of the soldiers being Elven, they would be traveling at an even more labored rate.

"Be on alert, men. That fallen tree was probably not a coincidence," Ilaird called out to his Rovers. Although he had been briefed on the eminent ambush, he was specifically told not act as though he knew about it.

At this point, it was Wiccer's job to flush out any and all Black Rabbits that were skulking about. Both Calsoon and Timber took to the trees. Trek and Rulan used their combined tracking skills to hunt the Rabbits, while Blayvaar and Lear stayed at the caravan's rear. Essie was on standby with the Rover medic, awaiting any sudden emergency.

Wiccer attempted to rest his pulse as he kept his senses strained for any sign of danger. As a White Cloak he was trained to expect attacks, but never had he expected an attack that he knew about in advance. This was the single most nerve-racking moment in his life. If he were in the heat of battle he would feel at home, distracted from his fears and anxiety, but the anticipation of battle was more than he could bear.

A whiffling sound ripped through the air as a wagon driver let out a short scream of agony. Another similar series of sounds broke through the previously silent scene. Two more wagon drivers screamed, signaling that the convoy was under attack.

A screeching whistle echoed through the treetops followed by a careening arrow flying from one side of the road to the other. Wiccer watched as a shadowy Black Rabbit fell from his perch in the trees. Its body crashed to the ground, one of Timber's arrows lodged into his chest.

In a fraction of a moment, a hail of shurikens showered from the trees into the convoy below. Rovers slid under the wagons for cover as Wiccer scrambled for the nearby wood line. Keeping a steady mind set, he whistled commands to his nearby allies, telling them to scurry up the trees and relieve the Rovers from the hailstorm of deadly attacks.

Wiccer watched as the nimble soldiers rushed up the trunks of the trees, daggers clenched between their teeth. The clashing of steel rang out throughout the canopy as ARO engaged the Rabbits. One by one, assassins fell from the trees and smashed into the woodland floor below.

From either side of the caravan burst bands of Rabbits from the shadowy brush, all brandishing swords and hatchets. Wiccer shouted out several orders commanding ARO and the Rovers to defend the supply wagons at all costs. An all-out battle ensued as blade sparked against blade. Blood sprayed onto the nearby leaves and gathered in pools in the grass beneath the warriors' feet.

Between engaging the advancing enemies, Wiccer made sure to keep an eye on his own forces. He kept his ears open for reports from each area of the battlefield and watched as both medics ran frantically to the aid of any fallen soldier. Arrows whizzed past Wiccer and his allies as Timber sniped out any unaware Black Rabbits. Calsoon and Blayvaar lurked from behind the Black Rabbit lines, slicing open unsuspecting throats. Lear, Trek, and Rulan slowly battered back the Rabbit offensive. Wiccer grinned widely, the battle was won.

Outpost Wolfcry opened its gates as the caravan entered. Arrows and shuriken protruded from the splintered wooden sides of the three wagons. New drivers were assigned from the squad of Roving Guards.

"Well done, captain. We were weary of having ARO assist us in this mission, given the reputation of your commander, but you proved useful. You aren't the scumbags you are rumored to be," said a relieved Ilaird at the breach of the outpost's gate.

Wiccer nodded. ARO's had a reputation as a motley crew of losers and rogues that came together under the wing of the vilest criminal Long Whisper had ever known. Not only this, but they were sanctioned by the king to learn the very techniques that were used against other soldiers. It was easy to question ARO's trustworthiness with such a pedigree. And yet Wiccer witnessed first hand that ARO was worthy to carry the banner of Long Whisper. He was proud of his ragtag unit. He was proud to be a part of it too.

"Thank you, sergeant. We'll be heading back to Lost Dawns in the morning," grinned Wiccer.

"My men and I would be more than happy to have ARO watching our backs on future missions. You may never earn the complete respect of our forces, but I don't think that you'll lose much sleep over that. You seem to only care about getting your mission accomplished successfully."

"Aye, respect is overrated, Sergeant."

"Rogues who hunt rogues. The shadows that guard the light," mused Ilaird.

Wiccer smirked at the thought.

Ilaird threw a salute to Wiccer before joining his men in the soup line.

***

ARO returned to their city victorious in the following days. They all stood in formation on the parade Field. Before them Elucard stood beside a large, mysterious crate. Elucard himself was no longer dressed in his familiar training armor, but instead donned light armor that was a deep black. A black half mask covered his lower face and a crimson hood and a long red cloak covered the rest of his head. His ninjato was strapped behind his waist. His upper arms stuck out the most. On his right shoulder was the patch of Long Whisper's flag: An elaborate eight looped knot with a ring of leaves encasing it. On his left shoulder, a patch depicting a red lightning bolt with an eye in the foreground. Below that patch was the triple chevron and fulcrum of a staff sergeant, just like the one that Ilaird wore. Elucard was officially a Long Whisper soldier now.

"Looking slick, Elucard," Blayvaar said, grinning widely.

"*Sergeant* Elucard," Elucard corrected. He kicked open the crate, revealing a stack of black leather armor and red cloaks, "Wiccer

269

reported to me that you all ran into Black Rabbits." The squad smiled and chuckled. Elucard continued, "And despite some injuries, there were no deaths."

Several of the ARO recruits hooted in excitement

"Quiet down!" harped Wiccer.

"Thank you, captain," Elucard said, nodding toward Wiccer, "Men, you have preformed with precision and perfection. Three months of training. Three months! I have worked you like dogs. Hell, worse than dogs. Instead of snapping like a rust-eaten sword, you cut into those Rabbit bastards like a freshly forged blade. You are now ARO." Elucard paused, watching their grins grow wider, "More than that. You are now a clan. Every clan needs a name – a name that the enemy will utter in fear when your shadow falls upon them."

"What name would that be?" questioned Essie.

"The Watchers," Elucard replied with a sliver of menace woven into his tone, "And we Watchers need to look the part. Come get your new uniforms!" Elucard passed the newly sewn ARO uniforms to the soldiers.

"Elucard, a suggestion for our unit's motto?" Wiccer piped up dawning his new red cloak.

"What do you have in mind?"

"The shadows that guard the light."

58

The Verdant Academy's botanical garden was one of Koda's favorite destinations. Its winding pebble paths wove throughout lanes of exotic trees and vivid wildflowers. A small pond accented the garden with its lush lotuses growing from the lily-pads that calmly floated on its still surface. Koda rested dazedly on the pond's bank, a book spread open on his chest. Wildeye amusingly played with a toad.

"Imagine if this was our life, girl; just lazing about without a care in the world. So much has changed..." He trailed off, lost in thought. His armada was to leave within two days' time. He could not help but wonder how many young souls he had sent to die on the shores of Varis. But before those thoughts could send him spiraling into a deep despair, a voice called out, distracting him from all of his worries.

"You would be bored by the end of the week." Koda looked behind him to see Megan approaching.

"I suppose so. I guess we'll never find out, will we?" Koda smirked teasingly.

"Word on the wind says you were looking for me," Megan said, plucking an apple from a nearby hanging branch.

"I was. Then I got distracted by the allure of a lazy afternoon," he admitted.

"You wish that my school and I join your forces," she said bluntly. She did not need to be a seer to know what was on his mind.

If she was going to get right down to it, Koda figured it best to be frank, "And?"

Megan knelt down to scoop up the toad that Wildeye had been unknowingly frightening. Wildeye gave off a whine as her newfound playmate was abruptly taken from her.

"I can't," Megan replied, sounding genuinely let down.

"You *can't*?" Koda questioned, taken aback by the response.

"I am the Headmaster of a mage academy, Koda. The Mage Council forbids us to take sides in 'petty political disputes.'" She mockingly spoke the last words.

"But I need you by my side!" Koda insisted.

"My hands are tied, my pupil."

Koda took in a deep breath to calm his thoughts. He set his disappointment aside, seeking ways around the problem, "Could you send me volunteer mages? I can really use any skilled spell caster that I can get my hands on."

"I will see if we have any students willing."

Koda bowed before his master, "I thank you... for everything. You have gone above and beyond to not only be my teacher, but a guide and friend as well."

Megan bowed back, "Same to you, Koda.

**

The Serpent Sea separated Long Whisper from Varis. It was aptly named for the many snake-like sea serpents that lurked in the murky depths below. Once, long ago, the sea serpents were not the only thing that struck fear into the hearts of seafarers, but also the pirates that terrorized the Serpent Sea. However, the glory days of swashbucklers and buccaneers had long passed.

Koda's armada was two hundred ships strong and was now closing in on the northern beach after a two days' journey. However, it was not a dangerous voyage. Estinia currently dominated the waters of the Serpent Sea and was currently laying siege to Varis' capital city.

"How close are they now, captain?" Koda asked Captain Faircloud. He and several other nobles watched the line of Estinian ships slowly trudging closer to their position. Although they seemed a ways off, they were still a threat. As Koda's fleet drew closer to the northern beaches it was apparent that part of the sea had a "welcome party" of sorts waiting for them, consisting of several enemy ships.

"They be in our cannon range in half an hour," The captain said as he lowered his looking glass from his eye, "M'Lord, It ain't the blasted ships that be scarin' me, but them drakes in the sky." Faircloud pointed a shaky finger up towards the skies. He took a swig from a wine bottle to calm his sea-worn nerves.

Koda and the nobles peered through the sky, spotting the large shadows of the dragons. Soaring through the clouds, a flight of forty lesser dragons could be seen. Each being manned by a drake rider and flying in sync with one another.

"My king, it would seem we are sailing to our deaths," Lenfell Raindancer said fearfully, his cerulean eyes glinting in the high noon sun.

"Those drakes will decimate us, never mind the twenty ships on either side of us preparing to blow us out of the water!" exclaimed Sove Breezerunner. Her voice was just shrill enough to grant Koda a slight headache.

"Captain, Varisian banners await us on shore, do you see them?"

"I see banners, M'Lord, but not Varis," the captain said with slight disdain in his words.

"Southtail?" Koda said, slightly hopeful. But he knew the truth. The Estinains had been laying siege to Varis City for at least a week. Stonewall, the mountain pass city to the south, had been under Estinian occupation for even longer. The chances that Varis could actually send troops or aid to Long Whisper for their landing was a long shot. Koda would have to split his forces in order to both relieve Varis City and to reclaim Stonewall. But the question remained: How many forces could he safely land on the beaches?

"Estinians, M'Lord," said Faircloud, confirming Koda's fears.

Koda's face was stiff, but turned grim. His options were few. He had enough ships to win a naval battle, but with the drakes above and the forces on the beach, he was not sure how much of his army he would have left at the end of it all.

"What are your orders, your grace?" Lenfell asked.

"We suppress the ships with a cannon barrage while we push as many landing craft onto the shore as possible. We need to strike hard and fast. We'll win no matter what, but the victory is hollow if we lose too many of our forces. Varis awaits our aid!"

"What of the drakes?" asked Sove, a bit more calmly than when she spoke before.

"I will leave them for the Silent Ones. We shall see just how great Jedeo's might truly is."

59

Avalon knelt down on the deck of the Wave Skimmer. Adema slowly made her way toward her and knelt at her side. Avalon had already informed her Silent Ones about the drakes and they were all-too-eager to tackle the issue head on. Together, the Silent Ones discussed their plan of attack. After a long deliberation a plan was hatched. For them to be successful, they would need the help of the volunteer mages that were aboard the ship.

"Would it be possible for you and the other mages to get us into the skies?" Avalon had asked a young Kanis vernal mage name Tobian.

Tobian looked into the skies, as if estimating the distance from the ship to the drakes. He rubbed his chin as he thought of a solution to the question. Nodding, he called over two of his colleagues and then turned back to Avalon, "I have a plan, so prepare yourselves. You'll hit the skies fast and reckless. I'm not sure how you'll make it back down safely, though."

"We'll play it by ear," she responded, curious as to how the mages planned to launch her and her comrades skyward.

***

As the Long Whisper armada neared closer to the shore, a shuddering noise broke through the grassy plains like a rolling thunder, followed by the explosive crack of splintering wood as cannonballs blew through the anchoring ships. Orders rang out as numerous skiffs filled with soldiers attempted to make their way to the unwelcoming beaches.

As the Long Whisper soldiers neared the beach, a storm of steel tipped arrows launched from the Estinian rear lines and showered onto the army of skiffs. The men raised their shields to shelter themselves from the hailstorm, but several arrows found crevices between the shields and armor, piercing soldiers as the sailors desperately attempted to move forward to unload their passengers.

Blood stirred within the ocean as wave upon wave of arrows blanketed the skies, whistling down upon the grieved soldiers. An order broke out to push forward as the elves jumped into the waist deep salty waters. Their shields remained raised above their heads and their swords and spears were ready for battle.

Fiery globes spewed from the mouths of the war drakes and crashed destructively onto the clippers below, splashing an oily fire across the decks and onto the sails. Sailors screamed in agony as their skin melted under the intense heat of the corrosive chemical. The drake riders sent their beasts in for a swooping maneuver, heaving a stream of blazing fire across several more ships before pulling the drakes back into the safety of the clouds. Large plumes of black smoke rose, creating a fog that stung the eyes and choked sailors.

***

The thirty-one Silent Ones crouched on the deck, their Silencers poised upwards tracking the movements of the drakes. On either side of the platoon of holy warriors were vernal mages that awaited Avalon's call.

Avalon nodded to the Silent Ones before cuing Tobian, "Do it."

Tobian and five other vernal mages waved their arms in wide counter-clockwise circles before ending their cast in a powerful upward thrust. Underneath each Silent One popped a piston of wood that launched them into the air and through the smoky fog.

Avalon's eyes watered from the stinging smoke and air. Her white coat flapped wildly, trailing behind her as she careened toward her target. Unbeknownst to the rider, Avalon performed a graceful moonsault over him as she grabbed his head, flipped him off his saddle and landed in his place. The rider echoed a scream as he fell through the clouds.

Quick to check her surroundings, she found her Silent Ones dispatching their foes in a similar fashion. However, some were not as lucky and either over shot or grabbed onto whatever body part of the drakes they could.

Avalon raised her sword over her head and rammed it between the drake's shoulders. The scaly beast screeched in agony as it spun upside down attempting to rid itself of its unwelcome guest.

Instinctively, Avalon swiftly tangled her hands in the reins just before she found herself dangling from the saddle above her. Straining, she grunted as she brought her feet into the iron stirrups. As the drake spun right side up, Avalon used the opportunity to grab her blade which was still stuck in the drake's spine. Jumping cat-like onto the saddle, she carefully ran down the beast's neck. The wind whipped at her and tossed her from side to side. Avalon mustered all her skill and dexterity to stay balanced. Soon, her efforts paid off as she found herself on top of its spike-rippled head. With a sharp strike, Avalon drove her Silencer into the crown of the drake's skull. The kill was instant, and immediately the drake dropped into a dangerous free fall. Avalon knelt down, gripping her blade's handle as the drake's dead body picked up speed. To her right she saw two more limp drakes plummetingthrough sky. Above them were two falling figures. Avalon spotted a drake's talons driving at her from her left. Avalon was too surprised to react as the drake slammed into her in mid air, her Silencer flipped wildly from her hand.

Avalon gathered her senses as she flew, rolling around. She outstretched her arm and grabbed her blade before she crashed into the drake's tail. With one hand tightly gripping her blade and her other arm wrapped around the drake's tail, Avalon scrambled up its back and made her way to the riding saddle. She grabbed the Estinain rider by his collar and ran him through with her blade before kicking the rider from the saddle.

"That was a little too close," she muttered under her breath.

Streams of fire swiped across the sky as Silent Ones acrobatically leaped from drake to drake, leaving a trail of death in their wake. Avalon desperately pulled her reins attempting to tug a drake away from an oncoming fire breath, but to no avail. Before she could be burned to a charred husk, Avalon dove downward and landed on the neck of a swooping drake below. A hand reached out and pulled her to the safety of the seat.

"Never rode a horse before, Silver Wing?" Adema teased, glowing with the thrill of battle.

Avalon sucked in a long breath as the two veered to the right, avoiding a collision with a falling drake. She snapped her head back to watch the drake fall into a spin as two Silent Ones cut through its wings. Avalon looked back toward Adema and pointed to drakes all plummeting from the sky, "Signal to the Silent Ones and kill your drake. Our mission is complete!"

Avalon jumped to the side and landed a kick on a drake rider that flew close by. The rider's jaw rocked unnaturally sideways before the jolt knocked him through a cloud. Avalon watched as her sword burned a bright gold, giving her a sense of urgency to follow Adema. Plunging her sword into the neck of the drake, she twisted the handle and ran her

Silencer horizontally, brutally slicing the drake's head nearly off. All that was left was to find a way down.

Avalon searched for a solution to her rapidly arriving demise. If she landed with the drake corpse, the suction of the impact would swallow her quickly. Avalon released her sword from the drake and leaped forward before the body splashed into the ocean. Avalon sailed forward, aiming for a set of skiffs safely away from cannon barrage and the shore. Within a matter of moments, Avalon had sheathed her Silencer and dove in a beautiful splashless arc into the sea. Above her she saw a skiff floating just beyond her reach. With a stroke of good fortune or perhaps divine providence, a hand grabbed her and pulled her onto the skiff. Avalon collapsed onto the ground, grateful for any help.

"Oi saw what ya did, lass. Unbelievable!" the sailor said, patting her on the back.

"Jedeo was under my feet," she said, still coughing up seawater. Once she had assured herself enough that she was unharmed, she swiveled her head searching the skies for her descending allies.

"You be lookin' fer yer kin? Oi saw 'em fall not too far to our east. They were snatched up likes you. Jedeo may not control the winds like Nayovi but I be mad not to think she ain't got some 'ole magic fer ya," the sailor said reassuringly to Avalon.

A ram's horn could be heard blurting from the shores. Estininia's forces were quick to retreat as the bulk of Long Whisper's forces made it to the shores. Banners were struck into the ground to signify to the anchored ships that the Northern Shore was captured. By sunset a full encampment would be raised. Avalon's skiff arrived on the shore soon after. She did not have to go far to reunite with Adema.

"Any deaths?" Avalon asked anxiously.

"None. A few injuries, but nothing that will keep them from battle," reported Adema.

Avalon nodded as she removed her soaked coat and draped it on her shoulder.

"You did well, Silver Wing. Perhaps you wish to gather your Silent Ones and lead them in prayer?" Adema suggested as they both walked over to where the Silent Ones were gathered.

She searched the eyes of the Silent Ones. Some of their coats were stained black from the grime and smoke. Perhaps prayer was precisely what they needed.

Adema knelt next to the other Silent Ones and bowed her head, "Our Silver Wing wishes to lead us in prayer."

Avalon stood silently. She gripped her leather-bound sword handle as it cracked. She had been an assassin, a gladiatrix, and now a Silent One. In the end, she was raised to be a killer, lived to be a killer, and would die a killer. Alanna or Jedeo. It did not matter. They both used her for her skill with a blade. Jedeo had her heart, but Alanna still held her soul.

"Avalon, we are waiting," Whispered Adema.

'Until the final light of the final morn,
We will forever serve as Jedeo's Bloodborne,'

Avalon paused, wondering if she was jaded by her duties. The same duties that she held as a High Blade were the same she held as a Silent One.

Adema grabbed her and pulled her to the side, "Silver Wing, we must not falter in the Night. When we fall, we must pick ourselves up. We depend on each other as much Jedeo depends on us."

Avalon lowered her head and whispered in Adema's ear, "I sought Jedeo to be free from the blood that I bathed in. Now I am asked to return to that blood and bathe in more."

Adema lowered her hood and the mask that covered her lower face. Her black veins pulsed across her cheeks and her amber eyes searched Avalon's, "Jedeo has chosen you so that you can protect many with your skills. Do not run from them, but embrace them. These Silent Ones look to you as a leader. You need to lead them."

"Who will lead me?"

Adema lifted Avalon's chin and smiled brightly, "My friend, Jedeo leads you."

Avalon grinned meekly. She moved back to the kneeling Silent Ones and finished her prayer.

'And until that final light of that final morn,
We will forever guide those as Jedeo's Heavensworn.'

"Amen."

60

It took all day and night to establish a base camp on the Northern Shore. Large tents and canopies were erected – a quarter master, a medical bay, a chow line, a resting area, and one particularly enormous tent in the center that served as a war council.

Koda gathered the seven lords along with Avalon, Wiccer, and his commanding general, Ashmer. They looked over a large territorial map of Varis, sticking a dagger into the various points of interests. A dagger marked the location of the capital city of Varis, the mining city of Stonewall, a clearing just beyond the Southern Shore, and their beach camp on the Northern Shore.

General Ashmer was an older elf dressed in a green and gold dress jacket. His golden star insignia glinted on his collar. His unit patch depicted a spear in the foreground of a gold tree with eight branches protruding from it, representing the 1st Spearman Division. He lit his pipe, taking in the smooth tobacco before delving into his plan.

"Varis City is under siege, Stonewall is currently occupied by the enemy, and the Southern Shore holds the main concentration of Estinia's reserve forces," he paused as his pipe puffed up a ring of white smoke. The smoke danced in the air with a thick cherryroot scent, "Varis's forces won't be able to assist us until the city has been relieved. Stonewall both serves as a gate past the Sarkeir Mountains to the south and as supply complex for steel weapons and armor for the Estinian siege. The clearing beyond the mountains north of the Southern Shore would be an ideal spot for a final battle."

Wiccer rubbed his chin, looking over the map and nodding passively to Ashmer's briefing, "A good assessment, but what is your proposed course of action, general?"

Ashmer removed the Varis City dagger and thrust it into the large map next to the clearing's dagger, "We send a large force to stop the siege and rally the Varisian army to the clearing," he then took the Northern Shore dagger and the Stonewall dagger and placed them with the other two daggers next to the southern clearing, "The remaining forces liberate Stonewall, meet up with the forces from the southern clearing, and run Estinia out of Varis!"

Long Whisper's officers muttered in agreement. He pointed to several lords, "Lady Aisling, Lady Sove, Lord Fendrick, Lord Lenfrell, and Lord Eris – take your forces and drive back the siege to unite with King Dallin and head to the clearing. Lord Athar and Lady Cass, your forces will stay with the Silent Ones and myself. Together we'll reclaim Stonewall for Varis and rendezvous with the forces from Varis City."

Koda caught Wiccer looking aloof as he balked at the king's assignment of the dividing forces, "Your father is in Varis City, isn't he Captain Newsun?"

Wiccer looked up, caught a bit off guard. The White Cloaks originated from Varis City and his father had been recently stationed there to assist the Varisian army. Wiccer had been deeply worried for him. His anxiety had been exacerbated ever since the city fell under siege. He had hoped that it would be his unit that was sent to Varis City, and he could not hide the disappointment on his face, "Yes, my King," he replied.

"Do you wish to go save Varis City with the other forces?"

"I…" Every fiber in his body wished to say yes, but he knew he needed to stay with his Watchers, "…My place is leading the ARO"

"Good," said Ashmer, cutting his way back into the conversation, "because we could use the ARO to scout out the forest before Stonewall. The last thing we need is to be ambushed by Black Rabbits as we make our way there,"

Koda, both concerned and curious, asked, "ARO had three months to train. Are they ready to take on the Black Rabbits?"

I hope so. Wiccer thought to himself. That would have been the correct response, but was not the one he went with, "Our Watchers are an apt group of individuals that were rigorously trained by the best of the best. We are more than capable of dealing with anything that the Black Rabbits can throw at us!" Wiccer said with slightly feigned confidence.

"Excellent, captain. Gather your men and clear that forest of any Rabbit scum!" General Ashmer said with more than a hint of thrill in his voice.

"Yes, sir!" Wiccer responded with a neat salute. He bowed to his king and lords before exiting the tent.

***

"Don't you have medic things you're supposed to be doing?" Rulan asked, frustrated with Essie's insufferable giggling and teasing.

Trek had set up a chess board in one of the more quiet spots of the encampment. He and Rulan sat on logs with the checkered, wooden board resting on a barrel between them. Rulan shifted on his log, squirming as if he were being bitten by invisible ants. The thought of another loss to his more mentally agile brother made him fidget uncontrollably. Essie's commentary did not help the atmosphere. She hissed through her teeth every time Rulan made a foolish move that would cost him a piece.

"And what, miss watching your precious ego take another beating? I don't think so!" laughed Essie. She patted her brother on his head in a patronizing manner, "Come on Rulan, haven't you learned anything from Grandpops Sirbik? Never let your opponent control the middle rows."

"I know, I know!" yammered Rulan.

Trek smiled amusingly, "I miss those days. I miss all the goodies that Grandma would set out for family gatherings. She always had those wooden figures covering the shelves, and a few cats curled up by the hearth. She served the piping hot vegetable and lamb pies on the coldest of winter nights. Grandma Betts gave you that old white stuffed bear, right Essie?"

Essie chuckled, shoving Trek to the side to make room on the log besides him for her to sit, "Snowflake. I still remember him."

Rulan reached over and flicked Trek's ear tip the way he always had to get his attention, "Hey, stop concentrating on the past, and focus on the present, I just took your bishop!"

Trek rubbed his ear, "I have time to concentrate on the past when I move three moves ahead," Trek slid his knight into position and trapped Rulan's king, "Checkmate! You owe me three trit!"

Rulan zeroed in on his king's position, eying the checkmate in disbelief, "Wait a minute. I can... well I can... damn, I can't believe I lost again!"

Trek grinned from ear to ear, "Statistically speaking you should have won at least after the eighth game."

Rulan reached into his coin purse and pulled out three bronze coins. Each had a picture of king Jaelyn on the front and crescent moon on the back, "Three Jae-faces. There, are you happy now? I'm broke. How bout you let me win some trit back in a sparring match?"

Trek began packing up his chess set, a wide grin still plastered on his face, "How bout I give these trit to Essie and you spar her for them?"

Essie slid up to Rulan and flicked his ear, "How bout it Rulan?"

Rulan backed up, "Oh no, I err, just remembered – I'm pretty hungry. How about we find Timber and Calsoon and grab some chow?"

"Anything but fight your sister, eh, Rulan?" chuckled Trek.

"Anything!" blathered Rulan as he jogged away.

***

Blayvaar and Lear stood in line for fish stew at the chow tent with growling stomachs. Neither had seen so much as a bread crumb since they left for Varis. Blayvaar gripped his stomach to quiet his hunger, but to no avail. He sighed heavily, turning to his Yakahti friend, "This line needs to hurry up. My stomach is growing louder than a cat having its tail step–" he caught himself as Lear raised a brow, "...I like cats." Blayvaar finished blankly as he could not readily find a way not to offend the expert swordsman.

"This yikahti likes cats too," Lear grinned with a snaggletooth smile.

Blayvaar and Lear finally came to the front of the line and eagerly held out their tin bowls. The cook eyed their uniforms and scowled, "Move aside, I ain't got no stew for you lot."

"Excuse me?" Blayvaar questioned, flabbergasted by the rejection.

"You heard me, move aside. There's plenty of hungry soldiers more deserving of food than the two of you," the cook sneered.

"This yikahti doesn't understand. We waited in line just like the others." As calm as he seemed, Lear was furious on the inside.

A soldier shoved Lear from behind, "Get lost, Rabbit! You've got no right to our food!"

Lear spun around, a claw reaching for his sword's hilt. Blayvaar grabbed his wrist as he pushed himself in front of his companion.

The soldier thrust a finger into the former thief's chest, "Got something to say?"

Blayvaar smirked and he crossed his arms over his chest, relaxing his stance, "Don't I know you?"

The soldier shook his head.

"No, I swear we've met," Blayvaar insisted.

"I don't mingle with Rabbits."

"Yeah, I remember. Me and six of my 'Rabbit' friends handed you and twenty plus of your friends your asses that night in the Mystic Fang. Sad day in the 12th Spearman Division's short history, wouldn't you say?"

282

The soldier's face flushed red as he began to grind his teeth in fury, "Well there's two of you and all of us ready to have our payback! What do you say to that?"

Blayvaar drew his two daggers and licked his lips, "I'd say you're welcome to try!"

Before the chaos could ensue, a command broke out in the area, "Atten-*tion*!"

Wiccer pushed his way to the root of the commotion. He flashed a hard-nosed face at Blayvaar before addressing both hungry Watchers, "Get your food to go, we have a mission."

"I ain't serving those two," the cook butted in, repeating his stance.

Wiccer gave a cold, iron-eyed stare to the cook who might as well have crawled away into a dark corner.

"I say you will," Wiccer sternly growled.

"Yes, sir," The cook meekly said, quick to fill up Lear and Blayvaar's bowls.

Wiccer turned to the Spearman's face, "Do you have a problem with my men?"

"No, sir."

"What's your name solider?"

"Rith, sir," he said with much disdain.

"You won't start anything with my men again, or I will smoke you so hard the skies will rain with the tears of the gods from watching you sweat! Is that clear, Private Rith?"

"Crystal clear, captain," the soldier said, grimacing with every syllable, then swallowing hard as if he were swallowing a mouthful of glass shards.

"We're never going to get their respect," Blayvaar whispered to Lear.

"The shadows that guard the light, my friend," Lear whispered back.

61

The edge of the looming forest just beyond the encampment on the northern shore gave off a haunting presence. It sent chills down the spines of the youthful ARO members. Shadows reached out to each one of them with desperation as if the shadows themselves were trying to escape the clutches of the forest from whence they came. The silence was unsettling as well. No chirping, no sounds of small animals scurrying up trees. Nothing could be heard in the belly of the woods.

Elucard peered through the seemingly endless forest before signaling for his men to follow his lead. He, Elisa, Lear, Calsoon, and Timber leaped into the trees and made their way jumping lightly from branch to branch. The others followed silently on foot.

The Watchers trekked slowly through the thick forest, scouting a suitable path for the army to march through. The one that stood out was an old merchant route that had seen little travel over the recent years, but the ground was visibly worn. The trees had been cleared away to make room for horses and wagons. As far as Elucard could tell it passed through the forest and led into the mountains. Their mission seemed to finish without conflict and they made preparations to report their findings to Ashmer. Elucard signaled for those following him in the canopy to drop down to meet the ground squad.

Wiccer took a knee before taking a sip from his water skin. It was cool on the forest floor, but exceptionally dark without the presence of the sun. However, the strange forest toyed with his body. His chin and nose were numb from the cold autumn air and his eyes could not quite make out the far off figures of those ahead of him. He was the only one in ARO that had to work extra hard to train his eyes to adjust to the darkness. The Elves, Kanis and the yikahti were genetically gifted when it came to low light vision. They could easily see their surroundings in the dark. If he had only taken more than just three months of training with Elucard, his eyesight may have been more attuned. Although his skills had greatly risen to meet the challenges that Elucard had put before him, his eyesight was still a weakness. One, he would soon realize, that would cost him dearly.

"Where's Lear?" Wiccer said confusingly as he finished a quick head count.

Elucard stared blankly back at the trail towards the camp, "He took the rear. Who was adjacent to him?"

Calsoon piped up, still befuddled as to how Lear could be by his side one minute and gone the next, "I was; although I am at a loss as to where he went."

Wiccer was reminded of the lessons Avren had given him about this exact scenario. A squad leader was to do head counts regularly. Those keeping the rear were easily taken captive. It was exceedingly dark in this forest. Was Lear snatched up by a Black Rabbit or was he merely lost? He knew that there was a possibility that the ARO was walking into a trap. His troops needed to keep a clear mind and not panic.

"We–" Wiccer started.

"Split up in pairs," Elucard spat, quickly interrupting Wiccer, "Stay in the trees. Look for any sign of Lear and show no mercy if you cross paths with the enemy. This has Rabbit scum written all over it!"

"Belay that order!" Wiccer said sharply. He glared at Elucard who narrowed his eyes back at Wiccer, "Now is the time to think clearly. We'll get picked off one by one if we don't move in a pack. We have a better chance of survival if we stay together."

"Wiccer, do not forget I know the Rabbits better than you. We'll cover more ground if we split up!" argued Elucard.

"I appreciate your wisdom here, Elucard. However, don't forget your place. I out rank you and the ARO is under my command."

There was a moment of harsh silence between the two.

"Your inexperience is going to get them killed," spoke Elucard finally.

"Hold your tongue, sergeant," spat Wiccer, grimacing from the sharp remark.

"You're still thinking like a Cloak. When Cloaks underestimate Rabbits, they get killed," continued Elucard.

"I said hold your tongue, sergeant!" commanded Wiccer, his voice clearly rising.

"Have you learned nothing from me? At least learn from your brother's deat–"

Wiccer lashed out with a ruthless backhand across Elucard's face, silencing the cold hard truth that Elucard was treading upon. The former White Cloak stood over a sneering Elucard still on the cold forest floor. A resounding gasp followed by murmurs erupted from the onlooking ARO members.

Wiccer was breathing heavily, and slowly realization of what he had done set upon him. Finding his composure, he directed himself to his unit, "Stay together, keep an eye on each other. Search the forest for Lear. Don't let the Rabbits separate you." Wiccer waited a brief period as he saw no response or movement from his men, "That's an order!" Wiccer barked.

Elucard watched as the troops vanished into the shadows of the forest before eying his former rival slightly spitefully. Wiccer offered Elucard his hand to help him up to his feet.

"I'm sorry," said Elucard after he brushed pine needles and dirt off himself.

Wiccer's face was still sour, "You're in the military now, Elucard. You will listen to my orders or I will see that you are back in chains and in a cell."

"I shouldn't have brought up your brother," said Elucard, ignoring Wiccer's threat.

"Just drop it," said Wiccer, flatly. He shook his head and proceeded in the direction of his men, "Let's go find Lear."

***

The members of the ARO hustled through the woods with adrenaline coursing through their veins and determination burning in their eyes. The Rabbits had one of their own and they would pay dearly for such a brazen action.

Up ahead of the pack, Trek raised his fist to signal the group to stop. Each ARO member moved to face a separate direction, keeping eyes on each other's blind spots. Their hands gripped their swords with anticipation.

Rulan crept up beside his brother, careful to stay within the shadows. He looked up at the surrounding trees, sweat beading down the side of his face despite the cold air. His eyes were wide with strain and worry. His mouth had been parched since Wiccer's outburst.

"Trek, did you find something?"

Trek looked curiously at the scratchings on the trunk of a tree not too far in the distance. He narrowed his eyes as he followed the markings on the trunk upward and gasped as he saw the quick movement of a shambling blur in the tree's branches. Before he could piece the image together, he felt a sharp pain in his chest and he yelped in shock. He fell backward from the invisible force and writhed in the dead leaves that blanketed the forest floor.

Trek's vision blurred and his hearing was muffled by his own constant shouting. He heard an array of voices coming from all around him.

"Essie! I need you over here!"

"Find cover, find cover!"

"Where is he? Did anyone see where the arrow came from?"

Trek felt a desperate tug on his cloak as he was swiftly dragged behind a tree. The soothing voice of Elisa who was steadily calm during the calamitous time lulled him.

"Fret not, young one. All will be fine. Your sister in battle is here."

Reassuring as Elisa's words were, the pain was unbearable. He was sure the arrow tip had been coated in some type of poison or burning agent. Grunting and breathing hard, he shakily inspected the wound and confirmed his theory. His skin was corroded around the arrow shaft. He continued to scream in agony.

Essie shoved her face into his, "Trek, you need to get a hold of yourself. We need to know where the shooter is. You saw something and you need to point it out for Timber."

Another familiar voice came after Essie's, "Aye, in which tree did you see the marksman?"

The sound of his comrades' voices could be heard over the *thud* of arrows penetrating wood and dirt all around him. Trek heard Timber muttering to Essie, "It's no use, Es. Trek's out of this one. If we could flank that general area, I could find a good shot to deal with the marksman. We're all pinned down here. The situation is fucked."

Elisa took out and polished a grimy mirror the size of her palm. Timber raised a brow annoyingly, "This isn't the time to apply makeup, sweetheart."

Elisa smiled and winked playfully. Carefully, she guided the reflective glass around the cover of the tree, using it to view everything behind her. Despite her best efforts, the mirror did not give a clear picture. A well placed arrow shot the mirror out of her hand.

"The marksman is about twenty yards ahead of us. There's a cluster of about three trees over there. The archer is well hidden, even from my shadow elf sight," reported Elisa, frowning.

Essie nodded as she broke the shaft protruding from her brother's chest. She examined the wound as best she could, "Timber, Elisa, this arrow is in deep. He needs medical attention that I can't give him here."

Timber took off her cloak and propped it onto her bow. She poked it the opposite side of where Elisa attempted her mirror trick. Within seconds the cloak was punctured by several arrows.

"Can't get a clear shot with this kind of suppression," a frustrated Timber said cursing under her breath.

Essie waved to get the attention of her other brother and Blayvaar who were behind a dirt mound across the way. Rulan watched as Essie made a series of hand gestures and nodded, understanding the code. He quietly relayed the message to Rulan.

"Trek needs serious medical attention," Blayvaar said with urgency hanging onto his words.

Calsoon slowly crawled under the ferns until he reached Rulan and Blayvaar. Rulan moved slightly over to make room for Calsoon to share their cover. Calsoon arched his back to peer over the mound, "Ah, so that's what's keeping us pinned down," he said with a thin, amused smile.

Blayvaar took a turn to peep over the mound but saw nothing, "You see something, Calsoon?"

Calsoon nodded as he drew a dagger, "The archer is covered in heavy camouflage but my eyes are too sharp to be fooled." Calsoon scribbled a drawing in the dirt using acorns as their own position and pebbles as Timber, Essie, Elisa's and Trek's position. He marked an 'x' where he spotted the marksman.

"There isn't a way to get this information to Timber without giving away that we know where the enemy is," Rulan said as he came to the painful conclusion.

"Calsoon, where are Wiccer and Elucard?" Blayvaar asked, trying to formulate a plan.

"A very good question, friend. Elucard spotted a Black Rabbit in the shadows behind us and took off as if Dhalamar himself were on his heels," Calsoon chuckled to himself amused by the imagery, "Wiccer followed after him."

"Dammit," cursed Blayvaar, "We're on our own, boys."

"What's the plan, Blayv?" Rulan asked.

"You and I will run to Timber and your sister's position, acting as decoys while Calsoon flanks the enemy and takes them out," Blayvaar said, leaning a heavy shoulder on the still smiling Calsoon.

Rulan measured the distance between the two points, "That's about three seconds of distraction, Calsoon. Does that give you enough time?"

Calsoon grinned from ear to ear, his pearly teeth almost shined in the darkness, "My friend, there is nothing to worry about. It is a fine day and I am in high spirits."

Rulan shook his head, perplexed by Calsoon's response, "I suppose it's good that one of us is."

Blayvaar turned from his back and knelt into a sprinter's knee, "Let's pray to Father this all goes right."

"Or, whoever," shrugged Calsoon, cheerfully.

Blayvaar and Rulan dashed out from the cover, ducking as arrows whizzed past their heads. They ran, their hearts beating wildly in their chests and slid into position next to their comrades. Breathing heavily, Blayvaar frantically tried to spot where Calsoon was, but could not find him.

Timber tried to follow Blayvaar's gaze, "What? What is it?"

"Calsoon. Do you see him?"

Timber shook her head and then moved to the other side of the tree, quickly waving her hand out in the open in an attempt to draw more fire. But nothing happened. The wolf carefully poked her head around the trunk and began to crawl to a neighboring tree. She nocked an arrow as a figure approached from up ahead, a dagger drawn in both hands.

"Calsoon?" Timber called to the shadowy figure.

Eyes golden like an eerie moon shinned in the night before flashing to a familiar icy blue. Timber furrowed her brow in slight confusion before seeing Calsoon emerge from the darkness, "Calsoon, you startled me."

"Forgive me, friend," Calsoon said, elegantly bowing in apology, "I took care of our troublesome acquaintance."

Timber looked beyond him, "Did you keep him for interrogation?"

"He had very little to say. I do know where they are keeping our cat, though."

Timber looked back toward the others.

"Go help them with Trek, I will be fine on my own," offered Calsoon.

Timber looked back to Calsoon, but was surprised to find he was already gone.

***

"Elucard we need to go back! Our men are pinned down and need our help!" Wiccer shouted ahead of him to Elucard as the two dashed through the forest with explosive energy.

Elucard ignored Wiccer, blinded by rage from who he saw in the shadows. His mind was clouded from any rational thought, but he was dead sure he saw Baines.

Wiccer burst with an extra spurt of speed to grab Elucard's shoulder and spun him around to face him, "I don't know what you saw that made you take off and abandon your men in their time of need, but we have to go back now!"

Elucard's eyes darted beyond them, his lip arched up in a sneer. They were not alone.

"Did you hear me? I sai–" shouted Wiccer before Elucard gagged him with a hand.

"Quiet. He's here," whispered Elucard. Elucard swung his head around and threw a pair of daggers into the shadows behind him. He listened to the silence before he heard a vile snickering echo in the trees around them. From behind one of the trees appeared his former teacher, Baines.

Wiccer drew his blade as did Elucard. However, Elucard still searched the surrounding woods.

"What is it, are there more?" Wiccer asked, still focused on the threat before them.

"Where there is Baines, Ridge is close to follow," Elucard whispered sharply.

Baines' snickering quickly halted, his smile vanished from his face. He looked hard at the masked and hooded figure in front of him, "Alanna's bow! Is that you, Elucard?"

Elucard lowered his mask to around his neck, his magenta eyes sunken with pure hatred.

"You're supposed to be dead! What game is this?" Baines exclaimed, his voice louder. His eyes were wide and face was pale as if he were looking into the eyes of a wight.

"I've come back from the brink of Alanna's grasp to finish what I started!" Elucard snarled as he stepped forward.

"We Rabbits are the ones that will clean up your mess!" Baines said, smiling snarkily as his eyes jolted upwards.

Elucard had mere moments to look upward and even less than that to tackle Wiccer out of the way as Ridge rained down, driving his sword into the ground.

Elucard roared as he viscously lunged at Ridge, slashing upwards, but hitting only air. Ridge side stepped and spun around with his own attack. Elucard met the attack with a clashing block and pushed forward with enraging power. Ridge grunted, unable to hold firm as his feet slid back across the dirt.

Elucard broke the test of mettle and thrust forward, puncturing his enemy's side. With a savage kick, Elucard threw Ridge flying backward into a tree. Ridge clenched his teeth, calling for aid from his Blade

Brother, but found that he was already pre-occupied with Elucard's partner.

Wiccer ducked and slid a half-circle around Baines as the Rabbit slashed into the air. Wiccer plunged his sword forward but only grazed his enemy's side. Baines grabbed Wiccer's sword arm and flung him forward.

Wiccer tumbled over the forest floor and twisted to land back on his feet, adjusting his cloak that wrapped around him.

Baines twirled his sword in his hand, calling back to his Blade Brother, "Red and black assassins. It looks like Elucard found a new clan."

Ridge kicked Elucard away from him and wiped blood from his mouth, "Is that what you've been up to these last four months? Joining another clan of assassins?"

Elucard lunged into Ridge, jutting his elbow into Ridge's chest, following with a swerving slice. Ridge stumbled backward as Elucard finished his attack with a roundhouse kick that sent him sailing into the trunk of a tree.

Dazed, he called out for his Blade Brother, "Baines, I need you!" but there was no answer.

Now, seeing he was alone with an Elucard fueled with vengeance, Ridge stepped forward from the tree, his blood smeared on the bark. He gripped his sword's handle and rushed forward, slicing at his opponent.

Elucard was drowning in his malice for his former clan, but he was extremely focused. He would not allow his anger to be his folly. It drove him, but did not rule him. Defending with lightning fast reflexes and a well timed parry, Elucard made short work of Ridge, pushing him back into the tree again and impaling his blade into the Rabbit's shoulder, pinning him to the long trunk.

Ridge grimaced in pain, and desperately looked for Baines.

"Focus on me!" Elucard ordered, grabbing his chin.

"Baines, my Brother! Where are you?" Ridge called out in fear.

Elucard glanced over his shoulder spotting a victorious Wiccer wiping his blade over the corpse of his former teacher. Smirking, he turned his attention back on his prisoner, "You have info I need."

"Elucard! Is he still alive?" Wiccer called to his companion, "Tie him up and we'll bring him back to camp."

Elucard narrowed his eyes and brought his mouth to Ridge's elven ear, "Who killed Jetta?"

Ridge smirked, "A one track mind, eh Elucard?"

Elucard twisted his grip sending a spurt of extreme pain blazing into his captive's shoulder. Ridge roared in anguish.

"Who killed Jetta?" Elucard asked again, no change or fluctuation in his voice.

"I-I h-hope the answer to that question brings you more pain than what I'm suffering from right now!" Ridge spat, saliva dribbling from his lips and off his chin.

"You want to see pain?" Elucard hissed. He drew a dagger and with the same motion drove it under Ridge's ribs, twisting the blade wickedly.

Ridge cried out in sheer agony before Wiccer could wrestle Elucard from him, "Enough! You're going to kill him!" Wiccer ripped up Ridge's cloak and attempted to stop the profusely bleeding wounds. But the damage was done. Within moments Ridge was dead.

Wiccer pulled the sword from Ridge's body and threw it between Elucard's feet, "What was that? What is wrong with you?"

Elucard took his sword and sheathed it. He walked past Wiccer in a dark silence.

"Answer me!" Wiccer tried again.

"I caught a second set of tracks a little ways back here. Lear is this way," Elucard replied, deflecting Wiccer's questions.

"We need to be on the same level here. We're at war with Estinia! You're going to get us killed with your petty feud!"

Elucard stopped in his tracks. Without turning to Wiccer, he repeated his response, "This way. Lear is this way."

Wiccer opened his mouth to pursue his original question, but decided against it. He knew Lear was the bigger priority at moment and his questions for Elucard would need to wait.

Following Elucard through the forest, the two were surprised to find a scene of recent bloodshed as three Black Rabbits were strewn about, daggers in their chest, and throats slit. Untying a clearly shaken Lear, they found Calsoon.

"Calsoon, did you do all this?" Wiccer asked in amazement, stepping over the bodies as Elucard inspected the handiwork.

"Indeed, dear captain," Calsoon said, amused with himself.

"Impressive, Calsoon," Elucard said, taking pouches of shuriken and any daggers he could find off the corpses.

Calsoon grinned with satisfaction.

Wiccer checked Lear for any wounds, but found none, "Can you walk?"

"This yikahti would just like to get this day over with, Captain."

"I think we can all agree with that," Wiccer sighed, looking back at Elucard.

Elucard caught Wiccer's gaze. He stared back darkly. Helping to shoulder an exhausted Lear, they all made their way back to camp. A long and dangerous day was behind them, but they knew even grimmer times lay ahead.

62

The weary Watchers sat outside the medical tent in the Northern Shore camp. Essie assisted the surgeons dealing with Trek's egregious chest wound.

As they carried him on a makeshift stretcher made of boiled leather belts, his clothes began to soak through from hemorrhaging. Despite Essie's best efforts and determination to save her sibling, she knew Alanna wanted him more.

"I swear to Father…" A distraught Rulan started, mumbling under his breath just loud enough for Wiccer to hear, "…if he dies, it will be on your head." He rose from the log he was seated on and turned to face the two leaders.

Blayvaar rested a gentle hand on Rulan's shoulder, "It was a Rabbit arrow that hit Trek, not Wiccer's blade," he said, attempting to calm his friend.

Rulan turned to respond to Blayvaar but the sight of Essie emerging from the medical tent caught his attention. Her apron was drenched in blood and her hands were shivering uncontrollably as she wiped them clean with a rag. Her teeth were clenched and tears rolled down her cheeks.

"Tr-Tr–" she stuttered trying to overcome the pain that wrung her like a wet towel.

Rulan did not let her finish. He knew the truth even before she spoke. But it was not the loss of Trek alone that sent him into a spiraling rage on the inside. His anger was pointed directly at Wiccer and his incompetence as a leader on the battlefield.

Rulan charged Wiccer. He grabbed him by his red cloak and brought him close to his face. Rulan's eyes were red with tears and anger, "You! You did this! You did this to Trek! Your hands are covered in his blood!"

Wiccer was silent.

"You refused to listen to Elucard and then vanished when we were ambushed."

Wiccer continued with his silence.

Rulan pushed his captain, sending him stumbling backwards, "Say something! Answer for yourself!"

What could Wiccer say in his own defense? He agreed with Rulan wholeheartedly. He had failed his men once again. He was their captain, charged by their country to lead them to success and to protect them with erudite leadership. He accomplished neither in his eyes. His father was a fool to think he was ready to be a leader of men. Wiccer was even more foolish to have believed such a thing. Now Trek was dead and it was on his hands.

"Have you nothing to say?" Rulan shouted again.

"Stand down, private," a voice called out.

Wiccer looked behind him to see Elucard. Rulan gawked teary eyed and hot-faced.

"The Black Rabbits played us all. Something we should have expected. They are masters of manipulation. They've been training for years to deal with any form of threat to their ways."

"Then what was the point of all our training? If we can't beat them, why try?" Rulan spat, now angrier than ever.

"We are at war with the Black Rabbit clan. When you go to war with someone you must expect battles and defeats. Do not let a single defeat deter you from pursuing vengeance. They have trained for years, you have trained for months. Right now we have the taste of our own blood on our tongue, but not for long. Retribution will be ours!"

Rulan narrowed his eyes. A thin smirk appeared on his face. He continued to listen, swayed by the bloodlust in Elucard's words.

"We are not Koda's shield. We do not protect him from the Rabbits. We are not his sword. We do not fight along side him. We are his dagger. We hunt in the shadows, dealing sinister blows to the enemies that his soldiers can not see." Elucard moved his sight from battered man to battered man. He finally rested his gaze on Wiccer, who was paying close mind to Elucard's words. Wiccer had forgotten what he was transforming into. He had forgotten that he was no longer a White Cloak, "We are rogues who hunt rogues. We are the shadows that guard the light. We are the Watchers! Never forget that!"

A cheer erupted from his men. Wiccer nodded in approval to Elucard.

"We have a long march ahead of us, but before we head out, we must see to Trek's final walk to Alanna's embrace," Elucard said as he wrapped an arm around Rulan's shoulders.

***

Gathered around a shallow grave just beyond the dunes of the beach, The ARO members surrounded Trek's final resting place. A short tower of stones served as a grave marker. The rocks were smoothed from a small stream that washed out into the ocean.

Timber knelt down and placed an arrow shaft wrapped in wild flowers from a nearby field, "Alanna will train you to become her archer. Here is your first arrow, Trek. Use it well."

Elisa placed a silver coin on top of his grave, "Show your respects to Alanna. Give this trit to to her as a gift."

Lear unsheathed his rapier. It was his personal blade. He had been unsatisfied with the ninjato Elucard tried to assign him. He leaned it against the grave marker, "Take this with you. It will serve you better than any blade you will find in the Roaming Plane."

Blayvaar produced a small piece of black root with dark green stripes running around it. He dug a small pocket in the loose dirt of the grave and buried the root in it, "Blissroot, my friend. Illegal in Long Whisper, but you are in Long whisper no more," he stifled a smile as he chewed on a bit of blissroot of his own.

Essie took a knife and cut her hand and passed the knife to Rulan. Together they dripped their blood unto their brother's grave.

"Trek..." Rulan tried to speak, but lowered his head unable to finish.

"Trek, we are triplets. Forever bound like no other. Take a part of us with you and we will be with you for eternity." Essie's gentle voice warmed the hearts of her comrades.

Wiccer took out one of his daggers and thrust it hard into the dirt. He stood back up straight and gave a long salute, "You died a hero. No one could argue that. At ease, soldier."

Elucard bent down and took a small handful of dirt and trickled it back unto the grave. A small drift of wind caught it as it danced away in the breeze, *"Sen lmis Roam'Alan es lmes'cas Dala."*

Not all shadows are meant to be feared.

63

Koda strode upon his gray riding wolf through the forest. The elves of Long Whisper had long used these giant wolves as a mode of transportation as opposed to the common horses used by most other countries. They were only slightly smaller than a horse and easily carried the light weight of the elves. Athar Moonfall and Cass Baneberry rode on either side of him, both matching his slow pace. His familiar, Wildeye, trotted just ahead of the three as they followed the long train of their armies on the old merchant road. The morning light failed to cut through the thick canopy, transforming an otherwise serene morning into a dim one.

"I heard your ARO did a piss poor job of clearing out this forest. I also heard that one of the scoundrels died in the quarrel. Are you sure it's safe to take this route, my king?" asked Athar as his head darted about suspiciously.

Cass answered back, "That *scoundrel*, as you put it, died so that our men could pass through this forsaken forest with little to no strife. Luckily for you, it was he who took that vile arrow and not you. It'd be a shame to fill your fine cloak with poisoned arrows. What a waste of good cloth." Every word he spoke was coated in disdain.

Athar sneered without making eye contact with the lord, "We are fools to trust ARO. They were trained by the king killer himself."

"That may be the case, but if King Koda trusts them, I would be willing to trust them myself," Cass said without hesitation.

"Once a Black Rabbit, always a Black Rabbit," Athar responded snidely.

"It takes a Rabbit to hunt a Rabbit, my Lord," finished Cass.

The three of them turned to see Avalon galloping up from the rear on her own wolf. She caught up to their pace before pulling her reins to slow the wolf's speed. She made an extra effort to learn to control her mount as she remembered her utter failings as a drake rider.

"The mountains rise in the distance. We are close to Stonewall. Has the scout returned to report his findings?" Avalon asked pointing to the tall mountains seen from a clearing in the trees.

"We've heard no word from our scout, nor the one we sent before him," Koda said. When the first scout did not return he felt a justified concern, but Athar convinced him that the forest was large and it would be easy for one to get lost.

The realization set in and Avalon became distressed, "My king, we are walking into a trap!"

"Nonsense, Silent One. Stonewall has no clue we are even coming," Athar retorted lightly.

"Surely you jest?" Avalon replied in disbelief, "Stonewall has known of our arrival since we reached the shores. Why do you think the ARO ran into Rabbits two days ago? If you do not halt our men, I will do it for you!" spat Avalon.

Athar's face grew sour, "Do you forget yourself, Silent One? I should have you in chains for such insolence!"

Avalon turned to Koda with desperation on her face, "My king, listen to reason. What waits beyond this forest is death. We need to send Elucard to investigate what Stonewall has in store for us."

Koda turned to Athar and then to Cass, as if looking for an answer to a question he did not know.

"My king," Athar complained, "if we send Elucard to investigate, who is to say he won't join his former Black Rabbit companions? If I remember correctly, Captain Newsun did mention that Elucard chased after and killed a potential prisoner during their mission. Elucard is no soldier of Long Whisper. He cannot and should never be trusted."

A large crash and the splintering of trees filled the air from up ahead, interrupting their conversation. Blood curdling screams rang out as wooden shrapnel lodged itself into the flesh of dozens of men. Several more loud sounds came crashing in from the distance, as if a giant were barreling through the trees, shaking the forest by the roots. Panic ran rampant throughout the caravan.

"Athar Moonfall, you've doomed us all," spat Avalon as a scowl grew on her face.

Athar hid a cruel smile, he knew what he had done. He had played Koda to look like an inexperienced fool, but his work was not complete yet.

Koda swallowed hard, his face was a ghostly white. A voice in his head told him to take a deep breath and remain calm. He did as the voice said. He collected himself so that he could lead his army.

"Cass, Athar, Avalon, on me!" he ordered as he kicked his heels into the wolf's side and rode past countless soldiers, making his way to the front lines.

The leading point of the army was a complete disaster. Fallen trees had collapsed on top of unlucky soldiers. Blood was splattered across the dirt. Limbs were scattered about as mangled men crawled for cover. Far in the distance, the city of Stonewall was nestled in a valley of the mountains. A vanguard of Estinian soldiers and siege weaponry were set up beyond the edge of the forest. Ballistas recoiled and fired gruesome, flaming steel-tipped bolts into the forest as they collided into the frantic men below. The trees exploded from the impact of the bolts, cracking their trunks into deadly wooden shrapnel. Catapults launched large flaming boulders into the canopy crashing down with sundering force, decimating soldiers below.

"Fall back! Fall back!" the commands of General Ashmer could be heard cutting through the chaos like an axe.

Koda took another look at the destructive enemy force outside Stonewall before running back deeper into the forest, leaving the apocalyptic scene of his inexperience and failure behind.

64

Deep in the night, the soft sounds of scurrying feet could be heard as Essie moved across the forest floor. She used her ARO training to muffle her footsteps while the collar of her cloak masked her cold breath in the frigid darkness. In the distance beyond the forest's edge, the camps of Estinain forces could be seen. Large fires blazed as groups of enemy soldiers huddled around the welcoming warmth.

Koda's men had no such opportunity to light even an ember. A single spark would give away their position and another onslaught of attacks would befall the already shaken forest. During the first week, the king's mages were able to shield the soliders from most attacks. However after awhile their magic waned and several of the mages were killed. That left the remaining six mages hesitant and defensive.

Essie leaned against an uprooted tree. Its trunk was large enough to provide temporary cover as she took a moment to count her supplies. She bit her lip when she found herself low on dullweed, a plant used to numb the pain of a patient. She tried to think how her supply could have run out so quickly. They had been entrenched in this forest for the last week. She started with at least twenty pieces of the weed, and that was enough for forty patients. The attacks left soldiers completely mutilated and maimed. Dullweed was given out liberally at first, but all that changed after the third night.

I should find some bitterbark.

Bitterbark was not as potent as dullweed, but kept the pain low enough to avoid sending a patient into shock. Finding it would be the tricky part, but at this point it would not be as scarce as dullweed.

Noticing a flash of shadows weave into an adjacent tree, she whistled a low call to grab the attention of a fellow soldier. The soldier poked his head around the corner, showing that he was a fellow medic. Essie motioned for him to run to her, but the medic seemed too fearful to expose himself. After another failed attempt at convincing him to come over, Essie darted and slid to his tree.

"Private Essie Windfoot, first Anti-Rogue Ops," Essie rapped out her name, rank, and unit in a single heavy breath. Sure to keep her tone low so that he could hear, but not those around her.

"Corporal Jempsen Rivertread, second Medical Corps. I'm attached to the first Wolf Lancer Division. Can't find any of them though. Have you seen any Wolf Lancers, Private?" His eyes were tired and blank. The unit he was attached to was part of the front line. The Wolf Lancers were scattered after the first day, and Jempsen had been wandering among the forest ever since.

Essie instinctively checked Jempsen for any visible wounds. He was shaken to the core, but was not physically injured. She frowned and shook her head, "Sorry, Corporal, I've not run into your kin," She pointed a ways off, and Jempsen turned his head to where she pointed with a delayed reaction, "I know if you walk a bit that way, you'll run into a Sergeant Elimder Barkwick. He's a platoon sergeant for the second Tactical Information Relay Division. If TIR doesn't know where the Wolf Lancers are…Well, he'll know."

Jempsen continued to stare off in a daze. After a minute or two, he finally responded, "Thanks, Windfoot."

Essie grabbed him by the sleeve as he was getting up, "Corporal, do you have any dullweed you can spare? Maybe some bitterbark?"

Jempsen reached into his haversack and pulled out a stack of dullweed tied by twine and tossed it into Essie's shivering hands. She smiled weakly and carefully stashed the dullweed in her medical satchel. She watched as Jempsen slowly trudged through the forest once more. She took a long breath and moved out of her resting place herself.

***

The night grew colder as the pale moonlight revealed itself from the navy blue clouds. The night was at the pinnacle of danger when the moon came out. What was once a safe and quiet time within the foxholes became a troublesome rat race to keep from being hit by bombarding boulders and piercing ballista bolts.

Essie dashed quickly, sliding into the nearest foxhole as the delicate moonlight dawned on the forest floor. The frosty air hung silent. Not a howl from a wolf nor a peep from a soldier could be heard throughout the lines.

Blayvaar and Lear smiled lightly, happy to see the familiar face of Essie as she dove into their foxhole. They wrapped their cloaks around themselves to keep warm. Lear nibbled on the carcass of a vole he found in the loose dirt. He tried sharing the mutilated rodent with Essie, but she made a squirming face and politely refused the offer.

Blayvaar prodded Essie on the arm and used his ARO training to whisper lowly, "Hey Es, any word on when more rations are coming this way? We haven't eat–" he scrunched his face at the sight of Lear happily chewing the small critter's bones and intestines, "*I* haven't eaten in three days."

Essie took out her last loaf of bread and broke off a sizable piece. She then tore that piece in half and gave the pieces to Blayvaar and Lear.

"Chew slowly. When you eat too fast after having not eaten for so long, you can get awful stomach cramps," Essie warned as she inspected her two companions for any physical damage, "Which way to the captain's foxhole?" she finally asked after being satisfied with her inspections.

"This yikahti saw him taking a piss further to the east. Be careful Essie," Lear said between mouthfuls of bread.

Essie nodded as she jumped out of the hole and sprinted to the east.

***

Essie crawled on the flat of her stomach as she moved closer to Wiccer and Ashmer's foxhole. Once already, a fiery boulder had careened through the night, crashing somewhere in the northern lines. Cries for medics broke through the thin air, giving away the fact that Estinia had landed another triumphant strike. Essie squeezed her eyes shut, drowning out the screams of anguish, attempting to concentrate on the task at hand. She needed to find out if there were anymore supplies coming from the north to refill her dwindling resources, and hopefully garner word on any reinforcements.

"Captain?" Essie whispered at the edge of the foxhole. She was surprised to find that the foxhole was filled with several people. Along with Wiccer and Ashmer, Avalon and Elucard were in the foxhole as well.

Wiccer reached over and gingerly pulled Essie into the warmth that the several bodies gave off. They were huddled in a circle looking over a topographical map of Stonewall and the surrounding forests and mountains. Several 'x's' were scratched onto the map, each indicating the locations of the different units and overall forces of Koda's men. A set of lines and circles marked the Stonewall side of the map, indicating Estinia's large force.

"I've reported to King Koda, Lord Athar, and Lady Baneberry that we've lost a quarter of our men to wounds, injuries, and sickness. Another quarter is also in rough shape and will probably add to our casualties if we stay in this position another week," spoke Ashmer in a low raspy voice. He coughed and hacked as he attempted to the get the string of words in one go.

Essie took out her water skin and a few herbs. She placed the herbs into a wooden cup and poured in the water she had to make a crude paste, "It's not hot tea, general, but this will help with your cough."

Ashmer gratefully accepted. His face puckered from the bitter taste, "Could use some sugar, private."

Essie frowned lightheartedly, "Fresh out of sugar, sir."

"Fresh out of a lot of things," added Avalon grimly.

"When are we getting fresh supplies, captain?" Essie asked Wiccer.

"We were supposed to get new supplies two days ago. We've heard nothing from the quartermaster. No raven, no scout, nothing." His mind was heavy with the entire situation, not just the lack of information coming from the Northern Shore.

"Elucard, what are your thoughts? Are Black Rabbits cutting off our supply caravans?" asked Ashmer between wheezes.

Elucard looked at Avalon as she nodded the answer that he already knew, "No doubt, General."

Ashmer's mood soured even more. He took the final sip of the cold paste before turning his attention to Wiccer, "I don't know how many Rabbits are on the road to the north; obviously enough to interrupt a large supply caravan. Can your ARO recapture that access road?"

Wiccer's eyes darted to Essie, then to Elucard, before finally giving his gloomy answer, "General, my men haven't had rations in at least three days. They are stricken with sickness and have not slept in a week. To ask them to deal with a squad of Black Rabbits would be unwise. I would advise taking a platoon of men to secure that road."

Ashmer frowned from the answer, "I will advise Koda and the two lords to make a decision. As of now, we have no food, no medical supplies, sick men, and nowhere to bring our injured. If we do not take swift action, the king's best option will be to surrender and hope that Estinia takes prisoners!"

Essie scrambled up the foxhole. Supplies or not, defeat or not, her job was not done. She pressed onward into the cold, somber night.

65

While it was true that Varis's army was occupied defending the capital, its police force still roamed the countryside. The men of the Varisian mounted police, who normally responded to bandit attacks or simply escorted travelers to their destinations now did their part to perform harassing actions against Estinian troops wherever they could, performing hit-and-run style guerrilla warfare, made possible by their quick and nimble courser horses. The mounted police would enter Estinian scouting camps in the forest, kill as many men as they could, and then leave before they could suffer a single casualty of their own.

One such force, the Arborvale County Gendarmerie, under the command of Lieutenant Lucerne Foseman, had arrived on the outskirts of the forest were ARO and the Long Whisper regulars were surrounded.

The police had followed the trail of Estinian bodies that their allies had left in their wake to this section of the wood. Lieutenant Foseman had every intention of joining up with them. This was before he saw a regiment sized group of Estinian troops close in on the area and surround it. His men had to wait until nightfall to attempt to break the encirclement. Now that the moon was up, they would not allow their comrades to suffer any longer.

A group of sixty policemen stalked through a poorly lit forest trail in the undergrowth with their horses, riding as quietly as they could towards the trapped army of Long Whisper. The trail was straight and narrow, flanked by thick ferns on either side. What little moonlight the men had trickled through the thick forest canopy.

The men kept their mounts calm and silent by stroking their manes and whispering in their ears as they walked. All it would take for them to lose their advantage of surprise was a single Estinian lookout.

"Sir," said one of the men, "I hear the sound of a bowstring stretching."

"There are all kinds of trees here, Ferenc," whispered Lieutenant Foseman in reply, "I'm sure it's a branch or something."

In the back of his mind, Foseman agreed with Ferenc – that was a bowstring. But he desperately wanted to be wrong. There was very little he could do to react to an ambush in this darkness anyway. The men were following sounds – foreign voices in the darkness. Under the low visibility of the moonlight, the horses were leading the men down the forest trail just as much as the men steered the horses.

Another stretching creak came from the treetops.

"There it is again," Ferenc mumbled.

Foseman said nothing in reply. He just wished that the archers – if they were truly there at all – second guessed themselves and believed that there was nothing to shoot at. If he could perfectly mimic a deer or an elk to throw them off, he would. He could almost feel the eyes staring at him from the trees, but the feeling of helplessness was very real.

A quick whistle cut through the air, ending in a loud thud.

"I'm hit! Sir, I'm hit!" cried a voice from the middle of the formation.

The horses began to neigh and rear – no smooth caresses or gentle whispers could calm them now.

Without a second thought, Lieutenant Foseman wheeled his mount around and galloped towards his screaming companion. As he did this, more whistles came down from the tree tops – there was not enough moonlight to see where they came from.

"Shields up, men!" Foseman bellowed as he saw to the first man that was hit. He felt around in the darkness on the injured man's body, checking for the protrustion of the arrow or the stickiness of blood.

"What's this? What are you screaming for?" Foseman said as he grabbed the shaft of the arrow and broke it off, "You're fine, you idiot! Your armor saved you!"

The policeman let out a nervous laugh and opened his mouth to speak, but was interrupted as an arrow struck him through the top of his unprotected head.

More arrows rained down from the forest canopy. The men now joined their horses in panicked screaming as arrows struck the men's shields and the ground around them. Foseman himself grabbed his small buckler and raised it over his head, just in time to stop an arrow.

"Damn it! Troop – on me! We're getting the hell out of this kill zone!"

The men did not wait for another word – with loud shouts, the mounted police sped through the forest at full gallop, with branches and leaves smacking the faces of riders as their horses raced towards anywhere-but-there.

"Stay in formation, men!" Foseman yelled as he spurred his horse to catch up with the broken troop, "Regroup on me! We have to rescue the Lost Dawn contingent!"

It was no use. The horses were scattering in the darkness. Arrows pierced thighs, heads, and hands. A lifeless policeman clung to his still fleeing horse with an arrow sticking out of his neck that pinned him to the animal.

Foseman could say nothing more than "Go!" as he rode as fast as he could to get out of the woods.

He could see a clearing just a few meters ahead. If he could reach it in time, his men could regroup and form a counter-charge. There was hope for a moment.

Then it was gone – an arrow struck Foseman's horse and threw them both to the forest floor. As he landed, he heard the sound of a bone breaking – his leg refused to obey him. Mustering up what strength he could, he crawled towards his horse, which lay thrashing and screaming on the earth.

"Ember!" he said as he cradled the animal's head in his arms. The horse had been with him for years, and had saved him from countless enemies. Now it was time for him to rest, "There's no need to suffer anymore."

As the rest of his men who were still mounted galloped aimlessly around him in a rout, Lieutenant Foseman pulled out a dagger and stabbed his horse in the throat. The creature's pitiful crying ceased, and Foseman allowed himself to cry before an arrow struck him in the side of the head.

66

"Ve hev King Koda jus vhere ve vant him, cowering en de forest vith his men dying all around him," said Commander Unrick, smiling with bloodthirsty satisfaction. He was the leader of the Estinian force occupying Stonewall. He was a weaselly man with a long nose, a thin minute-hand mustache, and a boney chin that matched his cheeks. At the tip of his chin, he sported a neatly trimmed tuft.

Unrick gazed out of a circular window as his siege machinery continued their horrific onslaught on the forest. Turning around, he sat back down at the desk within the room that once been the office of Stonewall's mayor. He spent a solid minute wiping his teeth clean of any remnants of pheasant meat before turning his attention to the two men that waited patiently to be addressed.

"Inle, vhat news of de Northern Shore do you bring me?" he finally asked.

Inle bowed graciously, as he had learned quickly to do in the presence of his volatile allies. They were easy to upset and quick to be offended, "My Lord, my High Blade has sent a large squad of our kin to capture the roads. Please allow him to make the report."

Unrick nodded towards Legion, indicating for him to pick up where Inle had left off.

"My men have captured and burned several supply caravans and reinforcements heading to Koda's front lines. We also shot down several messenger ravens both requesting more supplies and warning the front lines of the road being captured. We have effectively stopped all flow of support to Koda." Legion reported. His voice was monotone and without emotion. It was unsettling to Inle.

"Dis es good news to hear! De Div'Rah vill be pleased vith my performance," Unrick said, sitting back and smiling.

"As you can see, my Lord, we Black Rabbits are an excellent al–" Inle started.

"De Div'Rah vould indeed be happy vith you Rabbits, ef you could preform von more task."

Inle looked at Legion before responding to Unrick, "What task would that be, my Lord?"

"Koda needs to die tonight. Can you do dat, Rabbit?"

"Of course that can be arranged, my Lord," said Inle as he bowed pompously.

Outside the office, Legion glided gracefully but aggressively into Inle. Grabbing him by the collar, he slammed him against the wall, "Do not let this power trip go to your head, First Blade. I am High Blade; I am in command of this operation. I accept the missions, I deal with everything while the Silent Master is not at hand!"

Legion was fierce and a legend in his own right; one to be feared and revered. Inle knew this, but he also knew Legion was in no position to make threats. The Div'Rah saw Inle as the commander of the Black Rabbits and so long as they were to continue this campaign, Inle would be sure to play that part. He was a performer after all and he saw himself fitting this part perfectly. But he would have to handle Legion delicately all the same. Without Legion on his side, the rest of the Rabbits would not give him his due respect.

"My High Blade, I would never overstep my boundaries. I am simply the liaison of our clan for the Estinain people. Nothing more, nothing less."

"Do not play coy with me, Inle. I am fully aware of the kind of elf you are capable of being," snapped Legion, tightening his grip.

"Let us not forget who is partially responsible for crafting me into that elf," Inle hissed.

Legion narrowed his eyes and released him, "Take Dest and Vemrick with you."

"Koda is but a mouse in a corner. I will go alone."

"A cornered mouse will bite. Take them. The collective experience will be good for the mission."

***

The moon was cloaked in a veil of clouds as it had been for the last several nights. The lack of moonlight made for excellent cover as the Black Rabbits slipped through the front lines of Koda's forces. The trio moved around several foxholes, searching each one for Koda.

"Look how they slumber Inle, it would be a shame to not kill each one," Dest mused as she loomed over a nest of soldiers sleeping in a huddled clump within the foxhole."

Inle took a brief moment to watch a soldier stir innocently before going back to searching for Koda's foxhole, "We have work to do, Dest. Don't get distracted."

Dest unsheathed her blade silently and chuckled, "Well, what about you Vemrick? Want to slit a few throats while we're here?"

Dest's smile disappeared as Vemrick's response did not reach her ears.

"Vemrick?" Dest turned to find her companion missing. She swiftly scanned her surroundings, calling for Vemrick as loud and as far as her whispers could reach, but still no answer back from the elf.

Inle took in a long sigh, clearly annoyed with the performance of the supposedly experienced Dest and Vemrick, "Will you two quit fooling around?"

He, too, was met with silence; twice the silence as before. Quickly he spun around, blade at the ready. To his curious delight, he found three oddly dressed assassins. They looked like Black Rabbits, but instead of the traditional black and violet colors, they bore crimson and black uniforms. Inle's curiosity got the best of him. His perplexed face grew a wide smile once he saw the bodies of Dest and Vemrick laying at the feet of the three strangers.

"Assassins from Varis?" Inle asked, tapping his sword on his shoulder in a casual manner.

One of the assassins removed her hood to show off her exotically beautiful shadow elf face. She twirled a dagger around in her fingers, "It's been a long time, Shadow Kin."

Inle's pleasure was slowly turning into quivering rage at the sight of Elisa, "I see you are running with a new clan."

Lear removed his hood revealing his keen yikahti eyes, "We be no assassins, Rabbit!"

Blayvaar lowered his mask and took a pair of daggers from a set of sheathes behind his waist, "We're Watchers. Born and bred to hunt assassins. Now watch us work!"

Inle was furious. Had Elisa trained Koda's men in the Black Rabbit ways to hunt Black Rabbits? He did his best to mask his anger and simply bowed. A new show was about to start. His audience had taken their seats and it was now time to be the show stopper he was born to be.

Blayvaar, Lear, and Elisa rushed him, enclosing on all sides. Lear's reach was longer, forcing Inle to deal with the yikahti's rapier first. Inle spun into the inside reach of Lear, and struck the cat's chest with an elbow, knocking Lear backwards.

Blayvaar sliced furiously with his set of knives, but Inle leaped and flipped over Lear, gathering distance away from the ARO members.

Elisa cartwheeled with a single hand to match the speed of Inle's movements, finishing off with a graceful roundhouse kick at Inle's head. Inle snapped his forearm up and blocked the kick, dropping his own body down and sweeping his leg into Elisa's legs, tripping her backwards. Inle took advantage of his off-balance opponent and thrust a side kick into her ribs. The blow sent her flying into a nearby tree.

Inle spun his sword in his hand as he neared Elisa's crumpled body, but was caught by a dagger driving into his side. Furious at the sneak attack made by Blayvaar, Inle viscously back handed the former thief. Blayvaar was knocked into the air, twisting like a rag doll and slamming into the cold ground. Inle raised his blade to strike down and finish Blayvaar, but Lear slid into sight, parrying Inle's blade to the side.

Inle huffed in annoyance, attempting to reach for his weapon, but Lear slapped it further away.

"Before ARO, this yikahti was an accomplished swordsman, perhaps better than you, Rabbit."

Inle feigned to reach for his blade again, but pulled out and threw several daggers into Lear's throat and right shoulder. Lear reached for his wounds in shock, giving Inle ample time to grab his blade and thrust it into Lear's stomach. Inle finished his advance by kicking the yikahti off of his blade.

Inle grabbed Blayvaar by the tuft of his hair and brought the elf's head close to his, "Where is Koda?"

"Find him yourself," hissed Blayvaar.

Inle glanced about his surroundings, no doubt the commotion from the fight would bring others to investigate. He was wasting time dealing with this nuisance. With a hefty backhand, he rendered Blayvaar unconscious, "Very well," he whispered as he left to look for Koda's foxhole.

***

The back of the forest was quieter than the front lines. Although the cold night enhanced how sound traveled through the forest, the rearward lines were relatively undisturbed by Inle's skirmish with the Watchers.

The shadow elf crouched over the foxhole of Koda and his two tribal lords. Koda stirred in his sleep as Cass and Athar slumbered in the much needed peace that the unattacked forest provided. Taking out a thin garrote wire, Inle carefully wrapped it around the throat of the mage king, raising the two ends ever so slightly so that the wire

310

tightened at a slow pace. At first there was not much movement from Inle's victim, but soon Koda's feet fidgeted as he began to choke and struggle.

"Drop him, Inle."

A burning memory shot through Inle's ears and drove deep into his mind like a meteor crashing through the atmosphere. That voice. A voice he could never forget. The voice that was carved into his heart, mind, and soul. But it could not be him.

Inle hesitated, haunted by the familiar voice. He turned around to face where it came from, nearly gagging on a flood of emotions.

"M-Master? Is that you?" whispered Inle. He raised his mask from his face to get a better look. He struggled to quell an enormous amount of questions and revived hopes and dreams.

Elucard's cold, dead stare would have slain any common man, but Inle was no common man. Elucard signaled for the remainder of his ARO team to surround the smitten Inle.

The wire in the Rabbit's hands slacked and Koda lurched forward gasping for air. Inle's hands shivered as he tried to quell the clutter of feelings. Anger, longing, confusion, and love coursed through his heart and mind, "M-Master, you are a-alive? How can this be?" Inle sputtered.

Elucard attempted to step closer, but Inle snapped out of his stupor and snatched Koda by his collar and brought him into his arms. A sharp dagger rested under Koda's chin, pressed hard against the king's throat.

"I've seen your tricks my king. Make a move and I'll bleed you dry, right here!" Inle threatened. The young elf had always had a firm grasp on his actions and emotions, but now he was a mess. His thoughts were erratic and this night had been a brewing storm of unpredictability and failure. How could Elucard be alive? Why did he wait until now to reveal himself? Inle lowered his mask.

"Inle, drop him. There is no winning this battle," said Elucard, ignoring Inle's questions and trying to reason with his former student.

"Master, you will be proud to know I am the First Blade now. I have sway in the clan. Come back with me and you can rejoin us. All can be forgiven, Master. We can be a family once more," said Inle as he slowly backed away with his hostage.

"Let him pass!" Wiccer exclaimed, "Timber, keep an eye on him."

Elucard gingerly kept up with Inle as the shadow elf retreated.

Inle recanted tales of a happier time for him, "You and I were an unstoppable team. Can you imagine what we could do together now?

You can even be First Blade again, I wouldn't mind. I'd do anything for you, Elucard."

Elucard knew the situation was delicate. His student was as delusional as ever, but now he had Koda's life at knife point.

"Inle I don't want you to die this night. Not by their hands. You and I could be together, but not if my team kills you. You need to let the king go and come with me." Elucard spoke as calmly as possible. Thoughts raced through his head as he tried to defuse the situation as best he could, with whatever words he thought would appease the delusional Inle.

Inle breached the clearing bordering the Estinian siege line. He pressed the dagger's edge into the flesh of Koda's neck until he drew blood.

"Is that true? You and I are no longer enemies?" a hopeful Inle asked his master.

"Inle, I only wish I could forgive you," Elucard said.

"Even in death, Jetta twists your soul."

Seeing that Elucard and Inle were now distracted with the baggage of their past, Calsoon slid a dagger down his arm into his palm. With a flick of the wrist the knife whistled through the air and impacted Inle's steel mask with a loud '*thud*.' Inle's head reeled back in an awkward stumble. Elucard dashed forward and pulled Koda to safety.

Wiccer made a quick glance to Timber, "Now!" he shouted.

Timber let loose an arrow straight for Inle's chest, but Inle was fractions quicker, grabbing the arrow just as it penetrated his leather armor. He danced lightly into the shadows making a gracefully bow, as if the theater curtains had drawn to a close.

Calsoon indulged the clown with a long and exaggerated bow of his own, "Until next time, friend," he whispered under his breath.

***

Inle walked the streets of Stonewall, thoughts swirling in his head like a tropical storm. Too distracted to even see where he was going, he passed Legion leaning against the side of the local tavern.

"You failed your mission. Your Estinian friends won't be happy about this," Legion sneered, almost smugly.

Inle held his mask in one hand, the other held his heavy face. He was in no condition to be the First Blade tonight. In the past he had come to the terms with the fact that the love of his life was dead, but now that reality had been crushed into a fine powder.

"What's more, you let Dest and Vemrick fall under your watch. They were useful veterans of our clan. I will not forget this failure, nor will the Silent Master," Legion's callous words continued.

Inle slowly raised his gaze to meet his High Blade. His eyes were sunken and watery from tears. His mental state was a shambled mess.

"What do you have to say for yourself, Inle?" Legion finished.

"He's alive," Inle choked out a short whisper.

"Who?" Legion asked.

"Elucard."

67

Koda knelt at the side of the injured Lear, holding his hand tightly as Essie did her best to tend to his bloody wound. A bandage was wrapped around the bruise on his neck. It throbbed, but it let him know he was alive. Alive, that is, thanks to Elucard's efforts. The man that had slain his father and left him alive as an act of mercy had now saved his life as well. He was at Alanna's feet; even a single second of hesitation and he would have been dead.

Lear winced as Essie cleaned the wound with a bottle of whiskey that she had scavenged from the neighboring Eighth Spearman. Her dwindling medical supplies did not deter her from working at her utmost peak with what she had.

"Is he going to be alright?" Koda asked, his eyes wide with hope and worry. The yikahti was a hero to him. All of ARO proved to be more than he expected. The amount of dirt they had to endure from himself and his military had all been unwarranted.

"Well, I'm using the last of my dullweed on Lear here. I have to clean his wounds with this half empty bottle of whiskey. I don't have any blistercloth to close his wound. On the bright side the Rabbit's blade missed any vital organs and I think the bleeding will stop once I get him stitched up. So as long as he doesn't fight any more Rabbits and break his stitches, he should be fine. Of course, if he does break them, he'll bleed to death because I don't have the supplies to save him. But we'll cross that bridge when we get there," Essie said, her tone rife with dark humor and sarcasm. Koda did not find the dire situation as humorous, however. Essie was pleased that her cat-folk friend meekly chuckled.

"Bring word of any changes to Lear's condition, positive or negative," commanded Koda as he stood and brushed the soil from his trousers. He moved quickly, making his way back to the northern lines.

***

Cass moved quietly through the back lines, checking on the weary and sleepless men, reassuring them that the end of the nights in the "Forest of the Splintered Skies" was at its end. Men with bloodstained bandages swathed around their faces and arms in slings were happy to see their Lady. They swore an oath to serve their tribe and would not falter, however this forest was known to make weak even the strongest men. No common elves such as these were safe from the demoralizing effects of another two weeks of dire straights. Koda's army had been held at Estinia's mercy for nearly a month now. They had no supplies, they had no access to fresh men, and they had no way to retreat. They had only themselves and the hope that their leaders gave them.

Cass slid into the foxhole with her king and fellow lord. Cass knew her situation was grim, but she kept her misery low. Athar, on the other hand, let his misery shine.

"My King, this is the twenty-third sunrise that we've endured in this forest. We have run out of fresh water and when we sent men to find a river, only half of them returned. No doubt Black Rabbits were the culprits. We have run out of food, and the same fate that befell the water scouts have struck the foragers as well."

Koda stared bitterly at Athar. He had given his report every day since they arrived in this mess. Koda ignored Athar, but he continued.

"My King, our medics say that over half our army is either injured or have fallen ill. We can not wait to die any longer, action must be taken."

Koda slowly turned his head away from Athar. Indeed, something needed to be done. A full on assault was never advised by Ashmer. At their best, his army would have been decimated by the siege engines.

"My King, an Estinian officer requests a parley to speak with you," called out a voice, breaking Koda's depressing thoughts.

Koda looked up to see a messenger staring back down at him. His young, dirt covered face bore witness to the fact that he had seen too much for one lifetime. However, there was still vigor in his eyes. He was still ready to fight for the freedom of Varis and Long Whisper.

"Athar, come with me. Cass, fetch Wiccer, Avalon, and Ashmer, then come join us on the front lines. We shall see what Estinia has in store for us."

On the field between the Estinian lines and the forest border, Koda and his company stood facing Estinian soldiers on white horses. They were not in any sort of armor, but in clean and pressed tan military tunics adorned with various medals and ribbons. By their sides were sheathed ornate golden sabers.

"King Koda, et es a pleasure to finally meet you. I em Commander Unrick. I command dis great army of Estinian soldiers. As you can see ve hev come to vish you to be en no more harm's vay."

Koda bowed politely, "Commander, what do you have to say?"

315

"King Koda, ve are prepared to march ento your forest en slaughter every von of your men to capture and enslave you. However, dat is not necessary. Ve hev the resources, do not forget dat. Ve are allowing you to surrender your men and your crown. Your men vill be taken en to continue dere service, but in de service of the von true king. De Div'Rah."

"Surrender?" said Koda, taken aback. He saw this ultimatum coming from leagues away, but to have it stated to him so plainly caught him slightly off guard. It was all too real.

"Ve vill give you entil dawn to dink et over. Good day, King Koda," finished Unrick before nodding and trotting back to Stonewall.

***

"You must surrender, my King," Athar urged.

Koda, Avalon, Wiccer, Ashmer, Athar and Cass stood in a secluded, but well guarded section of the woods. Athar's negativity must have finally worn through Koda's mind, because it seemed like the best option.

"Ashmer, can anything else be done?" Koda asked his general, desperation throttling his voice.

"My King, our men are prepared to fight–" Ashmer exclaimed but was cut short by Athar.

"You mean prepared to die!"

Avalon shoved herself in front of Athar to pull Koda's attention to her, "My King, we can no longer pretend that a soldier or king's way will solve this dire situation."

"What do you suggest, Avalon?" asked Wiccer, although he had a keen guess as to what the Silent One was alluding to.

"We must think like a Black Rabbit," Avalon said, cracking a thin smile, "Hear me out. I was trained as a Rabbit before I became a Silent One. I can not help but to still think like one. Your soldiers and noblemen see a bleak situation. As a Black Rabbit I see an obvious action to be taken by you, my King."

"You wish to assassinate Unrick?" asked Koda, already irked by the thought.

"Take him prisoner. He commands the Estinians. Cut off the head of the dragon and it can no longer breathe fire. With Unrick in our possession, he will command his army to surrender and open Stonewall's gates."

Everyone around Avalon nodded to the plan.

"Who do you suggest sending?" Wiccer asked.

"Myself, Elucard, Calsoon, and your sharpshooter, Timber," she said, counting on her hand. She then pointed to Wiccer, "You and the rest of ARO protect Koda. He could still be in danger. I don't trust this Inle."

Wiccer nodded and turned to Koda, "My King, do you approve of this mission?"

"I do. May the gods grant you strength in your hearts and sanctuary in your souls."

68

Slipping through the siege lines as silently as the clouds passing through the sky, Elucard, Avalon, Timber, and Calsoon made their way to the walls of the mountain pass city. The walls reached high and were not smooth. Stones jutted out and were riddled with various cracks, allowing them to serve as fine footholds. The shadowy team crouched in the darkness of the walls waiting for a pair of night patrolmen to pass. Elucard had his team inch closer to the wall to avoid the rim of the illuminating torchlight. Once the two patrolmen had passed by completely, Elucard nodded to Timber. Timber moved to an appropriate angle from the wall and a watch tower on top of the battlements and, with excellent accuracy, shot a guard above. The arrow was well placed and quick to kill, piercing the throat. Beyond the reach of the ever watchful eyes of the enemy, the infiltrators made their way up and passed their first obstacle.

Upon making it to the battlements, the squad leapt like the Rabbits they were from rooftop to rooftop. Timber held the rear, spotting and taking out several rooftop archers guarding the city sky.

"This seems too easy, Elucard," Timber whispered as she sniped a third archer, "Or are we just that good?"

"A little of both, I suppose," smirked Elucard, although a bit on edge.

"Rabbit!" Avalon hissed as she spied an assassin fleeing a neighboring building.

"I'm on it!" Timber called out in a low voice. However her arrow did not fly true. It skimmed off the Rabbit's right shoulder as he dropped out of sight behind an adjacent building

"Calsoon, take him out! We'll continue forth," Elucard ordered.

Calsoon swiftly leapt after the enemy. He soared through an open window and hurdled through the upper room, landing next to the now surprised assassin.

The assassin did not pause for introductions and dashed out of the building with breakneck speed, knocking over crates and hopping over wooden fences. Calsoon followed closely by making his way through the makeshift obstacle course.

The chase made its way throughout the wide array of alleys and across the cobblestone streets. They raced, passing over hay carts, under horses, and around wagons. Finally Calsoon stopped dead in his tracks as the Rabbit crashed into the doors of a large temple. Just inside the archway, the assassin could be seen. His labored breathing echoed off the walls. He stumbled on his backside, further into the church as he watched the motionless Calsoon.

Calsoon smiled a wicked grin. His toes barely grazed the border of the temple's doors.

"Sala'Esh Ru'Ala Vey'Dako." *'No angel's embrace will save you from my reach,'* Calsoon hissed in a bizarre ancient tongue; a tongue that no elf or any priest of that temple had ever heard.

Calsoon's eyes drained into a dark amber, he beckoned to the now frightened assassin, "Come friend, you and I are kindred spirits. We both worship the same god. We both want to walk out of this night alive. In another lifetime we could have been friends."

The Rabbit shivered uncontrollably as he walked toward Calsoon, "I don't want to die. Promise me I won't die."

"Hush now, my friend. Allow me to sing you a soothing song; a song that will put your mind at ease in such a troublesome time as this."

May the angels sing to you my dear child
May they bring comfort to the king and the exiled
Let them come forth when you are helpless and scared
Let them give heart to the cowards and the unprepared
Until sunset, angels will fight until they must sleep

The assassin now stood before Calsoon swaying in the cool night breeze. He was calm, locked in Calsoon's hypnotic gaze. Tears rolled down his cheeks. Somewhere deep inside, he knew he was in the deadly grasp of an adder. With a flash of steel and a cool slice, the assassin's head bounced onto the ground.

"Until sunrise, in the darkness I shall reap," Calsoon whispered, finishing the song. His eyes returned to a cold blue once more as he wiped his sword clean from the Rabbit's blood.

Calsoon looked up at the stain-glass window that embellished the archway above the entrance's keystone. It was decorated with an image of the All-Father. His eyes seemed to look saddened. Calsoon bowed to the decorative piece.

"Not everyone can be saved, my friend."

***

A trail of blood made its way through the city hall's courtyard and up its steps. Soldiers' bodies lay crumpled on the ground, throats neatly slit. Through the lobby, guards leaned against the walls, daggers and arrows pinning them upright. Elucard, Avalon, and Timber made their way up the curling stairwell silently. Each step was measured so as not to burden the old wood with too much pressure. The last thing they needed was for the floor to creak, alerting their prey of their presence. Avalon reached the top floor and glided to the door. With her Silencer at the ready, she pulled the door open, but stopped short of rushing inside.

In front of her stood thirty soldiers armed to the teeth. A barrage of polearms thrust forth with surprising speed. Avalon was caught off guard as one of the iron spades pierced her shoulder. She leapt backwards, nearly stumbling down the stairs. Elucard grabbed her by the coat to keep her stable. Timber fired several arrows in rapid succession, trying to cover the retreat of her companions, but the platoon of soldiers barreled through the storm of arrows and forced the trio down the stairs.

Elucard pushed Avalon against the banister on the lower part of the stairs just long enough to examine her wound.

"I'll be fine, do you have any blistercloth?" Avalon winced as she flexed her sword hand. The pain would be too much of a burden, so she opted to use her left hand instead.

"I'm pretty sure Essie would kill me if I had blistercloth," Elucard said jokingly as he ripped off a piece of his red cloak and wrapped it tightly around Avalon's wound.

"Will you two stop bantering? I'm dangerously low on arrows here!" Timber yelled. Her arrows flew wildly at any solider that dared make his way around the bend.

"Master," a familiar voice called from on top of the stairs, "did you really think Legion wouldn't have thought that you and your little Red Rabbits would come and take our commander this night? The final night before the great King Koda's historic surrender? You disappoint me."

Elucard narrowed his eyes and made his way to charge back up the stairway, but was caught by Avalon.

"Don't be so foolish Elucard. He's toying with us. He wants us to be on his territory. Let us make our way back outside and figure out a way to out maneuver him. Don't play into his hand!" She could feel the hatred seething off the young elf.

"You're right," Elucard said, nodding to Timber to follow him and Avalon as they ran to the city hall's exit.

As the trio barged out into the courtyard, it became exceedingly clear that they had just walked into the actual trap that Inle had set. Forty guards quickly swarmed them while the others closed in behind them. Commander Unrick and his lieutenant waltzed up to the defeated squad as they were having their weapons confiscated.

"So, dis es how Koda dinks he can vin dis battle?" The lieutenant scoffed as he lifted the chin of a furious Avalon, "By sending his biggest failures to assassinate you, my commander?"

Avalon clenched her teeth and palmed a dagger beneath her sleeve. In a flash, she took the officer by his head and sliced his throat open. The lieutenant gurgled blood as he lurched awkwardly toward Unrick before collapsing in a bubbling and bleeding mess at his boots.

"You vill be de first to die, girl!" Unrick shouted. He snapped his fingers to have a soldier move forward, but a shadowed figure stepped between him and Avalon.

"Commander, my clan will pay your Div'Rah handsomely to keep these three as our prisoners," said Legion as he eyed Elucard. Elucard glowered at the sight of his former master.

Unrick gazed at the three would-be assassins and thought for a long moment, "Very vell. Take dem to the prison tower."

Calsoon watched from above, hidden in shadows of the rooftops as his companions were ushered forward, unable to help them.

69

The cell where Elucard, Avalon, and Timber were being kept was silent, save for the pattering of the soft rain outside the cell window. Moisture drizzled down the rusty bars.

Lying on a damp pile of hay, Timber counted the many stones that tiled the ceiling. For each crack, she snapped her fingers. For each web she counted, she clapped her clawed hands. Avalon flinched in annoyance at Timber's monotonous game.

"Will you quit that? I'm trying to think of a way out of here!" Avalon snapped.

Timber held still, then sat up, "It's nearly dawn. Estinia will soon be marching to trample over Koda's army. They'll take the king prisoner, they'll capture the northern beach camp, and then they'll send a large army to take take over Long Whisper and burn Lost Dawns to the ground." Her voice was thick with defeat.

Elucard stirred in his silent stupor, but said nothing.

Avalon shot an angry glare at Timber, "We haven't failed our mission yet. We need to keep our senses sharp."

"A blade is only as sharp as the Rabbit wielding it." Legion appeared from the shadows of the cell, walking closer to the prison bars. His face had a grim look to it. He peered into the prison cell and examined Elucard and sighed greatly, "Elucard... I..." he began, but hesitated. He struggled with his words as if they were caught in this throat, "I wished you died when I threw you over that waterfall. The fate planned for you now will be far worse than death."

Elucard slid his eyes to glance at his former Master.

Avalon stood from the stool she was sitting on and approached the bars, "I have traveled the world and killed many more after I left the clan, but even I eventually found peace. Peace in Jedeo. She is a merciful goddess, even to Rabbits like us. You can find peace in her as well. Serve a new clan, serve as a Silent One, old friend."

Legion lowered his head and shakily rubbed his hands together, "No, I think mercy is out of my reach, Avalon."

Elucard swiftly moved to the bars, gripping the black iron tightly in his hands, "You taught me nothing but lies! Twisted lies. Your philosophy, your way of life, it's worthless!"

Legion stepped closer to his former student, "My lessons kept you alive in a world that would have otherwise swallowed a whelp like you whole."

"I survived, but Jetta didn't," Elucard hissed in a raspy voice.

Legion lashed out and snatched Elucard by the throat, squeezing tightly, "You want to know who killed Jetta, Elucard?"

Elucard gasped out, "Tell me!"

"You did!"

Elucard screamed in anguish and struggled to grasp at Legion through the bars.

Legion pulled him into the bars and brought his face closer to Elucard's ear, "That will be the closest you ever come to the truth. Now bury your hatred and move on with your life."

Elucard quivered, clenching his teeth in frustration, "Why won't you tell me? You were my father when I had none. I loved you and now you torture me by withholding from me what I need to know!"

Legion struggled to hold his cold demeanor and loosened his grip on Elucard's throat, "I hold back the truth because I know it would ruin you as it has ruined me."

Elucard peered into Legion's sorrowful, crimson eyes. Legion took a hold of Elucard's shoulder and raked his fingers downward, dragging his shaking hand down Elucard's armor. He bowed his head and fell to his knees. The weight of the guilt was too much to bear, "Elucard, it was the only way to save you."

Elucard stumbled backwards and slid down the prison wall, he stuttered as he began to bawl, "M-Master h-how could you?"

Legion grabbed the bars and rattled them. He knelt silently before glancing over his shoulder, "You know the truth, now do what you must." He picked himself up and exited the prison.

Avalon knelt beside Elucard to comfort him, "You must forgive him now, Elucard. He has confessed his sins. For both of you to heal you must drop your vendetta."

Elucard turned to face her, "He deserves no forgiveness, and I no peace." Elucard squeezed his fist tightly, his leather glove cracked, "The only one who deserves peace is Jetta and she will have none until every Rabbit pays for it in blood!"

Avalon furrowed her brow, "I will pray for you."

The clanking sound of keys brought the attention of the three prisoners to the cell door where they found Calsoon hastily opening it.

"Calsoon!" Timber exclaimed in surprise.

"Come quickly, we haven't much time! I found your weapons, we must complete our mission before it is too late!"

Elucard nodded, "We've wasted too much time already, the fate of Koda's army rests on our shoulders."

70

"I suppose this is as fine a morning to die as any," Koda whispered; half to himself and half to the leaders at his side. The king had gathered his men at the edge of the forest. The front lines were made up of whatever men could stand. Any who were not bound to crutches and arm slings stood as the final bulwark of their king. These men, as battered and bruised as they were, were Koda's last hope; barely strong enough to hold their swords and only strong enough to take a command.

Koda stared in fear at the Estinian forces. To surrender now would save many lives, but in the end Varis would fall, and without their king, Long Whisper would follow soon after. With that, centuries of tyranny would befall Cypress. He had failed King Dallin, his lords, his people, but most of all, he had failed his father.

"It's over," Koda finally choked.

From across the field, Commander Unrick called out, "Do you surrender, King Koda?"

Koda reached for his words. At first he spoke nothing, unable to grasp the reality of his situation. Then he felt a hand grab him by the shoulder. Koda followed the hand to find it hand belonged to Adema. Until now Koda had never got a good look at Adema. She was an elf of some sort. Her hood hung low over her face and she wore a gold mask that covered the lower portion of her face. The shadow of her hood covered her eyes. She wore silver leather gloves that neatly accented her white long coat. A dark orange trim finished the coat's detail. She wore light silver armor beneath her coat, and her beautifully crafted sword hung sheathed on her left side. She was indeed a mystery, rarely ever speaking. She preferred to let her actions speak on her behalf.

"My King, this is why we were sent to aid you. Allow us to handle this," she said in a low, calm voice.

"Handle? As if it were so simple." Wiccer turned to her looking as confused as his king.

Adema slowly walked beyond the front lines and pressed forward down the field. She stopped halfway between the two armies. Without turning to look, she commanded her thirty Silent Ones to fall in behind her, "Silent Ones, to me!"

Immediately, flashes of white darted in a row behind her. Adema began to walk again, but at a brisker pace this time. She gripped her blade and drew it from its sheath, creating a piercing sound. Unrick clenched his teeth and winced at the noise.

"When all hope fades, we will continue to fight. For we are her courage, her strength, her light. So draw your blades touched with Jedeo's might," Adema chanted as she hastened into a sprint, her Silencer raised in the air.

Upon uttering the third verse, the thirty Silent Ones pulled out their blades in unison. The ringing was so sharp and loud that the front lines of the Estinian army dropped their weapons to cover their ears in agony.

Unrick realized that this mysterious person was a true threat and despite the overwhelming odds against the Silent Ones, he was afraid, "Attack dem! Do not let dem reach de lines!" ordered Unrick as he scrambled further into the back lines of his army.

"And together we shall silence the Night!" Adema called out as she crashed into the front lines, viciously hacking into soldiers too caught by surprise by the sudden advance to react properly. The thirty Silent Ones clashed into the fray, joining their leader.

Together the Silent One forces pushed back the Estinians as they toppled over each other to get away from the deadly Silencers. From far behind his army, Unrick could be heard shouting orders to destroy the Silent Ones. But the zeal of the Silent Ones was not to be underestimated. Each had been tested by the trials of the Blade Range and was willing to die for the glory of their goddess. The Estinians were ill equipped to deal with such a foe, and that disadvantage gave Koda's forces the upper hand.

Koda looked on in awe at the spectacular feat as less than forty men pushed back a force of one thousand. His men took notice too. They cheered with a new spurt of hope in their hearts, waving their hands and weapons in glee.

"I think it's time, my King," said Wiccer, stoically.

Koda trotted his wolf onto the field ahead of his men and raised the Long Whisper banner, "Chaaaarge!"

Koda's men ran across the field crying blood and thunder in their battle cries, most limping, some refreshed in a dead on sprint. All with vinegar pulsing through their veins as they broke into the now terrified Estinian lines. The enemy forces clambered backward, falling over the corpses of their fallen comrades as they broke into a fearful retreat. However, they were halted in their tracks by the sight of Unrick, who had a dagger to his throat. The Estinians dropped their weapons and cowered on their knees, unsure of what to do.

Koda broke through to where Unrick was crying out for a formal surrender. There he found Elucard holding a thin knife under the chin of the Estinian commander. Timber, Avalon, and Calsoon had several other officers tied and gagged.

"Well done, sergeant. I'll take it from here," Koda nodded to Elucard to let go of his prisoner. He then peered into the furious eyes of Unrick, "I admit, you had me beat, but it wasn't me you needed to defeat. It was the spirit of Long Whisper that defeated you."

"You vere a vorthy adversary, King Koda. It vill be a delight to vatch you squirm vhen my Div'Rah burns your Lost Dawns to de ground."

Koda's smile faded quickly, "Take him away," he said solemnly.

***

"You let them escape! You let them win!" Inle snarled at Legion.

The two Black Rabbits stood on a ledge in the mountains overlooking the now liberated city of Stonewall.

Legion turned to look at the young shadow elf. His steel clown mask cast a dark shadow in the sunset, "This is not how we want to beat Elucard. Imprisoned by Aric and handed to our clan as some kind of bargaining chip to be at the mercy of the Silent Master." Legion thrust an index finger into Inle's chest, pushing him off balance a bit, "That's not how you imagine his death. Is it?"

Legion read Inle like a book and even as clever as Inle was, he knew Legion was right. He continued to let Legion talk, "You want Elucard all to yourself. You need him to see that you aren't just his student, but his equal. Elucard sitting in some scum filled cage isn't the proper ending for him." Legion walked past him back to the road, "It's not how I imagined his death either."

Inle took one final look at Stonewall before chasing after his High Blade. Elucard had to die by his hands and his alone. No one deserved Elucard more. No one.

71

Night had settled on the newly liberated city of Stonewall. A calmness hung in the air as the exhausted soldiers found their way to the warmth of soft beds and cozy inns; a sharp contrast from the weeks before. The townsfolk were more than willing to share a home cooked meal and open a fine wine for Koda's weary men.

Wiccer, Ashmer, Athar, Cass, and Koda sat at a dining table in the home of the mayor. Dinner plates were cleared away as a much needed meal was eaten by the five guests. Small glasses were refilled with the mayor's finest brandy, once hidden from the Estinian men.

"We will stay in Stonewall one more day, and then we march hard to meet up with our divided forces and the Varisian army on the other side of the mountains," Ashmer stated as he sipped a glass of the smooth alcohol.

"I think we should keep our most injured and ill here in Stonewall. They will be no good to us if they can't march," suggested Cass.

Koda curled his hands together, resting his chin on top of his knuckles, "How many men do we have if the injured and ill stay here?"

Ashmer calculated on his fingers and did a quick bit of math in his head, before finally answering, "About seven hundred, including the thirty-two Silent Ones, and six Vernal Mages. We picked up about twenty working catapults and ballistas too."

"Well, we've seen the Silent Ones work. They each fight like twenty men," Wiccer mused as he remembered the incredible feat from earlier in the day.

"Then it's settled. We'll stay one more day in Stonewall and then take our most well-off men and march through the mountain pass," Koda said, perking up after taking a swig of the welcoming drink.

***

The Crooked Sword was filled to the brim with soldiers desperately seeking a cold drink and a warm hearth after the hellish experience in what they named "The Forest of the Splintered Skies." The ARO members, save for Elucard, Wiccer, and Lear, relaxed to the best of their abilities as they sipped on their ales and slurped down the hot beef stew. But no one spoke between them, for their once sharp wit and keen senses were now dull like rusted blades.

Blayvaar broke the silence, "We should bring Lear some ale when we get a chance."

"This yikahti would appreciate a cold one," Rulan grinned as he joked.

Smiles broke from the tired Watchers as they agreed that they should pay Lear a visit.

"Well, look who it is," a familiar and unwelcome voice broke through the good spirits like a war hammer.

Blayvaar turned to find Rith and a large gathering of the 12th Spearman division chuckling crudely with their arms crossed over their chests.

"Me and the boys were about to head out and find some fun in this town, but there seems to be some fun to be had right here," Rith said, cracking a snide smile. He nudged one of his fellow spearmen.

"Not now Rith, I don't have the patience to deal with your bullshit," Blayvaar spat before turning back around to his stein.

Rith's face curled as he grabbed Blayvaar by the collar and spun him around in his seat to face him, "I see you don't have your captain here. Me and my boys are going to get some hard earned respect from you ARO bastards, even if we have to beat it out of each one of you!"

Immediately seats could be heard screeching back across the floor as each one of the ARO members came to the aid of their companion, "Now is not the time to mess with us, spearman!" Timber snarled.

Rith moved to Timber, but Rulan stepped into Rith's face until the elf was close enough to see his reflection in Rith's eyes.

"Stand down Rith, we've both been through some shit and none of us want to be tested." Rulan spoke calmly, though his eyes were stressed and sunken from the lack of sleep

"Get out of my face, Rabbit," Rith sneered.

Rulan narrowed his eyes and butt his forehead into the bridge of Rith's nose. A hard thump followed a sharp crack as Rith's nose bent unnaturally. A thick, long droplet of blood dripped to the wooden floor. Rith was taken by surprise as he stumbled backwards into the arms of his fellow soldiers.

Swords were quickly drawn all around the ARO soldiers as Rulan and the others prepared for a melee to ensue. However, a loud order rocked the tavern, "Stand down, spearmen!"

Pushing his way between the two units came a scarred and gray haired elf. A heavy woolen bandage covered his left eye and the rank of Staff Sergeant was stitched on his shoulder, above it was the "12th Spearman Division" unit patch.

"Sergeant Aloth!? We were just–" Rith wheezily tried to explain himself.

"You take me for a fool, Rith?"

"No, sergeant!"

"You think I didn't see you harass these soldiers?"

"No, sergeant!"

"Are these the Estinains?"

Rith held silent, knowing full well what kind of trouble he was in.

Aloth's face turned beet red and a vein protruded under his skin, "Then tell me why you are harassing this unit!"

Rith clenched his teeth trying to think of a suitable enough answer that did not land him in an endless session of push-ups, "They are Rabbits, sergeant."

"Rabbits?" spat Aloth.

Another soldier pipped up, "They were trained by Elucard, sergeant. They shouldn't be treated with the same respect as any of the other soldiers."

Aloth nodded and then turned to Blayvaar, "You, private. Did you just spend three weeks in the Forest of the Splintered Skies?"

"Yes, sergeant," Blayvaar said, his face still sour.

Aloth pointed to Elisa, "What about you?"

"Yes, sergeant."

Aloth pointed to Timber, "And you? Were you there too?"

Timber grinned, "Indeed I was, sergeant."

Aloth turned to his unit, "ARO shared the same experience as all of you in that god-forsaken forest. They slept in the same shit-holes, they bled the same blood, they shed the same tears. They are as much as part of this army and country as the rest of you. Trained by Rabbits? Yes, but they were trained by them to fight and save you pieces of shit from the Rabbits. Don't you forget that!"

The spearmen all lowered their heads.

"I want all of you outside after you apologize to each one of those ARO soldiers. We're going for a discipline jog until you learn how to give proper respect to your peers!"

The Watchers looked at each other in bewilderment but each grew a new smile on their faces as it seemed that they finally gained the respect they yearned for.

***

Elucard sat in the large temple of Father. The moonlight danced in fragmented colors as it passed through stained glass windows depicting battles against an evil that came from the skies. His head was bowed and eyes were closed shut as he muttered words of prayer and confusion to the goddess he was once faithful to, "Alanna can you hear me? I know you must be disappointed in me. I know I served you without question at one point. Or at least I thought I was serving you. I was really serving a twisted version of you."

He opened his eyes, now red with tears from remembering such a tumultuous period in his life. He had no one to turn to for guidance, no god to lean on for understanding. Everything in his life was a lie and now he did not know whether he wished to live in that lie or be free from it.

"Alanna, I seek your blessing. I am on a path of war and many will die. At one point I believed I did your work and that I was your hand. Now I seek to kill for myself and I need to know if you will not shame me when I run my blade across the necks that deserve my wrath." Elucard held silent. He used this moment to reflect on his own thoughts and words, "Not for myself, but for her. I wish to kill for Jetta. I know she has Alue, but Alanna, she lived a life full of trauma and strife. She needs protection. Please, while I slay those that harmed her, watch over her soul. Maybe some day Jetta and I can meet once more and I can finally have my peace..."

"Peace can be sought without the shadow of hate in tow, Elucard."

Elucard's eyes widened at the sound of what he thought was the voice of the one he so desperately missed, "Jetta?" He turned looking for his lost friend, but found Avalon sitting in a pew behind him instead.

"Is it she who drives you?" Avalon asked thoughtfully. She had seen many tormented hearts since she had begun her service as a Silent One. It was her duty to protect and spread the word of Jedeo. Naturally, putting the restless at ease was also a large part of her duties.

"No," Elucard spoke simply.

Avalon leaned forward and spoke quietly into Elucard's ear, "I was once like you, a Rabbit betrayed by her own life. I traveled the lands, seeking redemption. I was a slave to an endless nightmare of hatred and sorrow, but then Jedeo found me. She gave me my Silencer and a new purpose. I still fight. I still kill. I am still an assassin, but now for a greater purpose. I fight for the light and the truth," she said, gripping her sword's handle tightly.

Elucard stood up and began to walk out of the temple. Avalon grabbed Elucard's hand as he passed her, "Elucard, don't let the darkness swallow you. If you let that happen, you will never find peace."

Elucard snapped his hand away from her, "You want to know what drives me? The darkness drives me. I want it to swallow me so that I can be strong enough to face my demons!"

Avalon lowered her head in prayer as Elucard stormed out of the temple.

Jedeo, give Elucard the strength to walk away from the path he walks. Give him the strength to find his way to the light and find his peace.

72

Koda's remaining forces marched through the long mountain pass, knowing the journey would last two days. Despite spending an extra day in Stonewall, Koda's men were not revitalized enough to start another trek and even less ready for a battle at the end of that trek. The mountain pass was a narrow stretch of road that sliced through a single mountain. A set of high rock-face walls bordered the road and wind rushed through the makeshift valley with its cool autumn air.

Wiccer and Elisa marched behind the train of troops, watching its rear. Wiccer was still very tired. Leading ARO and acting as a military advisor had taken its toll on his body and mind. His eyes drooped and his movement was slow, as if he walked through mud. His joints creaked stiffly as he trudged along.

"You should get some rest. There are a few wagons not too far ahead. No one would look down upon you if you hitched a ride," Elisa said softly.

Wiccer jolted his head in a quick shake to wake up. He sleepily smiled at the shadow elf, "I've always treated you like dirt, but you've been nothing but kind to me."

Elisa paused before responding, "I was a prisoner in the past. I've killed many and caused much strife to many others. I would treat me like dirt too."

"You've changed so much, Elisa. Do you know that?" Wiccer asked. He rapped his scabbard with his thumb while trying to choose his words, "It's like you're one of us now. No it's not that, it's more like ever since you and Avren were together you've just been trying to make things right."

"Avren..." said Elisa faintly, still pained by his loss.

"You've gone above and beyond to show me that you really cared for him, I think I was too upset with myself to see that," Wiccer swallowed his shame hard, "I'm sorry Elisa. You are a true friend."

Elisa smiled gently, blushing up to her ear tips, "You've changed a lot yourself, Wiccer. You no longer see ARO as just some asset. You really care for each and every one of us."

Wiccer nodded and looked away, "It took a war for me to finally see that the lot of you are my family."

"Even Elucard?"

Wiccer held silent, not ready to admit he now saw Elucard as a friend.

"Someday, perhaps," Elisa sighed.

***

Timber and Calsoon looked down from their perch, high on top of one of the stone walls. They sat looking down at the marching army, silence filling the gap between them. Finally Timber spoke up, although seemingly to herself, "My grandmother was a wise wolf shaman. She was very religious and often told me stories of times long ago. She once told me a story of five individuals and the sacrifices they made to vanquish an evil that descended from a new moon."

Calsoon turned curiously to his companion, but she did not return the gaze. She continued all the same as she regaled the tale:

"Long ago, before there were no gods. A time where there was only 'Nihilio.' The world had its magic, but only for a select few. Man lived in fear of the wickedness that the shadows brought. At the time, the wicked were ruled by the vampires and the Night was not nearly as frightful as it would soon be. For once the Black Moon appeared in the sky, the Night would rule. Demons descended from the new moon, and with them brought a war that man would fight for one hundred years.

At first, man did not fight alone. Following the demons came the angels. Skin like gold, wings as pure as pearls. The angels fought valiantly, but were overwhelmed by this menace. Save for six, the angels retreated from whence they came. The six angels were indeed fantastic warriors in their own right, but the demons were greater.

It seemed all hope was lost, until Nihilio stepped down from his celestial throne and gifted five mortal beings with the power of a second soul. The second souls were of a new magic, a magic crafted to hunt the demons. Embedded with the souls of the Jade Hawk, these five men and women fought back the demons in a final bout. The demons were defeated, but not destroyed. They crept back in their shadows. The five Jade Warriors vanished, now that their purpose was complete.

The six angels ascended to become gods, a mortal leader was chosen to ascend with them. Once the new gods were established, they saw Nihilio as their All-Father. After one hundred years of a brutal war for survival, man found peace again."

Calsoon grinned, "I've been told that story before, but you tell it so eloquently.

Timber finally turned to face Calsoon. Her eyes were steely and her face was grim to match, "My grandmother told me that the demons still lurk among us. She tells me to watch for anyone with amber eyes that the Night shines through like an amber moon."

Calsoon chuckled lightly, "You granny is full of stories."

Timber smiled thinly, "Perhaps…"

But stories are always born from a shred of truth.

73

The gigantic Estinian camp was bustling as Legion and Inle entered. Soldiers sparred and blacksmiths repaired armor. On the outskirts of the encampment, they found Vada leading fifty new Black Rabbits in a kata. They were fresh faced and of Estinian blood. However, despite being green, they looked well trained and strong. After all, Estinian soldiers were known as merciless and tenacious in the first place. Now that they trained as Black Rabbits they would be a force to be reckoned with. Vada finished her kata and bowed to dismiss them before turning to her High Blade and First Blade.

"Fifty Rabbits trained and ready, my High Blade," Vada said, proud of her quick work.

Inle inspected the new Rabbits as they walked off, "They look a bit rough."

Vada winced at the criticism, but made the best of it, "They are indeed rough around the edges, but the bones are there. They will do fine in combat."

"Inle, report to the king—the Div'Rah—that we have returned and share what we know of Koda's army," said Legion, catching himself. He waited for Inle to bow and hustle off before pulling Vada off to the side, "Vada, there is something we discovered while we were in Stonewall."

"Go on," said Vada, slightly confused.

"Avalon is alive and is with Koda's forces."

Vada stumbled backwards, her jaw slouched open in bewilderment, "H-how can this be? I-I was sure she was enslaved in the gladiator pits of Scorch!"

Legion grabbed hold of Vada, shaking her to her senses, "Whatever the case may be, can I count on you to finish your mission?"

Vada furrowed her brow, still taken aback, "M-My mission?"

"To finish off Avalon!" Legion snarled.

Vada ran her hands over her head. She needed to sit down and reflect on this news, but Legion did not allow her such time, "Avalon will fall under my sword, my High Blade," said Vada finally.

"Good. I have no doubt you two will meet on the battlefield," nodded Legion, pleased with himself.

Vada walked slowly away. She was now focused. She was confident she would see Avalon on the battlefield, but now hoped to meet her before then as well.

***

Koda's army had made camp under a large overpass of rock. The Silent Ones slumbered as Adema conversed quietly with her Silver Wing across the glow of a dimly lit fire.

"You know who the first Silent One was?" Adema asked Avalon. Not a true question, but a test to begin a conversation. Her long white and orange jacket rested beneath her, serving as a pillow against a boulder. Her pale white skin gleamed in the fire, as did the black veins that seemingly clutched her cheeks. Her Amber eyes hauntingly cast in the night.

"Autumn, sister of Jedeo," Avalon responded.

"Do you know why she was the first Silent One?"

"What do you mean?" Avalon asked, slightly confused by the question.

Adema sat up, "I've heard stories about you, Avalon. I've learned about who you were before you dedicated yourself to Jedeo's blade."

Avalon shifted nervously.

Adema shined a toothy smile, "No need to worry, dear Avalon. As you can see a lot of us came from troubled and dark pasts. I'm a tainted elf, for example; an elf born with the blood of the Night."

"What have you learned about me then?" Avalon questioned Adema, now more curious.

"You were once an assassin. One of the best in your clan. You had a sister of sorts and were very close."

Avalon lowered her head. She had never forgotten about Vada. She thought about her constantly, and it hurt her heart each time her memory surfaced.

"You left her behind in your old world so that you could ascend to the high honor of being a Silent One. You, Avalon, are Jedeo. Your Blade Sister is Autumn. Separated by an entire world, your sister stayed behind to carry on the work she believed in. One day you two will be reunited. But unlike Jedeo and Autumn, you will have to make a choice," Adema continued.

Avalon widened her eyes with the realization of that choice.

"The choice of whether you will save Vada or kill her. I pray you find the strength to make the right decision," finished Adema.

"I-I need to take a walk," Avalon said as she took her leave from the fire.

Avalon wandered far from the sleeping army, deep in a whirlwind of thoughts. What would she do if she had to confront Vada? "Blade Sister, we must speak," she whispered to herself, unable to clear her head.

"I am here, my sister," a voice called from the shadows as a figure dropped from a low hanging cliff.

Startled, Avalon instinctively drew her blade. Peering into the shadows, she whispered to the stranger, "Vada, is that really you?"

Vada approached from the reaching shadows. She placed her hands out so that Avalon could see she was no threat, "I see you still wield a blade like a Rabbit."

Avalon arched a brow, unable to tell if Vada was here for a fight, "A fragment from my past. I doubt I'll ever relearn to fight like anything other than a Rabbit," responded Avalon.

"Avalon, there is a battle on the horizon. You and I will be on opposite sides of that field. We will be enemies, and truthfully, I do not want that," Vada said stepping closer to her Blade Sister.

Avalon sheathed her blade and offered her hand, "Then come with me, Vada. Become a Silent One. We can stand together as we once did!"

Vada sneered at Avalon's offer, "You wish me to forsake my ways? The only path I walk is that of Alanna. You of all people should know this."

Avalon looked at her own empty hand and and curled it into a fist. She bit her lip in frustration, "Ever still the stubborn one, Vada. Once again you stand on the precipice of a new destiny and you still do not see that the ways of the Rabbit are wrong!"

Vada looked away silently. Avalon continued.

"I have been in your shoes. I have seen the errors of my ways. Jedeo will save your soul. She will shape you into a warrior of the Light. Where Alanna turns her back on you, Jedeo will embrace you in her crimson wings."

Vada opened her mouth to speak. She could see it herself, dropping the ways of the Black Rabbit to run and join Avalon. However, she was afraid. Afraid of the clan and afraid of herself, "I-I can't Avalon. I-I have to go," stuttered Vada as she leaped back on top of the wall and vanished into the shadows.

Avalon watched as her friend disappeared once again. Tears began to swell in her eyes, "You are not too far gone, Blade Sister. I will wait for you," she whispered, knowing Vada was not around to hear her.

338

74

Koda's army pushed through the morning at a quickened pace and arrived at the Varisian encampment by noon. Koda's forces were relieved to finally get some proper rest and meet up with old friends from different divisions. Wiccer found his father discussing plans with his friend and fellow White Cloak, Petrov. Wiccer was hesitant to approach his father, but Petrov nudged Marcus, alerting him of his son's presence.

Wiccer threw a smart salute, "General Newsun, I–" Wiccer was broken off by the heavy embrace of a bear hug from his overjoyed father.

"Wiccer, it's good to see you. I'm so happy you survived Stonewall!" Marcus shouted in a booming voice as tears streamed from his eyes, "I've heard the reports of what you had to go through. I prayed to Alue for mercy and Jedeo for you to have the strength to pull through!"

Wiccer blushed, crushed by his father's large arms, "Father, not in front of the men!"

Marcus chuckled, dropping his son, "Right. It's good to see you alive and well, captain," he said, finally returning Wiccer's salute.

Wiccer smirked, going in for a hug of his own, "I'm happy to see you too, Father."

Marcus sat down, pulling a barrel for his son to sit next to him, "Speaking of your men, you must tell me how ARO turned out."

Wiccer flashed a wide grin, "We are the scourge of the Black Rabbits. I've learned much from Elucard and I'm inclined to believe I could even beat you in a sparring match."

Marcus chortled a belly laugh and slapped his knee, "Well then, I'd like to take you up on that offer once we win this war."

"It's really good to see you again, Father," Wiccer mused

"Aye, the same to you, my son."

***

Koda walked into the large war tent set up for the various leaders. There, he met with King Dallin of Varis. The King was about thirty, but his face was weathered and his hair was dark with streaks of gray. He had a well kept beard that was red at the tips. Despite his age, he looked tired and dreary, the way a king should when his capital was under siege. The seven Long Whisper lords stood conversing around a circular table with a large map of Varis spread on top of it.

King Dallin relayed his information to Koda, "Now that you're here, Koda, we can begin this meeting. The Estinians are three thousand strong. Their forces are well rested and well fed, a stark contrast from my own. We were at siege for weeks with our supply routes cut off from Stonewall. We have the numbers with our forces combined, but my men are in no shape to fight. How are yours?"

Koda gulped nervously, "I was hoping your men could carry mine to victory. Three weeks in that forest have left my men just as battered."

"The two of you have sentenced us to death with your arrogance!" spat Athar.

"Silence, Moonfall!" snapped Koda.

Athar's negative attitude over the course of the war had grounded Koda's patience into a fine powder, and Athar knew this. He was delighted to see Koda's defenses finally giving way.

"Koda, your constant foolishness has cost us dearly," pushed Athar.

"I said enough!" Koda shouted, clearly stressed by a combination of Athar's criticisms and his own failures as a leader.

"You see, my fellow lords, Koda can not handle the crown. Unlike his father, he is not–" a sharp backhand from Koda reeled Athar backwards. He was then lifted in the air with his arms tightly bound to his side by an invisible force. Athar watched in horror as Koda stared at him menacingly with his raised hands quivering in anger. His breathing was labored and deep. Athar clenched his teeth and pushed on defiantly, "I would be a fool to think our king is a coward. But to say that he is drunk with power would be a catastrophic understatement. How can we entrust the realm to such a volatile child?"

The other lords gasped and whispered amongst themselves. Koda's eyes darted around the tent before he released Athar from his Magi-infused grip. He was in complete shock of his short temper and unforgivable actions. To strike a lord was appalling, but to use the Magi against him was unforgivable. He stormed out of the tent embarrassed and afraid. Dallin ran after him.

"Koda, wait!" Dallin called to him.

Koda turned, his face tense as tears streamed from his eyes, "I d-don't know w-what happened. I just lost it. A-Athar is right, I am not my father and I am no king!"

Dallin grabbed Koda's shoulder and lifted his chin, "I was the youngest in my family, fourth in line for the throne. I hadn't a care in the world..."

Koda sniffed and rubbed his eye, "You're making me feel worse."

Dallin smiled and continued his story, "I had my whole life planned out. I was going to marry my long time love and travel the world, but then the Baneblood plague spread through Varis. I lost everyone. I was alone with no family and no mate. At seventeen I had to take the throne and lead my nation through a troubling time." Dallin paused as he remembered the painful memories, "Koda, I know about the pressures of the throne. I know what it's like to take the crown young. You need to stay strong for your people and yourself."

Koda wiped his tears away and nodded.

"Take some time and then come back and lead your nation."

***

Koda sat in his private tent with a chessboard between him and Elucard. The two were locked in epic duel of wits. Finally, Elucard moved his knight in place, cornering Koda's king.

"Checkmate," Elucard said as he knocked the king over with his knight.

"Who taught you to be so good?" asked Koda as he reached for a cup of water.

"My master. He wanted to train my mind as hard as he trained my body." Elucard picked up the wooden knight piece and felt the grooves that made up its mane, "He always said, 'A blade is only as sharp as the Rabbit wielding it.'"

"A wise man," nodded Koda, approving the quote.

"He was like a fa–" Elucard started but halted so as not to offend Koda, whose own father was taken by Elucard's blade.

Koda frowned, but then smiled gently, "It's true, you were responsible for my father's death. By all rights we should be enemies. However, you are my ally now. You serve to protect me and my people. It's funny how life works out sometimes."

Elucard opened his mouth to respond, but quickly stood watching as the tent flap opened and in stepped the seven lords.

Athar kicked aside the chess board to stand in front of Koda, "I see you are with your pet Rabbit. No matter, this will be short."

Elucard sneered behind Athar's back.

Koda stood and put his hand up to calm Elucard, "Athar, what do you want?"

Athar smirked and turned to the lords. Sove Breezerunner stepped forward and spoke up, "Koda, we seven have discussed the crown and your future with it. We have come to the decision to elect Athar Moonfall to take your place as the king of Long Whisper."

Koda gawked at Sove, floored by the news, "How can the seven betray the Dawnedge? My father forged this nation with his own hands!"

Athar bobbed his head and chuckled, "You father was a great elf, but you are not your father, nor are you the same caliber of an elf."

"We can not falter now! We can not break our binding with such a great battle on the wings of dawn!" exclaimed Koda as he looked desperately into each one of his lord's eyes, finally resting on Cass Baneberry, "Even you Cass? You were my mother's best friend. The Baneberry were the first to support the construction of Lost Dawns! You must still respect the Dawnedge tribe!"

"It is not about respect for the Dawnedge, Koda. You have driven yourself beyond reason. You are drunk on the Magi. You are blind and unstable and must abdicate," stated Fendrick.

"I–" Koda stopped, he knew he had lost the crown. He knew he lost it all.

"As king I will make a deal with Aric Stine to salvage the freedom of our country under his guiding rule," said Athar, almost smugly.

Elucard flashed in front of Athar and drew his blade, "Shall I kill him, my king?"

Athar stepped back and shouted in a shrill voice, "Keep your Rabbit's leash taut, Koda!"

"Lower your weapon, Elucard. He may speak treason, but only because he is a coward," snapped Koda.

"I speak treason?" spouted Athar in mock bafflement, "You forget that the same elf by your side slew your father and brought our country to its knees! You let Black Rabbits into your home, you sent away the White Cloaks, you sent us to war ill prepared, you marched us to our deaths, and when hope and prosperity presents its self to you, you dismiss it for further destruction. You are unworthy of that crown, now hand it over!"

Koda shook his head, hot tears dripped down his face, "You can't do this!"

"It is already done," sneered Athar.

Koda slowly removed his crown and handed it over to Athar.

"You utterly failed as a leader, but I will make sure you are spared if you bow to me now," said Athar as he snatched the crown and placed it on his head.

Koda trembled, but before he could move, Elucard put his hand on Koda's chest and faced the lords, "Koda will not bow to a traitor. Will none of you five stand by this man's side? The burden he carried was more than the weight of the crown. The war is not over, this upcoming battle with prove that to us. Leave to lick Stine's boots and Long Whisper will fall. Stand by Koda's side and we will overcome and triumph, I promise you this!"

Cass balled her fists and stepped to stand by Koda's side, "I can not carry on with this. Bowing before Stine is wrong," she turned to Koda, "I will stand with you, Dawnedge. I would rather die than serve under a traitor to our nation!"

Athar snarled in disgust, "Very well Cass, be the worthless dog I've always known you to be," Athar snapped his fingers and walked out of the tent with his five lords following behind.

"We may have lost an overwhelming number of men, but the Baneberry will fight with honor along side your men, my king," Cass said reassuringly.

Koda lowered his head. In his own mind, he was no longer a king. He had failed himself, his people, and most of all, his father.

75

Dawn's sun had finally risen and two armies stood on opposite sides of a grassy field. Where once two forces stood, equally matched, Varis' forces were now dwarfed by the combined armies of the Estinians and the traitorous forces of the newly deemed king, Athar Moonfall.

Koda sat saddled on his riding wolf. Wildeye was by his side, geared in a lightweight leather armor set. She looked up anxiously and whined. Koda reached over to calm her nerves.

"I know girl. This may be our last day together. If that is the case, it was an honor to be your familiar," cooed Koda.

Wildeye rubbed her muzzle against his leg in compliance. Dallin nodded to Koda, signaling him to follow him to the center of the field where Aric and Athar waited.

The four nobles gripped their leather reins while an uncomfortable silence swirled around them. Finally Dallin spat on the ground and yelled across the field at Athar, "The crown doesn't fit you, traitor!"

Athar only raised his chin and grinned.

Aric gathered Dallin's attention before speaking, "King Dallin, I advise you to surrender. Your men are grossly outnumbered now dat Long Whisper hev come to dere senses and turned on you. As Div'Rah, I em merciful end reasonable. I vill lit you rule Varis under my banner, as I hev allowed Athar to rule."

"Even sharing the same sun with you and your swine this day is an insult to my men and I. I will look for you on the battlefield!" Dallin snapped.

Aric looked taken aback by the ruthless insult, but regained his composure, "Very vell King Dallin, as you say."

***

The Silent Ones and ARO knelt in a large circle behind the main lines of battle. Wiccer relayed his plan of action to Avalon and Elucard as they listened intensely.

"Aric will no doubt send his Rabbits to take down King Dallin. They will easily break through the lines in the chaos of the battle. We need to protect the king."

"Legion, Inle, and Vada will lead the Black Rabbits, together we three need to intercept them," said Avalon as she nodded at Wiccer's assessment.

"Our boys will form a circle around Dallin and Koda to stave off any Rabbits, but we won't last forever," Wiccer added.

"Leave the outer ring to the Silent Ones," Avalon offered.

Wiccer turned to Elucard, "Elucard, can I count on you to stay focused."

Elucard flashed an iterated glare, the same glare Wiccer knew he was going to receive, "Inle will be there. Are *you* going to stay focused?"

"Point taken," said Wiccer, wincing from the retort.

"We all have our grudges with these Rabbits. They've all caused us great pain, but we must all stay focused. If we stumble, we will fall," Avalon said sternly.

Wiccer rose and looked at the members of ARO. Each had tired but ready faces. Each feared the outcome of the eminent battle.

"Listen up Watchers! Today will be a day of reckoning. We stand at the edge of a battle of unsurmountable odds. Among our enemies are a God-King, the deadliest assassins in Long Whisper, and those we once bent our knees to," he paused, taking a large sigh as he thought about how participating in this battle made him a criminal in his own country, and the challenges the coming onslaught would be. He took a deep breath and continued, "Well, we serve no God-King, and we are not in Long Whisper. Each one of you has tasted Black Rabbit blood. We also no longer serve a king. What we once sought to protect, we must now seek to destroy. As you are no longer part of the Long Whisper army, you may turn and walk away now. No one will shame you if you do."

Each ARO member looked at each other and nodded. Rulan spoke up, "We're all with you, Wiccer."

"To the end!" called out Timber.

A large group of men, mostly made of remnants of several units that once belong to the various lords surrounded the ARO members.

Blayvaar looked in disgust, "What do you want, Rith?"

Rith gestured to the various scattered units, before speaking, "We are no longer whole as an army, which is why we need to stick together now more than ever. You had our backs from the very beginning. Now it's time we had your backs, ARO."

Blayvaar stood and offered his hand. Rith responded by shaking it.

Wiccer flashed a joy filled smile. He looked onward to the Estinian army, they were ready.

76

'May the bards of time and lore,
Sing a song of my fate in this war,
A ballad that will not crumble with age,
Nor its ink fade from the page,
Its story will tell of soldiers' blades that clash,
Fallen warriors taken by angels, wings like ash,
And among the chaos of this blood soaked field,
I will forever rest or a victory shall be sealed.'

-Song of the Soldier

A stillness hung in the air as each and every soldier clenched their teeth in fear and intimidation. The grass waved in the wind, carefree and unaware of the anarchy that would soon sweep over the field like a giant wave crashing through the forest.

The Div'Rah raised a single hand from the rear of his lines, prompting a standard bearer to wave a red flag. Immediately, hundreds of arrows were nocked and relased into the air, flying like a flock of sparrows careening down onto the Varisian forces below.

"Shields!" Dallin shouted as his men moved to raise wooden shields to deflect the shower of arrows. Thunks from the arrow heads piercing and splintering into the shields resounded through the ranks.

Another volley, then another, then another pounded down onto the now arrow covered shields. Suddenly, there was silence.

"Recover!" Dallin yelled.

The men lowered their shields, relieved to find that many of them had survived. One or two soldiers had been nicked in their armor. Their chainmail had saved their lives. Relieved laughter resounded throughout the ranks.

"Battle groups will prepare to defend!"

The laughter died. Men began to jump on their heels in anxiousness, while others began to whimper in fear as spears were lowered and swords were held at the ready.

Across the field, the men could hear a single Estinian officer shout, "Chaaarge!"

The ground shook as thousands of men and horses rushed towards them.

Koda leaped his wolf over the the protection of the ARO and Silent Ones and ran to the Vernal Mages, "Quickly, we must disrupt them!" in unison the six mages and Koda made an elegant but swift motion with their hands and channeled their energy into the grass, commanding it to grow wildly and capture the charging force in a jungle of choking grass blades. Cavalrymen were thrown from their own horses as infantrymen struggled to chop through the new forest of grass.

Koda smiled, pleased with his actions. He turned back to his fellow mages and said, "Lift us up!"

Once again, Koda and the mages made intricate casting motions with their arms and with a final upward thrust, pushed gigantic roots from under their own forces and led them high over the tall grass and over the trapped forces.

"Attack!" Dallin shouted to the men running from the large roots and jumping down onto the helpless enemy.

Furious, Aric called for his catapults to blow through the roots and choking grass, not worried about the lives of his own men.

Koda watched in horror as boulders slick with oil and fire sailed through the air, crashing in plumes of black smoke into the center of both forces. A command for the Varisian forces to fall back rung through the chaos. Fire roared as it spread through the roots and grass. More boulders were released into the skies, this time launching further into the Varisian main forces.

Koda channeled magic to spring up massive wooden hands to catch one of the boulders, but the rest fell into a destructive impact, sending bodies and limbs flying.

"Forward – march!" Aric ordered as his men finally overcame the magically grown obstacles. As soon they were close enough for another head on charge.

"Prepare to defend!" Dallin called out as the Estinian and Long Whisper forces clashed into a full on battle with the Varisian forces.

Koda hurdled alongside Wildeye over bodies and fighting men, but a bolo tangled his familiar's feet, sending her tumbling across the ground. Koda jumped off his saddle to come to his wolf's aid. A vision of several soldiers charging behind alerted him to the oncoming dangers. He swung around and lifted his hands into the air. Emerging roots tangled the bodies of the enemy soldiers with stunning efficiency.

Koda quickly untied Wildeye's legs. Once free, she instantly jumped up to snatch a swordsman's arm within her jaws. The swordsman cried in anguish as she threw him to the ground. Quickly, Wildeye lunged for the throat of another enemy that came to flank Koda. Koda found himself overwhelmed as he earnestly tried to keep more and more men at bay with serrated leaves and whipping vines, but finally a pike plunged into his side. Wildeye yelped in pain as she collapsed to the ground. A magic empathic wound formed the familiar, seeping warm, red blood just as the pike wound did on her master.

Koda roared in agony as he sent the assailant flying with the crack of a vine whip. Marcus and several White Cloaks fought hard to reach Koda.

"You don't look so well, Koda. We need to get you to a medic!" yelled Marcus, between heavy breaths.

Koda gripped Marcus's cloak in pain, and hovered his hand over the gaping wound. His palm began to glow a faint cerulean as his wound slowly began to close. Koda grunted through the strain to use the Magi under such a great deal of pain and stress, finally giving up with a half-way closed wound, "Protect me, I need to rest a bit. Then I'll be able to fight more."

Marcus smirked, "You heard the elf, form a ring! Let's get this mage back to tip-top shape!"

77

Through the dark smoke created by the great fire, Black Rabbits glided through the ranks of the battle, making their way to King Dallin. Under the cloak of low visibility and the chaos of the ensuing battle, the fifty Black Rabbits made quick work of the unsuspecting Silent Ones, causing the ARO members to react in order to protect their Silent One allies from being completely swallowed by the ambush. The circles were broken.

Elucard, Wiccer, and Avalon swiftly attempted to join the fray with their men. However, they were deterred by a new set of shadowy figures. Legion, Inle, and Vada intercepted the three, catching them off guard.

Legion swiped in a horizontal arc, pushing Elucard away from his companions. Legion chased after him, locking his great sword with Elucard's own blade. Inle ran and drop-kicked Wiccer into the chest, sending him flying backwards. Inle drew his blade and slowly approached him, grinning under his mask.

Avalon stood motionlessly facing Vada.

"Make your move, Sister," smiled Vada.

"I take no pleasure in this, Vada," replied Avalon.

Avalon ran headlong into Vada, caressing her blade against the grassy ground, ending in a furious slash. Vada dodged to the side and followed through with her own attack, but frowned as Avalon easily parried the strike.

Avalon circled around Vada and lunged forward. A quick slice connected into Vada's side. Avalon followed up with a side kick that sent her Blade Sister sliding backwards. Enraged, Vada charged forward and leaped over Avalon's head, landing a slash to the Silent One's cheek. As she landed on the other side of Avalon, Vada flipped and kicked off the ground with her feet to boost her speed.

Avalon inspected the gash on her cheek with barely enough time to dodge the next attack. Avalon twirled around and slashed at her Blade Sister's back, landing a gruesome strike. Vada tumbled across the ground, seething in anger.

"You can't win, Blade Sister," spoke Avalon, a hint of sadness trembling in her voice.

"The day isn't over," snapped Vada.

Avalon sighed before dashing at Vada once more. The two traded strikes with each other before Avalon sidestepped and grabbed Vada by the back of the neck, thrusting her knee into Vada's face. A brutal crack let the assassin know her nose was broken. She tried to break free, but Avalon launched her other knee into a heavy blow under Vada's chin.

Vada sailed through the air, landing hard on her back. She lay motionless in a complete daze. The side of Avalon's sword slapped her cheek to awaken her from her stupor.

"I learned much from the pits. I learned to fight better than you. Much better," Avalon said coldly.

Vada tried to scoot backwards to escape her sister's edge, but Avalon held the blade firmly at her throat.

"I'm prepared to end this," Avalon continued.

"Then end it!" spat Vada.

"Join me. I will fight you no longer!"

Vada narrowed her eyes, "Join you or die?"

Avalon tossed her blade to the side, "Join me or kill me. I am done fighting you."

Vada grabbed her sister's blade and swung it at Avalon stopping a hair's inch from her throat. She furrowed her brow and snarled, "Damn you, Avalon!" she threw the blade away and embraced her long lost Blade Sister in a tight hug, "I won't fight you any longer either. I'll join you. I'll join you."

***

Legion swirled his large blade in an arc, keeping Elucard at bay while cutting into Elucard's chest. Elucard jumped further backwards before dashing into the edged fray. Catching the great sword in mid swing, Elucard grunted under its immense weight as he pulled a dagger from his belt and struck out to Legion's gut.

Legion smiled fondly before spinning around Elucard and slashing at the elf's back with ease, "You haven't been training as hard. A common disadvantage to training the youth."

Elucard growled as he attempted a set of slashes followed by spinning across the grass on his knees and jumping up with a ferocious upper slash. The combination of attacks surprised Legion as he desperately avoided the final slashing attack, catching a slice to his armor and chin.

"I didn't have a scar there yet. I was wrong, you have grown stronger, my student."

"Why do you toy with me?" Elucard shouted, his voice shaking and tired.

Legion unleashed a vicious kick to Elucard's chest, sending him onto his back. Legion stomped down, cracking Elucard's ribs.

"I don't want you to die here,"he said as he looked around, sensing an unworldly power emitting from somewhere in the battlefield, "The tides are about to turn, I can feel it. It's like a force I've never felt before… It frightens me."

"So you're running away, I've never known you to be such a coward!" spat Elucard.

"If you still wish to finish it all, meet me in the place where it all began," said Legion before thrusting his sword into Elucard's thigh.

Elucard screamed as he grabbed his leg in agony, "There will be nowhere you can run, Legion! I will find you!"

Legion walked away, but called back to his student, "Trust me, I'm not going to run."

***

Wiccer dashed angrily at Inle, slashing savagely at the shadow elf. However, Inle parried before catching Wiccer's right wrist. With a flick of his hand, Inle ruthlessly held Wiccer in a painful wrist lock. Inle put more pressure on the now numbing wrist and rendered Wiccer to his knees.

Inle smiled, "Little White Cloak is now a Red Rabbit. My, how the world has changed."

"Damn you! I will have my vengeance!" Wiccer winced.

Inle pulled Wiccer's arm forward and drove his sword at his opponent's stomach, but Wiccer was quick and grabbed the blade's edge firmly. Wiccer grunted under the sharp pain of his slicing hand, but raised his deathly eyes up at Inle.

"Ruining the fun?" sneered Inle.

Wiccer stomped a foot into the soil from under him and slowly rose with a rush of strength pumping through his blood, "The fun is just about to begin!"

Inle twisted Wiccer's wrist to its breaking point and attempted to thrust his sword into Wiccer's stomach again. However the sword did not budge. Wiccer roared as he rammed his shoulder into Inle, toppling them both over and freeing him from the clutches of Inle's torment.

Wiccer made sure to move a knee against Inle's chin. The pressure put the Rabbit's face against the ground. Inle thrashed his hand around wildly trying to grasp Wiccer's red cloak. Wiccer grabbed Inle's arm with both hands and fell to the side, locking Inle in a straight arm bar.

Inle desperately struggled to free himself, but Wiccer mercilessly pressured Inle's elbow until his arm snapped in the grim hold. Inle screamed in pain, rolling over to favor his splintered arm.

"We're not done yet, clown," Wiccer spat, as he situated himself on top of Inle.

"No, I think we are done," giggled Inle half-heartedly, as he gestured to the Black Rabbits now overtaking King Dallin.

Wiccer watched in horror as the Black Rabbits pushed back the remaining Silent Ones and surrounded ARO, who desperately guarded the king. Wiccer looked over to the battlefront to find Estinian reinforcements thundering though the Varisian ranks and powered onward to a sure sighted victory.

"It's over, Red Rabbit," chuckled Inle.

***

From the fog of the black smoke, fifty Black Rabbit trained Estinians rushed the Silent One lines. Their blades were furious as they overcame the holy warriors. The Silent Ones fought with the force of twenty men each, but these new Rabbits were able to adapt to the style of Jedeo's knights.

Adema fought hard as she parried and slashed. A set of knives were flung at her side as she retreated back into ARO's lines. More Estinians rushed her as she struggled to hold her own, eventually falling onto one knee. She grunted as sweat stung under her eyes. The immense weight of several swords clashing down upon her was too much to bear.

A barrage of arrows flew past and relieved her of her strife as the Watchers sprinted to the aid of the Silent Ones. Elisa somersaulted to Adema's side as she slashed the neck of an oncoming Rabbit. She helped Adema to her feet.

"I don't think I'll ever get used to fighting those who used to be my allies," huffed Elisa as she spin kicked a Black Rabbit off his feet.

"I said the same thing when I killed my first demon," said Adema as she inspected her blood soaked side.

"Worry not Silent Sister, the are no demons here," said Calsoon, giving a sly wink.

Adema nodded awkwardly, unsure if Calsoon knew of her linage. She wobbled on her feet as the pressure of the daggers ached in her side and thigh. She dislodged each knife and focused on her silencer until it glowed a bright white. Laying the blade on her wounds, she grimaced as her flesh seared and closed shut.

Calsoon watched curiously while deflecting several attacks around him, "That's a useful trick."

Elisa rolled over Calsoon's back dodging several shurikens, "You two can talk later. We have business to attend to!"

Adema groaned as she limped back into battle, "The shadow elf is right. Enough chatter! Let's get these Rabbits cleared from the king!"

Calsoon nodded happily, "I suppose we should do that."

Timber let loose several close ranged shots from her bow as she hopped nimbly from side to side. Behind her, Lear gracefully danced, disarming Rabbits and diving forward lethally with his sword. He grunted as one hand held onto his stomach. He frequently checked the hand for any sign of his stitches breaking.

Timber glanced behind herself and called to the cat folk, "Essie is going to murder you herself if you keel over now."

Lear chuckled. The light threat reminded him of his shameless begging not to be left back in Stonewall, "Fret not, Timber. This yikahti can handle a bit of bleeding."

Timber dodged a wayward arrow, leaning backwards against Lear so that it would miss him too, "Well 'this yikahti' better take extra care of himself."

Lear kicked away an Estinian soldier, "Cheeky," he replied, amused by Timber's impression of him.

Rulan jumped backwards and clattered down his sword against a pair of Estinian attacks as Essie slashed her sword across the two Rabbits. She slid back to the side of her brother and wiped her brow.

"I miss those days where we just followed Trek in the woods all day. This is too stressful," sighed Essie. She looked upon the battlefield and found that despite their hard work, the Estinian forces were still encroaching closely to King Dallin, "Rulan, we might not survive this."

Rulan grunted as he locked a Rabbit in a head lock before snapping his neck, "Essie just do your best and watch my back…"

Essie growled as an Estinian rushed her with a spear. Grabbing the pike with both hands, she leapt backwards and landed hard on the ground. The enemy unsheathed his sword and raised it to strike down on the medic, but fell in a heap as Rulan drove him through.

Rulan knelt down next to her shivering sister, "Like I was saying, watch my back and I'll watch yours. All we have is each other now."

Essie smirked and reached to flick the tip of her brother's ear, "I can live with that."

Blayvaar held the final ranks next to King Dallin, watching as the Rabbits continued to push through the two lines of Silent Ones and

Watchers. His hands were moist from the sweaty grip of his daggers. His mouth was parched from his crumbling nerves. His heart pounded, still weak from the weeks before. As more and more Estinians broke through the lines, his adrenaline finally overcame his fear. Lunging headlong into the fray, he diced left and right, slicing into necks, arms, legs, and chests of Estinains. Finally, a slash ripped into his side, bringing him onto his knees.

He looked up into the autumn sky, watching as the sun set, perhaps for the last time. However, as he began to faint from the trauma of his wound, a blurred shadow drove his spear into several oncoming Estinians. Blayvaar collapsed into the shadow's arms. He heard a familiar voice as he began to bleed out.

"You can die later, Rabbit. The twelfth Spearmen are by your side, now!"

Blayvaar smiled as Rith dragged him to the safety of the medical corps, "You glory hounds."

Rith chuckled, "You got us read like a book, Rabbit. Rest now, let us have a shot at these guys."

Blayvaar nodded as he laid back to let the medics work on his large wound.

***

"Sire, we are being overrun! We need to retreat!" Marcus grunted at Koda as he pushed away yet another attacker. Bodies piled all around the circle of White Cloaks as Koda sat propped up by his familiar, both breathing heavily.

"This is not how it ends. Not here, not today," Koda wheezed, exhausted. He struggled to stand, resting one hand on Marcus's shoulder.

"There's nothing we can do. We've been overwhelmed. We need to retreat."

Koda limped past the circle of White Cloaks, a large horde of enemies rushing toward him with spears poised forward. Koda was steadfast as he raised his hand outward, "It's time I let go," he whispered.

A shockwave exploded from the young mage's feet knocking the rushing soldiers off balance. Koda raised his other arm and pointed away from his side, pulsing an energetic, invisible force that pushed hundreds of enemies in a wave across the ground. This got the attention of Aric and Athar.

The two trotted toward the weakened Koda on the backs of their cream white horses. Athar gingerly approached Koda, "What are you doing, Koda? The battle is lost for you. Do what must be done and surrender already!"

Koda's nose bled profusely. Sweat dripped and soaked into the ground creating a small puddle at his feet. He was hunched over, bleeding through his now drenched side and down his once vibrant emerald robes.

"I-I w-will not f-fail my father..." Koda murmured, half conscious now.

Athar smirked, "It's far too late for that."

Koda's eyes snapped open and rolled to the back of his head, unleashing a blood curdling roar, "I will not fail my father!!!"

A teal aura turned bright red as it exploded all around Koda, sending thousands of orbs of Magi streaming through the ground and up the feet of every enemy soldier on the battlefield. Each of the still attacking Estinian and the Long Whisper forces struggled in vain as they found themselves frozen by the alien energy.

"Vhat es de meaning of dis Athar?" Aric screamed at the top of his lungs to his ally.

Koda's eyes burned an array of vivid colors and flared much like the magical flare his wolf gave off. He slowly lifted each of the captured soldiers into the air and suddenly clenched his fist. A resounding crunching sound rang through the ranks of thousands of soldiers as their bodies twisted and contorted. Athar and Aric could only watch in grotesque horror as their once overwhelming force was reduced to crumpled up corpses.

"Enough! Please, Koda!" Marcus's terrified scream called out to the unresponsive mage.

Koda's eyes sparked and sputtered out less and less Magi as he reeled his fist closer to his chest, flinging both Athar and Aric closer to him until they were eye level.

"Do you yield?" Koda growled, his voice booming a loud echo across the field.

Athar and Aric looked at each other's frightened faces, before stuttering a 'yes.'

In unison the lifeless, mangled Estinian bodies fell to the ground like a heavy rain. Koda stumbled forward as his eyes returning to normal before he collapsed in complete exhaustion.

78

Koda was groggy when he finally woke. His mouth was parched and his body was still very weak. Propping himself up in the grand bed was out of the question, so he simply turned his head to view his surroundings. The room was rather large. Sunlight drifted through the windows giving the silk curtains a soft glow. The room looked eerily similar to his own bedroom back in Long Whisper. It was beautifully furnished with a rosewood writing desk and wardrobe. A small, round table accented the center of the room with three comfortable chairs placed around it. In a chair next to his bed he found King Dallin looking curiously at him.

"Welcome back to the world of the living, Koda," said Dallin with a light chuckle escaping him.

A blinding pain spurted from his forehead, making Koda wince, "Ugh, It doesn't feel that way. How long have I been out?"

Dallin stood up, stretching his back, "About a week, maybe more. As you can see, you are in Varis City. There is much for you to–"

Koda rapidly spat out a succession of questions that nearly bowled Dallin over, "What of Aric? Is the war over? What will happen to Long Whisper now that Athar is king?"

"Easy, easy, Koda. You are far too weak to deal with Long Whisper's troubles at this time. Just know that Athar and the five traitorous lords are in my prison."

"Well, what of Aric?"

"Aric is also locked up and we are currently working with Queen Natal on an agreement for his release in exchange for their surrender to Varis."

Koda sighed with the relief. The war was finally over. With much of that stress having now passed, he found himself sleeping once more.

***

Another week had passed. Koda stood beside the throne of Dallin leaning on a crutch. He was still weak, but no longer bedridden. It was time to address the future of Long Whisper. He looked at Cass who was on the opposite side of the throne. She was loyal and fierce. She stood by his side throughout the war. Perhaps she was even more fit than he to lead Long Whisper – another question to add to the pile in his mind.

"You six stand before us for committing the crime of treason during a time of war. What say you?" barked Dallin at the chained up King Athar and his five shackled lords.

Athar wrestled with his shackles, still astonished that he was in such a dire situation. When he convinced the other lords to betray the young Dawnedge king, he thought things were finally going his way. He was promised more power and riches than he could ever dream of when Aric Stine showered him with dreams of victory. Now he was locked with iron bolts in front of the wretched human, Evritt Dallin. To throw salt on his already deep wounds, Koda may well be the one deciding his fate, the boy that he so easily manipulated. The boy whom he regarded as nothing more than a fool was now the single greatest threat to his life.

"I am the king of Long Whisper by rite of the eight tribes! Release me and I will forget this incident!" Athar snarled in humiliation and rage.

"You dare call yourself king of Long Whisper? I should hang you by your slimy neck right now! You betrayed our alliance at our most vulnerable time!" Dallin spat before turning his attention to the cringing lords, "You five, do you still see this man as your king? Speak wisely or share his fate!"

Athar attempted to step forward but the guards at his side raised their pikes to his neck. He shouted from behind the spear tips instead, "What kind of choice is that?" You dare bully my brethren into insulting their crown?"

Dallin stood, shouting at the top of his lungs. His booming voice echoed off the walls of the throne room, "Silence! Which of you stand by the side of the true heir of Long Whisper, Koda Dawnedge? And which of you stands by the side of the traitor, Athar Moonfall?"

The five lords stepped forward away from Athar, their heads lowered in fear and shame.

Koda looked on with sunken eyes, still drained from his overuse of the Magi. The sounds of the throne room were muffled as memories of the past war drowned his thoughts. Only fragments of those thoughts breached the surface of his mind – thoughts of his lords betraying him. The same families that swore allegiance to his father were so quick to turn on him. They would rather side with a tyrant that would enslave his own people than fight alongside their rightful king. How could he trust these lords? He couldn't. That was the answer.

"These five lords..." muttered Koda, half dazed, Dallin and Cass turned to the drowsy Koda, "these five lords do not deserve amnesty..."

Cass Baneberry gawked at Koda's words, "Koda they have distanced themselves from Athar."

Koda drooped his head and took a large breath, "They are just as guilty as Athar. They betrayed Varis and Long Whisper in a time of war. They have committed treason and therefore must be punished."

"You are still weary from the battle, you are not thinking straight," Cass said, attempting to quell Koda's wrath. She walked over to him and placed a gentle hand on his shoulder.

Koda jolted his shoulder away and hobbled over to the five lords, each watching with an intense fear, "How dare you treat me as some child! My innocence died when I watch my father's head roll at my feet! My foolishness died when I watched my men starve in the blasted forest! Today I am a man, and today I must no longer be weak minded! You say I am not thinking straight. I have never thought so clearly in my life. These five lords will swing beside their beloved king. If they wish to follow him to war, then they can follow him to death!"

Cass stepped back to her place as Dallin stood from his throne, "Koda is the rightful king, his word is law."

Athar's eyes brimmed with fury as he began to spit his words, "You think you are no longer a child? You think wearing that crown hides your failures from your people? You do not des–"

Koda thrust his hand forward, silencing Athar. The shackled elf froze, still struggling against the painful grip of the Magi's binding.

"T-this is h-how you handle criticism?" stuttered Athar.

"Be quiet, worm," Koda snapped ruthlessly. He released Athar from his ethereal grip, dropping the prisoner to his knees.

King Dallin waved his hands to send the six elves back to their cells, "You will all be hung in morning, may Alanna have mercy on your souls."

"It is more than they deserve," whispered Koda.

79

The Varis City infirmary was a large building with multiple floors and several rooms, each filled to the brim with soldiers recovering from wounds inflicted during the war. The small group of ARO members jumped onto the small medical bed, rudely awakening an injured Blayvaar. He groaned as he gripped his freshly bandaged side. Sitting up gingerly, and after his initial grumpiness, he found himself excited to see his visitors.

"Glad to see some pretty faces. The only company I've had was a nurse and my neighbor's ugly mug."

Everyone looked to see that Rith was on the bed next to Blayvaar. Rith put down the book he was reading, puckered his lips, and blew Blayvaar a teasing kiss, "You know you can't get enough of me!"

Blayvaar chuckled and turned back to his friends, "I'm ready to get back out there. Being laid up in this bed is driving me crazy!"

Lear gave a sour look, "This yikahti wished he had been laid up in a bed and not in a cold forest, bleeding out."

"Some guys have all the luck, eh Lear?" joked Blayvaar.

Essie moved to Blayvaar's wounded side and gently undid the bandage to inspect the healing wound, "Pretty good stitching. That must have been a pretty, big slash."

"It was a big sword," added Blayvaar, widening his arms to show how big the sword actually was, perhaps indulging a bit.

"Blistercloth is too small for that one, but the stitches seemed to be doing fine, your wound will heal just in time."

Blayvaar arched an eyebrow inquisitively, "Just in time for what?"

Rulan spoke in a low voice so that only trained ears could hear, "Elucard wants to strike the Black Rabbits as soon as we get back."

"The compound?" gasped Blayvaar.

"It's time we finished them while they can't recruit," Timber growled.

Blayvaar flashed a smile, "Then let's end it!"

80

Wiccer stood in the dank and dimly lit prison cell. Shadows danced around the cell from the torches that hung on the walls. He jeered through the bars at an unmasked Inle who sat alone in his cell. His healing arm was still wrapped in a bandage and resting in a wool sling.

"You will finally hang for the crimes you have committed," sneered Wiccer. He glared with venom across his face.

Inle turned to look up at the former White Cloak, "I will hang, but it's because I killed your brother. Isn't it? You seek vengeance. It was never about justice. The whole reason why you became a Red Rabbit was to kill me," He ended with a nasty smile.

Wiccer grabbed the bars in anger, "Do not play your mind games with me, Rabbit!" he howled. His face flushed with rage. He first planned to approach Inle to find some closure, but he thought he'd have more control over his emotions. He seemed to underestimate Inle's cunning. He seemed to always underestimate the Black Rabbits, a mistake that had constantly haunted him.

Inle ran to the bars and placed his face as close to Wiccer's as the bars would allow. He chomped his teeth with a crude smile that made Wiccer back up, "You play mind games with yourself, dear friend. A game you already lost when you buried your brother."

Wiccer fumed as he opened the cell and entered. He savagely backhanded Inle against the wall and thrust out his hand to choke the Rabbit. Wiccer tightened his grip as Inle gasped for any air that he could.

"I will end your pathetic life here and now!" Wiccer shouted.

Inle's eyes cracked red as he let Wiccer squeeze his throat, "I-It f-feels good to give into your e-emotions? D-Doesn't it?" Inle croaked.

Wiccer's eyes widened and he released his grip. Inle collapsed coughing and sucking in air. He lifted his chin to look up. Although his face was always a light gray complexion, he was slightly paler now. His neck began to bruise with a bluish-purplish color. Inle smiled a maddened smile, "Finish it Cloak! Take your vengeance! Avenge him! Avenge your brother, Cloak!"

Wiccer looked at his trembling hands and stepped backwards. He shook his head whispering to himself, "No, I mustn't be blinded by my hatred. This isn't what Avren wanted."

Inle snatched Wiccer's wrist and pulled it to his neck, "Finish it!"

Wiccer pulled his hand away and swiftly left the cell after locking it back up. Inle laughed loudly as Wiccer made his exit.

"See you around, Wiccer!"

81

The town square of Varis City was bustling like a festival. Traders peddled balloons and roasted snacks. Clowns and jugglers entertained on the sides of the streets. Minstrels sang jingles of silly tales in up beat tunes. Peasants crowded around a large wooden platform with the Long Whisper lords and Inle Ebonpath standing on top of it. Their necks were inside nooses, preparing to be hanged. Off to the side on top of a stone second platform sat King Koda and King Dallin on their respective leather-bound thrones. Dallin calmed down the excitement of the crowd with a raised hand, before calling out to the six lords.

"Any last words?"

Athar's face was pale with fright, he pleaded to Koda to listen to him, "My king, I regret how I wronged you. Please show mercy!"

Dallin leaned his chin on his hand, "What say you, my friend. Will you show mercy to these criminals?"

Koda stood so all could see him, "When Ryjin Leafsong attempted to assassinate my father, my kind and just father spared the Leafsong tribe from the same fate their kin shared. I won't be so foolish. Your families will be stripped of their lands, their wealth, and titles. They will be exiled from our country and I will find new lords to take their place. Consider that my mercy!"

The former lords gasped as a trapdoor fell beneath them and their ropes snapped taut. The gallows creaked as the six elves hanged dead from their nooses.

Dallin looked at Inle, repeating the same question to him, "Inle Ebonpath, any last words?"

Inle's face held still and cold. He showed no fear or any emotion at all, "My final words are for Elucard Freewind!"

Dallin looked down to Elucard and nodded, giving permission to walk up the steps of the gallows.

Elucard ascended the wooden steps. He paused for a brief second to watch the swaying bodies of the former noblemen before coming face to face with his student. Several years had passed since he considered the young shadow elf as an ally and a friend. Perhaps even more than a friend. Had his life not turned into a mess, he could have been happy.

Happy with Inle, Jetta, and his world within the Black Rabbits. But life has a funny way of pulling you away from the comfort of your happiness and burying it under pain and suffering. For when you survive what life throws at you, you become a stronger person.

"What do you have to say, Inle?" Elucard asked Inle. At first Elucard made no effort to make eye contact with Inle. It wasn't shame nor hate. He dared not look at a former life when he still secretly longed for it.

Inle gave a meek smile, "I was once masked, but no longer am. I think it would be fair to stand on equal footing," the words were familiar to Elucard.

Elucard finally glared with his cold magenta eyes into Inle's, he was not playing any games with Inle.

"Please, master..."

Elucard gave a long sigh, but then lowered his mask and removed his hood. Inle smiled again and looked lazily at Elucard's features. He was now older and more refined, but Inle still found him the handsome elf he had fallen in love with.

"Is that all, Inle?" Elucard asked, impatiently.

"A final request?" whispered Inle.

"What is it?"

Inle leaned into Elucard, the rope around his neck tugged, but he was as close as he needed to be. Inle brushed his lips against Elucard's and kissed him. At that moment, for those few fleeting seconds, Inle was at peace. Even amids the chaos of war and despite the hatred carved into his heart, he still had feelings for his master.

Elucard closed his eyes and remembered a simpler time as a Black Rabbit, but then pushed away those memories as he pushed Inle away, "Goodbye, Inle."

The trapdoor fell beneath Inle's feet, but before the rope could go tight, a dagger whizzed past Elucard and severed the rope. Inle fell underneath the platform, in complete shock. A strange cloaked figure grabbed him and together they sunk into the shadows as if they were being transported through a void.

The town square was in complete disarray. Dallin and Koda barked orders to the guards to find and recapture Inle. Elucard stood in silence, locked in a stupor as memories of being a Rabbit clashed with being part of ARO. He would have his vengeance whether Inle lived or died. He knew it was all coming to a close.

***

Miles from Varis City, within a lush forest, a shadow seeped from the ground. Growing rapidly until its darkness overtook the surrounding area. From that shadow two figures formed from ashes. Inle was still collapsed on his knees, his arms bound tightly to his sides. The remains of a noose hung limp around his neck. The stranger cut his bindings and threw the noose to the side. He helped Inle stand up before lowering his hood and unraveling a black scarf from his face. It was Calsoon.

Inle stumbled backwards in bewilderment, "Y-You're one of Elucard's Red Rabbits! I recognize you from the night in the forest, when I tried to assassinate Koda!"

Calsoon bowed gracefully, "At your service, Inle."

Inle stepped closer, looking at the shadows that webbed around the forest, almost choking it, "You are no normal elf."

Calsoon raised his hand to cover his face then moved it away to reveal a new scaly black face. Straight black horns protruded out of his head, slightly curved towards the tips. His eyes were the color of burning amber instead of his normal icy blue. He grinned, exposing deadly pointed teeth. His hands were now sharp claws and he had a thin, long barbed tail.

"You're a demon!" Inle exclaimed. He had heard old wives' tales of demons taking the form of others to spy on men from the bards in his troupe. However, they were just that, old wives' tales. Inle was still taken back from the reveal. He collected his wits, "Why did you rescue me?"

Calsoon licked his fangs before speaking, "This world that we live in is a complex chess game. You and everyone you know are the pieces."

Inle squinted his eyes, carefully choosing his next question. This demon spoke in riddles, but if he asked the correct questions, he would see the answer, "Then who are the players?"

Calsoon let out a cackle, "Ah yes, a fine question, my friend. Come with me and find out for yourself!"

82

Snow gently drifted in the cool night as lofty clouds roamed across the skies. Shafts of silver moonlight barely lit the Black Rabbit compound as the Watchers slid past the gates one by one. Within the frigid shadows, the ARO members strangled sentries with thin stretches of garrote wire and dragged their bodies into the woods. The snow was still light on the ground with little chance of making noticeable tracks. The Watchers were well-trained assassins and the Varisian War gave them experience with the Rabbits that no training could have provided.

At the center of the compound, the Watchers gathered in a circle, each member keeping a sharp eye out for additional Rabbits. As they kept their wits heightened, the door to the Silent Master's quarters slid open. The Silent Master approached the center of the grounds. Scars criss-crossed on his imposing frame. His tattoos seemed to ripple as he moved forward. He wore only a long, dark leather kilt. His right hand was no more than a bandaged stump – a memento from his prior encounter with Elucard. Veins raised and pulsed down his left arm and over his only hand. By his side was a solemn looking Legion.

Elucard stared at the pair, raising his sword in caution, "This is the end of the Rabbits, Ryjin."

A vile sneer lurked upon the Silent Master's face, "Legion, it is time you dealt with your whelp."

Legion stepped between his master and his student, drawing the long and heavy claymore in a single hand. The Watchers immediately surrounded the two Black Rabbits. Legion turned his head to look at each Watcher before turning his eyes back onto Elucard, "Withdraw your men. They don't have to die tonight."

Wiccer shuffled himself closer to the Silent Master, "Elucard, we'll handle the Silent Master, you deal with your old master."

"Be careful. I maimed him, but he's still deadly," Elucard said, nodding in acknowledgment to Wiccer.

Legion took in a long breath, "I want you to know that I am sorry it has come to this. You were never meant to be my enemy."

"Somehow I believe you, but it's too late for apologies now, master," Elucard said softly. He gripped his blade's handle tightly before lunging forward at Legion.

Legion shook his head and spun quickly to land a back kick into Elucard's chest, launching him backwards. Legion ran headlong, twirling his large sword in his hand before dropping the edge in a chopping swing. Elucard held up his sword horizontally, watching sparks burst as the blades clashed together. Inching his arms upwards, Elucard struggled to push Legion's sword away from him and jumped up to snap a kick under his master's jaw. Legion's head rocked backwards as he swayed sideways.

Dazed, Legion bent over as Elucard launched a flying knee into his gut. Elucard used his momentum to twist his body upside down and land a hard kick to the side of Legion's face. The strike threw Legion off balance and he crashed into the stone ground.

Elucard stood over Legion's crumpled body, pointing his sword at him. He used a foot to turn the elf over onto his back. Legion knocked the sword away, thrusting his body from the ground. He flew into his student, catching Elucard in a headlock. Legion's fingers interlaced around the back of Elucard's neck and he sent a series of devastating knees slamming into Elucard's chest and side, with the final strike cracking Elucard's ribs. Legion grabbed his student's hood and let loose a brutal uppercut that clasped his jaw shut and flung him into the air.

Elucard landed on his back and tumbled several feet backwards. He sluggishly picked himself up and moved his hands in front of his body, readying for another painful round of attacks.

Legion picked up Elucard's blade and wielded it alongside his own sword. He tossed the smaller blade to Elucard and shook his head, "We can fight until the sun comes up. We can beat each other into a bloody pulp. You can kill me, I can kill you. None of it will get us closer to peace."

Elucard caught his blade. He spun it expertly in one hand before dashing at Legion again, "This is our fate—eternal damnation. Neither of us deserve peace!"

Elucard slashed a succession of attacks at Legion, half were parried to the side, while two found their mark. The swings carved into Legion's upper arm and lower side. Elucard snarled and took a dagger from his belt, attempting to drive it into his master's shoulder. Legion grabbed his wrist and his back into Elucard before throwing him over his shoulder. Elucard slammed down on his backside, his dagger clattered and slid across the snowy, wet ground. He tugged on his arm but found that his wrist was still locked within Legion's grip. Legion pulled Elucard toward him and held his neck in his forearm, choking him.

"Look at them!" shouted Legion, tightening his hold and forcing Elucard to watch the other battle unfold, "My Silent Master will destroy them, and then you! Is this what you wanted? How many more will suffer? How many lives will you take until your hate and anger consume your entire world?"

The Silent Master sidestepped and countered as each Watcher leaped and dashed at him with blades glinting in the moonlight. Timber fired several arrows from the rear, each found their mark burying themselves deep into the Silent Master's back, but it did not quell his fury. Instead, he shifted his attention to the Kanis and dove at her.

"Rulan, Elisa, use your weighted chains to slow him down! Lear, Calsoon, Essie and Blayvaar attack him while he's bound!" Wiccer shouted, throwing out a flurry of commands.

Rulan and Elisa whipped a pair of chains with heavy iron weights attached to the ends. Together they ran circles around Ryjin and tied the Silent Master's arms behind his back. They grunted as they pulled the chains tight.

As soon as the Silent Master was chained, Lear dashed in to cut at the Silent Master's legs. Blayvaar jumped onto his back, wielding dual knives, and Calsoon and Essie dove to impale him through the stomach.

With a roar, the Silent Master flexed his muscles, popping the links of the chains until his arms were free. Wrapping the remains of the chains in his left hand, he pulled both Rulan and Elisa into his awaiting arms. Elisa and Rulan flipped head over heels as they collided with his muscular right arm.

Turning to Lear, he lifted his leg and nailed a solid kick into the yikahti's jaw. Lear's eyesight lit up and then faded to a blurred darkness as he smashed down to the ground.

Rocking his head back, Rjyjin bashed his skull into Blayvaar's face. Blayvaar's jaw snapped shut with a loud pop as the former thief reeled backwards, falling with a loud thud onto the floor.

With Ryjin's free hand, he thrust at Calsoon's neck. Clenching tightly, he lifted the elf up and smashed him into the ground, creating several cracks into the stone tiles. While the Silent Master was distracted by Calsoon, Essie managed to run her blade partially into Ryjin, however the large elf stiffened his abs, bending the sword until it buckled and snapped from the force. He savagely backhanded the young Windfoot into a frightened Timber. Both flew backwards, rolling into a mess on the ground.

The Silent Master turned to Wiccer and smiled, "Your clan lacks the skill to defeat me."

Wiccer shot a worried glance to Elucard.

Elucard began to fall in and out of consciousness. His eyes rolled back into his head as Legion continued to squeeze Elucard's neck. Elucard gargled out a response the best he could, "J...ust tw..."

"What was that?"

Elucard grabbed onto Legion's arm and sunk a large bite into it. Legion yelped as he lunged backwards, holding onto his now bleeding arm.

"Just two," Elucard wheezed. He smirked as he steadily got to his feet. He looked over his shoulder to see his Watchers strewn about, barely able to keep up with the surprisingly nimble Ryjin, "I need to end this."

"Indeed," Legion said sternly.

Both rushed at each other, swinging, clashing, and slicing. Elucard dodged right as a heavy strike came crashing down. Thinking fast, Elucard stomped onto the blade with one foot and jumped into the air as Legion pulled it upwards, struggling to free it from the ground. Elucard sailed up and over Legion, Plunging his sword deep into Legion's shoulder.

Legion fell to his knees as his shoulder sagged, letting his arm fall limp. Elucard painfully yanked and rested the blade against Legion's neck.

"I taught you well, Elucard," Legion managed to say despite the overwhelming pain he was in.

"You taught me *well*? You taught me nothing but lies!" shouted Elucard as he swung Legion to face him, "You filled my head with delusions of honor and purpose – and for what? So that I'd turn my back on the real people who cared for me!"

Legion looked away from Elucard in shame. The drive to protect his clan and kill Elucard had eroded over time. He was now just a husk of the Black Rabbit he once was. He wanted only to die at the hands of the last person he cared for, Elucard, "I taught you only what I thought would keep you alive. I taught you to think and fight. I didn't want to make you the perfect weapon, but a perfect man," Legion turned to face Elucard once more and tears swelled in his eyes, "I am honored to say you turned out well; a good and just adult. You've grown into the leader I always hoped you'd become. You are my humanity, for I never had it on my own. I am proud of you...my son."

Elucard brought his face closer to Legion's, "You don't deserve that huma–" he couldn't finish the sentence. He clenched his teeth as the words choked in his throat. Tears formed as they dripped down his cheeks. Legion may have killed Jetta, but he still loved him like a father. Like the father that was there for him. Like the father that raised him. Like the father that protected him. Like the father he needed. That he would always love.

"You were always too weak, Legion," Ryjin's familiar low growl cut through the winter night. In his hand he held Wiccer by the face, dragging him on the ground as he walked over to Legion and Elucard.

Elucard gently laid Legion onto the ground and met Ryjin half way, "You are the root of all this! You take the innocent and contort us into vile killers! Bred to turn on our own world and do your bidding! You are the true reason why Jetta is dead! You will corrupt the youth of this world no more!"

Wiccer groaned as he was released from Ryjin's clutches. Ryjin grabbed Elucard by the cloak and brought him close to his face, "I did not corrupt your mind! I merely surfaced your desires!"

Elucard squinted, holding his face slightly askew from Ryjin's, "What desires?" he asked.

Ryjin flashed a nasty smile, "Your desire to serve and your desire to kill!"

Elucard let loose a blood shivering roar as he tried to strike out at Ryjin with his blade, but the Silent Master threw him aside. Elucard clattered onto the ground, weakened from his long battle with Legion. With his newfound rage rising, he mustered the energy to stand.

Ryjin barreled towards Elucard, punishing him with a punch to his gut, following with a hefty elbow to his upper back. Elucard lay flatten on the ground. As he struggle to stand again, Ryjin smashed his foot down onto Elucard's head. Elucard's face bounced off the ground as blood splattered into several directions.

Ryjin knelt down and lifted Elucard's bloodied face by the tuft of his hair. He sneered sadistically as he spoke lowly into the elf's ear, "You led a glorious life."

Elucard gagged and spurted blood as he clawed at Ryjin's grip.

"A shame that it ended so anti-climactically," Ryjin continued.

"His life isn't over yet," Wiccer's voice called out from behind Ryjin.

Ryjin dropped Elucard, turning around to face Wiccer, "You alone will not be able to save this one."

"It's a good thing he didn't come alone," Blayvaar said, limping to Wiccer's side and flipping a dagger in his hand.

Ryjin jeered as one by one each Watcher came to Elucard's aid, "I've already defeated you all. What makes you think you can win this time?"

ARO readied their weapons. Wiccer smiled, "Because now we are whole."

Ryjin growled in confusion as a sword grew from his stomach, spraying a fountain of blood onto the snowy ground. Ryjin spun to find an exhausted Elucard smiling with half slit eyes.

"Watchers attack!" Wiccer called out as each ARO member hacked and sliced at Ryjin.

In a ballet of blood, the Watchers danced around the Silent Master as he desperately attempted to overcome the flashes of steel before finally falling to his knees. Blood flowed like several rivers from hideous wounds all over his body. His head slouched forward as his breathing became labored.

Elucard raised Ryjin's chin with the tip of his blade, "The Black Rabbits are done."

Ryjin grinned a ghastly smile, "The Black Rabbits were but one day in an endless winter."

Elucard snarled and ruthlessly sliced Ryjin's head off. He took a great sigh. He dropped his blade and stumbled backwards. He was lightheaded from exhaustion and the loss of blood. He took a knee and whispered a low prayer.

Alanna, tonight I have slain a man,
I have shown him no love, no remorse,
Alanna, take this man's soul in one hand,
With the other mend my hatred's source,
Finally sever our bond and give me my release,
So that I can remember those I've lost in peace.

Elucard fell silent after finding his atonement before making his way back to his resting master, "Essie, can you patch him up?"

"I'll do what I can."

Elucard cradled Legion in his arms. His nightmare was over and all he wanted now was to dream. Dream for a time of peace. A peace to share with his new family, perhaps even with his old one. To share with Legion, "Master…I…"

Legion winced as Essie examined Legion's gruesome wounds, "You saved us all, Elucard."

"Master...I..." Elucard started, unable to find the right words—much less the perfect words for this moment.

"She would be proud of you..." said Legion, as slowly fell into a slumber.

"Master...I forgive you."

83

In the newly refurbished Ruens abbey, Elucard relaxed on the floor next to Avalon as they watched the new Silent Ones train under Vada's watchful eye. Elucard stirred uncomfortably in his new finery. His waist coat was tight around his ribs and his fluffy ascot made his throat itch. He was older now and wanted to focus his attention on a new life instead of bloodying his hands and hunting down those responsible for his hatred. He had finally found a world of peace and wished to hold on to it.

"Vada is falling in well as your First Blade once again," Elucard said as he desperately scratched at the ascot.

"She returned from the Blade Range as an Iron Wing, rising through the ranks faster than I ever did. She requested to serve under me, which is good because I seem to be attached to her," Avalon explained, fondly watching her Blade Sister move through a kata.

"What of Adema?" Elucard asked, remembering the fierceness of the mysterious woman.

"She was assigned to me only to aid in the war and establish this new temple. Although this was once an abbey for Ruens, it will now serve Jedeo well. I believe Adema is being assigned to the Holy Front. I wish her the best. It's not a pleasant assignment." Avalon took a sip of wine from the glass sitting next to her and brushed her hair away from her eye, "These new Silent Ones will be the first of many generations that will be taught to fight like Rabbits. We learned much from the war in Varis. To mix teachings will craft the perfect weapon for Jedeo."

"A blade is only as sharp as the Rabbit wielding it," Elucard mused.

"Speaking of which, it's been almost a year since you and the rest of ARO put down Ryjin. How are things going?" Avalon asked.

"It has, hasn't it? Despite our best efforts, Dallin has reported that new assassin clans are popping up in Varis. Black Rabbit copycats no doubt: the Ghost Fox clan and the Twisted Skies clan."

"Looks like Varis will need to form an ARO unit," Avalon said grinning.

"We're already on top of that. Wiccer is being sent to Varis City to start the unit. I'll be taking over command of ours."

"Wiccer is off to Varis? Who will be your second in command? Lear? Blayvaar?"

"Legion, actually. He picked up the military life very well. Go figure. I'll really need his help too because ARO has tripled in size! Several new faces came from the 12th Spearman Division alone."

"Will Long Whisper need ARO to be so large?"

"The Rabbits are dead but not finished. No doubt someone will pick up the mantle of Silent Master once again," Elucard said grimly.

"Any word from Inle? I heard rumors that you were responsible for his escape."

Elucard balled his fist and grit his teeth. All the work put into gaining the trust of Long Whisper nearly decimated by the hidden stranger, "No one has seen or heard from Inle since that day. If it weren't for Koda, Dallin would have arrested me for conspiracy to commit treason. Hopefully Wiccer will be able to smooth out our relationship with Varis."

"Well it looks like we have our work cut out for us."

Elucard stood up, quick to pat off the dust on his new clothes, "We'll see."

***

Elucard walked down the streets of Lost Dawns. Since his promotion to captain, he had a lot more trit to burn. He had loaded his wardrobe with the latest in Long Whisper fashion and found himself filling up a newly furnished book case. Things in his life he once shrugged off now seemed to be coming to the forefront. He was domesticated now.

The streets were becoming lively as the noon sun sat high in the sky. He stopped to look into the glass pane of a store front. Staring at his reflection, he adjusted his green and orange waistcoat that seemed to have slightly climbed his chest while he was at the Silent One abbey. He took a comb from his pocket and brushed his hair into a neater look. Before he had the chance to put it back into his pocket a small boy bowled him over.

"Sorry, mister!" the elven child said.

Elucard propped himself up and took a good look at the boy. He was around twelve. Dirt covered his fair skin and messed up his stark white hair. His eyes were a vibrant green. He wore a filthy tunic and patched up trousers. Elucard lifted himself up and patted the dirt off his pants, "Not a problem. I've had my shares of bumps in the past."

The boy snickered, "I'm sure, mister," he made an over the top face as he picked up a silver trit resting on the ground, "Mister, you dropped this!"

Elucard smiled, "Honesty should be rewarded. You keep it. Run along now."

The boy flashed an over exaggerated smile and dashed off.

"Nice kid," Elucard said to himself. He wondered exactly how many of his coins had dropped from his purse before realizing that his coin purse was missing. He frantically scanned the ground before it dawned on him that the boy had conned him. Elucard sneered as he looked at where the child had scampered off to and gave chase.

Elucard leaped onto the shoulders of several citizens before pulling himself onto the roof of a shop. He ran to the edge and looked down into an alley to see the boy counting the contents of Elucard's purse.

"Hey! Hand over the money and I won't hurt you!" Elucard shouted down at the street urchin.

The boy looked up in surprise. He tied the purse on his belt and hopped over the fence behind him. Elucard dropped down and flipped over the fence, chasing after the thief.

The boy fled, climbing a ladder to the nearest roof and leaping over wide alley gaps. He glanced behind him and found the strange "nobleman" keeping pace, not tiring from dodging strenuous obstacles. The boy spotted a gap ahead that this man would be mad to attempt to jump. Picking up his speed, the boy mustered all his dexterity and energy to leap across an incredibly wide berth between two buildings, but despite his best efforts he came up short. He fell inches from the target ledge and thrust out a hand in a desperate attempt to latch onto the building. There he dangled, certain death waiting for him below.

An older hand grabbed the boy by his tunic and lifted him onto the safety of the building. It was the nobleman.

Elucard kept his grip tight so the boy could not escape, all-the-while contemplating the insane lengths the boy took to get away from him, "You've got some talent, kid. That potential is going to waste out here in the Roots. How would you like to work for me?"

The boy squirmed himself free and pouted his face, "Doing what?" he asked in a nasty voice.

"Doing the world some good."

The child sneered, "The world ain't done nothin' for me."

Elucard smirked, "What's your name kid?"

"Kyzo."

Elucard dropped down to one knee so that he was eye level with the boy, "Kyzo, the world hasn't seen what you can do yet. Come under my wing and I will give you that opportunity. Come under my wing and learn from me."

Kyzo looked curiously, "What will I learn?"

"To hunt assassins."

84

The sacred island of Nashoon was not at all how Koda and Wildeye
left it. The once verdant forest was now blanketed in vivid white.
Withered leaves fell from the grasps of their branches and danced on
the snow covered forest floor below. Koda looked on in astonishment as
winter had found its way to Nashoon for the first time.

Xile sat on a stone with a litter of wolf pups playing on his lap. Koda
slowly approached his grandfather, yet Xile did not bother looking up
at the grandson he had not seen in such a long while. His voice was
tired and worn, and he coughed hard in between his words, "I traveled
the world as you told me to and I found a pupil. She is an elf of Stratus
descent. She is not well accustomed to warm climates, but she shows
great aptitude and willingness to learn. Her name is Lore Starfrost.
Perhaps you will become friends in time." He gently pushed the pups
away and gingerly used his staff to stand. His joints popped and he
grunted and his back ached, "It seems the Dawnedge were not meant to
be Guardians."

Koda rushed to support him, but was brushed away, "What were we
meant to be?" Koda asked.

"Leaders," smiled Xile.

Koda grinned, but his face turned serious. He pointed to the
glistening ice that gripped the canopy above, "I've never seen seasons
change on Nashoon. What is happening?"

Xile shuffled over to pet Wildeye, who arched her back to get an
extra bit of attention from the ancient elf, "Koda, I am dying. As the
Arcane Guardian, my life force is connected to this forest. When I finally
pass, the forest may well never come out of this winter. When that
happens, evil will swallow this land whole."

"What of your student?"

Xile's face wrinkled, "Lore is wise beyond her years, but not ready to
protect the seal."

Koda's brow perked up, "Seal?"

"The Celestial Seal of Cypress. One of five, each one written on each
of the Dragon Realms. They ward the gods from the mortal plane.
However, if broken, the gods will continue their deity wars on our

world and Draak Terra will crumble. Even now the seals are slowly cracking and fading. I am too weak to repair the seals and Lore is far from being fully trained still."

Koda shook his head, "I thought the Arcane Guardian protected the Magi?"

"They protect all of the world's secrets. The Magi is just one of them."

"Why didn't you tell me about something with such dire consequences? I could have helped!" Koda fumed, angrily.

"I was wrong to think you were prepared to become a guardian. I know how much you latch onto the Magi as if it is some sort of nectar. I have felt you growing darker. I only envisioned your fate as a flicker, but as time passed... Koda I fear the worst."

Koda's face hardened like the frozen ground beneath him, "*Darker*? *Fear the worst*? I have grown vastly stronger than the child I was when I left!"

"It's far too late to prove yourself to me. However, it is not too late to prove yourself to those that depend on us."

"Tell me how, grandfather!"

"Use your influence to find the seals and protect them. I sense I am not the only one that knows of the seals' waning," Xile wheezed. Wildeye leaned her large body against the aged elf, so that he could rest.

Koda nodded solemnly, "I will do this for you."

Xile placed a trembling hand on his grandson's shoulder, "Do this for the world."

85

Inle walked for what seemed like an eternity to the shadow elf. He trekked alone through a dark void. The walls were black but shimmered with a magenta light while the road was lit with a soft, white glow. The path seemed to twist and rotate with each step he took.

"How much further?" he asked, although he felt like he was talking to himself because Calsoon seemed to have vanished months ago. Inle had no choice but to walk down the strange corridor without the aid of his mysterious guide. He did wait at first. However, much like the journey he was on, the waiting seemed to be never ending as well.

Calsoon's delightful voice came from behind Inle, "We've just arrived, my friend."

Inle spun around, surprised by Calsoon's sudden reappearance, "Where have you been?"

Calsoon grinned and bowed, "A thousand apologies, my friend, but perhaps it is best if you didn't know."

Inle narrowed his eyes. The abundance of vague puzzles were starting to wear on him, "How long have I been here?"

"I mean not to confuse you any further, but time has no meaning here. Once you leave to go back to the mortal plane, it will be as if you never left."

Inle shook his head in disbelief before asking one final question, "Where is *here*, exactly?"

Just as the question left to escape his mouth, the world around them warped and vanished. Around them appeared a large room with a circular table in the center. At the table sat five men and a woman. Each one wore a long black cloak and an oversized hood that masked their face. The table was made of dark ebonwood with a large, black, eight-pointed snowflake carved into the table. The carving was outlined with a thin line of silver paint so that the black design would be better seen on the dark colored wood. In the foreground of the snow flake were twin crescent moons painted blue that faced away from one another. Circling the room were stone walls and invisible pillars that took the form of falling snow. There were two empty seats, one of which Calsoon took.

Inle looked around confused. He stood silently, waiting for an explanation before finally speaking, "Are you the players of this game?"

Calsoon clapped his hands in delight. A man next to him rose from his seat and and unveiled his face. He was a devilishly handsome man with delicate features and faintly silver eyes. His skin was pale and matched his short, platinum hair. He spoke with an elegant dialect, as if he were highly educated and had noble blood, "Welcome Inle, to Dead of Winter—A collection of unique individuals such as yourself."

Inle was even more confused, "How did you know my name?"

"We always keep an eye on those we take a special interest in."

"Who are you?" Inle asked. A whole batch of new questions hatched in his mind.

The mysterious gentleman bowed, "I am known as Wraslyn to my peers. However, others know me as other names. I will introduce the other members of our guild, but over time you must take it upon yourself to learn each of their strengths." He moved his hand to each of the six other members. As he stated their name, they stood and bowed, "Uther, Aazeren, Strife, The Collector, Sable, and you have already met Calsoon who serves as Sable's servant."

Inle nodded to each but looked blankly at an eighth seat, "Who sits in the last seat?"

Wraslyn walked over to the empty chair and rested his hands on its back, "His name was Ryjin Leafsong. I believe you knew him?"

Inle looked flabbergasted, "The Silent Master was one of your members?"

"He was merely a Leafsong. Who did you think trained him?"

"We all assumed it was one of the warrior tribes who disapproved of the founding of Lost Dawns," Inle responded.

Calsoon snickered out loud, "We trained him, we set up his funds, and we gave him his opportunity for the vengeance he craved against the Dawnedge."

Inle shook his head in confusion, "The Black Rabbits were all a part of your game?"

Calsoon strolled over to comfort Inle, "My friend, I told you that you and everyone you know are just pieces in our game."

Inle pushed him away, "Why? Why go to such lengths?"

Wraslyn flashed a wide smile, "Now we are getting to the good questions. By straining Jaelyn's power, we knew he would send for Koda to come home. By further pressuring Koda, he would become king."

Inle furrowed his brow, "How does Koda becoming king have anything to do with this?"

"You see, without Koda in Nashoon, a new Arcane Guardian can't be trained. Soon the seals will be ready for us to make our move."

Inle leaned against the wall, "I still don't understand."

"But you will in time," Calsoon finished.

Wraslyn motioned to the eighth chair, "Take a seat, Inle. A new Silent Master must be named."

Inle grinned and slowly stepped toward the seat, but halted shy of sitting down, "I wish to be a player, not a pawn."

"We knew you were more ambitious than Ryjin. That is why we sought you out," Calsoon said, giving a cunning smile.

"Then I will join and become the new Silent Master," Inle answered as he finally took the eighth seat.

"To the dawning of a new season, darker than the last," Wraslyn toasted, a pleased look was strewn across his face.

Liked the book? Want to help the book grow? Write a review and help to get the book out there. For news on future the Dragon Realms Saga books, check out:

Facebook:
www.facebook.com/Dragonrealmsaga

Twitter:
@Vendettas_Rise

Also:

Read the Web Comic:
http://vendettasrise.smackjeeves.com/

Join the official Discord:
https://discord.gg/hpsEx8J

ABOUT THE AUTHOR

I was raised in New England on cartoons, comics, and fantasy books at an early age. As I grew older my love for fantastic characters and epic adventures didn't diminish. I was soon sucked into the world of creating my own stories through the means of table top rpg's with my friends. This hobby would even carry with me serving in the US Army in Iraq. It was these stories that I harnessed into Vendetta's Rise and its future books in the same series.

15185868R00225